WINTER SOLSTICE

WINTER SOLSTICE

Frozen in Time

DONNA PFANNENSTIEL

abbott press

Abbott Press books may be ordered through booksellers or by contacting:

Abbott Press
1663 Liberty Drive
Bloomington, IN 47403
www.abbottpress.com
Phone: 1 (866) 697-5310

ISBN: 978-1-4582-2237-4 (sc)
ISBN: 978-1-4582-2236-7 (e)

Library of Congress Control Number: 2019908033

Print information available on the last page.

Abbott Press rev. date: 6/26/2019

Dedicated to:
Bill Pfannenstiel, the love of my life.
My lover, my inspiration, my best friend.
My husband of 43 years.

Special Acknowledgement:

To Larry Waterman, who pushed, prodded, and never stopped believing that I should finish this story.

Thanks, Uncle Larry.

Acknowledgements:

Each of the following people have played a part in helping me to finish what I started. Thank You for the support and encouragement I have received from:

*Audra (Durham) Blattel: My head cheerleader. Thanks, mom, for always reminding me that, "we will not know until we try." And, a very special "Thank you" for reading this piece.

*Erica, Karl, and Caleb McKimmey: Your unwavering love and support, (emotional and tech), means more than you will ever know.

*Colleen Waterman: Thank you for reading, and listening; for your ideas, and your encouragement. Also, for letting me use your name.

*Barb and David Phillips: Love you both so much, Thank you for always being there. Check that snow-globe very carefully.

*Cindy McIntyre/ Jim Tucker: The support I always receive from both of you touches my heart. From Jim sharing every post I create, and Cindy for your inspiration, heartening, and reassurance.

*Janet Branch/Tracy Branch/ Lesli Hendrix/ Kati O'Quinn/ Regina Esther/Sara Gartin

For reading my rough drafts, your guidance, and then asking for more. Love you ladies. I am Blessed.

*Finally, to Hunter Dismang (former student): Thank you! Not only were you the first person to read my 'short story,' the first chapter of this book; but you also expressed enough interest to ask a very pertinent question: "What did you do?" Well, Hunter, keep turning the pages and all will be revealed.

Dark and Light
Darkness overtakes the light,
Trapping, smothering
Argent light perseveres--
Burning deep within the Fold of Darkness,
Bursting forth,
Radiance dances with shadow,
Each struggles with the other.
Dominating, receding, again, and again.
At days end,
Compromising, blending,
Becoming one.
Dusk
-DP-

Prologue:

The rocking sensation comes first, then the blizzard. The snow is blinding, obscuring the scene before me. I can barely see the flames of the fire that is flickering through the whiteout. I feel nauseous from watching the swirling of the snow...around and around. Finally, it stops almost as quickly as it had started. The room is so familiar...I can see people in the room sitting near the fireplace and lights twinkling from the tree in the corner. I can remember the sound of a fire crackling, and I can almost feel the warmth of the flames. Warm and dry---Oh, how I miss the feeling. Will I forever be stuck here, alone, in this stagnant watery world? Will I ever get to take my rightful place in the world again? Or, will I spend eternity staring out at the world while the world stares in at me? How long have I been here? I have no idea of how much time has passed. How many Christmases ago?

TOSSING HER LONG BLONDE HAIR OVER her shoulder; Terese stepped back to survey her handiwork. The tree was up and looking quite festive; hung with delicate antique angels, hand-blown glass ornaments, and bells from around the world. Unique tree ornaments acquired from their travels and antique store finds.

"It's magnificent this year, even if I do say so myself," Terese announces to the currently empty room. "I love Christmas!" Terese singsongs aloud as she pirouettes around the expansive receiving room of Bilford Mansion. So, named for the Bilford family of New Hampshire; as is the town in which she and her husband, Gordon Bilford III, call home.

Terese felt very fortunate to have Gordon, a very handsome, a very indulgent husband who shares her love of the holiday. They had started collecting Christmas decorations before they were wed nearly ten years ago; married on Christmas Eve, of course. Studying the room, Terese runs through the items of her mental checklist, one more time, in preparation for the holiday gathering she and Gordon have planned for tonight; their annual Winter Solstice celebration.

"I want everything to be perfect," Terese thought. The caterers would be arriving shortly, and she checked the buffet table one more time. The cream-colored linens, which had been passed down through generations of Bilford's, were edged with gold embroidery. She ran her hand over the table covering to smooth a small wrinkle and made a minor adjustment to the greenery that graced the center of the table. Feeling giddy with excitement as she smiled approvingly at the cedar boughs caught up with large glittery gold bows draping the curved banister leading to the second floor. Flames crackled brightly in the fireplace; its mantle festooned with more cedar and a pair of authentic mercury glass hurricane globes that held golden candles waiting to be lit. Tiny pewter deer peeked out from the greenery, but the center of the mantle sits empty for now; because, Gordon has promised her a surprise, something special for the place of honor on the mantle.

"Silver and gold--- silver and gold," Singing to herself, Terese hurried upstairs to the bedroom she shares with her husband. She needed to make sure Gordon's clothes were laid out for tonight and to begin readying herself for the party. Gordon had said that he needed to make a stop before coming home to pick-up her surprise. He wouldn't' give her any hints, *"It must be an exceptional find if he wants it placed on the mantle where they normally placed their favorite angel collection,"* Terese thought as she twisted and turned to scrutinize herself in the full-length antique tri-fold mirrors, *"Just like all the ladies of the Bilford Manor have in the past,"* she mused.

For tonight, Terese had decided to wear her white-blond hair curled and piled high on her head, accentuating her long neck along with the gold chains graduated from her throat to her cleavage. Checking on her dress, hanging on the closet door suspended from its satin hanger, yet again, Terese thinks how perfect it will be for the party tonight. Not to mention how pleased Gordon would look when he saw her in the floor-length off-white chiffon gown. Once again, she took a moment to admire the intricate gold embroidery that was splayed across the shoulders, the same embroidery highlighted the ruching of the empire waist and the edging around the hem of the perfectly draped skirt. Uncharacteristically, Terese had splurged on herself and had the dress made to compliment the decor of their home for the party. Indulging in a moment of daydreaming, Terese imagined herself in the arms of her raven-haired husband, her skirt swirling, his dark eyes staring into her face as they danced tonight.

Breaking from her brief reverie, and glancing at the tiny clock on her make-up table her clear-blue eyes widen as she took note of the lateness of the hour. Quickly slipping on a pale-gold dressing gown, she hurried downstairs. *"Gordon will be home any second,"* she thinks, with anticipation, *"with my Christmas surprise."*

Gordon Bilford III unlocked the front door and stepped into the foyer of Bilford Manor. He never tired of walking through that door; *"I always feel such a deep connection with Bilford Mansion, and well I should,"* he thinks, *"Considering the price that has been paid by my family."* Carefully, Gordon placed the gift he has promised Terese on a Queen's Anne table that has graced the foyer for decades, anxious to see Terese's reaction when she opens the box. *"Terese is so expressive and so beautiful,"* Gordon says to himself, *"What is it that people say? Beautiful on the inside as well as the outside, but with Terese, it isn't just a platitude. She is truly a joy to be with."* And, Gordon begins to ache with the loneliness he knew he would find when she was gone; but he had lived it with before, years ago when he had lost his first wife. *"I just didn't think I would have to go through this again. But, if I want to go on living,"* Gordon thought, ironically, *"I will have to go through the heartache again."*

Gordon watched with appreciation as Terese skipped happily down the wide curving staircase to greet him. Her silken hair pulled up and wearing the dressing gown he had given her for her birthday. Her porcelain complexion glowed with the anticipated excitement of the evenings' festivities. *"As usual,"* Gordon thought, *"she looks gorgeous."* He bent slightly to receive her greeting in the form of a lightly placed kiss, so as not to smudge her lipstick.

"Oh, Gordon I've been so excited to see my surprise," Terese trilled. "I know it must be something special if you want it to take the 'place of honor' on the mantle from the Holt Howard angel collection."

"It is," he said smiling indulgently as he retrieved the box from the table, "and if you come along in by the fire, you can open it and see for yourself. I think you will find it quite unique."

Squealing with anticipation and childlike delight Terese carefully opened the box and lifted out a snow globe that is unique indeed, due to its unusually large globe. The intricately carved base is tarnished with age, but the deceptively simplistic scene inside is intact and perfect.

"It's exquisite!" exclaims Terese. "Where did you find it? I've never seen one quite like this. The globe is rather large for such a sparse little scene."

"Actually, I have had it packed in storage for a while...it's a family heirloom. Passed from father to son."

"Gordon! You have been holding out on me," Terese exclaimed with mock reproach.

"In my defense, I have been waiting on an appraisal. I have, also, been waiting for the perfect opportunity to give it to you. Tonight's party seemed to be *the* perfect opportunity."

"Gordon, you're so sweet" patting the cushion, Terese beckoned him to sit beside her, "tell me more about the story behind this globe." Peering inside Terese observed a young woman in a full-length forest-green shirtwaist dress with long puffy sleeves, walking along a path, with a semi-circle of snow-laden pines set behind her. The trail started at a little bench nestled into the trees then followed next to the banks of a small pond set to one side. "The detailing is so incredibly life-like; I feel as if I could step inside and walk with her along the path around the pond," Terese marveled.

Gordon re-told a condensed version of the history of the globe. It was made in Scandinavia, yet the tiny statue had long dark hair and dark eyes; not traits you would typically associate with any Nordic lands, certainly not at the time this appeared to have been crafted. His great-grandfather had acquired it as payment in a poker game, and it was said to bless whoever owned it with prosperity, and long life.

"I guess it must be magic," Gordon said, with a touch of irony that only he understood, "Great Grandfather Bilford built his business... that in turn, built this town and people still marvel, given the era, that he lived well into his nineties."

Terese gave the snow globe a gentle shake, and a shower of snow engulfed the scene.

"It's just beautiful Gordon, and the tale behind it makes it all the more special. I know you said you wanted it for the mantle, but, just for tonight...for the party, I want to put it on the buffet table. That way everyone will see it, and it would make such a lovely centerpiece."

With a coy little smile, she added, "Besides, I want to show off my lovely gift from my wonderful husband, and the mantle is so tall no one will truly be able to appreciate it."

"What do you like best about it?" Gordon queried.

"That you gave it to me...trusting me with an heirloom from your family."

"No," Gordon said shaking his head with a chuckle. "Not the sentiment behind the gift. You are the most appreciative person I know, even with the littlest of things. I mean the gift itself. The snow-globe."

"I don't know; there is something about it that draws you into the scene; almost as if it has its own gravitational pull. There is no denying its beauty, and the craftsmanship is superb. Although, she looks a bit lonely and cold...strange, don't you think? Usually, the people in a snow-globe, are portrayed in coats, hats, and fur-lined muffs for the female figurines. And, laughing or at least smiling. She has a bewildered expression as if she has somehow lost her way. She appears to be dressed more for a soiree or gala; rather than taking a leisurely stroll on a wintry day." Terese gave a little shudder that brought her out of her reverie. She drew back her gaze from the globe and re-focused her clear blue eyes on Gordon, as she sheepishly explained, "I have always imagined myself inside the perfect little dioramas, like a *Currier and Ives* winter wonderland, come-to-life." Terese ducked her head and peeked from under her lashes at Gordon. "Too childish? Too silly for the Lady of Bilford Manor?"

"On the contrary," Gordon replied, with an indulgent smile. "I think your answer as the Lady of Bilford Manor, is more perfect then you will ever know. I also think you're sweet and that it fits you perfectly, my imaginative little elfin. So, why don't you place it exactly where you want it for tonight? And, you might want to check on the caterers ensuring everything meets your specifications, and while you do that, I will take a quick shower and change. You can take your time dressing; I will be ready and here, along with Joseph to greet our guests awaiting your grand entrance," he said with a wink.

"Oh Gordon, you're such a tease," Terese laughed. But, with a quick glance at the grandfather clock and a small cry of alarm when she saw the time, Terese carefully placed the snow globe to nestle in the center of the greenery that adorned the buffet. Then blowing Gordon a kiss she turned toward the kitchen.

After showering and changing, Gordon stepped into the hall outside the bedroom and hearing Terese's light tread on the servants' back stairs, Gordon started to make his way downstairs. Suddenly, what sounded like a tremendous sonic boom rattled the windows, at the same time the hallway was plunged into darkness and Gordon heard a small cry from Terese, but just as suddenly the lights flooded the hall again.

Downstairs, Gordon checked on the kitchen staff to assure the electrical interruption had not presented any problems. *"Terese would have undoubtedly been devastated if anything were to go wrong,"* Gordon thought, as he headed to the Hall's drawing room. There, he poured himself a drink and dropped into one of the leather wing-backs that flanked the fireplace. *"Alone again,"* Gordon brooded, staring into the fire. *"Hopefully, I won't be alone for too long,"* he thought.

Gordon, along with his steward Joseph, greeted the guests and poured drinks all around. He played the perfect host. Everyone asked for Terese, and he made her apologies blaming the sudden onslaught of yet another migraine, and relayed her request to please forgive her for not joining them tonight.

"However," Gordon announced, "as most of you know Terese does have a certain fondness for Christmas." Nearly all of the guests, especially those that knew Terese well, laughed at such an understatement. "So, she has asked me to say *'please, please stay and enjoy'* and I second it." Raising his glass to his many guests, Gordon toasted, "To Terese, we will eat, drink, and be merry."

Their oldest and dearest friends, Fran and Shaun O'Malley, had brought along their niece, Colleen, (pronounced with an Irish lilt as Call-leen) who was visiting from upstate New York. The O'Malley's were a unique family dynamic. Brothers O'Malley, Shaun, and Shamus had married sisters Fran and Fiona Kelly. Colleen was the daughter of Shamus and Fiona O'Malley; both of whom had been killed in a tragic accident when their daughter was barely a teenager. And, although, Shaun and Fran had given their niece a home, and spoke of her often, Gordon and Terese had never met her. Gordon recognized her from a portrait that graced the entryway of the O'Malley home.

"She certainly grew-up very nicely. She's quite lovely," Gordon thought, *"the portrait does not do her justice."* With deep red hair that sparked when the lights caught it, a sprinkle of freckles across her high cheek-bones, an engaging smile and a body that had caught the attention of nearly every man in the room, Colleen O'Malley had grown-up quite nicely. *"She must have inherited her coloring and height from the O'Malley side,"* Gordon surmised. Shaun O'Malley was a great red bear of a man, with a quick wit and winning smile, who was also, fiercely loyal to family and friends. Fran, his wife, a striking dark-haired beauty that could charm the birds from the sky.

In much the same style as her Aunt, Colleen had charmed everyone she had met tonight with a soft laugh and a certain grace. *"She certainly has caught my attention,"* Gordon thought, as he observed her from across the room when he noticed that she was gingerly holding the snow-globe from the center of the dining table, and was peering intently inside. Excusing himself, from yet another boring anecdote from John Bishop, a neighbor that Terese had insisted they invite, *"Because it's the polite thing to do"* she had said. Gordon approached Colleen.

"Good evening, we haven't been formally introduced, I'm Gordon Bilford," he said as he drew near to stand next to the stunning red-haired beauty. Gordon was a bit flummoxed by the peculiar pull he was feeling from the young woman, but schooled his features as he said, "I noticed you seemed intrigued by this Christmas trinket."

Colleen turned to Gordon and replied with a dazzling smile, "Snow globes are my favorites, and I collect them. However, I have never seen one quite like this one; the detailing in the figurines are quite impressive, wherever did you find it?"

When she had turned, and Gordon was faced with the full force of her smile, he was momentarily disconcerted. "Actually," Gordon began, "it has been in the Bilford family for generations. I gifted my first wife with it, for our first Christmas."

"Oh, I'm so sorry for your loss..."

"Yes, it was tragic, but then Terese came into my life. I consider myself a fortunate man."

"Yes, of course," Colleen replied appearing a bit flustered. "I'm sorry I didn't get to meet her tonight."

Changing the subject, Gordon inquired if she would be staying with her Aunt and Uncle for the holidays. When she said that she was not sure how long she would be in Bilford, Gordon replied, "I'm sure you will meet Terese at another time, Fran and Shaun are not only our closest neighbors but our dearest friends. It's amazing that we have never met before."

Dipping her head, and peeking up at him with wide green eyes, she replied, "I've been away at school, and then took some time off to travel. It's been years since I've been in Bilford."

Later in the evening, after the last guest had left, and as the temporary hired help cleaned the kitchen, Gordon poured himself yet another drink.

"Sir, you might want to slow-down," Joseph suggested, indicating the glass in Gordon's hand, "How many have you had?"

"Not nearly enough," Gordon replied, "I'm not completely numb yet."

Hearing Joseph heave a heavy sigh, Gordon retrieved the snow globe from the formal dining table and moved it to the mantle in the great hall. Gordon stepped back to admire it and raised his glass in a salute as he studied the scene inside.

The dark-haired beauty, Jeanette, was no longer alone, or lonely, for there was another. An equally beautiful woman with white blonde hair curled and piled high on her head. She wears an off-white dress with intricate gold embroidery across the shoulders, around the high waist, and across the hem of her swirling chiffon skirt and is sitting daintily on the bench at the apex of the path.

"*Another acquisition to appease the devil's deal, so that my life will go on,*" thought Gordon. Peering into the mirror that hung over the mantle he spoke aloud to his reflection, "Well, old man, Mr. Gordon Bilford the...what is it now? Oh yes, the third isn't that what father said? Regardless, third, fourth, or fifth you're alone again."

Turning his attention back to the snow-globe he musingly thought: "*Hmm-mm pure cliché, but, with a brunette and a blonde; perhaps, a redhead is needed; Ms. Colleen O'Malley is exquisite, she would complete the set in this globe, and make a nice addition to the others tucked away in the vault.*"

GORDON TWISTED HIS WEDDING RING AROUND and around on his finger. He stood at his second story bedroom window watching the line of vehicles slowly approach the front of Bilford Manor. Crawling up the long-curved drive making their way to the center of the circle at the front portico of the manor was no less than three limos, four Bentley s, two Aston Martins, and a Rolls.

There was enough luxurious rolling metal and chrome in his drive to make even the most elite of autophiles salivate. They stopped long enough for drivers to jump out and scurry around to hold the doors open for some of the more prominent members of his social and business circles. More than a few political figures and a small number of minor celebrities would be attending. He was comforted knowing they were each receiving a solemn and dignified greeting at the entrance to Bilford Manor by his houseman, Joseph; who handed them off to be greeted by the O'Malley's.

The entrance hall and drawing rooms were a floral delight to the senses of both sight and fragrance. Fran and Joseph had scoured every greenhouse and florist for miles in search of fresh lavender to be added to the arrangements, Terese's favorite. The catering servers moved discreetly among the growing throng, making sure everyone's needs were being met. Glasses refilled, canapés offered, and directions to the powder rooms for the newcomers; all being handled deftly under the watchful eyes of Joseph as he stood on the wide dais at the front entrance. Debussy's *Trois Nocturnes* played softly in the background to quiet introductions and the muted conversations of the mourners. Gordon had been dreading this particular event since he had boarded the plane in Switzerland one week ago today. The memorial service for Terese.

Turning away from the bedroom window that faced the front lawns, Gordon wandered to the French doors on the opposite end of the bedroom. The weather had cooperated quite nicely for New Hampshire in the middle of January. It was cold, but the sun was out, and there had not been any new snow for several days allowing the shoveled walks and drive to remain clear. Gordon stepped out on the balcony that faced the east, he welcomed a deep breath of the chilled salt air. His balcony overlooked the back of the Bilford property that leads to the water's edge.

New Hampshire has only 18 miles of coastline, and Gordon treasured his piece of the coast. The timelessness and the repetition of watching the waves roll in to grasp at the grains of sand and then roll back out, scattering those grains into the vastness of the ocean always felt apropos. He likened it to his place in the world. The balance "... *take a little away here and scatter it to find a foothold there,*" he mused silently.

As he watched the water, Gordon allowed his mind to wander back to the days that followed the Bilford's annual "Winter Solstice Christmas" party. For days after the party, Gordon had intercepted the phone calls that flooded in from concerned friends who had attended the party inquiring after Terese's health. Finally, on the 'eve' before New Year's Eve, he made a phone call to their neighbors, the O'Malley's.

He told them that he had been doing some research, and had found a clinic in Switzerland that specialized in the treatment of migraines. Terese seemed to be getting worse he had explained;

and this clinic had an excellent reputation for, if not curing, at the very least alleviating the worst of the symptoms. Their departure for Switzerland would be immediate. Two days after his arrival in Switzerland he had called to tell them of her demise. It turned out that Terese had had an aneurysm.

"They tried everything, but they couldn't save her," he had moaned into the phone. "I've lost her, I've lost her," he sobbed.

Gordon had sounded so bereft on the phone the O'Malley's had offered to fly over and help him with the arrangements to bring Terese home. *"The O'Malley's' are unusually good people,"* thought Gordon, *"but I may have over acted."*

"No, no," Gordon had told them, "I couldn't ask such a thing of you. Repatriating Terese could take weeks. I will take care of everything here. Actually, if everything goes smoothly, I will be returning home before too long. Terese and I had a serious discussion years ago after attending a funeral service for a friend, and Terese had made me promise then not to put her on display if she should die before me. She insisted on cremation." Gordon paused to listen to their murmurs of sympathy over their speakerphone. He could hear Fran quietly sobbing in the background.

"Listen, I have an appointment at the American consulate in Bern in about three hours. I need to get myself pulled together to focus… so I can make sense of the paperwork involving Terese's death on foreign soil and what that entails. So, I really must go, it's at least an hour and a half to Bern and with the fresh snow maybe longer. However, I did want to let you know about Terese and that I'm staying at the Gstaad Palace Hotel. I will call again in a day or two; but, in the meantime, Fran I do have a request."

Still sniffling, Gordon could hear her clear the tears from her throat before she asked, "The Palace? Oh, Gordon isn't that just too difficult for you? Didn't you and Terese go there for your second honeymoon?"

Pausing, Gordon lowered his voice just above a whisper and answered, "Yes, I thought it would bring us luck. Terese loved waking up and looking to the Alps every morning before we started our day. She was so happy here, and the clinic is near. I had thought we might extend our stay if the treatments went well for her."

"I am so sorry Gordon. Anything, anything I can do at all. You must know how much we adored Terese."

"I am a bit hesitant to ask," Gordon said, forcing his voice to break slightly, "It may be too difficult for you to go through."

"Please," Fran replied, "I would be honored to do what I can for dear Terese, and for you Gordon."

"As you know," he began, "Terese had no family." Hearing an affirmation from the O'Malley's on this point, Gordon continued. "However, being the kind, generous, and loving person she was, Terese had collected so many dear friends. Would you make a few calls to let people know? I will, of course, send a formal announcement to the local papers and media, but I thought a more personal touch from someone so close to us might be a more appropriate way for our mutual friends to be told."

"Yes, yes, of course," Fran said, "I will start making calls within the hour."

"Thank you both so much. I don't know what I would do without such good friends to rely upon."

"Yes, the O'Malley's are outstanding people," Gordon thought, as he wandered through the exquisitely appointed suite pausing to appreciate the view afforded him through the floor-to-ceiling windows that could be found in every room of the suite facing the mountains. *"That wasn't nearly as hard as I had thought it would be... Fran was so eager to please, nearly begging to do the favor."*

As Gordon drank in the scenery, he remembered introducing Terese to the Swiss Alps. She had been enamored with the grandeur of the Alps when they had spent their month-long second honeymoon here in this very suite. Thinking back to that very pleasurable interlude he recalled how mesmerized Terese was by their beauty, and yet, feared their danger. When they were not out exploring the picturesque village of Gstaad; she was entirely satisfied to gaze upon the mountains for long periods of time, safely ensconced, from every room, and every angle. Even while soaking in the enormous jetted tub that faced the peaks with the same floor-to-ceiling windows that could be found as in the rest of the suite; Terese would watch as the shadows of the morning clouds would play across the face of the mountains. After her morning ritual, she would then spend hours attempting to recreate the majestic vista on canvas while he went skiing. Actually, Terese had a bit of an artistic flair. Even now, one of the Alp canvasses hung in her dressing room. He honestly did miss her. Pity though, he never could convince her to try the skiing with him. And, now she never would. Which is why he believed one should never squander an opportunity.

Firmly setting aside all thoughts of Terese, and checking his watch, he had grabbed his down jacket from the chair and headed out for the elevator. He had just enough time to make his appointment. The concierge had called, just before he had spoken with the O'Malley's, to tell him that all reservations had been taken care of for the afternoon, and Gordon didn't want to be late.

Gordon had made an appointment with a beautiful dark-haired, dark-eyed seductress from Florence. The Italian beauty had shared his connecting flight from Zurich to Switzerland. They had run into each other several times since he had been here; and, again last evening at a local cafe' where they shared a few drinks and decided to make plans for this afternoon. They would lunch here in the hotel at the La Fromagerie Restaurant and then hit the slopes via Air-Glaciers. It was January after all, the peak skiing season; it would have been a shame not to take to the trails at least one more time before heading back to the States. And, the lovely Katrina, was nearly as much of a ski enthusiast as he.

"She is the exact opposite of Terese in every way, and made for a pleasant distraction while he had been there; especially, in light of his reason for the trip," Gordon thought with a sigh.

A blaring car horn abruptly brought Gordon out of his reverie. Feeling an odd, yet familiar sensation, he touched the key through his shirt, an ancient twin to another, which he always wore on a heavy silver chain. *"Andrew!"* The name fairly screamed across Gordon's mind. Going to the front windows to look down on the drive, Gordon saw a low-slung, midnight blue, sports car of some obscure make that he couldn't identify located among the austerity of the BMW's and a Rolls that were slowly making their way to the entrance. Knowing Andrew as he did, he presumed that he could have purchased two Rolls for the price of that little beauty. But this wasn't the time to be admiring the man's newest toy. He had a house full of very influential people mourning the death of his wife, and Andrew wasn't the type to appreciate the solemnity of the occasion. To the contrary, the man was more prone to flaunt his extremely non-conventional viewpoint of polite society. What was Andrew doing here?

Gordon decided to wait in the bedroom. The last thing he needed was to greet Andrew in front of the mourners. The last thing needed today, of all days, was Andrew. *"He will find me soon enough,"* Gordon brooded as he once again fingered the key.

Within minutes, Gordon could hear Andrew's boisterous voice as he made his way up the stairs.

"Joseph, old man, how are you? It's been a long time." Gordon couldn't hear Joseph's muted reply; but he could detect the sudden silence in the great hall where the mourners had gathered.

"Go back to your duties, Joe." Gordon cringed at the unrestrained volume of Andrew's voice. "I'm sure Gordon knows I'm here and is waiting for me. I'll catch up with you later."

Throwing wide both of the double-doors that led to the sitting area of the bedroom, Andrew Bilford walked-in with his usual swagger. Gordon turned to face a near mirror image of himself. The same dark wavy hair they both wore longer than today's current style, roughly the same six-foot-plus athletic frame; but whereas Gordon's eyes were as dark as night, Andrew's eyes were a deep emerald green. Although the physical differences were minimal, their personality traits were near polar opposites. Gordon, portrayed the epitome of refinement and decorum; and the boisterous Andrew could give lessons on impropriety. Speaking loudly enough for any interested ears to hear he said, "Gordon, my dear, dear cousin, how are you?"

QUIETLY, WITH A FURROWING OF HIS brow as the only indicator of his anger, Gordon asked, "Andrew, what are you doing here?"

Answering the question with one of his own, Andrew replied with a smirk that belied his tone of concern, "Why Gordon, we're family, where else would I be at a time like this?"

"Close the doors Andrew, and please lower your voice. I think we should have some privacy, don't you?"

Pulling the doors closed, Andrew turned to face Gordon, "So you're going through this charade again, cousin?"

"This is not a charade," Gordon replied indignantly. "Terese is gone, and these people are here to pay their respects. There is no pretense in their mourning, nor mine. Terese was a loving and lovely person."

Cocking his head to one side, Andrew studied Gordon's continence for a moment before speaking, "Oh I have no doubt the people below are genuinely sorrowful. But, you?" Andrew sauntered across the room to survey the ocean view before turning to face his cousin and mockingly asked, "Was she as lovely as Miss Katrina?"

"How...?" began Gordon.

"Have you forgotten cousin that my existence is connected to yours?" Andrew asked as he pulled from his shirt a key, identical to the one that hung around Gordon's neck. "You see I was beginning to think that you had. So, since you seemed to be dragging your feet, I took care of things on my end; which prompted a visit to our friend Dr. Gustav in Switzerland for the necessary paperwork. By the way, brilliant move on your part for bringing the good doctor into the Fold. Anyway, I digress...I wasn't *married* to the girl, but we had been seen together enough that I needed some sort of plausible explanation. So, I took her for a romantic getaway, and there was an accident." Pausing to pour himself a drink from the monogrammed whiskey decanter that set at the ready on the dry bar, Andrew continued, "A *skiing* accident."

Andrew paused once more to sip slowly at his drink, but primarily, to give Gordon time to digest this bit of information. "I was roughly three hours from you, down in Zermatt skiing on the Matterhorn, while you, dear cousin, squired the delectable Katrina out and about Gstaad."

"You son-of-a-bitch," Gordon roared, as the lights in the room flickered.

"Ah ah ah, -- Gordon, please! Remember the guests. Remember your manners." Andrew sneeringly reminded Gordon. More pointedly he asked, "No need to raise *Hell*; is there?"

Gordon immediately snapped his head around and strode to the bedroom entrance. Opening one of the doors just a fraction, he listened for a moment. Hearing nothing but the subdued sounds of conversation from below, and strains of Chopin's *Pavane for Dead Princess*, "*a fitting tribute*," he thought, as he quietly closed the door and rested his forehead on the frame.

Chuckling, as he observed Gordon's reaction, Andrew added, "And Gordon, to be more accurate, shouldn't it be 'son-of-a-bastard'?"

Gordon hated that Andrew was the one person that could goad him into losing his temper, he always could, even when they were children. Drawing a deep calming breath, while still facing the door, Gordon quietly asked, "Am I correct in assuming that you have made a stop at our offices in Boston?" Turning to face his cousin with a modicum of his former composure he said, "Tell me you didn't bring it here."

"Of course, I stopped in Boston, I'm not a fool. That's when I found Terese," Gordon raised an eyebrow at that remark as his dark eyes bored into Andrew's green eyes.

Backtracking, Andrew immediately amended, "Okay, okay... perhaps I should have said that's when I found *out about* Terese. I know how distressed you can get about it all, so I thought a visit would be in order. Honestly, Gordon, I don't understand why you allow yourself to get so involved in these relationships. Why do you feel compelled to marry them?"

"Did it ever occur to you that maybe I just want to feel normal, even if it's just for a short amount of time?"

"Normal," Andrew scoffed with a shake of his head. "We'll have time to argue the virtues of normality later, I believe I hear Joseph hovering at the doors."

With a sharp warning rap, Joseph opened the door, and looking directly at Gordon said, "Sir, it's time." Turning his attention to Andrew, Joseph gave him a nod of acknowledgment, and continued, "Sir, your rooms have been readied, if you would care to rest."

"Thank you, but I don't need to rest, Joe," Andrew said with mock politeness while using the shortened form of the butler's name knowing how he and Gordon hated it. "I will be right by my Cousin's side in his time of need." Heading for the exit, Andrew added, "Family can be such a great comfort at a time like this, wouldn't you agree with that Joe?"

Joseph and Gordon shared a look of disdain. Gordon, experiencing the strange, yet familiar sensation put his hand to his chest to touch the key again through the silk fabric of his shirt. At the same time, he heard Andrew's laughter floating upward from the stairs.

Gordon straightened his shoulders and stepped into the hallway, crossed to the top of the wide curving staircase as Debussy's *The*

Girl with the Flaxen Hair began to play; his cue to make his entrance. It was a favorite of his, and he paused in the middle of the staircase to remember Terese as the music washed over him. This particular piece had been chosen from the vast collection of classical music that Gordon had acquired over the years; he had played it for Terese on one cold winter New Hampshire night. He had called her his 'flaxen-haired girl' and they had made love in front of the fireplace. Heaving a great sigh, Gordon continued down the stairs; he would never make love to Terese again, nor, would he ever listen to this piece of music again. It had been far more challenging to let Terese go than it had been Jeanette; he actually liked Terese.

Reaching the bottom of the stairs, Gordon made his way to stand next to Terese's portrait; it had been placed on an easel to one side of the dais, framed on each side with formal arrangements of her favorite flowers. Gordon could barely look at her image; he could hear the murmurings of those close-by attributing his behavior to that of a grieving husband, rather than the gut-wrenching guilt that plagued him.

Drawing a deep breath and facing his guests, Gordon said, "I want to thank all of you for coming out on such a blustery day to celebrate the life of my beloved Terese...our beloved Terese." Surreptitiously, Gordon's eyes scanned the crowd for Andrew as he continued by asking everyone to feel free to share a favored memory about Terese. Terese had always been highly respected for her charity work; and she could be described as the type of person that could be just as comfortable rubbing shoulders with an ambassador at a gala as she was chatting with a local store clerk. Everyone she met loved her. Gordon took his seat as one person after the other spoke their praise of Terese; his dark eyes continually scanning for Andrew.

For over an hour they spoke, until he caught Fran's eye and with a small inclination of his head she came forward and asked the mourners to please enjoy the refreshments, continue to share their stories of Terese as they visited. "But we really must let Gordon have a few minutes to himself."

Heading back upstairs after promising that he would return, Gordon entered his bedroom. Feeling the cold ocean breeze sweep across the room, Gordon immediately turned to the balcony to find one of the doors open. He could see Andrew through the opening, and he wasn't alone. Striding across the room and stepping out he turned to find Colleen O'Malley standing to one side, looking toward the water.

The fresh salt breeze caught her long flaming red hair, pushing it away from her face, and lifting it to expose her graceful neck. Aware of his body going taut, not to mention that strange, magnetic pull from the O'Malley beauty, Gordon cleared his throat to announce his presence, and said, "Andrew, don't you think it's a little too cold to be entertaining Miss O'Malley on the balcony?"

"Gordon," Andrew answered, "so you already know Miss O'Malley?"

"We met at the Solstice Party," Colleen interjected. "I had just arrived in Bilford to visit my Aunt and Uncle." Flushing, from remembering that was the night that Terese took sick, Colleen warmly said, "Mr. Bilford, please accept my condolences on your wife's passing."

Giving her a nod of acknowledgment Gordon answered, "Thank you, and thank you for helping with the arrangements for today."

Colleen looked surprised, so Gordon continued, "Fran told me what a wonderful assistant you were, Miss O'Malley, with the flowers and over-seeing the menus."

"Although I have never met Terese, I'm glad to have been of some assistance," she answered, "And, please, would you both call me Colleen?"

"Agreed," Andrew smiled, "if you will call us Andrew and Gordon."

Inclining her head in agreement, after looking to Gordon

for confirmation, she drew her wrap tighter against her body as another gust of wind blew in, Colleen turned, "Gordon I think you're right it is chilly out here, and I would like to go back in now." Taking Andrew's immediately proffered arm she continued as they went back inside, "I had been in the conservatory admiring all the flowers when Andrew found me. I realized that you must have an extraordinary view of the ocean from somewhere inside the house and Andrew said it was best viewed from this balcony. I'm so very sorry to have intruded into your private quarters, I would not have been so easily led had I known." She seemed to very pointedly say this last part to Andrew, Gordon observed.

"Ah," thought Gordon, *"so she does have some sense of deportment, which is more than I can say for Andrew."*

Taking both of her hands in his, forcing her to drop Andrew's arm, Gordon said, "Please don't concern yourself. The view from up here is extraordinary; but you look absolutely chilled to the bone." Still holding her left hand, he led her to the doorway and said, "Why don't you go warm yourself by the fire downstairs with a brandy. I need to speak to Andrew for just a moment, and then we'll both be down."

"Thank you, I will," Colleen murmured.

Softly closing the door behind her, Gordon turned to his cousin, "No Andrew."

"What do you mean, *No Andrew?* I simply brought her up for the view Gordon."

Dark eyes collided with green, as Gordon gave Andrew a look that clearly said he didn't believe him.

"Okay, look," Andrew said, "She's very familiar to me, and I just wanted to spend a few quiet moments with her to try and figure out where I have run into her before."

Gordon still skeptical, retorted, "I know you Andrew, and I know how you operate. Colleen is the niece of the O'Malley's...just leave her out of it. Granted she is a beautiful woman, but we don't need to intrude into her life."

Andrew narrowed his eyes as he scrutinized Gordon's face, "You're attracted to her! That's why you don't want me to be around her. You're afraid I will make her my next conquest, and my next tribute!"

Gordon inwardly groaned, *"Not only could Andrew get under his skin quicker than anyone else ever could; but he could also see straight through him. Gordon never could run a bluff on him with much success."*

Seeing no point in denying it, given their relationship, Gordon replied, "Yes, I find her attractive. However, I have no intentions of pursuing her. I will admit I had considered it, but it would be too difficult with her family living next door. So, no I will not, and more importantly, Andrew, neither will you."

"Gordon…" Andrew began.

"No more Andrew, we're expected downstairs. For that matter, Colleen is waiting too. This day has been difficult enough." Gordon leveled a look on Andrew, and with a raised brow, more pointedly said, "And I have had enough surprises for one day."

Once downstairs, Gordon began to make the rounds among the mourners accepting sympathetic platitudes from business acquaintances, along with the sincere sympathies of the people that knew Terese well. He kept an eye on Andrew and was relieved to observe that for once Andrew was behaving in a gentlemanly manner. Nearly everyone commented on the remarkable resemblance between the cousins. Some saying they had to look twice to tell them apart. Andrew had charmed them all by declaring that he, of course, was the better-looking cousin. Gordon was pleasantly surprised by Andrew's solicitous manner with the guests and felt comfortable enough to leave him for a bit. He knew Andrew was perfectly capable of being quite charming; but, given his flamboyant entrance earlier, Gordon found his willingness to be so affable entirely unexpected.

Gordon had spotted Colleen near the conservatory a little earlier and gradually made his way in that direction. He stopped to tell Joseph to keep an eye on Andrew for him…just in case. Joseph nodded and headed to the main hall to stand near the front entrance as people began to take their leave.

Entering the greenhouse Gordon was immediately struck by the various fragrances of the flowering plants and moist earth combining to hang so heavy in the wet air that he could nearly taste nature's perfume.

The additions of new species were carefully chosen to create fresh groupings that complemented the existing plants. In constant flux, the conservatory became a welcoming respite to the harshness of a New England winter. The octagonal shape of the enormous space provided interesting nooks and corners in which to arrange comfortable seating to while away an hour or two reading. Or, one could just rest in the double hammock located between two of the waterfall fountains that were connected by a man-made brook. Terese had taken great delight and pride in helping to create such a magical place that had been featured in several magazines, and at least two books by well-known interior designers.

Spying Colleen at the far-side of the glassed-in room Gordon paused to lean against the door-frame and observe her unawares. He watched as she gently ran a finger over the delicate petals of an orchid and bent to take in its fragrance. She then trailed her hand through a clustering of ferns to her left as she moved deeper into the greenery. She meandered forward and found one of the many small benches that were placed among the greenery. In one graceful, fluid movement she sat down and bent to remove her shoes, her thick hair falling around her obscuring her face from Gordon's view. Straightening, she slightly arched her back to stretch, and while still looking straight ahead she asked, "Are you going to join me?" She then turned to look in Gordon's direction. "Or, are you just going to continue to watch me?" she asked while gesturing with a wave of her hand to indicate the windows that now mimicked mirrors due to the setting of the sun.

Gordon was a little taken aback, *What is wrong with me? Caught ogling my guest and at my wife's memorial.* Giving himself a mental shake to focus, as he straightened, he replied with feigned indignation, "I was simply coming to 'Thank you' once again before I retire for the evening. It's been a long day." Gordon gave her a curt parting nod before turning on his heel to leave.

"Oh… Gordon," upon hearing his voice, Colleen jumped up and quickly started to move toward him, "I'm so sorry, I thought you were your cousin. Please forgive my presumptuousness."

Stopping, to allow her time to reach him, Gordon smiled inwardly; outwardly he schooled his features into a stoic mask before turning to look down into her green eyes full of concern.

"Has Andrew been too forward with you, Miss O'Malley?" Gordon caught her slight wince when he addressed her formally, and he took note of the embarrassment that reddened her cheeks. *"Good,"* Gordon thought, *"best to keep her a little off-balance."*

"Not really forward, perhaps just a little too familiar. Your Cousin Andrew seems to think that he knows me from somewhere. I really don't have any idea what he is talking about," Colleen explained. "Maybe I just have one of those ordinary faces that seems familiar to lots of people," she said smiling up at her host.

Gordon returned her smile with a glimmer of his own, as he bent closer to her unable to resist the urge to drop a fleeting kiss on her parted lips, before he said, "There is nothing ordinary about you Colleen." Leaving her staring after him, Gordon made his way up the servants' staircase to his rooms on the second floor.

Throwing the doors open and without breaking stride, Gordon went straight to the bar and poured himself a generous shot, which he preceded to throw back in one gulp. While he could still feel the burn of the whiskey coursing through him, he poured a second. With his back to the softly lit room he spoke aloud, "Go away, Andrew."

Chuckling faintly and rising from a wing chair in a shadowed corner of the room, Andrew said, "So dear Cousin, you warn me off, while emphatically stating that you have *'no intentions'* of pursuing the lovely Colleen." Andrew came around to Gordon's side and softly commanded, "So, tell me, what in sweet Hell was that?" When Gordon didn't answer, Andrew continued pushing, "Change your mind? Couldn't resist a little taste? Think you might want to find your way into her pa--"

"Don't be boorish." Gordon retorted, cutting off his cousin's line of highly inappropriate questions.

"*Boorish?*" Andrew repeated mockingly. "Do you even hear yourself, man? You really do need to update your vocabulary cousin."

"Not everyone appreciates the crudeness of your vernacular Andrew." Gordon noticed Andrew's derisive sneer at his choice of words; before continuing, "In the shipping business...*our* shipping business, we have offices around the world. I must speak with people from all walks of life, from dock-workers to ambassadors. I don't have the luxury of being offensive, we have an image to uphold. I certainly haven't noticed you refusing any of your generous dividends."

"Geez, okay, okay," Andrew held up his hands, tired of the dressing down, "I won't bring it up again; however, you haven't answered my question. What was that little scene with Colleen?"

Furrowing his brow and, unconsciously raising his hand to his chest, Gordon asked, "Are you watching my every move?" Gordon chose one of the overstuffed chairs that faced the French-doors and sat down. "I've already got Joseph, I really don't need another watcher,"

Shaking his head, Andrew laughed, "You're avoiding the question."

Heaving a great sigh, Gordon knew Andrew would make his life intolerable until he gave him an explanation, but how could he explain when he didn't know? "I really can't give you an answer. Sitting here with you now, I can honestly say there will be no relationship between Colleen and me."

"But...?" prompted Andrew as he took the chair opposite of Gordon.

"But, when she's around, I am inexplicably drawn to seek her out. It's a need, not a want. When I first came home from Switzerland, I couldn't stay here on the chance that she would be here with Fran. Colleen helped her Aunt with the interview process for temporary wait-staff, met with the caterers, and florists." Gordon gave an uncharacteristic snort as he recalled his arrival at Bilford Manor, "From the moment I walked in the door, I knew there had been a shift, but I couldn't identify it; then Fran and Colleen, came in to greet me." Looking Andrew in the eyes, he said, "One look at Colleen, and I nearly forgot the reason they were in the house, Terese."

With an arch of his brow and a tilt of his head, Andrew urged Gordon to continue.

"I stayed long enough to sign a handful of blank checks and give final approvals for some of their choices. I left Joseph to handle the details while I went down to Boston. I have been staying at the corporate apartment over our offices for the past week; I only returned yesterday. I must have just missed you."

"I told you earlier there is something familiar about her, but I can't put my finger on it… yet. Maybe she has been sent here?"

"Don't you think I thought of that?" Gordon asked, impatience tinging his voice, "I've already had Joseph to check. She is not from our inner circle or any of the outliers of the Fold. Besides, that wouldn't explain my reaction to her. I'm as out of control as a testosterone driven teenage boy when she's around. It's been that way since the first night I met her."

Gordon noticed that Andrew was quietly shaking with laughter. "You're amused?"

"No, no, of course not!" Andrew denied, but the mirth in his voice belied his words. "Well, maybe a little."

"I shouldn't have tried to explain to you," Gordon said wearily.

"C'mon, Cousin, you're the one that plans every minuscule detail of every move you make. You're the astute, intelligent, and responsible one. The one that always says and does the right thing;

so, give me a moment to relish this out-of-control, libido-driven Gordon," Andrew said still laughing.

"Andrew!" Gordon admonished.

"Oh, hey now, I could have been far cruder-"

"Undoubtedly," Gordon retorted cutting Andrew off, "please Andrew, I am begging you; we can talk tomorrow I promise."

Rising from his chair, Andrew paused to pat Gordon's shoulder in what Gordon took as a gesture of understanding; but, as Andrew walked to the doorway, he threw one last taunt over his shoulder, "Sweet dreams Cousin."

ORDON AWOKE THE NEXT MORNING TO find a tray with a carafe of steaming coffee and the Boston Globe paper next to his bed courtesy of Joseph. He didn't care to 'click' his way through the news. Computers and smartphones were essential to his business. Gordon liked the fact that, through technology, he could work from nearly anywhere in the world, including his residence; however, for Gordon, computers, and smartphones equated work. When he was trying to relax, or just waking up, he preferred 'old school' by way of print papers and hard copy reading materials. *"They don't need to be charged, and if you accidentally drop your book or newspaper, they don't shatter,"* thought Gordon.

Showered and dressed, Gordon grabbed the paper and preceded downstairs for breakfast; and was surprised that Andrew was already sitting at the dining room table.

"Good morning Andrew," Gordon greeted his cousin in an attempt to get his attention away from the phone he held swiping and tapping.

"Gordon," Andrew answered, without taking his eyes from the gadget.

"Andrew, would you please put the phone away? Since you're up, I thought we could talk over breakfast."

"Give me a minute. I'm reading something of great interest," Andrew replied.

Dryly, Gordon said, "The pornography will always be there, Andrew."

Andrew looked-up with surprise, and then in a tone to match Gordon's said, "Now who is being *boorish?*"

Gordon nodded once to Andrew, "Touché." Chuckling softly, he asked, "Care to tell me what has so completely caught your attention?"

"It might catch your attention also," Andrew said. "I am waiting for a background check on Miss Colleen."

All traces of humor were erased as Gordon reminded Andrew, "I told you to leave it alone. Colleen will go about her life, and we shall go about ours. She will probably be gone soon, back to wherever she came from, and that will be that."

"Plan to sell Bilford Manor Cousin?"

"What?" Gordon asked sharply, "Of course not! Why would you ask such a thing?"

"Well," Andrew asked, "didn't she tell you?"

"Tell me what?" Gordon asked.

"She's not going back to where she came from...," Andrew began.

Gordon could tell that Andrew was relishing seeing him squirm, "Out with-it Andrew," he demanded.

"She's moving into the O'Malley's guest house. She is staying here in Bilford; just a couple of miles up the road," Andrew announced with glee.

Gordon slumped back in his chair, *"Well Hell,"* Gordon thought, *"all traces of a 'Good Morning' are gone now."*

"I see that has caught *your* attention," said Andrew, closely watching Gordon's face.

"Well this is ridiculous," Gordon thought. *"It's not as if he and the O'Malley's lived out of each other's back pockets. They frequently dined together in the past, but that was mostly due to the friendship between*

Fran and Terese." Out loud, he said, "It really is of no concern to me where she lives, Andrew. Remember, I am a recent widower, still in mourning; therefore, I can always make my excuses for any social invitations the O'Malley's might issue. Now, do you think we can finish our breakfast, and then turn our attention to our business for a little while? I have some things you need to sign."

Not to be detoured, Andrew asked, "And where was the *'widower-in-mourning'* last night, Gordon?"

Sighing heavily, Gordon responded, "Andrew, there is nothing particularly unusual for a bereaved widow, or widower to act out-of-character. I will send Joseph over later this morning with a note of apology to Miss O'Malley. Let's be done with this...agreed?"

"Sure Gordon," Andrew affably agreed. "Just as soon as I figure out where I have seen her before, we'll be done."

Gordon groaned mentally but simply said as if speaking to a child, "Eat your breakfast, Andrew. We have work to do before you take off on your next whim."

Andrew glared at Gordon for a beat, and then abruptly changed the subject, "You know Gordon I really do like the changes that have been made to the manor. The addition to my suite is quite comfortable, and the conservatory is nothing short of extraordinary. The new has been blended with the old seamlessly."

"I would have to credit the improvements to Terese, particularly the conservatory. She spent many hours there planning, and planting for that matter." Gordon said wistfully. "Never afraid to get her hands dirty she always worked side-by-side with the gardeners."

"Don't get maudlin on me Gordon. Terese was a wonderful woman, so was Jeanette, but you knew what you were getting into when you made the deal. If I recall correctly when our fathers brought us into the Fold so they could...ah...let's say retire, you were more than willing to sign-on-the-dotted-line, so to speak," Andrew tapped his chest, forcing Gordon to once again feel the weight of that decision from the chain around his own neck.

Gordon desperately wanted to end this conversation; sure, that if they continued, Andrew would detect the threads of doubt that had been weaving through Gordon's mind, for some time now. "You're right, of course, a deal is a deal; so, if you're finished, let's go to the office, and seal a few deals for *Bilford Shipping*," Gordon replied.

Gordon and Andrew had been pouring over the books for two hours, and were now on the last document, "I want to add this local trucking firm to our short-run transport fleet," Gordon said, as he indicated where Andrew needed to sign.

Suddenly Gordon froze, staring at the closed door. "What is the matter with you?" Andrew asked, looking around the room.

"Don't you feel that?" Gordon hissed.

"Feel what?"

"The shift..." Gordon began, but a knock at the office door cut him off before he could explain.

Joseph walked in, and looking directly at Gordon said, "I need to speak with you immediately, sir." Casting a glance at Andrew, he added, "Privately, please."

Hurriedly, scrawling his name on the last page of the contract, Andrew rose, stretched, and said, "Fine by me. I have some calls to make. I'll be in my rooms." Stopping at the door, he added, "By the way Gordon, I don't think I will have any traveling whims for a while. For the foreseeable future, I will remain here in Bilford Manor."

Following Andrew to the door, wanting him out of the room as quickly as possible, Gordon simply said, "Welcome home Andrew." Gordon closed the door as soon as Andrew had moved well out of earshot, he turned to Joseph and said, "She's here, isn't she?"

"Yes." Seeing the fire in Gordon's eyes, Joseph immediately continued, "I did exactly what you told me to do. I delivered your note, along with the orchid, and waited for her response, as you requested. It's just that her response was to come here and speak to you personally."

"Tell her I'm not here," Gordon instructed.

"I tried. In fact, I told Ms. O'Malley, I thought you were leaving the manor to run a couple of errands in the village. I told her that you had left just as I was leaving to deliver the message and orchid to her. She said, and I quote: *'If he's gone, I will just wait until he returns.'* Then she said something about not getting to spend enough time in the conservatory. That's where I left her."

"Damn her!" Gordon growled.

"We could do that, but it would be hard to explain to the Aunt and Uncle," Joseph replied dryly.

Narrowing his eyes at Joseph, Gordon said, "This isn't a joke."

"No sir, it isn't."

"This is ridiculous, I'll take care of it," Gordon said with determination.

Gordon headed straight to the conservatory, determined to put an end to any contact with Miss O'Malley. Upon entering he found Colleen sitting in the same spot as last night; *".... only this time I will not be pausing at the door to ogle her,"* Gordon told himself, trying to ignore the enticement he was already experiencing.

"Miss O'Malley, what can I do for you?" Gordon called from the entrance. He watched as she made her way to him. She had dressed very informally today; jeans and a black sweater. A tight pair of jeans, and a tight black sweater, both emphasizing all of her curves. Gordon drew a steadying breath wishing that he would have had Joseph to just send her on her way.

"Gordon, I thought we agreed that you would call me Colleen," she said, as she stood in front of him.

"Well, so much for keeping her off-balance with formality," thought Gordon, *"she appears to have recovered her equilibrium rather quickly."*

"Yes, you're correct, I'm sorry," Gordon said, "I am rather busy just now, so ---"

"I'm the one that owes you an apology for inviting myself over, and ignoring Joseph's excuses," Colleen said, cutting him off before he could finish. "Please don't blame Joseph, I refused to take no for an answer," she said with a knowing smile. "But, after receiving your note… Thank you, by the way for the orchid…I knew we needed to speak in person," Colleen paused for a breath before continuing, "Gordon, you have been under terrible stress for weeks now, and last night was a culmination of that stress." When Gordon didn't reply, she went on, "Due to your relationship with my Aunt and Uncle, I'm sure we will see each other from time-to-time. You see, I am moving to Bilford, and staying in their guest house. I don't want things to be awkward between us. So, let's just put that one small incident aside, and start from here. All right?"

Gordon had stood quietly during her little speech, watching her up-turned face for signs of deception; but he saw no indication of deceit. What he did see were the sprinkle of freckles across her nose and high cheekbones; the same freckles he had seen the first time they had met. Searching her eyes as she spoke, he noticed little flecks of gold that shimmered in their green depths, and he noticed the scent of her spicy perfume that seemed to wrap around him.

Closing his eyes, he told himself, *"C'mon man pull it together. Tell her whatever she wants to hear, and get away from her."*

Alarmed, Colleen reached out to place her hand on his arm, "Gordon, are you, all right?"

Gordon's eyes flew open at her touch. Gently pulling his arm away, he replied, "Yes, yes, I'm fine. You are very kind to overlook my indiscretion from last night. As I said in the note, I just wasn't myself, and I can assure you it will not happen again." Taking a step back to put a little more distance between them, Gordon said, with what he hoped would pass for a smile, and not a grimace of near pain, "I hope you will be happy here in our little hamlet."

"Thank you, I'm sure I will be quite happy here," Colleen said, with an infliction in her voice and a look in her eyes that Gordon found to be extremely disconcerting. With a smile, she said, "And, I will excuse myself now; so, you can get back to the work you were doing before I so rudely interrupted." As she started to move past him, she stopped, putting her hand on his arm once more, she reached up, and kissed him lightly on the cheek before softly saying, "Um, Gordon, don't make promises that we both know you can't keep." With that she was out the door, crossing the dining room, and heading toward the front entrance, as Gordon stared after her.

For a couple of moments, Gordon was absolutely stunned into stillness, barely breathing. Recovering, he went to the foot of the stairs, and bellowed, "Andrew!" His voice ringing through the manor.

Andrew appeared on the upper story landing, and peered over the balustrade at Gordon below, "You need something Cousin?" He asked with a smile from ear-to-ear.

"Pack," Gordon barked at him, as he headed up the stairs.

"I beg your pardon? Pack? Am I being asked to leave my home?" Andrew queried.

"Yes. We're both leaving our home. We will be in Albany in time for a late lunch." Gordon replied, taking the stairs two at a time, and his tone left no room for argument.

"Oh…skiing. Okay, give me 45 minutes, and I'll be ready," Andrew said.

"You have 30 minutes, and I will meet you by the car," Gordon threw back over his shoulder, as he entered his rooms from the opposite side of the large open landing between his and Andrew's quarters.

Gordon could hear Andrew's ringing laughter through the closed doors of his rooms. He wouldn't give himself time to think right now, *"…just focus on getting what I need for a few days. Don't think about anything else right now. Just throw some clothes in a bag, and grab a laptop."* Running through a mental checklist, he thought; *I have everything I need for the slopes at the house. The bathrooms are kept stocked with toiletries, and we can eat-out or order-in for our meals. Joseph needs to stay here to keep an eye on things."*

About 20 minutes later they were on the road heading North on Highway 16 that ran just inside the New Hampshire side of the state line separating New Hampshire and Maine. Albany lay just outside of the White Mountain National Forest and just a little over an hour from Bilford. Gordon had bought a house there for himself and Terese about four years ago, for the quiet, the views, and of course, the skiing.

They, Gordon and Andrew, rode in silence for the entire trip. Upon their arrival in the little village, they stopped at a local cafe' for lunch. They kept their conversation light while they ate their meal, and then made their way to *Bilford Getaway,* so named by Terese.

Not as grand as the manor, the *Getaway* offered comfort and relaxation. It had two masters on the second floor, a large family room/dining area with a rock fireplace that took up one whole wall to the apex of the vaulted ceiling, an office/library off to one side, along with a guest suite, and the kitchen opened off the dining area to the other side. Large decks surrounded the house that sat on a little over two acres. Private, but not totally isolated; Terese had described it as having a 'cozy feel.'

Gordon had wanted to make Terese happy for as long as he could, so he bought the house. She had a wonderful time decorating it. Choosing large overstuffed couches in neutral colors, sprinkled with colorful throw pillows. Not the hard, little squares covered in fancy lace, and ruffles kind; but, specially made pillows, large enough and soft enough, so that you could actually rest your head on them for an afternoon nap while covered with one of the thick crocheted throws that also graced the room.

For the dining room, she had chosen a large, round, dark oak table for a more intimate, informal feel she had said. She had chosen well in the office/library also. Volumes of their favorite authors, contemporary and classics, lined the shelves that stretched across two walls, along with an old record player Terese had found in a thrift shop and had restored. She had also accumulated quite a selection of music on vinyl, scouring the internet and every antique store wherever they went. She had opted for Chaise loungers rather than couches to curl up on, and spend a relaxing evening with the latest whodunit. Terese did cozy very well.

But Gordon wasn't feeling very 'cozy' at the moment. He had no choice but to ask for Andrew's assistance. He had to figure this out before it drove him crazy; or worse yet, he started making mistakes, and all Hell would literally break loose.

The walls on either side of the great fireplace were actually panels of glass that slide open for access to the deck surround. Gordon paced from one side to the other looking out on the drifts of snow that turned the decks, and the lawn beyond into a winter wonderland. Terese would have loved to see this. It had snowed last night. Funny, how the snow that had fallen last night was just a dusting a few miles away in Bilford; but, here in Albany with its higher elevation, a three-inch blanket concealed the lawns and the planks of the decks.

Gordon touched the key at his throat and thought of Andrew, and within seconds heard him call from his room upstairs, "Hang on Gordon, I'll be right there." Gordon smiled. It had always been like that. Maybe it was stronger between the two of them due to the shared DNA. All they had to do was think of one another, and the other one would answer.

Unbeknownst to anyone, their fathers included, if the cousins were in close enough proximity to each other, and they chose to do so; they could pick-up not only the others thoughts, but could feel and see, what the other was experiencing in the moment. That's why Andrew knew what had happened in the conservatory with Colleen last night, and again today. It's why he had not argued about leaving today after Gordon's meeting with her. Andrew had been *watching*.

"How does that idiom go?" Gordon wondered, *"Ah yes, they could be quite a 'force to be reckoned with' due to their extraordinary capability of reading each other."*

"Okay, I'm here," said Andrew, as he came to stand beside

Gordon carrying a drink in each hand. "Let's sit down, and try to sort this out."

"I honestly don't know where to start," Gordon replied wearily as he took the drink.

"All right let me ask you a question…do you think there is any way that Colleen knows…about us I mean? About what we are?" Andrew asked as he gently swirled the golden liquid in his glass.

"I don't know," Gordon answered honestly as he sank down onto one of the couches. "Here's what I don't understand: why can't you feel her presence if I can."

"Good question," Andrew said, taking a seat across from Gordon on a matching couch. Watching Gordon closely he said, "Maybe I have, and I'm just not as sensitive to it…explain it. What does it feel like?"

"At first there is this shift---"

"You keep saying that," Andrew interrupted. "What does that mean…a shift in what?"

"The atmosphere? The environment?" Gordon answered, and asked simultaneously. Observing Andrew's frown, he did his best to explain, "It's as if her presence fills the entire space. My space. I have to focus on breathing; it's a hyper-awareness of everything around me, but she is at the core…overshadowing everything else. Including my good sense."

"And this?" Andrew asked, tapping the key beneath his sweater.

"No, it's not the same as what we share," Gordon answered, unconsciously reaching for his own key.

"What about when she isn't around?" Andrew asked.

"The intensity of the sensation is absent." Gordon shrugged, "Oh, I think of her, I am attracted to her; but, that sensation, that feeling…no."

Taking a deep breath, Andrew asked what he knew Gordon was avoiding, "Should we summon them?"

Gordon shook his head, and quietly replied, "Only as a last resort."

AFTER A SHORT HIKE ON ONE of the nearby trails, and an early supper that Andrew had brought back from the village; Gordon decided to retire early, leaving Andrew to his own devices. Of course, leaving Andrew to prowl on his own could be risky, but Gordon needed some solitude, to think...to remember. *"To do a little soul-searching of my own as it were,"* Gordon thought, nearly groaning out loud at his own pun, *"that is if I have one left."*

He removed the chain from around his neck, and placed it in the small ornate container he always carried. Although they were still aware when the other was near; it was wearing the key that would allow *'watching'* by the other...the capability of tapping into the senses of sight, sensation, and emotion of their counterpart. Therefore, during the more intimate moments of their lives it was removed, and moments like the present, when they wanted to be alone with their thoughts.

Gordon had pushed away thoughts of his father since this afternoon when Andrew had suggested the possibility of summoning the duo. But, now alone, so very alone, in this room he had shared with Terese, lying back on the king-sized four-poster bed, he let his thoughts wander through the past, and to those things he knew of his legacy.

There were certain things he knew for absolute truth; who his parents were, when and where he was born, and that their shipping business had been handed down from father to son *supposedly* through the generations, now when that actually started was hard to say. These small truths he knew for fact, but, as for the history of his family, some details were sketchy at best, and some were non-existent.

Gordon's father and his uncle came into this world minutes apart, twins. Gordon Andrew Bilford, and Andrew Gordon Bilford, for whom he and his Cousin were named respectively. The exact year, decade, or century they came into this world is still a mystery. The twins, in their reckless privileged youth, had come across a different way of life somewhat by accident, or that was the way it appeared at the time, so they said. Coming from wealth, they were both spoiled young men accustomed to buying whatever took their fancy, and when they no longer fancied it, they tossed it aside. And, if they couldn't buy it, they took what they wanted. If they were caught taking, they would then buy their way out of trouble. There was always palms that could be crossed that would get them off the hook.

One of his father's stories occurred in the twins twenty-first year, Gordon and Andrew the II had been sent to several ports-of-call by their father on the premise they were to learn the shipping trade from the deck-up; the business they would someday inherit. The trip had a two-fold purpose; not only would they receive practical knowledge, but it would also get them away from their latest scandal involving two local young ladies; sisters, just one year apart in age. The young ladies' father, while not as wealthy as the Bilford's, did have enough money and power to raise quite a ruckus.

It seems the twins had made promises to the girls for certain favors compromising their virtue. Promises they had no intentions of keeping. So, Grandfather Bilford packed them up, and shipped them out, hoping that some time away would allow the girls' father to cool down, and the twins' time to grow-up.

While in port near Sicily, they met the Acoorsi sisters, Adriana and Angela. This is where the details began to get sketchy. Gordon's father first told him the story of the sisters on the evening of his twentieth birthday. On the surface it seemed to explain many things, yet, years later upon closer examination, as Gordon tried to sort it in his mind, he realized that it actually didn't explain anything at all.

The young women came from one of the ancient mountain villages near Sicily overlooking the Tyrrhenian Sea. The sisters were twins, just like his father and uncle. That in itself, might possibly explain the instant attraction or wonder that the young Bilford men had felt...finding another set of twins... beautiful, exotic, young women, close to their age, and nearly half-a-world away. But, why were they there at just the same time? Coincidence? Maybe. Or, had they somehow foreseen the arrival of the cocky, yet, malleable young men.

Although it was anyone's guess to how much of any stories told, by the now elder Bilford brothers, was true; the meeting of the Acoorsi twins was the one part, of his father's and Uncle Andrew's story, that remained consistent. Gordon allowed his mind to dredge-up the memory of the first time he had heard of the Acoorsi twins.

When Gordon Andrew Bilford the III turned twenty, his father had summoned him to his office. The same office that he and Andrew had worked in this morning at Bilford Manor. Upon entrance to his father's inner sanctuary, Gordon the II told him to sit down, that he had a proposition for him.   Gordon took the chair opposite of his father's leather topped work area and quietly waited for his father to speak. But, before he spoke, his father opened the bottom drawer of his desk and pulled out two highball glasses followed by a bottle of bourbon. He filled the first half full and the second, he filled nearly to the rim; this one he sat in front of his son. Gordon was shocked. His father had not objected to him having an occasional glass of wine with dinner since he had turned eighteen, but he never encouraged him to drink hard liqueur; quite the contrary.

Gordon could remember one night whenever he and Andrew came back to the manor drunk out of their minds. Stumbling through the front door, singing to the tops of their lungs, laughing boisterously at a prank they had pulled on a nearby neighbor, and his father standing at the top of the stairs to greet them. His father stood, legs akimbo-fists on hips, eyes blazing; the nearby neighbor had already sent a message. He didn't say a word, but we sure sobered up fast. Early the next morning, his father made clear the extent of his displeasure. Every day, all day for a month afterward, he and his cousin, spent their time swabbing the decks of one of their ships, which was currently in dock. The entire ship. The Cousins spent their nights that month passed out in their beds, not from drunkenness, but, from exhaustion.

Yet, here was that same man offering him a topped off glass of bourbon. Gordon knew that whatever was coming, must be very serious. He had no clue how serious, nor how devastating it would be to his future.

His father started with the night, he and Uncle Andrew, had met Adriana and Angela Acoorsi. Gordon could still remember his precise words, *"...bewitched, spellbound, charmed...I don't know how to describe the enchantment I felt whenever I stared into Adriana's eyes. Andrew felt the same way with Angela."*

Gordon had probed his father for more information about them. But all his father would tell him was that Adriana and Angela were the ones that had brought them into the Fold of an ancient power that he, Gordon, could not possibly understand, just yet. They had shown them a way to live as they pleased, taking whatever, they wanted, and never looking back. To live with no mortal repercussions and no regrets. He and his brother Andrew had stayed with them for quite some time, learning the *'ways of the Dark Fold. The Genesis.'* Both had immediately agreed to take whatever steps were needed to embrace this new-found power and embrace it they did.

First, they would be responsible for recruiting others to join the Fold, people of like mind. Gordon could remember that his father had laughed at that phrase… 'People of like mind.' In other words, he had explained, greedy. Greedy for everything this world had to offer---good or bad. Greedy to experience it with no regrets-no repercussions. The kind of greed that he and his brother understood. That was the easy part, he had said. "The world had a surplus of greed, and always would." The second part was a bit more involved. They would also have to supply tributes if they wanted immortality. Tributes--people that would be frozen in time…suspended, to keep the balance in the universe.

When Gordon had bluntly asked him about the underworld, Satan, and demons, his father had laughed. This power, he told him, predated anything known to mortal man. The power of the Dark Genesis could only be described as the epitome of darkness opposing the epitome of light; however, if Gordon wanted to think about it that way, it was as good an explanation as any other.

When Gordon pressed for more information, an explanation, his father had simply said, "…you can't have darkness without light, and you can't have light without darkness. How would you know which is which? One without the other is nothingness, void." His father continued, "Think of it this way. How would you know what happiness is if you had never experienced sadness? Or, vice versus? How would you know if you were sad if you have never been happy? You have to have one to recognize the other."

After giving his son a moment to contemplate what he had been told, Gordon Senior, said, "Think of the balance like the Winter and Summer Solstice. Putting those two days together there is a perfect balance of Dark and Light. What we are, your Uncle and I, are necessary to the world. Balance is the key to all." He had then opened another drawer and pulled from it an empty snow globe and an ornate box that contained an odd-looking key suspended from a silver chain. The bow of the key lay separated at the shoulder from the shaft; yet, Gordon could tell they fit together seamlessly. A key for the key. A key that fit into a secret compartment on the bottom of the snow globe. A key that would open a gate to Gordon's eventual nightmare and heartache.

By the time his father had explained the significance of the globe and the key, Gordon was reaching for his glass with a shaking hand, only to discover that it was already empty. His father watching him closely, poured him three fingers more, and said, "Son, I have one more thing to tell you. I am your father, Gordon Andrew Bilford II, but this is the *fourth time* I have been Gordon Andrew Bilford II." With this revelation, Gordon Andrew the III grabbed his glass and downed it in one gulp.

All Gordon could muster was, "How?"

"How? Good question. The answer lies in the number of tributes, and how one chooses to live. If you live a nomadic life, never staying anywhere for very long putting down roots, it's quite simple. There are those in the Fold that do just that. Living a near lifetime in one place, then one can leave, and either, never return or return as someone new to the area years later. Now, in order to live as I and your uncle have, it takes some planning. Not so much for Andrew, he has a bit more of the wanderlust than I.

For me, I stay put here, live my life and then when I am somewhere in my late sixties, I move abroad for 30 or 40 years running our businesses from overseas. Shortly after my move, I send announcements, to acquaintances, of a marriage, generally to a younger woman…that's always good for my image," pausing, he gave his son a wink, then continued, "A year later, I send another announcement about the birth of our son. When the time comes, I come back to Bilford as Gordon the II, the son. Everyone I knew before is dead. *If* there is still someone around, I simply explain that my father, Gordon the Ist, has passed after a long and prosperous life; and that I have come to take over the business." His father halted and studied Gordon carefully before resuming.

"But things are different now. This time I did have a son. This time when I go away, I won't be coming back, at least not in this role. It's your turn now. I'm afraid it will be more difficult for you in some ways; different methods of communications are moving so rapidly it won't be as easy to make your whereabouts unknown."

"How old are you? How is it that you look--"?

"So young?" His father had finished the question for him. "Tributes. The right number of tributes will not only give you more years, but will actually reverse the aging process allowing you to start over, more or less. As for my age...well, let's just say I have walked this earth for a very long time," he said with a knowing smile.

"And my mother? Did you trap her in one of these things?" Gordon demanded, gesturing to the snow-globe.

"Your mother died shortly after giving birth to you. I loved her. I did not 'profit' from her death," his father bristled. "Your mother had nothing to do with any of this. I would have grown old with her until she succumbed to a natural death."

Something in his father's voice lead Gordon to believe him on this point; or, maybe he just wanted to believe him. Having that question answered, he asked another, "So is there any truth to your story? I mean about Grandfather sending you away, the girls the two of you compromised?

Laughing out loud his father replied, "You will find that you should always add a grain of truth in whatever you tell people. The exact order, the timing, these are things that get a little skewed. You get used to being vague, when necessary."

"And, vague is your euphemism for lying?" Gordon asked, his disdain growing by the minute.

"Does it really matter, in the long run?" his father asked. "Who would remain to call you a liar?"

Changing the subject, because he knew he wouldn't get a straight answer, Gordon asked, "When you say you're going away?"

"Oh, I'll be around if I'm needed, and I'm not going anywhere for a while," he said. "You and your Cousin have much to learn, about the business, and about other things before we will take our leave, permanently, or as we like to phrase it, *retire*." Noting his son's look of surprise at the mention of his cousin, Gordon the II added, "Your Cousin Andrew will be brought into the Fold in two months...on his twentieth birthday his father, your Uncle, my brother, will be having this same conversation with his son."

For a few days after Gordon's twentieth birthday, his mind kept trying to reject the horror of everything his father had told him on that night. In fact, his mind did such a good job of rejecting it, that for small periods of time, he could convince himself it was just a bad dream. It wasn't that hard to pretend it hadn't happened, particularly given his father's behavior during the following days and weeks.

The morning after, his father had behaved as if the conversation had never taken place. Over the next few weeks Gordon observed as his father went about his regular routine, keeping to his schedule. He kept his appointments with prospective clients, he met with his bookkeepers, visited the docks; he even hosted a small dinner party about two weeks later. Gordon would find himself watching his father constantly; however, Gordon Bilford II, never batted an eye. When he noticed his son's scrutiny, he would just smile, and would either tell Gordon about some mundane event that had occurred that day, or, question Gordon about his day. Gordon was going on the assumption that his father was giving him time to digest the information; time to accept that the man he called 'father' was a.... to this day Gordon still couldn't put a name to his father's alter-ego. However, as time passed, the more he thought about it, the more it explained certain things that he had always wondered about, yet couldn't understand about his father.

Two months passed and the time had come for Bilford Manor to celebrate Andrew's twentieth birthday. His cousin would be told the same extraordinary tale by his father. That night after the party, Andrew and his father adjourned to their study and closed the door. Gordon prowled the great room, adjusting a picture here, straightening books there, until his father ordered him to sit down, and read something. Gordon needed Andrew to know. He needed to talk to someone about this; to figure it out.

More than two hours had passed when Gordon suddenly grabbed at his chest, the key he now wore seemed to have come alive; it pulsated, and he became intensely aware of Andrew just down the hall. Gordon's father smiled with approval, and said, "We couldn't be sure it would work the same, since you are cousins and not brothers. But, from your reaction, I am assuming it does." With that said, his father pulled out a key similar to Gordon's, but, not exactly the same. "Your Uncle Andrew wears the mate to mine. Your Cousin Andrew now wears the mate to yours."

Gordon didn't need to talk to his Cousin, he could feel what Andrew was feeling, and it made Gordon sick to his core. Andrew had embraced the darkness and was reveling in the power. When he and his father emerged from the study, Andrew's emerald green eyes sought Gordon immediately, and with a gloating smile, he said, "You've been holding back on me Cousin."

Andrew learned quickly and was anxious to put into practice the knowledge he had gained. Gordon wanted to find a way to reverse it all, to make it go away. Despite his father trying to tell him their ways were necessary to the balance of the universe, Gordon wasn't convinced. He could not reconcile such evil with necessity to the world and humankind.

For months, Gordon had hounded his father with questions about the sisters. His father would consistently reply, with a smile, "The 'dark messenger' cast a spell of enchantment over me and my brother."

Not understanding what his father's cryptic remark had meant, and needing answers, Gordon had researched everything he could find on Italy, Sicily, ancient societies, ancient religions, and the name Acoorsi. Nothing he had found made a connection. Until one day, on a whim, he looked up the meanings of the sisters' first names, in an attempt to make any kind of connection between what his family had become, and the sisters. He discovered that Adriana means 'dark' and Angela means 'messenger.' Together they were the *'dark messenger.'*

Finally, Gordon confided in his father that he wanted nothing to do with Fold. He would move to the west coast, change his name, make his own way, and live his life as a *'normal,'* then die when his time came.

Speaking softly to belie the steel in his words, Gordon II said, "If you do not adhere to the tenets of the Fold, both, you and Andrew will die, but it will be long before "your time.""

Gordon had felt a gnawing in his gut, since the night of his birthday; but, now looking into the depths of his father's eyes, he had been consumed with a type of fear he had never experienced before. Apparently, his father picked up on the fear Gordon knew was radiating off of him in waves; because he continued, "Do not fear me, son. But there are those that you should fear; your Uncle for one. If you refuse to become part of the Fold, you also seal the fate of your Cousin, his son. If it were turned the other way, and Andrew was putting you in jeopardy; nephew or not, I would not be kind."

That was sixteen years ago. Since then, he had been married twice, and twice had used his wives as tributes. To say his father wasn't pleased, with his choice to enter into any marriage, would be an understatement. So, when the time came for his father to start traveling, as he phrased it, he had left his cohort, Joseph, to be Gordon's watcher and mentor. Joseph would also serve as a liaison between Gordon and his father if the need arose.

Gordon couldn't remember a time when Joseph wasn't a part of his life. He had been a substitute father when needed, and truth be told, a substitute mother. Joseph had been by his side when Gordon had made Jeanette his wife when he turned twenty-one, and when he had made himself a widower at twenty-two. Jeanette had been his confirmation tribute. Dooming Jeanette to existing without an existence had been challenging; but a confirmation tribute had to be brought to validate his commitment to the Fold. About a year later he met Terese. A woman full of warmth, kindness, and generosity; the complete opposite of Jeanette.

Terese embodied normalcy in Gordon's life, and gave him a glimpse into the world of the Normals. A world that he so desperately wanted. Three years, after Jeanette's *demise*, Gordon and Terese had married on Christmas Eve. Gordon kept Terese by his side for much longer than he should have. He had let his heart become involved to a certain extent. In his defense, he was thoroughly convinced that given enough time he could figure a way out of this cursed situation. But, he didn't, and over the past year, Joseph repeatedly reminded him of his duty to the Fold; not to mention the safety of both himself and his cousin.

Just yesterday, Andrew, had reminded Gordon that he had known what he was getting into, and had been more than willing to "sign on the dotted line." Except Andrew didn't seem to realize that Gordon felt he had no choice without endangering both of their lives. Gordon didn't try to fool himself into thinking all of his motives for staying in the Fold were altruistic. He accepted his responsibility for the things he had done, and would accept responsibility for deeds of the future; but, unlike Andrew, he would never stop trying to find a way out.

Pulling himself from his reverie, Gordon looked around the darkened room, realizing his trip into the past had taken longer than he had anticipated. He still wasn't any closer to knowing what to do about Colleen O'Malley, and too exhausted to think anymore tonight. He knew he would have to find out more about her, *"Maybe Andrew's background check would yield some answers,"* Gordon thought. The only thing he knew with any certainty is that he did not want to 'summon' his father, nor his uncle.

FTER A FITFUL NIGHT, GORDON ONCE again was awakened by the fragrant aroma of coffee; however, on this morning it was not accompanied by his Boston Globe. Today, his morning jolt came accompanied with Andrew; sitting in one of the striped club chairs near the window, swinging Gordon's key back and forth like a pendulum.

"Andrew, I would appreciate you *not* going through my things," Gordon said evenly, as he stretched and pulled himself up to a sitting position to face his cousin.

"And I would appreciate *you* not being out-of-touch for so long," Andrew replied.

"Overnight? It's hardly the first time one of us has needed some privacy while in each other's company, Andrew," Gordon said, as he sipped at his coffee, relishing the taste and the warmth.

"There was no need," Andrew said, as he continued to swing the key that caught the morning sun streaming through the window. "Neither of us was uh…what phrase would you find acceptable? Oh, I know, *entertaining* last night. Unless you snuck someone in here."

"No, I wasn't entertaining," Gordon scoffed. "A little too soon after the loss of my wife, don't you think? We just had her memorial two days ago."

"You didn't seem to have a problem in Switzerland," Andrew reminded him, with a smirk.

"That was Switzerland. Albany is barely 50 miles from home. I have a nodding acquaintance with some of the locals here, and Terese knew everyone in the town," Gordon said, adding wistfully, "She made friends wherever she went."

"There you go again," Andrew complained, as he tossed the key to Gordon, who deftly caught it. "You're getting overly sentimental about a woman you chose to become a tribute. I keep telling you not to get so involved. Don't marry them! It would make your life so much easier."

"Did it ever occur to you that it's my way of paying penitence for choosing them to become tributes in the first place?" Gordon asked, knowing that Andrew would never understand the remorse he felt; nor, could he tell Andrew that he had firmly believed that he would have found a way out of the Fold long before it would be necessary to make Terese a tribute. Andrew looked at Normals as if they were beneath him and their existence was of no consequence.

"I want what time they have to be the best that life has to offer. It's the least I can do before they're trapped for all eternity. I want them to feel loved, spoiled, and coddled. I could do that with Terese, have tender feelings toward her, and to protect her," Gordon continued, "but she wouldn't spoil; always so appreciative of the least little thing, and never asking for more."

"Maybe that *was* her way of getting more," Andrew said under his breath. Catching Gordon's narrowed glance; Andrew said, "You could still do all that; give some woman a weekend, a week, or a month, they will never forget, but, you don't have to marry them, live with them for years, only to tear yourself up when the time comes."

"You just don't understand," Gordon said with a sigh. "I'm not like you Andrew. Sometimes I wish I were. I want something more out of my existence."

"More? We can have anything we want now," Andrew exclaimed.

"Except a normal life," Gordon reminded him. "Why don't we drop this for now? My coffee is cold, and I need to dress. What do you say to a late breakfast at that little place where we stopped yesterday, and then we hit the slopes?" Gordon asked as he gathered his clothing from the suitcase, he had not bothered to unpack last night.

"Maybe, I understand more than you think I do," Andrew began, as he leaned back in his chair, stretching his legs out, "I know that you really didn't want to join the Fold as I did. I know that you were coerced into embracing your birthright."

"Birthright? What are you babbling about?" Gordon challenged, irritated that Andrew had apparently decided to ignore his suggestion.

"You were born into this the same as I, but you felt forced to go along with our fathers' vision for our future." Andrew rejoined.

"I will give you that we were born into this, but our sires were not. They were Normals before meeting up with the *dark messenger*," Gordon sneered as he used his father's descriptor. "They chose this way for themselves, and they are to blame for putting us in this position."

Andrew rested his head on the back of the chair to make eye contact with Gordon, and asked, "Are you sure about that? Are you sure they were ever Normals? We only have their word for that cousin, and you know what that's worth."

Gordon turned away, wanting to brush aside his cousin's questions. But something in the way he looked, the way he sounded, had Gordon feeling ill at ease. Did Andrew find out something while embracing the tenets of the Fold that Gordon, who had spent his time trying to find a way out, did not? If their fathers were never Normals, that would change their positions in the hierarchy of the Fold; which in turn would alter the positions of himself and his Cousin.

Gordon rounded on Andrew "Do you know something that you need to share with me, Andrew?"

"I *know* what you know; however, I have often wondered if their story was accurate," Andrew answered. "If you think about it, our fathers being closer to the Genesis of the Fold than what they are claiming would explain a lot."

Gordon had to admit that he had wondered about that, but he had not been able to find any substantial proof, just an observation. Over the years, he and Andrew had met other members of the Fold, and the one thing that always stood out to Gordon had been the deference shown to his father and uncle. Apparently, Andrew had also noticed something.

He had even mentioned this observation to his father once. The elder Bilford had just shrugged and said, "Well Gordon, how would you have them to treat us? They are visitors to *our* home, in *our* town. They are simply being polite and showing respect. Would you not, be polite and show respect, if you were to visit one of them?"

Gordon had let it drop there, but he had never forgotten the conversation either. He turned to Andrew, "So what makes you doubt them? Outside of their being such consummate liars, that is?" Gordon added wryly.

"Just by watching how others treat them. It's as if they, our fathers, have a higher authority or power over them. Surely, you have noticed the way others seek their counsel. Not just their recruits, but the heads of other Houses. I find it hard to believe they are on the same level as the rest," Andrew answered.

Gordon asked, "Did you ever talk about this with your father?"

"I tried to once," Andrew said, "He said something about decorum and respect due to their tenure. You?"

Gordon studied Andrew carefully, "Yes, once, and I received much the same answer. We are the House of Bilford, that seemed to be enough of an explanation." Deciding that since he wasn't going to get breakfast any time soon, and Andrew appeared to be in the mood to divulge this morning, Gordon pressed Andrew for another piece of information, "Andrew, what did your father tell you about the use of the snow-globes? I mean, why snow-globes?"

"Well, that's another thing that sets our fathers apart from the others that we have met; most members of the Fold use paintings or statuary. Photographs would be the easiest don't you think?" Andrew asked. "But, to use the globes is an altogether different vehicle, exclusive to the House of Bilford, and quite inconvenient at times."

"I would say a much crueler vehicle," Gordon replied. "They are not just suspended; they are aware they're suspended. I can barely think about it."

"Yes, Gordon, I'm aware," Andrew said, impatiently. Then added, "I know you believe me to be completely heartless, but you are blood. I simply don't understand why you suffer so over the fate of a few Normals; however, I take no pleasure in seeing you suffer."

A part of Gordon was surprised to hear Andrew admit to a more tender side; yet, the cousins had grown-up together, as youths they had always had each other's backs. Still Gordon, couldn't understand Andrew's callousness toward Normals; his Cousin had absolutely no capacity for compassion or empathy.

Gruffly, Gordon replied, "Are you sure about that? Right now, I'm suffering from hunger, and we are not going to solve any of this presently. I will speak with Joseph this evening, he has been looking into a couple of things for me concerning the O'Malley's niece; and you're still waiting to hear from your background check, right?"

With Andrew's affirming nod, Gordon continued, "Then let me get dressed, we'll go eat and then hit the slopes."

Gordon didn't really care about eating; what he desperately wanted, no, needed, was the release of flying down the trails. They would be going to Cranmore Mountain in North Conway, just a few miles away, and it boasted a mile-long run, enough to feel the speed. It also had enough varying terrain to demand his focus, thus allowing him to free his mind for little while.

Yes, a day on the slopes is precisely what he needed. The cold air, the sun bouncing off the snow, relishing the feel of your own strength as you defy gravity. Gordon had always looked at skiing as a metaphor for life. Choosing your trails, gliding along smoothly on the straight runs, being prepared for the challenges of the turns, bumps, and mastering any surprises that came along.

Gordon had a healthy respect for the mountain, because it could take you down; yet, he never felt more in command of his destiny. He never felt freer. The only other thing that came close was standing the deck on the high seas, but that usually involved business. The snow equated pure pleasure.

It had been a glorious outing. The skiing had been precisely what Gordon had needed. Not ready to let go of the easiness of the day, Gordon and Andrew decided to dine that evening at a little place in North Conway, before making the short trip back over to Albany. The restaurant they chose set in the shadow of the mountains, and boasted the best steaks and bourbon. The L-shaped building housed a restaurant and pub; it wrapped around a busy street corner that had convenient entrances from both streets. It's one of those places that catered to the tourists and the locals. Rough hand-hewn beams crossed the vaulted ceilings, the dining tables were made of thick slabs of wood, low-lighting, and high-backed booths offered cozy corners for an intimate meal, while the pub-side sported a twenty-foot curved bar, high-top tables, and a small dance floor. The pub also hosted a big dart tournament a couple of times a year. Gordon and Terese would frequent the establishment regularly when they were in town, and Gordon, although more adept at archery, had entered the contests once or twice, with Terese cheering him on.

For tonight, Gordon refused to dwell upon what he couldn't have and decided to just enjoy the shared camaraderie with Andrew. Regaling one another with exaggerated tales of athletic prowess, checking-out the pretty little waitress that had taken their order, and laughing at the other's jokes. Gordon had missed this, all but forgotten, closeness with Andrew. The carefree atmosphere almost felt as if they were teens again. Gordon defined his life by before and after the night of his twentieth birthday. Up until that night, he had led a life of normalcy; after that night he had led a life of torment.

Just as Andrew launched into his second anecdote concerning himself, a woman, and what was thought to be an absentee husband, Gordon abruptly went very still.

"Gordon, are you listening to me? I'm just getting to the good part," Andrew said.

"She's here," Gordon said.

"She...?" Andrew started to ask, then with understanding said, "Colleen."

Gordon and Andrew immediately began to scan the room. They both spotted her at the same time, along with her Aunt and Uncle, Fran and Shaun. They were near the restaurant side entrance, waiting to be seated. Gordon drew a sharp breath upon seeing her. Dressed in a chocolate brown sweater that highlighted the color of her hair, and cream-colored pants. The way she filled the sweater, combined with her long red hair, long legs, and her lilting laugh, had been enough to draw the attention of every man in the room, Gordon noticed. Having made a split-second decision, Gordon touched his key and looked at his Cousin; Andrew nodded once, and Gordon stood to make his way toward the O'Malley's.

"Hello, neighbors," Gordon greeted them. "Why don't you join us, unless you're meeting someone? It's pretty busy here this evening." This afternoon Gordon had finally come to the conclusion that he would never get any answers to the mystery surrounding Miss Colleen if he kept avoiding her. On the mountain, it had been easy to convince himself that he needed to face her and the situation, but now, in such close proximity to her, his resolve was wavering. Gordon swallowed the mild disgust he felt for being such a coward; and perhaps, unjustly, felt a little peevish toward Colleen for making him feel that way.

"Well thanks, buddy, they did say it would be a while, and I'm starving," Shaun said without hesitation.

Laying her hand on her husband's arm before he could take off, Fran interjected, "Gordon we don't want to intrude."

"Franny, he wouldn't have asked if it was a problem," Shaun argued with his wife.

"Nonsense Fran," Gordon said laughing, "We would love to have the three of you to join us," Gordon indicated toward the table where Andrew sat. "Go ahead to the table, and I will get the waitress before Shaun passes out from hunger."

Colleen had stood by quietly during this little bit of byplay, with an indulgent smile for her Aunt and Uncle. Catching Gordon's eye, she tipped her head to the side and winked at him. Inwardly wincing, Gordon excused himself to track down the hostess to find their waitress and send her to their table. Locating her, as she seated a patron at the bar, he went to intercept her, before she moved to the next customer. Gordon slipped a fifty into the palm of the hostess as he took her hand. She looked a little startled, but curious; Gordon warmly introduced himself and told her they would be five for dinner rather than two. Then with a slow, easy smile, he asked if she could, please, have the kitchen to hold the meals that he and Andrew had ordered until the O'Malley's meals were ready also. It was evident, the woman was captivated by his charisma, and when she looked in her hand at what he had placed there, she readily agreed.

Gordon had expected Colleen to follow Shaun and Fran to the table; therefore, he was surprised to find her still near the entrance. Not only was she still there, apparently waiting for him, but she had been watching his performance with the hostess. Her green eyes were dancing in amusement.

"*Damn it!*" Gordon swore in his head, as his body screamed to be closer to her, "*She has an unerring way of setting me on edge. Well, I said I would meet this vixen head-on…no time like the present.*"

As he approached Colleen, she extended her hand leaving

Gordon no choice, in the bound of good manners, but to offer his arm, and lead her to their table.

"Nice," she murmured, "I don't think she knew what hit her."

Colleen's voice was filled with bemusement, but Gordon thought he heard something else too, *"An underlying challenge?"*

Deciding to go with a more formal touch and fabricated misunderstanding, Gordon replied in his best offhand voice, "I'm sure I don't know what you're speaking of Miss O'Malley."

With another attention-grabbing lilting laugh, she murmured, "Oh but, I'm sure you do, Mr. Bilford."

Upon reaching their table, Andrew and Shaun started to stand, but Colleen waved them back into their seats and said, "Please gentleman keep your seats," then turning to Gordon, she raised a perfectly arched brow, and said in a soft, smooth voice, "I'm sure Gordon will see to all of my needs."

Gordon stood stock still. *"Maybe I misunderstood her,"* Gordon thought as he looked about the table at his dinner companions. Her Uncle had simply sat back in his chair, and continued to study his menu, Fran smiled warmly; but Andrew's eyebrows had nearly disappeared into his hairline. *"Nope, I heard her correctly,"* Gordon thought with a sigh. When Colleen very pointedly looked first at Gordon than to the chair next to her uncle, and back again, Gordon automatically held out the chair for her. They had been seated at a round table, and she would sit between himself, and her Uncle. Fran was to Shaun's right, between her husband and Andrew. *"Well, this could take some finesse,"* Gordon thought.

"J.C., what do you think you'll be having?" Shaun O'Malley asked as Colleen was seated, "your Aunt Franny is having the lobster, and I think I want a steak."

Furrowing his brows, now that they had returned to their normal position between his eyes and hairline, Andrew repeated inquisitively, "J.C.?"

Shaun immediately looked contrite, and with a grimace said, "Ooh, I'm sorry Colleen, I know I promised no more childhood nickname," shaking his head and with a shrug of his shoulders, he continued, "hard habit to break, lass."

Patting her Uncle on the shoulder, and giving him a dazzling smile, she said, "It's okay Uncle," to Andrew and Gordon she warned, "Just as long as it doesn't become a trend, that is."

Taking up the dare, Andrew leaned his elbows on the table, squarely looked at Colleen, and said, "Okay, I won't call you J.C. if you tell me what the 'J' stands for...I assume the 'C' is for Colleen?"

Nodding, she replied, "Yes, and the 'J' is for Janet."

Fran smiled fondly at her niece, and said, "Yes, it means, *God's gracious gift*, and Colleen means *girl*. So, our girl is God's gracious gift, and I think she lives up to her name."

Colleen gently chided her indulgent Aunt by saying, "Aunt Fran, you're embarrassing me,"

But Fran's attention was drawn to Andrew sounding as if he had strangled after taking a sip of the wine they had ordered earlier, "Oh Andrew! Are you all right dear?"

Andrew waved her off as he cleared his throat.

Gordon quickly answered for his Cousin, "He's fine, Fran," throwing Andrew a look of warning, he remarked, "Ah, here comes our waitress, does everyone know what they want?"

"I know precisely what I want," Colleen murmured as she gave Gordon a sweeping appraisal from head to toe. After a small pause, she then looked straight into Gordon's eyes, and said, with a demure little smile, "I'll have the blackened shrimp and a salad."

"WHAT THE HELL?" ANDREW ASKED WHEN he and Gordon finally got back to *Bilford Getaway*. They hadn't said a word on the short drive back to the house.

"I am not discussing this until I have had a long, hot shower, and I have a drink in my hand," Gordon retorted.

"Are you sure you don't want a drink now, and then have a *cold* shower?" Andrew quipped with a smirk.

Gordon shot Andrew a look that would have quelled a lesser man; but Andrew just laughed. *"No, actually he chortled. I'm glad someone is getting some enjoyment out of this situation,"* Gordon thought caustically as he climbed the stairs to his room.

Seeking some sanctuary, Gordon removed the key before stepping into the shower. He braced his hands against the shower wall as he let the steaming water wash over him. *"It had been difficult enough to sit beside her, listen to her happy chatter with her Aunt and Uncle. She had even been quite cordial with Andrew, although, she didn't seem to care for him much. Not to mention that she had completely charmed the wait-staff, except for that one waitress who flirted with me."*

Gordon recalled the evening minute-by-minute. *"Colleen's face is so expressive, made even more so by her quick and easy smile. But I felt as if every statement, every question, she directed toward me was a double entendre, sexual innuendo, which nearly became my undoing. Or, did I just take it that way because I want her? No, obviously, from Andrew's earlier query, I wasn't reading her wrong. But, why? Did she not care that he was recently widowed? But, that kind of callousness didn't seem to fit into the persona that she portrayed."*

Toweling off, and pulling on a pair of sweats, Gordon headed back downstairs barefooted, the heat of the water had loosened his muscles, and he felt more in control of himself. He thought he had heard his phone ringing, and Joseph was supposed to call tonight. As he reached the bottom of the stairs, he could hear Andrew chuckling. *"That's odd, Joseph and Andrew didn't get on very well. Veiled civility, the most either could muster with one another,"* Gordon mused. But, as he moved into the room, Gordon knew immediately that Andrew and Joseph were not conversing.

"How on earth did she grow-up in New England, and not learn to ski?" Andrew asked. When he saw Gordon, he pointed to the phone and mouthed, "Speaker." Then Gordon heard Fran O'Malley's voice on the other end.

"Oh well, Colleen's parents were snowbirds, always moving to warmer climes in the winter," she answered, "She could give lessons on water skiing," Fran added with a laugh. "I just remember Terese remarking at how patient Gordon had been when working with some of the young people in town. I was hoping that he might be able to give Colleen some pointers?" She had phrased this last as a question.

"You're in luck," Andrew said with a sly smile, ignoring Gordon as he shook his head no, "Gordon just walked in, and you can ask him."

Nothing would have given Gordon more pleasure, at the moment, then to knock the smirk off of Andrew's face; but, instead, he took a deep breath, and spoke out, "Hello Fran," he greeted, "is there something I can do for you?"

"Gordon dear," she began, much to Andrew's glee, "I have been telling your Cousin that Colleen doesn't know how to ski very well, and she very much wants to learn."

"Fran, I'm not a ski instructor," Gordon begin--

"I know that, dear, but she seems so comfortable around you, which is quite unlike her, honestly. She doesn't always take to people so quickly. We tried to book an instructor for her, but they're either, all booked-up, or not taking on new students due to the lateness of the season." Pushing her advantage, Fran continued. "Everyone knows you are an avid skier, and, since she's here and you are too, I hoped that you could just give her a few pointers. Andrew had said earlier this evening that you planned to be here a few days."

"Isn't Andrew just too helpful," Gordon fumed inwardly, to Fran he said, recognizing defeat when he saw it, "If you think I can be of assistance, Fran, it would be my pleasure."

"Oh good, Colleen will be delighted," Fran crooned, "I'll give her your number, and the two of you can set a time that will be convenient for you. Goodnight dear."

Gordon's phone went dark. Andrew approached him with a drink in hand, "Well, *dear*, it sounds like you might have a skiing date in your near future."

Taking the proffered drink, "Are you aware of how much I really hate you?" Gordon asked with very little rancor, and a great deal of weariness, as he dropped down on one of the couches.

Undaunted, Andrew continued, "I will go along with you so you won't be alone with her...kind of, like a chaperone. Except, it will be *your* virtue I will be protecting," he added with a grin.

When Gordon didn't take exception to this ribbing and come back with a stinging retort, Andrew sat down across from him, and said, "Seriously Gordon, all joking aside, I don't know what to make of the fair Colleen. The report I got back, while you were showering, from my investigator reveals very little, and she, along with her team are quite thorough."

Andrew pulled out his phone, located the memo app, and began ticking off the stats his investigator had unearthed. "Colleen O'Malley attended the best schools here in the states, high marks in all of her academics, graduated with honors. In college, she studied architecture, design, and went to a finishing school, quite a juxtaposition wouldn't you say?" Andrew interjected, before continuing, "Although she doesn't work for a firm, her name is associated as a consultant with several fairly large building projects. There are a few Society notes in the papers, mostly charity work. No serious relationships could be found. Just various escorts to Broadway debuts, or a charity gala, while she lived in New York. No scrapes with the law. She has been with the O'Malley's since the age of thirteen when her parents' car was hit by a train; having no children of their own, Shaun and Fran took her in immediately to finish raising her as their only heir. I can't figure out what her game is, but there is no mistaking her interest in you."

Setting his glass aside, Gordon got up and started pacing before speaking, "That is pretty much what Joseph found. He, also, discreetly checked with several key members, and so far, has not found any connection to the Fold. He is still waiting to hear from one or two others. I thought that was him on the phone when I came down, I'm expecting his call when he knows one way or the other."

On his second trip around the room, Gordon stopped, turned to Andrew, and asked, "Andrew what do you know about the 'light beings'?"

"Light beings?" Andrew echoed.

"It's something that my father said, on that night sixteen years ago, about how we were necessary, or needed, for the universe to, *"...keep the balance."* I didn't pay much attention at the time, I guess I was too shocked, sickened by what he was telling me," Gordon said candidly, undaunted by Andrew's frown, "I was in total denial. He knew that, and when I thought about it later, I assumed he had just made it up in an attempt to justify what he is, and what he was expecting me to become. But, if there were any truth to it, wouldn't it stand to reason that if a balance needs to be kept, and we are one side of the scale, then opposite beings must also exist for the other side of the scale?"

"You mean a kind of 'yin and yang' thing?" Andrew asked trying to follow Gordon's line of thought.

"Not exactly, more like balancing a scale," Gordon replied, "I think it makes sense. Many Normals readily believe that God's angels walk the earth; but, I'm not sure they give those, such as you and me, the minions of the underworld as much credence, or any real thought at all. Perhaps, that's one of the reasons the Fold is so successful in staying hidden." Continuing with his line of reasoning, he said, "So maybe we should not make that same mistake."

"My father didn't talk to me about that," Andrew said, "but, then again, I didn't have to be convinced either."

"I remember," Gordon sighed, "As you recall I was already in possession of the key. The second you touched your key we were connected."

"If I understand you correctly, you think that Colleen could be like us in the opposite?" Andrew asked, from his position at the hearth. As Gordon had paced, Andrew had placed logs in the fireplace, added some kindling, and lit the fire. Replacing the screen, they both watched as the flame caught, and the starter wood began to crackle. They remained quiet, each lost in their own thoughts until the fire flared and danced around the logs.

"You know, Gordon, the more I think on it, the more I think you might be on to something," Andrew paused, his face in deep concentration, "Yeah some kind of do-gooder warrior; it would explain a lot. The way she has zeroed in on you...appears to know your feelings for her, and she is intentionally playing on those feelings. I mean honestly, "...Gordon will see to all of my needs." I also noticed how she took every opportunity to touch your arm, or brush against you. Then when that pretty young waitress came by and---"

"Andrew, you don't have to replay the entire evening, I was

there," Gordon admonished, recalling his emotional response, with each look and touch, was not only unsettling but embarrassing as well. "I'm well aware."

"Don't forget," Andrew said, tapping his chest, "believe me, I was well aware, too. I got a jolt every time she touched you; I felt like I was hanging onto an electric fence throughout the whole evening. Perhaps, the little girl that is, *God's gracious gift*, is your *light* messenger," Andrew, half-jokingly exclaimed, referring to the enchantment their fathers claimed when they had met the Acoorsi sisters. "I just wish I could either, remember where I have met her before, or be rid of this damnable feeling of familiarity every time I see her."

Gordon had finally stopped pacing to sit and watch the fire's flames. He wanted to rebuke Andrew for comparing Colleen with the Acoorsi sisters, and for comparing him to their fathers, but to be fair, hadn't he wondered the same thing? The draw to Colleen was growing stronger with every meeting. Even when he wasn't consciously thinking of her; unbidden images would pop into his head, almost like flipping through a handful of photographs. Colleen smiling at him when he had first introduced himself to her. Her hair caught by the wind, the startled look in her eyes when he had kissed her. The look in her emerald eyes right before she had brushed her lips against his cheek, the way she had winked at him tonight; every moment spent in her company was burned into his brain as individual pictures.

Was this the feeling his father and uncle had experienced when meeting the Italian women? Was Colleen attempting to allure him into some other cult? He needed to speak with Joseph. He needed answers; but how far could he trust him? After all, Joseph was his father's confidant, and had been left behind to be his 'watcher.' Gordon had never tested the extent of Joseph's loyalty. Did the strength of his commitment lay with him, or his father?

"Gordon...Gordon," Andrew was nearly shouting his name.

"What?" Gordon asked, coming out of his trance-like state.

"You're not wearing your key again," Andrew peevishly pointed out.

Gordon sighed, and said in a voice full of weariness, "I will put it on in the morning. Doesn't it bother you to have me in your head whenever I choose?"

"Not really, I don't have anything to hide," Andrew answered, lazily. "I have come to view it like a safety feature." When Gordon gave him a quizzical look, he explained, "We're stronger together."

"Agreed, I was thinking last night that we are, quite a force to be reckoned with when we are working together," Gordon said with a smile. "However, I'm not hiding anything, cousin. What would be the point? You would find out eventually."

The ringtone of Gordon's phone interrupted their conversation. Gordon had put his phone in the pocket of his sweatpants after speaking with Fran; yet, he knew who it was without looking, "Colleen," he informed Andrew before pulling it out of his pocket.

"Seriously?"

Glancing at the screen, she was using Fran's phone, he nodded once toward Andrew, and mouthed "quiet." He then pushed the speaker, "Colleen, what an unexpected pleasure. What can I do for you?"

Her lilting laughter filled the room, "Really? I doubt my call was unexpected... a pleasure? Well, time will tell; I suppose that will depend on what pleases us. As to what you can do for me, I do have a list," her voice all but purred through the phone, "but we'll start with some pointers on skiing."

Gordon exchanged a look with Andrew, whose eyebrows had disappeared again, and said, "Yes, Fran mentioned that---"

Laughing again Colleen interrupted, "Aunt Fran mentioned my list or the pointers?"

Rubbing his temples in exasperation, Gordon decided to ignore the question, and asked, "Since you're staying at Shaun and Fran's place in Conway; how about we pick you up for breakfast in the morning, and then the three of us will get an early start before the trails get too roughed-up?"

"Three of us? Are you giving pointers to someone else too?" she queried.

"No, but Andrew will be skiing also. We will probably be going back to Bilford in another day or two, and since there isn't much season left, he will want to take advantage of it while he can," Gordon said.

"Of course," she said, congenially, "Andrew would want to take advantage of the opportunity."

Gordon glanced to Andrew who shrugged his shoulders; continuing, he said, "Andrew is as avid a skier as I, which will be of benefit to you. Two for the price of one, shall we say?"

"Yes, let's say that," Colleen replied, with amusement tinging her voice. "What time will you be picking me up?"

"Eight?"

"Eight it is," she agreed, "And Gordon?"

"Yes?"

"Sweet dreams, I will be counting the minutes," she breathed.

"Sheesh...brazen, isn't she?" Andrew chuckled after Gordon had ended the call on his end, "Makes me glad you're not wearing your key I don't need it to know what you're thinking or feeling now."

Ignoring Andrew's crude remarks, and for what seemed like the hundredth time that night, Gordon asked, "But, why? If she is nothing more than the O'Malley's niece, why would she be making overtures towards a man that is in mourning for his wife?"

"The usual culprits in the world of the Normals don't seem to apply," Andrew said, tapping his chin. "Money? She's independently wealthy. Desperation? She's beautiful, cultured, well educated, she could have her pick of men. Revenge? You don't know her, you're on good terms with her Aunt and Uncle; there doesn't seem to be any connection between Colleen, and our acquaintances. Maybe, she thinks you're safe and willing to have let's say..." Gordon almost laughed aloud as he watched Andrew struggle for words that would be the least offensive for what he was thinking, "a good time without the strings?"

Gordon snorted, "Safe? She's not safe around me."

Andrew nodded, "Yes, well --she doesn't know that...I guess. Maybe you simply present a challenge. Some people get off on that sort of thing, you know?"

Choosing once again to ignore Andrew's crudeness, Gordon said, "That leaves, either, another house within the Fold, or ---," Gordon began, but for the third time that evening he was getting a call. Glancing at the screen, he saw this was the call he had been waiting for, Joseph.

Signaling to Andrew that he had to take the call, Gordon answered as he made his way to the office. Closing the door behind him, he crossed the room to sit behind the desk.

An hour later that is where Andrew found him, sitting at his desk, his head resting on the back of the chair, and his eyes closed. The strains of Vivaldi's Four Seasons filling the room; *Winter*, Gordon's favorite had just begun. Vivaldi had published *Four Seasons*, his most famous piece in 1725; Gordon nearly laughed aloud as he idly wondered if his father had attended one of Vivaldi's live performances.

Without moving, Gordon said, "We have to go back to Bilford Manor. We are expecting company."

"Our fathers?" Andrew asked.

Sitting up and reaching for a remote, Gordon muted the music, *"I suppose I should be grateful they're not the company,"* Gordon thought, but aloud he said, "No. It's Darius Alanis, and his son, Stavros."

"I have met Stavros a couple of times," Andrew replied, "but not his father. Any particular reason for their appearance?"

"Joseph thinks there could be something, considering that both heads of Alanis House are dropping by to visit, but Joseph can be a bit paranoid at times. According to the message, they are docking in Portsmouth on business, and, you know...Portsmouth is just a couple of hours south from Bilford," Gordon shrugged, as he answered, "...in the neighborhood and all."

Frowning, Andrew said, "I don't know that Joseph's intuition should be dismissed too quickly; like I said I've met Stavros before, I don't trust him."

"I have also met Stavros, and I didn't say we should trust him," Gordon retorted, to himself he added, *"I don't trust any member of the Fold,"* continuing he said, "I am merely pointing out that Joseph can act like an old woman sometimes, looking for danger around every corner."

Letting it go, for now, Andrew asked, "Did Joseph have anything else to report?"

"Yes, he has heard from his informants...no rumors, no recognition, nothing about Colleen," Gordon said with a sigh.

"When do we leave?" Andrew asked.

Referring to his notes, Gordon answered, "They are to dock in Portsmouth tomorrow, and arrive at Bilford Manor sometime Thursday evening. Today is Tuesday, so, I will return tomorrow afternoon, after the skiing lesson," at this Gordon shook his head, still not quite understanding how he had gotten wrangled into that, continuing, he said, "I can get a car if you want to stay on here, but, I want a little time at home before they arrive. We do have some minor business dealings with them; I want to be prepared."

Andrew gave a short laugh, and said, "Thanks, but no thanks, I will return with you. I'm afraid Fran would take pity on me, and try to keep me entertained. You know, it's hard to refuse that one."

Gordon smiled at Andrew, thinking, *"Oh yes, I am well aware that's how I got wrangled into the ski lesson...Fran."* Then said to Andrew, "I know. Fran is the real deal; she genuinely cares about people."

"Yeah, but I don't think her niece particularly cares for my company. I'll leave her to you."

"Thanks," Gordon replied dryly, as he stood stretching, "I'm heading for bed, we have an early date tomorrow."

Once he had reached his room, Gordon wandered over to the windows to check out the night sky. It was clear, and with so little light pollution in this particular area, the stars shone like jewels waiting to be plucked from a dark velvet cloth. Gordon struggled to put aside thoughts of Colleen, actually being left to him, as he readied himself for bed. He couldn't allow himself to think about her, and yet, he would be in her company most of tomorrow morning. Gordon suddenly felt the weight of all the decisions, events, and emotions that he had kept bottled up for the last few months. Reaching for his key, nestled in its little box on the nightstand, Gordon stopped, "Maybe I do have something to hide from Andrew; I wasn't cut out to be this inhumane. I wasn't cut-out for sharing every aspect of my life, every emotion, and every thought. The Fold has taken away all of my choices, but for tonight I can choose to be alone."

Using Terese as a tribute had been his undoing. That night, the night of the party, and for the days that followed he had tried to feel a callousness toward the whole of the situation; attempting to channel Andrew, but it was forced, a pure act of bravado. He had done what was required of him; but still, he had tried to blot it out on the mountain slopes, with a bottle or two of whiskey, and in the bed of another woman. When Gordon had returned from Switzerland, when he had to face what he had done, and the charade of what still lay ahead, he had vowed to find an end to it, no matter the cost, but there was Colleen. The woman knew something, but what? She was such a contradiction of personality traits. One minute, she conducted herself with the utmost propriety, while in the next moment, she was behaving as a seductress entirely outside of the societal bounds of appropriateness given Gordon's circumstances.

The key could wait, or rather, Andrew could wait 'til morning as he had said. Tonight, he needed to, once again, be alone with his thoughts.

WEDNESDAY MORNING CAME QUICKLY WITH A brilliant glow peeping through the snow-laden branches of the evergreens. Even though he had had another restless night, Gordon was up with the sun. The sky promised to remain clear, although a storm was brewing to the north just up the coast, and predicted to circle back in and make landfall by the weekend. But, for now the sky was a clear blue, the morning sun turning the trees into diamond encrusted sentinels, and the front lawns into glittering white blankets.

Gordon told himself that he was up early just because he was anxious to get this day over with, but in truth, his eagerness to see Colleen again, had him up with the sun. Perhaps he would be able to pick up a clue as to what was making him act so out of character while in her presence. *"Who am I trying to kid here?"* he chided himself. *"Just the knowledge that she is so near makes me feel off-balance. I want to see her because I want her. This has got to stop. I am the person that maintains control, conducts myself with the utmost decorum in the stickiest of situations. I refuse to let desire override my common sense, to control me… I refuse to let this woman get the better of me."*

Slipping the chain over his head and letting the key settle on his chest, he was immediately bombarded with Andrew. Apparently, Andrew was anxious to start the day also. *"Or, anxious to watch me make a fool of myself,"* Gordon thought. Immediately, after that thought, he heard his cousin's laughter coming from downstairs. "It's going to be a long day," Gordon said aloud.

If Colleen had thrown Gordon off-kilter before, it was nothing compared to this morning. She had been most congenial during breakfast. She had engaged Andrew in conversation and had not made one off-color remark to Gordon. After their meal, they had made their way to the slopes, and she had proven to be an apt pupil, listening intently, and following both his and Andrew's directions to the letter.

"She's a natural planker don't you think," Andrew asked Gordon as they watched her grab the rope lift after gracefully gliding down the short run and making a perfect turn to stop.

Gordon nodded in agreement, then said, "I don't get it. Last night she was incorrigible, and today she is behaving as if none of that transpired as if she were a different person."

"Split personality?" Andrew questioned wryly.

Turning to Andrew, Gordon asked, "Do you think we misread the whole thing? Our minds in the gutter? Maybe, we're getting paranoid?"

They both applauded as Colleen arrived with red cheeks, and a broad smile. "You were right, Andrew, I wasn't using the edge properly for my turn." Pulling her goggles down to hang around her neck, Colleen then turned to Gordon, and said, "Thank you for agreeing to a lesson," then with a little smirk playing about her mouth and the arch of her brow, added, "a couple of more and I can mark number four off of my list."

Looking down, Colleen busied herself with removing the skis; Gordon and Andrew exchanged a look, *"Well here we go,"* Gordon thought, while simultaneously touching the key, Andrew nodded.

Once she had removed the ski's, Colleen, turned to her companions and brightly suggested, "Let's go get some hot chocolate."

"Sounds like a great idea," Andrew began, "you two go ahead,

I think I'll take a run first." Gordon touched his key, *"You said you would stay with us."*

Andrew nodded and replied, *"I will be."* Giving them both a jaunty salute he made a turn for the downhill run.

Colleen and Gordon made their way back to the resort to return Colleen's rented skis. Deciding to relax at the same restaurant they had dined last night, they walked the two blocks in silence. Entering the cafe' Colleen immediately grabbed Gordon's arm for balance, after the blinding glare from the snow the darkened restaurant was disorienting. Gordon automatically laid his hand over hers and felt an incredible sense of protectiveness towards this woman surging through him.

Colleen requested a private corner table from the same hostess that had seated them the night before. Settling in after giving their order to the waitress, Colleen leaned across the table and said with a teasing smile, "You know that is the same hostess from last night?" Gordon nodded.

Continuing with the same teasing smile, Colleen said, "So, you are aware that she is waiting for you to give a repeat performance of your debonair charm... right?"

"Don't be silly," Gordon retorted, although, in all fairness, he had caught the young woman winking at him behind Colleen's back as she took her seat. It wasn't out of the norm for Gordon to find himself on the receiving end of mild public flirtation, but he didn't want to admit that to Colleen.

"Okay, I won't argue with you about that, not when we can discuss much more interesting topics," she responded. "For instance, like the way you and Andrew hold private conversations while in the presence of others."

With a sharp intake of breath, Gordon demanded, "What are you talking about?" Gordon stared hard at her as he watched a distracting little smile playing around her full mouth as she answered.

Chuckling softly, she replied, "Don't be so serious Gordon. I was merely making reference to the way you both seem to be of one mind, so much of the time. You know, finishing each other's sentences; almost, as if you each know what the other is thinking." Tipping her head to one side, and still smiling Colleen asked, "What did you think I meant?"

"I don't know," Gordon replied. "Sorry, I'm just a bit touchy I guess." Deciding now a good a time as any to start finding some answers, he took a deep breath to steady his nerves, and asked, "What did you mean when you said the skiing lesson was number four on your list? What else are you expecting from me, Colleen?"

Leaning in across the table, Colleen stared deep into Gordon's eyes; lowering her voice just above a whisper she said, "Many things Gordon...so many things." Tipping her head to one side and with a speculative look in her eyes, she added, "I think I could learn a lot from you."

Just then the waitress arrived with the hot chocolate served in thick earthenware mugs, with whipped cream swirled high on top. Colleen pulled her arms back from the table allowing room for the frothy drink. Without taking her eyes from his face, she dipped her finger into the cream, and proceeded to pop it in her mouth, licking it from her finger, "I love whipped cream and hot chocolate, don't you Gordon?"

At the moment, Gordon wished for a tall glass of ice water, to soothe his dry mouth; the only word he could manage to speak, "Why?"

With a toss of her hair and giving him a quizzical look, Colleen asked, "Why do I love whipped cream and hot chocolate? It tastes good silly!"

Gordon shook his head, "No, why are you--"

"Gordon, Colleen, there you two are I thought I had lost you," Andrew called in a rather boisterous voice, as he made his way through the lunch crowd to their table. "Sweetie," Andrew said addressing the waitress, "I'll have one of those too," indicating the steaming mugs.

"Andrew, I thought you were going to make the long run," Colleen remarked, as she sipped her drink.

"You're right...that was the plan," Andrew replied, "but, I received a call right after the two of you left...business, Gordon and I need to return to Bilford first thing this afternoon, and I realized I wouldn't have the time."

Frowning, Colleen said with a pout, "Gordon, I thought we would have time for at least one or two more lessons."

"It really is a shame isn't it?" Andrew said, in an attempt to draw her attention away from his cousin, allowing Gordon a few more moments to regain his composure. "You were doing so well out there today. You know, I might know of someone, a real ski instructor, that you could work with for the next few days if you would like."

"That would be lovely, Andrew," she accepted, and turning her attention back to Gordon, she added, with a deep sigh, "It is a shame that we couldn't continue Gordon, we are such a good fit..." as Gordon's eyes widened, she continued, "As teacher and pupil that is...like a key in a lock."

With that statement Gordon and Andrew both begin talking over one another, making excuses to leave within the hour. Andrew stood first; Gordon seemed to be glued to his chair. Throwing a fifty on the table for the chocolate, Andrew held Colleen's chair for her stand, and motioning for Gordon, with a jerk of his head to follow, they quickly made their way to the exit.

On the way to Shaun's and Fran's house, Andrew chattered non-stop to Colleen sitting up front with him, while Gordon sat as still, and quiet as a stone statue in the back, his thoughts swirling. Upon arriving at the front of the house, Andrew jumped out to get her door; as he hurried around the front end, Colleen turned and said, "Gordon, I want to say Thank You again. It was so very kind of you to give up part of your holiday to work with a novice."

His upbringing and good manners demanded that Gordon

respond. Clearing his throat, he said, with a tight smile, "It was my pleasure to be of assistance."

Disregarding Andrew standing by her door, she replied, with a small frown, "You're so formal again, I thought we were past all that." And then with the same quirky little smile that Gordon had seen playing on her full lips before, she said, "I am rather disappointed you have to go so soon. I'll have to think of some way for you to make that up to me, won't I? Perhaps number three on my list," she added with a wink. Colleen then turned to Andrew, as she popped the door handle, and gave him a dazzling smile, "Thank you for everything Andrew."

Andrew nodded and ran back around to the driver's side. As soon as Colleen opened the front door to the house, he hit the gas and shot away. Leaving Gordon to stew in the backseat.

Andrew stopped by the ski shop intending to offer five hundred dollars to the first instructor he came across to give a couple of lessons to a beautiful young redhead. Quickly scanning the room, Andrew noticed a young, blonde, and well-built man in his late twenties. Judging from the gaggle of young women surrounding him, Andrew assumed women thought he had the good looks of a Nordic Viking.

Andrew thought this guy might keep little Colleen entertained for a couple of days; but he got a non-verbal warning from Gordon who was still sitting in the SUV. Thinking quickly, Andrew promised to mail him another five hundred if she came back with an excellent report. The guy jumped on it. Exchanging information, Andrew handed over the first installment, her contact information, along with, a stern warning that he was paying for skiing lessons only.

"No problem sir, I'll treat her as if she was my mother," the young man said lazily.

"Be sure that you do," Andrew replied, and so there would be no mistake, he added, "or, I will be back." Andrew leveled a look on the Viking wannabe, and something in Andrew's eyes must have told the young buck, "...this guy is deadly serious," because he "Yes sir-ed" Andrew all the way to the door.

At the 'Getaway' Andrew took to the stairs to grab their bags, while Gordon called the cleaning service. He left a generous tip on the dining table for their trouble and called Joseph to let him know they would be home in a little over an hour.

Once in the car, and on the highway, Gordon asked, "Why did you stop me from questioning her?"

Andrew, studying the traffic ahead responded, "Because she was running over you like a freight train. You weren't thinking... you were reacting." Andrew took note of the *harrumph* from Gordon and quickly said, "Don't take that as a criticism, from what I could see I can't say that I blame you. I was a block away, but that little move with the whipped cre---"

"Shut-up Andrew," Gordon ordered, not wanting to relive that moment right now.

"Okay, okay," Andrew conceded, "but, I've never had a front row seat to watching you being seduced...not that blatantly. And, to answer your question from earlier, I don't think we're paranoid, nor misreading the situation. She has to be connected to the Fold in some way; I mean, that stuff about you two fitting together like a *lock and key*? Another sexual innuendo or does she know about the globes?"

"You really think she's part of the Fold?" Gordon queried, "Joseph couldn't find anything, and neither did your people." Gordon laid his head back on the seat, and closed his eyes, only to pop them open again. The mental pictures of Colleen were back, and they were more vivid than before.

Andrew swerved, almost crossing the center line, "What is going on with you? Stop thinking about her, at least while I'm driving. What the Hell was that anyway?"

"Me? Why are you driving all over the road?" Gordon shot back grabbing at the dash. Calming he asked, "What the Hell was what?"

"Look, Gordon, just try not to think about her for a little while longer, we'll be back to the manor shortly, I'll explain then. Think about Darius and Stavros. What business do we have with them? Bring me up to speed," Andrew encouraged.

Not fully understanding what was going on with Andrew, Gordon went along with him. He began to fill Andrew in on the export deal the Alanis Corporation had brought to him last year. "Like I said before, it's a minor contract." It had been Darius, the head of the Alanis House, which had approached him personally. Gordon had felt that he needed to be cooperative, lest he went complaining to their fathers. By the time Gordon had explained it all, Andrew was pulling up to the entrance of Bilford Manor.

As Gordon started to reach for the door handle, Andrew stopped him, "Gordon, I want to talk to you--out here--away from Joseph. It's about, before, when I swerved on the highway."

"Yes, I remember," Gordon said, his voice tinged with dry sarcasm.

"I'm not sure how to explain it, I've never experienced anything like that between the two of us. We are connected, of course, we know what the other is feeling if we're in close proximity, and can even see what is occurring in real time if we choose to, right?" Andrew paused, looking to Gordon for confirmation before continuing. "But that, back there on the road was different; it was like a vision, a vision I wasn't watching for, it came unbidden. It was a very, vivid still picture...nearly blotting out everything, that's the reason I swerved."

Before he asked, Gordon was sure he knew the answer, "What kind of picture?"

Taking a deep breath, and then blowing it out, Andrew replied, "It was Colleen. I think it was last night at the restaurant; she had a bemused look on her face, and I got the feeling she was expecting or waiting for something or someone." Andrew continued to watch Gordon's expression before saying, "I'm pretty sure she was standing up at the front, but she was alone with her hand out. Gordon, I didn't see her alone. The first time I saw her last night is when you saw her, with her Aunt and Uncle. When they came to the table, I was busy greeting them and getting more chairs. I didn't see her again until she came to the table with you, and she had her hand on your arm," Andrew finished.

Gordon stared out the front windshield recalling the moment Andrew was referring to, "Unbeknownst to me, she was watching while I charmed and tipped the hostess into holding our meals until our guests were also served. That was the reason for her amusement; she even made some remark about it, and then she held out her hand, so naturally, I offered my arm."

"She made a remark about it? I didn't pick that up, and I was watching," Andrew said with a frown.

"Yet, you picked one of the pictures out of my head," Gordon stated more than questioned.

"What do you mean *one of them*? Explain," Andrew demanded.

"I have been experiencing the same thing for the last few days. They have grown stronger, more vivid with each time I'm near her," Gordon rubbed at his temples, before continuing, "I get these unbidden images of Colleen, they're like photographs that will just pop into my mind. I don't have to be consciously thinking of her to have her face flash before my mind's eye."

"Has the 'shift' changed or stopped?" Andrew asked.

"Yes and no. No, it hasn't stopped," Gordon sighed, "Yes, there has been a change, and it's stronger, like with the phone call last night. She was using Fran's phone, but I knew it was her."

"Wow! So, you don't have to see her to feel 'the shift'? You don't have to be thinking of her to have her intrude into your line of vision." Andrew clarified. "Tell me, Gordon, did anything like this happen when Terese became a tribute? Or, Jeanette?"

"No," Gordon began his voice harsh with emotion, "With Jeanette, I'm ashamed to say it was a relief."

"Relief?" Andrew said incredulously. "I always found Jeanette to be quite exciting." Then added, with a wicked smile, "You know, in a dominatrix kind of way. Be honest, didn't you find Terese rather insipid in comparison?"

"Andrew, I am not discussing my sexual relationship with Jeanette, nor Terese with you," Gordon unequivocally replied, much to Andrew's disappointment. "To get back to your first question; no, I don't have images of my recently departed wife pop into my head unless I purposefully call them to mind. I do have feelings of regret and remorse for what I did to Terese. I miss her. I miss having Terese waiting at home for me, to talk with, and yes, to share my bed; but even before we married, I never felt this all-consuming desire to be with her,"

"I know about the regret and remorse, Gordon. I could feel that the minute I entered the house on the day of the memorial. I still pick it up from you occasionally, like now. But, this other, with Colleen is nowhere near the same thing." Andrew said.

"Damn!" Andrew exclaimed making Gordon jump, "Just saying her name has an effect on you, I can feel it like it's a tangible thing."

Gordon looked at Andrew, and said in a weary voice, "I don't know what to do, except to confront her. Yet, what do I confront her with? So, she's flirting with me, that's hardly a crime. Besides, I'm the one that kissed her that night in the conservatory," Gordon took a deep breath before continuing, "She is the niece of my neighbors, who happen to be my closest friends. I was in my early twenties when I met Terese, I was attracted to her, but I never felt the need to chase after her like a teenage boy." Gordon groaned, before saying, "Good grief, I never felt the need to chase after any girl like this when I was a teenage boy. I'm 36 years old now, and Colleen is probably ten years my junior."

"I hardly think the small difference in your ages has anything to do with this," Andrew scoffed.

"I suppose," Gordon agreed, but still unconvinced. "She's not exactly a child, but neither am I. That's my point. I feel as if I have, little to no, control of myself, over some woman I don't know."

"So, the conundrum is," Andrew began, thoughtfully, "are you out of control because you truly feel that way, or is she bewitching you somehow? Is Colleen *really* what she appears to be? After all, we're not."

They sat in silence for a moment before Andrew suggested, "Maybe you should take her up on her flirtations and see what happens."

"No," Gordon said emphatically.

"Why not?" Andrew came right back.

"The world believes that Terese died a little less than a month ago. I am in mourning, I cannot start dating," Gordon replied, as if tutoring a child.

"If you would follow my advice you wouldn't find yourself in this mess...how long do you have to be *"in mourning?"* Andrew asked impatiently while making air quotes.

"At least six months," Gordon said. "A year would be much better."

"No way are you going to last a year, maybe not six months," Andrew began, "not here. Perhaps you should stay in Boston for a while, or go check on some of our international holdings. Find yourself another Katrina."

"I don't know...maybe." Gordon couldn't bring himself to admit to Andrew that he didn't want to leave, not anymore; and he had no desire to find another Katrina. The idea of not being around Colleen was nearly as painful as seeing her and forcing himself to keep his distance. But he couldn't tell Andrew that, not yet. "Right now, it looks as if Joseph needs me," Gordon said indicating the front of the house where Joseph stood waiting patiently.

Gordon had often wondered about Joseph's age. As far as he could tell Joseph had not changed. Even from his first memories as a child, Joseph had always had the same medium build, dark brown hair with a hint of gray at his temples and closely-trimmed goatee. His eyes, the color of sapphires, could twinkle with mirth, or on rare occasions turn a cold steel-gray with displeasure. One of the things Gordon had always admired about Joseph was his self-assured, quiet manner. *'He is always the eye of the hurricane; still, calm, and confident never the storm. Andrew, would go out of his way to fluster Joseph with no success, and that in turn would fluster Andrew.'*

"Joseph, how are you?" Gordon greeted him as he exited the SUV and moved to the back to retrieve the bags before Andrew drove the vehicle to the garages. Joseph quickly walked over to help, and to inform Gordon that he had just received another message from the House of Alanis.

"Let's drop the bags by the back stairs, and we'll go to my office," Gordon said, as he knocked on the door of the vehicle giving Andrew the 'all clear' signal.

Once inside, Joseph took the bags, allowing Gordon to go straight to his office. Gordon was feeling more at ease, as he always did when he entered Bilford Manor. He immediately picked up the mail from the past two days and settled into his chair behind his desk. He was neatly stacking the items that would need his immediate attention in the center and laid the rest aside when Joseph returned.

"There's been a change in plans concerning the Alanis guests," Joseph stated, as he poured a short drink, and handed it to Gordon.

Gordon eyed the glass of bourbon, and then Joseph. Since he had not requested a drink, and it was a little early in the afternoon for him to start drinking, Gordon's feeling of ease and well-being was quickly being replaced by a growing apprehension.

"Go on, Joseph, just spit it out," Gordon said.

Taking a seat across from Gordon, Joseph said, "First of all they will be staying here, at the manor in the guest wing."

Gordon had expected as much, and with a shrug asked, "How long?"

"Darius is planning to return to his ship on Monday," Joseph said, and took notice that Gordon smiled; then added, "however, young Stavros will be staying on for an *indefinitely* extended visit, and he will be staying here at the manor."

Sitting back and closing his eyes, Gordon took a deep, steadying breath, and said, "No, we'll just tell him we can't accommodate him for more than a couple of weeks. We'll say that he is more than welcome to stay at one of the Boston apartments after that time, but, that Andrew and I will be leaving on business." Opening his eyes again he stared at Joseph who was shaking his head in the negative, "Why not?" Gordon demanded.

"Because," Joseph began, "he will be coming with a letter from your father, who has *requested* that you open Bilford Manor to the son of Alanis House, in a show of hospitality and alliance."

"And, by *requested,* I presume you mean demanded," Gordon stated bitterly, rather than asking.

Shrugging, Joseph said, "If you don't...there's a good chance he could show up, and I don't think you want that."

"He knows I'm in mourning," Gordon stated, "why would he expect me to play host *indefinitely* to some man I don't know?" Gordon was becoming more agitated by the minute.

"And, you know that he doesn't want you to marry your tributes, so you can't use that as an excuse," Joseph bluntly pointed out. "He taught you to keep the more intimate part of your life away from the business of the Fold."

Pacing back and forth around his desk, Gordon shouted, "I'm sick of the Fold controlling my life!" Feeling Andrew's queries, Gordon yanked the key from his neck breaking the chain, and flung it across the room, "And I'm sick of having a monitor in my head 24-7!"

Joseph, accustomed to Gordon's mercurial temper as he consistently battled with the tenets of the Fold, sat back quietly, waiting for this current show of temper to burn itself out. He had served as a mediator between father and son most of young Gordon's life. Joseph had tried to tell, Gordon Senior, that his son was not meant to take on this role; but he would hear none of it. Instead, the father had pushed the son, even as a little boy, to be measured and calculating in every move...every decision he made. To be strong-willed and independent with an eye to the future.

Gordon, who practically worshiped his father in his youth, strove to please him, learning his lessons well. But, on the night of his twentieth birthday, Joseph had watched as the father had dealt a devastating blow to his heir. Gordon, the son, had his entire world turned upside-down. Unlike, his Cousin Andrew who had embraced his inheritance, Gordon fought against it with every fiber of his being. The lessons of independence, willfulness, and calculating thought process while grooming his son had proven to work against the older Bilford rather than in his favor. The inherit leader, of the House of Bilford, had been crushed by his father's betrayal and wanted no part of his legacy.

Joseph was in the unique position of serving both men. He could take a step back, and understand the situation from both of their perspectives. Gordon Sr. was a powerful entity within the Fold, far more powerful than his son realized; not accustomed to being thwarted, certainly not by his only child, whom he was offering power, and nearly infinite control over the world of Normals. Gordon the III was not interested. He was his own man and chafed at being controlled by his father or the Fold, which in his mind were one and the same. Joseph couldn't help but admire the younger Bilford for his convictions. Gordon was a hard worker; he took pride in a job done well. He always maintained a sense of fairness about him, not only in his personal life but in his business dealings as well. Something in which Joseph found extraordinary, given the circumstances.

"Joseph!" repeated Gordon for the third time.

"Yes sir, sorry, my mind was somewhere else," Joseph replied.

"No, you don't owe me an apology. I owe you an apology for losing my temper--once again. And, once again, it is not necessary for you to call me sir," Gordon said with a sincerity that had Joseph smiling indulgently. Another trait that Joseph admired in Gordon, humility.

"Well," Joseph began, "there is one more thing I need to discuss with you. It concerns the O'Malley's."

Gordon stopped his pacing and dropped down into the chair next to Joseph, rather than returning to his seat behind the desk. Blowing air out as if he had been holding his breath he asked, "What now?"

"It's about the Valentine's Day Ball, the one that Ms. Terese was hosting," Joseph began to explain. Gordon began to shake his head 'no' before Joseph continued, "Mrs. O'Malley called yesterday to say that she would be taking it over and act as hostess in Ms. Terese' stead." Taking a breath Joseph continued saying the words quickly as if it would make it easier to hear, "She said, you won't have to do a thing, except put in an appearance, and of course, open Bilford Manor since it is being held in honor of Ms. Terese."

Gordon closed his eyes and groaned, "I thought I had left instructions to cancel that event."

"You did," Joseph said bobbing his head, "you did, but Mrs. O'Malley said that Ms. Terese had done so much to lay the groundwork, and was so passionate about the cause that she wanted to honor her memory," Joseph finished.

"Why can't I just send a nice big check to whatever charity it is, and be done with it?" Gordon asked.

"You can do that, of course." Joseph said with a twinkle in his eyes, "But if that is your choice, you will be the one to explain to Fran O'Malley why you don't want to honor your wife's memory, not me."

Gordon stood, and started pacing the room again, Joseph quickly added, "Mrs. O'Malley said they would keep it fairly low-keyed so it won't be weeks of preparation just a few days. Oh, and another thing, Ms. Terese had already sent out the save-the-date cards to the guests."

Gordon stopped his trek around the room, and said, "Maybe I could give her the house, a nice fat check, and spend a few days in Boston until it's over."

With a quiet and calm tone, Joseph replied, "Gordon, you can't keep running. I don't understand what is going on here any better than you, but you will have to figure it out." With that, Joseph went to the corner of the room where Gordon had flung his key. With a tsk of his tongue, he examined the broken chain. "This will take me a little time to repair, you know the key cannot be separated from the chain. You will need to explain to Mr. Andrew."

"Yes, I know…I don't understand it, but I know," Gordon said with a mixture of contriteness and scorn. In fact, Gordon didn't understand a lot of things about the mechanics of enshrining the tributes. As far as he knew his father was the only one of his acquaintance, within the Fold, that had witnessed an actual event. Gordon was only aware of his part in the enshrinement; separate the bow and shoulder from the shaft of his key, insert it into the hidden lock on the base of the snow globe and then walk away. That was it.

Gordon Sr. had assured his son that it was quick and painless for the tribute. Someone or *something* put the tribute into a deep state of hypnosis, then performed the necessary rites, and the deed was done. Gordon had inquired about the *entity* and the *necessary rites,* but his father would not discuss either with him, only saying, *"Perhaps, one day, you will be privy to that information."* He was ashamed to admit it, but a part of Gordon didn't really want to know.

Gordon watched as Joseph fussed with the broken links while still holding the key securely, to the chain, in his palm. Gordon thought the usually calm, collected Joseph seemed to be a little nervous, "Joseph is there anything else that you needed to tell me?"

Looking up from the tangle of metal in his hand, Joseph pinned Gordon with a look, and said, "She also said that her niece was a whiz at organizing such things and that she could easily pick-up where Ms. Terese had left off."

"Pick-up where Terese left off? That's what I'm afraid of," Gordon thought to himself, to Joseph he said with a weary sigh, "Of course she is a whiz at party planning she's *God's gift* so why wouldn't she be able to do this too?" Noting Joseph's quizzical expression,

Gordon explained, "It's the meaning of her *full* name; Janet Colleen, God's gracious gift-girl. Paraphrasing Fran, "...their girl is God's gracious gift, and she lives up to that, or so Andrew and I were told."

"Well now, that may change things," Joseph said, "I think we may have been looking in the wrong places for information on the lass."

"Honestly Joseph, tell me that you don't buy into all that prophetic name nonsense that father tried to warn me about." Gordon said, disdainfully.

"Are you forgetting the *'dark messenger'*?" Joseph asked. "Not to mention the meaning of your own name; *Gordon* means hero and *Andrew* means warrior. That's exactly how your father views you, a hero warrior for the House of Bilford. Even my own, Joseph, means add-on, which more or less describes what I do."

Before Gordon could launch into his argument, Joseph held up his hand to stop him, and said, "Let me look into it, I most assuredly could be wrong. However, I do need you to find some answers that I think only Miss O'Malley can supply. The lassie is truly an enigma."

Gordon sank into the nearest chair, and said, "I will concede that you're right about one thing Joseph, I can't keep running. I can't keep running from what I am, and I can't keep running from Ms. O'Malley." Thinking back to what Andrew had suggested, just a little while ago, *"Maybe you should take her up on her flirtations and see what happens."* A new idea took form in Gordon's mind, *"I could take her up on her flirtations... in private."* Gordon smiled, *"Then see what happens."*

When Joseph gave him a questioning look, Gordon thoughtfully continued, "So I will meet this situation with Ms. O'Malley like I do any other...head-on. I will gather as much information as possible, calculate my risks, make my decisions, and let the chips, so to speak, fall where they may."

Joseph looked at Gordon with skepticism and said, "So you

think to, um…*charm* the answers from her as a way to get your information?"

"If I have to, yes," Gordon replied. "I will have to be discreet, as I told Andrew before, social convention demands that I spend a certain amount of time in mourning."

"Just don't lose yourself to it, sir," Joseph warned, "That has happened before, you know?"

"I am my father's son, Joseph," Gordon retorted, "but I am not my father."

TOGETHER, GORDON AND JOSEPH LEFT THE office; Joseph headed off to see about dinner, and Gordon went up to his rooms. Going straight to his balcony, and throwing the doors wide, Gordon stepped out into the crisp salt air and stood quietly listening to what he referred to as his piece of the ocean. He never tired of the music on the shore. The crescendo of the windswept waves rolling in, then the quieting murmur of those waves as they momentarily rest on the beach only to be pulled back into depths of the ocean. Gordon stood quietly, with eyes closed, for a few moments to let the fragrance of the air and the sound of the water calm his mind. Snow had been forecast, and he most assuredly could feel the bite of cold in the breeze.

Suddenly, with breathtaking clarity, an image of Colleen flashed behind his eyes. Gordon's eyes flew open as he realized that she had followed them home and would be her making way to Bilford Manor. He had no idea how he knew, but he knew. *"It's nearly the same sensation as watching Andrew,"* Gordon thought, *"but how? Why?"* Although he found the experience unnerving, he didn't have time to think about it right now. Regardless of the why or how of it, he had no intentions of running; and, although he would have preferred a little more time to prepare, this time he would be turning the tables on Miss Colleen.

Pushing the intercom button on the bedside table, something Gordon rarely used, he told Joseph that Miss Colleen was on her way to the manor; instructing him to show her to his study and to inform her that Mr. Bilford would meet her there. Joseph began to sputter, so Gordon repeated his instructions. Andrew, having picked up on Gordon's heightened emotional state, immediately sent him a text, to which, Gordon replied: Don't worry, I have this. Will explain later.

Gordon decided to grab a quick shower, knowing Colleen wasn't too far away had him deciding to go without a shave. *"It's been my experience that some women like a little scruff,"* Gordon thought, as he chose a lightweight, red, V-neck cashmere sweater along with a pair of charcoal gray pants from his closet. When he would ask, Terese had always chosen red for him, saying the color in combination with his long curly black hair and dark eyes, gave him a devilish look. *"Oh, the irony!"* Gordon thought. Having decided to give back as good as she gave, giving over to his baser feelings, at least while they were in private had Gordon feeling a bit devilish at the moment.

After all, he thought as he pulled a brush through his dark wavy hair, *"The art of seduction is not exactly new to me."* It gave him a feeling of freedom to permit himself to stop avoiding Colleen, and if not actually pursue her, at the very least enter the game, in private, of course. When in front of others, he would continue to behave well within the parameters of societal acceptance for a recent widower, he still had his reputation and the reputation of his business to protect.

Stepping back to check his reflection in the antique floor mirror, he noticed a glint of light flash through the adjacent window. Turning to look down at the front drive he saw Colleen's car pull to a stop. Gordon smiled, *"Well here we go,"* he thought, and leisurely made his way downstairs to his study.

Taking a deep breath, he entered the study to find Colleen O'Malley sitting primly on the edge of a chair busily writing in a notebook that lay on her lap. She had her hair pulled up in a ponytail, and she wore a cream-colored sweater in a chunky knit, the kind Terese had always called her snuggly clothes, with what appeared to be a pair of the forever-tight blue jeans. In what was beginning to become the norm since meeting Colleen, Gordon immediately felt a sexual pull to the woman, which in itself might not be unusual; but there was something more, something that he could not quite identify; if he had to put a name to it, it would be something akin to feeling possessive.

"Colleen, it's good to see you again so soon, may I offer you something to drink?" Gordon asked, as he strode into the room and rather than going straight to his desk, he took the matching club chair positioned opposite from her. "Joseph would be happy to make you whatever you might like."

Gordon observed a quizzical look flit across her face as she watched him, "No I don't care for anything right now." Cocking her head to one side, she remarked, "You know Gordon, I do believe the skiing trip did you some good, you seem to be much more relaxed than usual."

Leaning toward her, he answered, "You know, I believe you're right. There is absolutely nothing like pushing-off at the precipice of a run, gliding carefully and smoothly at first as you begin to navigate the terrain, then leaning into it and as you find your rhythm you begin to push harder, picking up speed until you feel like you're flying, then ending the run in an explosion of snow crystals," Gordon said in a statement calculated to let her know that he too, could play her game, "It's exhilarating, and yet, quite a stress reliever." As he sat back in his chair, Gordon didn't take his eyes from Colleen's face.

He watched as Colleen's eyes narrowed infinitesimally, just for a second before allowing a little smile to play about her mouth as she leaned in to respond, "You make it sound so exciting." Dropping her voice just above a whisper she added, "I'm so sorry we had to cut our lessons short; perhaps another time. I would hate to miss out on such an experience with you."

"*Damn, she's good,*" Gordon thought. Then responding with a slow smile, he said, "I promise it would be an experience that you would not soon forget." As he spoke, Gordon observed a fleeting look of uncertainty in Colleen's face, rapidly replaced with a slight smirk, and a nearly imperceptible nod of her head. Switching gears Gordon asked, "How can I help with the party planning? That is why you're here isn't it, Colleen? Why you left Albany before taking advantage of the lessons that Andrew arranged for you? Fran left word with Joseph yesterday that you were ready to carry the torch, so to speak. She also said that you were very adept at planning a gala, and thought you would be willing to pick-up where Terese left off." Leaning forward again, Gordon asked, "Are you willing to pick-up where Terese left off?"

Giving herself a little shake and drawing in a quick breath, Colleen sat-up and consulted the notebook she had on her lap. Smiling she said, "Yes well, Aunt Fran seems to think I can do anything. She had just informed me of *her* plans when you dropped me off after skiing this morning." With a sigh, she continued, "I am truly sorry that I couldn't take the lessons that Andrew arranged for me, and of course, I will pay him back for any deposit that he might have made. I am also truly sorry you got stuck with this when I know you had wanted to call it off. I am intruding on your life once again. But in my defense, it is a worthy cause if that makes it any easier."

Gordon decided to ease up…a little, she seemed to be quite sincere, and he didn't want to overplay his hand, "I'm sure it is a good cause if Terese was so very passionate about it," Gordon responded, and to test her sincerity he added, "I just need to know what you want from me."

Waiting for another one of her asides with his last statement, Gordon was surprised when she smiled happily and said, "Since you have agreed to help, I will try to make this as painless as possible.

I can handle the press release, which will need to go out soon; along with the rest of the publicity." She flipped through a couple of pages and continued speaking almost as if she were talking to herself and had forgotten he was in the room. "Let's see...Terese sent out save-the-date cards on the first of December, although we may need to move the date, and she contacted a catering service. I can take care of staffing, such as the extra waiters and waitresses needed, parking valets, arrange for hired cars to pick-up any guests that would prefer not to drive..."

Gordon watched Colleen as she chewed her bottom lip jotting down notes and checking some items off her to-do list, only to add a few more. He wondered if the lip thing was a deliberate move, on her part, purposely meant to entice him, or merely an unconscious habit when she lost herself in concentration. Not that it mattered, because the results were the same...he was enticed and had been since the first time he had laid eyes on her. He wanted nothing more at the moment than to taste her mouth again. To Gordon, the night of the memorial felt so long ago, but in reality, it had just been a few days. He had spent nearly every moment since he had returned from Switzerland, running from this woman who now sat before him.

"Gordon?" Colleen had stopped fussing over her notes and was now leaning forward with her hand on his wrist, having reached across the space between them to gain his attention. "Gordon," she repeated his name and asked, "Are you okay?"

Gordon looked at her long-tapered fingers, and entertained the idea of flipping his wrist to grab her and pull her to him; he could just take her; no one would stop him. Wouldn't his father be proud? Just take what you want with little to no repercussions, because it was within in their power to make them forget, or remember only what you want them to; isn't that how the rest of his family lived? But, instead, he looked into her concerned green eyes and said, "Yes, yes I'm fine... just got lost in thought for a moment." Gently patting her hand with his free hand, Gordon made to stand, and Colleen settled back in her chair.

Colleen said, "Gordon if this is too difficult for you by bringing up too many memories too soon; I can try to handle it on my own."

Looking into her upturned face still etched in concern, Gordon felt a wave of self-loathing coursing through him for even considering using his powers on her. *"Maybe I'm spending too much time with Andrew,"* Gordon thought, moving to the window, to gaze out over the snow-covered lawn, and the gathering clouds that promised more snow soon. "So, what else is left on your list for the gala?" he asked, turning to observe her.

Referring to her notes once more, Colleen replied, "Well not a lot actually, uh-mm...decorations, flowers, hearts, something to go with the theme, re-setting the date, calling the caterers, and I thought a silent auction might be just the thing rather than a town raffle," she nodded to herself looking over her papers once again. "I already have quite a list of donations that I think would work wonderfully. Ski weekends, some athletic equipment, romantic dinners, some local artwork, and some exquisite antique jewelry pieces that were donated by a family from Newport after the passing of their dowager aunt."

Gordon was surprised by the list of donations and interrupted her by asking, "Terese did so much charity work I haven't even thought to ask, which charity is this gala for anyway?"

"Oh, I thought you knew; this is the charity that Terese founded, and it's a wonderful cause." Colleen enthused, "It's for people in this community. So many people live paycheck-to-paycheck that the least little thing can throw them into a financial spin that makes it difficult to recover. Such things as medical bills, an unexpected hike in their utilities, car repair, the sorts of things that happen unexpectedly, and one can find themselves in dire financial straits rather quickly. They will be able to petition the foundation and receive temporary help almost immediately. I'm a bit surprised you hadn't heard of it, Terese single-handedly started the organization on a smaller scale a couple of years ago, primarily for the locals here in Bilford." Pausing for a moment, Colleen stood and moved to stand next to Gordon at the window, facing him, "Care to guess what she named the charity?"

Gordon shifted, uncomfortably aware of her closeness, and answered honestly, "I haven't the slightest idea."

Laying her hand on Gordon's upper arm to gain his direct attention, she softly said, as she stared at his mouth, "She named it: Love thy Neighbor." Meeting his gaze, she once again allowed that little smile of hers to play about her lips, "A fitting title, don't you think so, neighbor? Something that everyone should aspire to do?"

Gordon stood mesmerized for the merest of moments before wrapping his arm around Colleen's waist and pulling her toward him. Feeling no resistance from her, only willingness, he lowered his mouth towards hers, when quite unexpectedly the door to the study slammed against the wall, and Andrew came strolling inside.

"There you two are," Andrew exclaimed, "Joseph sent me to fetch you both for dinner."

Gordon dropped his hand from Colleen's waist. As she took a step back away from him, Gordon's mind began to clear a little. He turned to stare at Andrew, but he spoke to Colleen, "Yes, Colleen, please stay. We can make it a working dinner and perhaps finalize a few of the preparations."

Colleen looked at Andrew and said, "Please tell Joseph that I happily accept. I will meet you both after a visit to the powder room." Before leaving she retrieved her notebook from her chair, and as she started to move past Andrew, she stopped beside him. Andrew looked down at her with a slight smirk; tipping her head to one side, Colleen said, "Your timing leaves much to be desired," and with that, she moved through the door.

Although Gordon wasn't pleased with Andrew's interruption, he found the dumbfounded look his cousin now wore mildly amusing. "She has a point," Gordon said. "Would you like to tell me what prompted you to come bursting in at such an inopportune moment?"

Quickly recovering, Andrew said, as he closed the door, "Dear Cousin, although you were able to rid yourself of your key, in a fit of angry I might add, I am still in close enough proximity to pick-up certain emotional reactions from you, and I got the feeling you might be heading down a road you might regret taking."

Shoving his hands in his pockets, as he turned away from Andrew to continue gazing out the window, Gordon replied, "Did it occur to you, *Dear Cousin*, that I was on a road of my own making? A road that would perhaps lead me to the answers we seek."

With a derisive snort, Andrew said, "With what I was feeling, it was more like a trail to get into her--"

"Enough!!" Gordon didn't shout, as he cut Andrew off, which made the utterance a far more ominous warning.

Andrew, knowing the power that Gordon could call forth when pushed too far, threw up his hands in a gesture of surrender. It was best not to bring Gordon to anger again today. "Whoa Gordon, calm down. I was just trying to make light of the situation. You know me, always the jester."

Drawing a calming breath, Gordon turned to Andrew and replied, "Sometimes your jokes go too far Cousin. Please do not goad me into losing control."

"You're right, but honestly Gordon, after the way you have behaved while in her presence over the past few weeks, how was I to know this was your plan and not an uncontrollable reaction?" Andrew asked, in exasperation. "We just returned *today* from a trip that we made to put some distance between the two of you."

Gordon nodded, in an attempt to be fair, he had to acknowledge that his temper, earlier this afternoon, had put Andrew at a disadvantage in understanding his motives. Coupled with the fact that he had not had time to explain beforehand. "You couldn't have known, and for that, I apologize." Gordon could see Andrew physically relax, "On the other hand, I am not accustomed to reporting every decision that I make to anyone. You need to trust me." Gordon said quietly with a note of warning in his voice. "I have set a course, and I intend to see where it leads me. Right now, thanks to Joseph, it leads us to dinner with Colleen." Clamping a hand on Andrew's shoulder as they made their way out, Gordon added, "This could be interesting."

As it turned out, Gordon did not need to be overly concerned. Joseph had set dinner in the family dining room. The smaller, more intimate, dining area had been added to the manor during the renovations and expansion of the conservatory. The smaller dining room had been built on a dais overlooking the conservatory. It had two glass walls that created the fourth corner of the room. During certain times of the year, with warmer weather, the walls could be slid opened into the greenhouse; sitting among the greenery gave one a feeling of picnicking in a forest. Or, the glass walls could be left closed, as they were tonight, still offering the occupants a glorious view of the various flora while dining.

Tonight, they enjoyed a relaxing meal, of tender roast beef, complemented with baby potatoes and mixed vegetables. Comfort food served on thick stoneware china, accompanied with a dry red Bordeaux, and apple tart-lets for dessert; in the background, lending to the relaxed ambiance, a selection of blues softly playing.

For the most part, Colleen had been on her best behavior tossing out only a few subtle innuendos, to Gordon's relief, he wasn't sure he wanted to go another round today. Playing the seducer, a pleasant enough diversion, in theory, had become a fine line to walk with the knowledge that he could not allow himself to see it through to its fruition. *"Good thing I have excellent balance,"* Gordon thought.

They had decided to hold the gala on Saturday the 17th of February. This way, Colleen explained, it shouldn't interfere with any romantic plans for the actual date of the holiday or any plans for a pre-holiday celebration. It was just a week past the date that Terese had picked for the save-the-date cards; they agreed that under the circumstances everyone would understand. She had also said that holding the gala after Valentine's Day might increase the bids for some of the silent auction items. When Andrew and Gordon had asked why, Colleen gave them a conspiratorial wink and said, "You know, for those men that didn't get their wives or sweethearts what they wanted for Valentines, or they completely forgot. The silent auction will give them a chance to redeem themselves."

"Brilliant!" Andrew had burst out laughing, and declared, "You are a clever girl Colleen."

Colleen laughed and said, "I can hold my own when need be."

Of that Gordon had no doubt. He had been observing her throughout the evening. Given they had been 'caught' in an embrace just a couple of hours ago, he expected Colleen to be more flustered, to display some embarrassment, but he couldn't have been more mistaken. She ate, she drank, she laughed, and she sparkled. He had never met anyone quite like *Janet Colleen O'Malley*. Due to his social and business circles, encountering beautiful, wealthy, and polished women was not new to him; but Colleen had an inner confidence, a quiet strength, that far surpassed the brittle self-assurance of those that possessed both wealth and beauty. The attitude of entitlement that sometimes-accompanied great wealth, and that Gordon had encountered on more than one occasion, had somehow eluded Colleen. She conducted herself as kind, thoughtful, and empathetic without being overly sympathetic; she presented herself as a very down to earth sort of person without pretenses. *"So how do I figure into her game? How much, if anything, does she know about my existence?"*

As the evening began to wind down, Andrew excused himself leaving Gordon to see Colleen out. They walked in silence to the foyer to retrieve her coat, as Gordon helped her into the lightweight coat that she held out, he peered out the transom window beside the front door and noted the snow coming down much heavier than what had been predicted, and resulting in very low visibility. He could barely discern the driveway from the lawns. The driveway was partially covered but the snow had blown in covering the windshield of her vehicle.

"Why don't you stay in here while I clean off your car?" Gordon suggested, "Or, I could drive you."

Turning to face Gordon, Colleen pulled the faux fur collar of her coat close to her chin, and while looking into his eyes replied, "Gordon I'm not as fragile as you appear to think I am. A little cold doesn't bother me, and besides, I only have a couple of miles to drive till I'm home. I will be fine." Leaning into Gordon, she put her palms on his chest, tipping her head back to look into his eyes, she added with a wink, "So unless you are going to invite me to spend the night with you, I will see myself home now, and I will be back tomorrow." With that, she patted his chest and turned towards the door.

Gordon was flabbergasted, but in a lightning-quick move, he grasped her elbow as she started to open the door. Pulling her back to face him, he asked, "Why?"

Colleen looked pointedly at her arm and back to his face, Gordon immediately dropped his hand from her elbow and raked it through his hair never taking his eyes from her face.

"Why what?" Colleen asked coolly.

"Why do you seem so Hell-bent on seducing me, a man that has just lost his wife, and is still in mourning?" Once he started questioning her, he couldn't stop, the words seemed to come tumbling out of their own volition, and tinged with exasperation, "Why does everything you say to me sound like sexual innuendo, an invitation? And don't try to tell me it's my imagination or wishful thinking."

Colleen, seemingly measuring each word, answered, "I won't question that you are in mourning; however, are you sure it's all due to the loss of your wife?" Gordon's eyes widened in disbelief as she continued, "Not yet, Gordon. You're not ready to hear the answers that you seek at this time."

"I demand to know what that is supposed to mean," Gordon said raising his voice.

Gone was the seductress who had just alluded to spending the night with him. The woman who stood before him now had stubbornly clamped her full lips together while wearing a look of defiance.

Gordon and Colleen were so focused on one another they both were unaware that Andrew had appeared at the top of the stairs, and that Joseph had moved past them. A gust of cold salt air swept over them as Joseph opened the front doors to welcome the newcomers standing on the other side.

10

"WELL, WELL, WELL GORDON, I DIDN'T expect to find you entertaining such a lovely young lady so soon after the demise of your dear wife," exclaimed a masculine voice with a slight accent.

Gordon looked past Colleen to see Stavros Alanis, followed by his father, Darius, entering Bilford Manor. Gordon stepped in front of Colleen, feeling oddly protective; he felt a need to shield her from the newcomers' scrutiny.

Wondering why the Alanis men had shown up a day early, and inwardly cursing their timing, Gordon quickly sized-up the men standing in his foyer. Stavros was barely seventeen the last time Gordon had seen him, but that had been about twelve years ago; no longer "just a kid," but, a man.

Like himself, Stavros wore his dark wavy hair quite a bit longer than the currently popular buzzed-off style, and it framed his face, emphasizing the chiseled features synonymous with the classic Greek profile. His eyes were a startling blue, made more pronounced by the olive tone of his skin. Stavros strongly favored his father, the same coloring, and the same chiseled features; broad-shouldered, long muscled, and both men easily topped six feet.

Darius had the added features of a little silver in his hair, and a few crow's feet; however, rather than detracting from his looks, the signs of aging simply added a distinguished air to his countenance. Currently, both men appeared to be highly curious about the drama unfolding in front of them; understandable considering that Gordon could almost feel the crackle of electricity sparking between himself and Colleen.

However, to Gordon's utter amazement, Colleen swept around him and with enthusiasm said, "Stavros, I can't believe you're here. How long has it been since we've seen one another?" Without waiting for an answer, she tiptoed to place a kiss on each of Stavros' cheeks, and quipped, "London, right?" Moving past the younger man, Colleen gave the elder Alanis the same Euro greeting as she had the son, before asking with a wide smile, "And, Mr. Alanis, you're as handsome as ever, how have you been?"

"Colleen," Darius Alanis exclaimed with a much heavier accent than his son, "you most assuredly do this old man some good." He held Colleen at arm's length, and said, "Here, let me get a good look at you paidi mou."

Gordon watched all of this byplay in stunned silence. *"Obviously, Colleen had some history with the Alanis family,"* Gordon thought dryly when Darius Alanis used an old Greek endearment for 'my child' as he pulled Colleen into a fatherly bear hug. Once again, Gordon's mind screamed, *"Who is this woman?"*

Coming to stand beside him, Gordon felt Andrew's hand on his shoulder, "Darius, Stavros," Andrew announced, "on behalf of my cousin, and myself, let me 'Welcome' both of you to the House of Bilford."

"I sincerely hope our early arrival is not too much of an inconvenience," Darius Alanis said, "but, we had been watching the weather when we arrived in Portsmouth, a day early, and thought it best to come straight here."

Andrew's presence seemed to calm Gordon for the moment and helped him to get his bearings. Picking-up on Andrew's greeting, Gordon said, "Absolutely, no problem at all. I second my Cousin Andrew's 'Welcome.' Please come on through to the salon," and for the second time that evening he took Colleen's arm guiding her toward the front door. "Joseph and Andrew will be more than happy to get both of you a drink," he said as he nodded to Andrew to get their guests out of the hall, "while I see Miss O'Malley to her car."

"I'm afraid she won't be driving out of here tonight," Stavros said. "The road has been blocked by a fallen tree. The thing fell right after we drove past it; I don't mind telling you it gave us quite a fright."

"Sir," Joseph said to Gordon, "I was just coming to tell you that our 'predicted snow flurries' for this evening has turned into the full-on storm predicted for the weekend. The radio is reporting that the roads are becoming treacherous with ice, in some places impassable, and a tree is down just past the driveway. They're asking people to stay off of the roads."

"Well, it looks like I *will* be spending the night," Colleen said. Turning to Gordon, she said, "I hope that's all right with you Gordon." Then widening her green eyes in mock innocence said, "Care to rescue a damsel-in-distress?"

All eyes turned to Gordon as he stiltedly replied, "It would be my pleasure, Miss O'Malley."

With a cheeky smile and blowing a kiss in Gordon's direction, Colleen took each, Stavros and Darius, by the arm and said, "Come along, gentlemen, let's go in by the fire, and we can catch-up on what we've been doing since we last met." Leaving Gordon, Andrew, and Joseph to stare after her in amazement.

Joseph was the first to break the silence, "So is the lass now the new mistress of the manor?"

Gordon had noted that Joseph had taken to referencing Colleen's heritage by continually calling her 'lass' or 'lassie.' "Not funny," Gordon fumed.

"I suppose not," Joseph replied as he tried to keep a straight face. "I will put the men's luggage in the two larger suites in the west wing, and prepare the smaller guest suite for the lassie," he said.

"Fine," Gordon agreed. Then with a purposeful glint in his eyes, said, "Except, put Ms. O'Malley in the suite next to mine."

Joseph, looking a little startled by Gordon's demand, simply said, "As you wish."

Raising his eyebrows in disbelief, Andrew asked, "Gordon, are you sure you want to do that? She seems to be well acquainted with the Alanis' men; I'm reasonably sure she would be comfortable there; why put yourself through that?"

"I want her where I can keep an eye on her," Gordon replied. "And besides I intend to finish our conversation before this night is over. I can't explain right now, Andrew, but, Colleen and I...we have much to discuss."

With a look of skepticism and a slight shrug of his shoulders, Andrew said, "I hope you know what you're doing Cousin."

Drawing in a deep breath, Gordon replied, "So do I Andrew, so do I."

Gordon, along with Andrew joined their guests in the salon just in time to hear Colleen's musical laughter, mixed with a deeper rumble of mirth from Stavros.

"Well it looks as if everyone is getting along all right," Andrew said, as he pushed his way around Gordon to enter the room. Gordon had stopped dead still at the entrance as he stared first at Stavros and then at Colleen.

"Mr. Alanis---" Gordon said, dragging his eyes from Colleen to address the elder of the two men.

"Please, no formalities are necessary, call me Darius," the older of the two men interjected.

"Very well, Darius," Gordon said with a tight smile. "Joseph is taking care of your luggage and Andrew will escort you, and Stavros, to your rooms in the west wing." Gordon settled his gaze on Colleen but directed his next statement to Stavros. "I'm sure you will want to see your father settled and to get some rest yourself after your harrowing trip this evening."

Stavros squared his shoulders and jutted out his chin, "Come along Colleen, I will see you to your room also, we can continue to catch up," he said warmly; then looking over at Gordon added, "and talk over old times."

"I'm afraid you'll have to continue your trip down memory lane tomorrow, Stavros," Gordon stated flatly. "Ms. O'Malley is not staying in the west wing." Arching an eyebrow at her, Gordon continued, "I will see to Colleen's needs." Gordon relished the blush he saw rising in Colleen's cheeks as he taunted her with the words, she had directed at him just last night, while at the restaurant in Albany.

"Oh yes, Stavros, you and your father must be exhausted after driving through this storm," Colleen said with such concern that Gordon nearly snorted aloud.

Looking back and forth between Gordon and Colleen, Stavros gently took hold of Colleen's chin, forcing her to look at him, and asked, with great obvious reservation, "Are you sure Colleen? I could get father settled and come back so we could visit more perhaps over a nightcap?

"I wouldn't think of it, you must be tired after your trip," Colleen quickly replied, shooting at glance Gordon, "As Gordon said, he will see to my needs. I'm sure I will be in good hands, and since I'm staying here, I will see you first thing in the morning." With that, she tiptoed to kiss Stavros on the cheek and gave him a gentle shove in the direction of the door.

Gordon followed the three men to the door, and quickly shut it behind them, leaving himself and Colleen alone. Securing the door, he turned to find Colleen standing in the middle of the room with her hands on her hips, and fire shooting from her glorious green eyes.

"How dare you! You have embarrassed me in front of your guests who just happen to be old acquaintances of mine!" She began pacing the floor as she continued, "This little tete-a-tete between us is one thing, Gordon, but others do not need to be privy to our little game of sparing!" She stopped pacing and stared at him indignantly, "You will show me to my room now," she demanded.

Gordon continued to keep his eyes on her as he leaned against the door. He had kept quiet during her rant, recognizing the 'best offense is defense' ploy.

"I'm tired, and I want to get some sleep," Colleen pouted. "Tomorrow will be a long day, we still have to finalize some of the details for the gala, you have guests you were not expecting this soon, and I have friends coming to visit me this weekend that I need to prepare for, that is, if the roads are cleared from this wretched storm by then."

Still leaning against the door, Gordon quietly said, "Tell me what you meant earlier, and I will be more than happy to show you to your room."

"Good grief, I was only joking, Gordon," Colleen scoffed, "You take everything so seriously."

"I don't believe you," Gordon said, still standing against the door. Gordon watched as Colleen lifted her shoulders in a shrug, and splayed her hands palms-up in an "I *don't know what you're talking about*" gesture, obviously feigning ignorance. No other doors led into or out of the room, or at least no others that she would know existed. As Colleen moved toward the door, Gordon continued to stand his ground blocking her exit. He had no intention of letting her out of the room until he had some answers.

Clarifying, Gordon quietly stated, "The loss of Terese was not a joke." Gordon watched as she slightly grimaced at his words. Deciding to push his advantage he continued, "What did you mean when you said, and I quote; *are you sure it's all due to the loss of your wife?*" Gordon asked.

Heaving a great sigh, Colleen replied, "You're right, the loss of Terese was not a joke. I shouldn't have said that to you. I'm so sorry; it was a horrible thing to say. I have absolutely no excuse."

Gordon wasn't ready to be swayed, regardless of the seemingly heartfelt apology. As she again started to cross the room towards the door, he raised his hand to stop her. "What about the part where *I'm not ready to hear the answers to my questions?*"

"Well, I should think that's obvious, Gordon," Colleen kept moving toward him until they stood nearly toe-to-toe.

"Just so there are no misunderstandings between us...why don't you enlighten me?" Gordon replied, determined not to let her closeness distract him from getting some answers.

She reached up and slid her arms around his neck, and whispering said, "I'm as attracted to you as you are to me, and have been since the first night I met you, but it's too soon to discuss it or act upon it. You're not ready."

He couldn't argue her observation, except at the moment he felt more than 'ready.' Having her, this close to him was muddling his mind. Which is why, rather than give in to his desires, he decided to let her go before he did something foolish. He disengaged her arms from his neck, and then turned to open the door, "You will find your room at the end of the hall, on the right, just past my suite. There are new toothbrushes and toiletries in the adjoining bathroom. Hopefully, Joseph found something for you to wear to bed." Flashing him a smug little smile, Colleen started past him, Gordon caught her hand and bringing it up to his lips lightly kissed her palm. In a husky voice edged in steel, he said, "I still don't believe you, and take this as your only warning; don't push me too far Colleen, I may be more ready than you realize or want."

Gordon watched with satisfaction as her eyes widened in surprise before snatching her hand from his grasp. He continued to watch as she made her way down the hall and toward the staircase, assured she was on the stairs, he closed the door and, as he turned, he heard a soft click from across the room. Reaching behind him to make sure the salon doors were secure he watched as a panel from the opposite side of the room slide open and Andrew emerged through the dark oak wall.

Gordon allowed a small smile as he nodded to acknowledge Andrew. They had discovered the secret passageway as children, unbeknownst to their fathers at the time. It connected to a linen closet near their bedrooms on the second floor by way of a narrow staircase; a second hidden door could be found under the main staircase connecting to this salon. The passageways had come in handy on more than one occasion when they would sneak in after a night of teenage carousing. They could slip in under the stairway and come straight to this salon, pretending they had been there all evening. For just a moment Gordon allowed himself to wish for the days that a curfew took top priority.

Andrew walked over to the portable bar-cart. He chose two glasses and poured more than generous shots of whiskey in each. Carrying both drinks, he moved to the wing-backs that faced the crackling fire that Joseph had thoughtfully lit earlier in the evening. He placed the second glass on the table between the chairs and sat down before quietly asking, "Get the answers you were looking for Gordon?"

Gordon crossed the room, picked up his glass and sat in the chair next to his cousin. He took a sip from his glass, looking forward to the fire of the fine liquor, as it hit the back of his throat, and spread its warmth through his chest. He studied the liquid as he swirled it around his glass before answering, "I'm not sure there are any answers, because I'm not sure of the questions anymore."

Turning slightly to look at Gordon, Andrew exclaimed, "Enough! I am fast growing tired of your riddles, Gordon."

Narrowing his dark eyes, Gordon glared back at Andrew, and said, "I've been pushed about as far as I can go for one night, Andrew. You would be wise to tread lightly."

Adopting a bit more genial tone, yet, still tinged with his own frustration, Andrew replied, "Then talk to me, Gordon. Tell me what the Hell is going on I have my limits too." When Andrew observed the hard set of Gordon's face, he quickly changed his approach, and tried for calm reasoning, "Gordon, since I pulled into that driveway less than a week ago, we have been running from Colleen O'Malley. This morning you were still trying to push her away, so unnerved by her that you were even contemplating leaving the state for a while."

Throwing his hand out gesturing toward Gordon, Andrew continued, "Suddenly, this afternoon, you're dressing and behaving like a man on the make. The hunter, instead of the hunted, and then I catch the two of you in an embrace in your office. I'm completely confounded. Over dinner, you're both throwing flirtatious little innuendos back and forth." At Gordon's look of surprise, Andrew replied, "Oh, yeah, I picked up on that too. Then, in the short time, it took for you to walk her from the dining room to the front door, you appeared to be at each other's throats." With total exasperation, Andrew asked, "Care to fill me in?"

As Andrew laid out his perception of the events covering the last few hours, Gordon had gone back to studying the amber liquid in his glass. He knew Andrew had a point; he had felt like he had been on a never-ending roller-coaster ride since he had returned from Switzerland; slowing just long enough to pull his Cousin on as a companion. He needed to catch his breath. He needed to breathe freely for just a little while. Gordon had found that release for a few short hours on the slopes yesterday, and it had continued through the start of dinner with Andrew. Then Colleen showed up. He had found it again walking through the doors of Bilford Manor, but then, once again, Colleen showed up. Perhaps he should follow Andrew's advice; maybe he did need to get some distance and time between them.

"Andrew, I know that I have been unfair to you, and after giving it some thought I intend to follow your previous suggestion," Gordon said with a decidedly growing assurance.

"Really?" Andrew sat back in surprise. "Okay, as soon as the roads are clear, I will have one of my people to hold her somewhere safe, we'll make her our next tribute, and we can be done with this."

Gordon jerked his head around, a look of astonishment on his face, totally speechless. Then he burst into a guffaw of laughter, Andrew had completely misconstrued his intent, but it was so completely Andrew to make such an assumption. However, his Cousin was watching him with such a look of confusion on his face that it made Gordon laugh even harder. Gordon had been wound so tight for so long, that it felt good to laugh.

"Care to let me in on the joke?" Andrew asked, affronted by Gordon's mirth.

"That's not at all what I had in mind, Cousin," Gordon replied while wiping his eyes. "First of all, I don't recall you suggesting that we make her a tribute. I was speaking of your suggestion to leave for Boston." Sobering, Gordon added, "And, since I *clearly* can't trust leaving you alone around Colleen you will be going with me."

"What about Stavros? You're going to leave him and Darius here in the Manor alone?" Andrew asked.

"Darius won't be here long, and Joseph is more than capable of taking care of Stavros," Gordon said.

Before Andrew could argue, the panel in the wall opened again. Jolted by the sound Andrew and Gordon turned in unison to see Joseph hurry into the room.

"There has been an attempted break-in at the offices in Boston," Joseph announced. Gordon and Andrew both started up, but Joseph waved them off. "I've spoken with the security company and the police. Entry was attempted, but not gained. The head of security is there now, and will be sending in extra guards around the clock."

Gordon spoke first asking, "Have they checked the camera feed?"

"Yes, of course, but it didn't show anyone around," Joseph replied, "At first, they thought it was an electrical malfunction that set the alarm off, or simply a malfunction in the alarm itself…"

"They found evidence? The vault?" Gordon interjected.

Joseph nodded in the affirmative, "Yes they found evidence of tampering on the outer door locks. The vault is as always secure."

"But nothing on feed? That doesn't make any sense," Andrew said.

"It does," Gordon countered, "if they found a way to intercept the feed electronically. Well, Andrew, I suppose we'll be heading to Boston as soon as the roads are clear then." To Joseph, he explained, "We had already decided to spend a couple of weeks at the offices. I will speak with Darius in the morning. Hopefully, the worst of the weather will be over, and they will start clearing the roads by afternoon."

"And the lass?" Joseph asked.

"I will speak with her also," Gordon answered. "And, I will expect you to assist her in whatever she needs for this cursed party." Looking back and forth between the two men, Gordon asked, "By the way, did either of you know that, according to Colleen, Terese named the charity 'Love thy Neighbor'?"

Struggling to keep a straight face Joseph replied, "Well sir, in this particular situation, I suppose that could give a whole new meaning as to what you might donate."

Andrew didn't bother at an attempt to hide his delight at the irony of Gordon's predicament, "Oh I don't think there is any mystery as to what Gordon wants to donate to his neighbor's cause."

Gordon grunted as he said, "I thought that might tickle your funny bones. Lighten the mood as it were."

Joseph stole a glance at Andrew and smiled as he unlocked the salon doors. To Gordon, he said, "Yes sir, it did at that. Thank you."

As Andrew chuckled at Joseph, Gordon just shook his head. "I think I'm going to call it a night. It's been a helluva long day, and I'm exhausted," Gordon declared rather uncharacteristically.

Sobering somewhat, Andrew asked, "So you definitely want to leave sometime tomorrow?"

"Yes," answered Gordon. "If someone tried to break-in by tampering with the security cameras, then it wasn't just someone looking for the petty cash. They were looking for something specific. And, since you're the tech guy, you will get to pick out the new toys that you want to beef up our security. But, Andrew, make sure you check the vault first," Gordon said wearily, leaving Andrew to finish his drink.

11

U PON ENTERING HIS ROOM, AND IN utter exhaustion, Gordon stripped off his clothing throwing his sweater and pants towards the nearest chair not really caring if the clothing landed there or on the floor. He pulled on a pair of pajama bottoms ready to fall into bed when he heard what sounded like a cry. Wheeling, back around he stepped out into the hallway, stood still cocking his head, and listened. Hearing nothing but the howl of the wind, Gordon shook his head, and said to himself, "I must be more tired than I thought. I'm hearing things." As he started back to his room, he heard the cry again followed by moaning. It was coming from the guest room.

Taping lightly on her door, Gordon softly called out, "Colleen are you, all right?" Not receiving an answer but, hearing another moan he opened the door slowly and peeked inside. The light spilling from his rooms and the low lighting from the hallway sconces softly illuminated the bed's restless occupant.

"Colleen," Gordon quietly called her name again from the doorway, not wanting to frighten her. When she still didn't answer, Gordon stepped into the room, as his eyes adjusted to the dim lighting, he could see a sheen of perspiration on her face. Thinking that she could be feverish, he quickly went to her bedside and gently touched her cheek. Her face felt cool under his fingertips. Twisting her head away from his touch she began mumbling in her sleep, *"She's just dreaming,"* Gordon told himself with relief, *"I need to leave before she wakes to find me standing in her room in the middle of the night."* Just as he had turned to leave, Colleen's mumbling became louder, and Gordon could make out the word's 'momma' and then 'daddy.' Suddenly, she made a strangled sound and sat straight up in the bed, and Gordon froze.

"Who's here?" She whispered, looking around in confusion, she then spotted Gordon and asked, "Gordon? What are doing you in here?"

Holding both of his hands out in a gesture of passiveness, Gordon replied, "I'm sorry, but I could hear you crying. I came in to check on you because I thought you might be sick, but I guess you were dreaming. Go back to sleep. I'm leaving."

When Gordon started to close the door behind him, he heard her sob and then say, "Don't go..."

Gordon halted in mid-step, not sure if he had heard her correctly; turning, he looked back at her, "Did you say something, Colleen?"

Sobbing harder, she caught her breath long enough to say, "P-Please stay with me for a little while."

Feeling hesitant, Gordon took in the scene before him. Sitting on the bed was Colleen, with her face buried in her hands, her long hair creating a curtain around her body racked with her sobbing. Gordon silently crossed the room in bare feet, stopping at the edge of the bed, casting a subtle shadow over her; Colleen moved over slightly, in what Gordon assumed was an invitation for him to join her. As he sat down on the side of the bed, Gordon turned his body toward her and asked, "Colleen, what do you want from me?"

Without a word, she leaned toward him, and he twisted sideways facing her, she lay her head on his chest, and he automatically put his arm around her shoulders. Colleen continued to cry, and he let her warm tears run onto his chest.

Gordon had witnessed this woman in many states of being; outrageously flirtatious, utterly charming, mischievous, all-business, lighthearted, defiant, and extremely angry. However, he had not seen her vulnerable. Gathering her in both arms, he pulled her up so that her head rested on his shoulder, and he leaned back on the padded headboard. *"This is going to be a long and difficult night,"* Gordon thought to himself, *"I'm probably going to regret this, but I can't leave her in this state."*

Her crying jag didn't seem to be letting up, so he began to rub her back and to make rhythmic shushing sounds in hopes of getting her to calm. After a few minutes, it seemed to work, or perhaps she had just cried herself out; either way, the worst of her torment appeared to have dwindled as evidenced by the hiccupping sounds, she was now making. Gordon tilted her head, and smoothed the damp tendrils of her hair away from her cheeks, and softly asked, "Want to talk about it?"

Without opening her eyes, she whispered, "Not yet."

"Want me to leave?" Gordon asked.

Colleen snuggled in closer, and with a catch in her voice, replied again, "Not yet."

Gordon allowed himself a small smile; he had imagined having Colleen in bed, wanting him to stay with her, more times than he cared to count; however, this wasn't exactly what he had envisioned; to hold her like a child, and yet, he felt oddly at peace by simply comforting her. Gordon assumed she must have been dreaming of her parents, given what he had understood from her previous tormented dialogue.

Awaking with a jerk, Gordon had a feeling of confusion that comes from having unexpectedly fallen asleep, particularly, when not in your own bed, and not alone. He didn't know how long they had slept, but he could tell that the sky was beginning to lighten, and judging from the quiet, the worst of the storm had passed. Colleen was draped over him like a throw over a chair. At some point, during the night, her leg had landed across his legs, her arm across his chest, and her face was still nestled in his neck. He chided himself for not moving immediately, but it felt so right. *"I shouldn't be allowing myself to do this,"* Gordon thought, *"I am already regretting this, but I want just a few more minutes."*

As Gordon relished the feel of Colleen's soft warmth against his body, he became aware of a hitch in her breathing. Quietly groaning, Gordon held his breath as he shifted just enough to steal a look at her face. Wide, startled, green eyes looked back at him. *"Oh boy...she's awake,"* he thought, *"wonder which way this is going to go."*

"Oh my God," Colleen whispered, as she extricated her body from his, and scrambled to sit up in the center of the bed; clutching the covers to her chin. "Wh-what are you doing? Why are you here?"

"So that's how it's going to go?" Gordon thought, his temper beginning to rise, *"Is she going to play the outraged Miss that's had her virginal bed compromised? When I fought myself for constraint?"* Aloud, he said flatly, "Because you asked me to stay."

"I--oh...," Colleen said as she struggled to remember. Gordon knew that the pieces had started to fall into place when she flushed red up to her roots, and hid her face in her hands, saying, "I'm so sorry. I'm so embarrassed. I---,"

Realizing that she truly was embarrassed, and this wasn't a ruse, Gordon calmed and stretched to relieve the stiffness of sleeping in such an awkward position for hours. He put his hands behind his head his fingers interlaced, and leaned back on the padded headboard, before interrupting her apology saying, "Don't stress over it. We can keep it our little secret?"

"That's very kind of you, especially after the abominable way I spoke to you last night," she replied.

Gordon shrugged, in an effort to appear nonchalant about the whole incident, and said, "We still need to work that out, I still want some answers; however, one thing has nothing to do with the other. You were distressed, and in need of some comfort; no need to be embarrassed about that. Simply one human reaching out to another."

"Always the gentleman," Colleen stated with a little smile, and turning to look at him asked, "Aren't you?"

"I try to be," Gordon answered, although, if he was honest, he couldn't attribute his magnanimous gesture to 'good manners,' so he amended his answer, "when I can."

Gordon, briefly lost in his thoughts, became aware that Colleen was watching him with too much interest. He gave himself a mental shake, and asked, "Do you have the nightmares often? Is that the reason you stay in Shaun's and Fran's guest house rather than the main house?"

'Yes, the dreams come often enough, especially this time of the year," Colleen replied. She hesitated for a few seconds as if trying to make a decision. Then seeming to have made her decision, she took a deep breath, and continued, "I don't know how much you know about my parents, but they were killed in a train accident during the month of February when I was barely a teenager."

When Gordon nodded, she continued, "They were also Aunt Fran and Uncle Shaun's siblings. Fran and Shaun have always been so wonderful to me. When my parents, Shaun's brother, and Fran's sister were killed, they didn't hesitate to take me in and to give me the best home they possibly could. They did everything within their power to compensate for my loss while ignoring their own grief." Her voice caught and became rough as she spoke about the relationship lost, and the love found to make up for that loss.

Not wanting to cause her any more pain then she was already experiencing, Gordon said, "We don't have to talk about this now, I really should leave so you can get some more rest."

But Colleen cleared her throat, and continued, "It hurts my Aunt and Uncle to see me go through the nightmares, and I don't like hurting them, so I stay in the guest house. It's for the best, I think, I'm close by, and yet it gives all of us a little more privacy."

"Understandable...you're a good niece. It's nice to see family taking care of family. Not just the physical, but putting the emotional good of those that you love ahead of your own wants," Gordon said, broodingly. Once again, he realized that Colleen was watching him, this time with a thirsty curiosity that he was not interested in quenching.

"As I said before," Gordon continued, "no one else needs to know I stayed in here last night. And, with that in mind, I need to vacate your room, and get back to my own before Andrew wakes up."

Gordon crossed the room, and just as he reached for the doorknob, someone knocked on the other side.

"Colleen?" Gordon recognized Stavros' voice and dropped his hand from the door. "Colleen, if you're up I need to speak with you." Feeling an unreasonable stab of jealousy, Gordon turned to level a look at Colleen, and raised a questioning eyebrow. Colleen shook her head and shrugged slightly as if to say; she didn't know why Stavros had come knocking on her door at such an early hour. Drawing in a silent breath, Gordon motioned for Colleen to wait as he went through to the bathroom, quietly closing the door behind him.

Gordon walked straight to the full-length mirror on the bathroom's back wall. He didn't try to make out the muffled voices from the bedroom; instead, he ran his fingers around the edges of the mirrors' ornate frame. *This is my home, I shouldn't be the one running and hiding like a teenage kid about to be caught in his girlfriend's room,"* Gordon thought, his agitation growing by the second, *"it's degrading and more than a little emasculating."* Finally, finding and pressing the concealed latch, Gordon held his breath expecting to hear squeaking and groaning, hoping it wouldn't be too noticeable, as he pulled one side of the mirror from the wall; but, to his surprise, it swung open smoothly and quietly. Stepping through the opening, Gordon ran his hand over the adjacent wall, finding, and flipping the switch that bathed the narrow hallway with soft light from the sconces high on the walls.

"For once, I'm glad Joseph chose to ignore my directions," Gordon thought wryly. *"When I told him not to bother with maintaining this hall, he had argued that someday I might want to make use of it,"* Gordon remembered. *"Once again, Joseph was right, even if it wasn't for the right reasons."* Gordon pulled the mirror back into place, and after assuring the latch had caught, he followed the hidden passageway that would lead to a wall in his closet/dressing room; another one of Bilford Manor's little secrets.

His father had included the construction of the passageway at the same time he had the manor built. He had also kept it renovated and maintained through his 'generations.' At some point, Gordon had learned that his father referred to the guest room, at the other end of the passageway, as, 'The Mistress Suite.' Gordon had taken his father's room when he left, but he had never made use of the passage and the room as such. But, in his frustration and anger last night, he had derived a perverse bit of pleasure by demanding that Joseph prepare that room for Colleen. *"Of course, now she will know there is another exit from the bathroom,"* thought Gordon, *"but, I highly doubt that she will ever stay in it again. No,"* Gordon, recklessly and ridiculously, promised himself with a smile, *"if she stays in Bilford Manor again, she will be staying in my rooms."*

Gordon came out of his dressing room, wearing only a towel after his shower in the adjoining bathroom, intent on checking the news to see what damage had been done from the storm last night. Waiting in his room was Andrew.

"So, did you get any sleep, last night Cousin?" Andrew queried, from across the room, as he looked to the sea through the balcony doors.

"Actually, I did," Gordon responded, as he walked to the small desk that held his laptop.

"Really?" Andrew sounded skeptical, "because, although you're not wearing your key; I was still picking up on some strange emotional vibes, they were that intense."

"Huh," Gordon grunted, as he kept his eyes on his computer screen, "What do you call strange?"

Andrew narrowed his eyes as he turned to focus on Gordon, "Well, let's see, first, I was feeling a little fear, or perhaps, wariness would be the best way to describe it, then some confusion, but, those feelings gave way to an overwhelming sense of contentment I think; but, there was also an underlying thread of frustration. Contented, yet, frustrated at the same time. Like I said--strange."

After checking the weather reports online, Gordon went to his closet, pulling out clothing, both to get dressed and to start packing. "I don't know what to tell you, cousin," he called back into the room, in what he hoped was a conversational tone, "I was, and I still am, concerned about the break-in at our offices. I was very frustrated with Colleen and very tired."

"Here's the thing Gordon," Andrew begin, "since I was getting all these weird feelings; you know, genuine concern, I decided to check on you. When I didn't find you in your rooms, I started checking downstairs; in the kitchen, the observatory, your study, my study, the library---"

"Are you going to list every room in the house, Andrew?" Gordon asked, dryly, as he stepped back into the bedroom, wearing only a pair of casual pants. Not expecting an answer, he continued, "Why don't you just ask what you want to ask...did I stay with Colleen last night?"

Before Andrew could either deny or confirm that was his question, Colleen walked into the room via Gordon's dressing room.

"**G**OOD MORNING ANDREW," COLLEEN SAID LIGHTLY, as she walked across the room and came to a stop in front of Gordon. Colleen gave him a slow, albeit, appreciative look, up and down, before tip-toeing to kiss him on the cheek. Softly, she said, "You left before I could say 'Thank you' for last night." With that, she turned, gave a visibly startled Andrew a wink, and then walked to the double doors, pulling both of them open. Before stepping into the hallway, she paused, looking back, and with a coy little smile, said, "Gentlemen I will see you downstairs."

Gordon followed her to the doorway feeling more than a bit bemused; he watched as Colleen descended the stairs. Closing the doors, he turned to find that Andrew still stood, rooted to the same spot and that his eyebrows had disappeared, yet again... *"She certainly seemed to have that effect on Andrew quite often,"* Gordon mused to himself, to Andrew he said, "Well now you know why you were picking up feelings of confusion, wariness, and contentment with an underlying frustration. Quite a woman, our Ms. O'Malley, wouldn't you agree, Cousin?"

Andrew blinked a couple of times, and gave himself a little shake, he then looked at Gordon, and said, "You can, and you will explain on the way to Boston, I have to pack."

Gordon inwardly chuckled, as their driver made his way over

to Highway 93 South. Although the roads weren't as icy going south, they still needed to take it easy. The county workers had made short work of the downed tree at first light, after treating the roads in the early morning hours making travel possible.

As it turned out Gordon and Andrew were not alone on the drive down to Boston. It had been decided over an early brunch that Darius would accompany the Bilford men, and spend a day or two in the city, looking up some old friends before heading back to his ship in Portsmouth. He was anxious to take care of his business with Bilford Shipping, and visit his friends so he could return to the sea.

As the elder Alanis had explained during breakfast, "I can't stay off of the water for long, if I had my way I would never stand on dry land." Colleen had laughed at this, but Stavros had rolled his eyes, and said, directing his conversation to Colleen, "He's not joking. I'm sure you've heard tell of the love affair between some sailors and the ocean? The sea is most assuredly his mistress. Although I do share a love for the sea, I prefer the company of a flesh and blood woman."

Stavros' attentiveness to Colleen was not lost on Gordon, and although she didn't appear completely averse to his attention, she kept him at arm's length. The young man had stayed by Colleen's side and monopolized her attention, certainly, since he had come downstairs; while at the same time directing hard dark looks at Gordon during the few instances when Colleen's attention was diverted from him. When it had come time to leave, Gordon had asked Colleen to meet him in his study for a few moments.

Allowing his mind to replay the morning's events in great detail, Gordon, shook his head thinking about the way Stavros had tried to push his way into his study behind Colleen, without success, "I need to speak to Miss O'Malley privately," he had said to Stavros. Gordon, in an attempt to reign in his temper had purposefully made the curt statement sound formal, but, with an edge of steel in his voice. Colleen had cleared her throat to get his attention, and when he looked at her, she gave him a small frown. Reluctantly, but quickly, Gordon turned back to Stavros and added, "If you don't mind," while leveling a look on the insolent younger Alanis that was meant to tell him what Gordon really thought; and just in case that didn't get his feelings across, then surely, the door shutting in his face had done the trick.

Once alone, Colleen sat down, and Gordon perched on the edge of his desk. "Would you care to explain why you came sashaying into my room this morning *knowing* that Andrew was there?" Gordon asked. "I didn't think you wanted anyone to know that I had spent the night with you," he added.

Shaking her head, Colleen replied, "I never said that, you did."

Gordon had thought back to their conversation, realizing she was right, but it still didn't explain her actions in his room this morning, nor, the apparent anger that was emanating from her now, "So, obviously, you're fine with Andrew thinking we spent the night together? Because that's exactly the conclusion he came to, especially after your Thank You."

"Considering you put me in a room specifically designed for a late-night liaison, don't you think everyone would reach that conclusion?" Colleen asked harshly, her voice rising. "I have Stavros at my door telling me all about the history of the room you put me in, and I argued with him, saying 'No, Gordon wouldn't do that.' I finally convinced him that I was fine, nothing had happened, and that he needed to leave, so I could get showered and dressed. Imagine my surprise when I went looking for you, and you were gone! When I couldn't find you, I knew he was right. I searched the room, and found the secret behind the mirror."

With her tirade complete, Colleen had sat back in her chair, her green eyes still snapping, as she glared at him. Gordon stood, took the two steps that separated them, staring down at her. He then placed a hand on each arm of her chair, trapping her with his body.

"Trying to intimidate me?" Colleen asked sarcastically.

"Me? Intimidate you? Please! But you do have a way of leaving a room while I still have questions," Gordon replied. He had leaned toward her, and with great intensity asked, "How did Stavros know about the room?"

Straightening her back, Colleen brought her face within inches of his, as she answered, through gritted teeth, "Really? That's your question? That's all you have to say or ask? You treat me like your whore, in front of a house full of men, and that's what you want to know? Get away from me."

Pausing in his reverie for a moment, Gordon looked out his window at the pavement as they continued down the highway. *"The snow that had fallen just a few hours ago has now been rendered a black muddy slush; a perfect analogy for everything the Fold touched."* Giving himself a mental shake, he thought, *"Who am I trying to fool here? It's a perfect analogy for everything I touch. Defiling purity with the Dark."* He forced himself to continue playing the conversation in his mind that he had with Colleen right before the three men had left for Boston.

He had been so surprised by what she had said, that he had frozen in place. Then regaining his composure, he had stood up and returned to his desk, exclaiming, "I did not treat you like my whore! What a ridiculous accusation, especially coming from you. You have thrown yourself at me on every turn. If anything, I was trying to protect you."

"Protect me? By setting me up in the 'mistress suite' in front of everyone" Gordon winced when she used the same label for the room that was used by his father. "Yes, Stavros told me *all* about it," she said with a condescending tone.

Gordon bristled at the mention of Stavros, "I asked you before, and I'm asking again--how would Stavros know anything about it?"

"Apparently, Mr. Alanis, Darius, has a long-standing relationship with your father," she replied. "Now, tell me that you were not prompted by some self-serving motive for **demanding** that Joseph prepare that particular room for me?" Once again, Gordon winced slightly, and Colleen pounced on it. "Ha! So that's true too," she said as she stood and started pacing in a small circle behind her chair.

Gordon closed his eyes and drew a deep breath to curb his exasperation before he allowed himself a full-blown fury. When he felt calmer, he spoke, "Look, I was angry with you last night, and yes, I told Joseph to put you in that particular suite; however, I didn't think you would want Stavros to see me, so I checked to see if the opening and passageway were still usable; they were, so I left." Then with a derisive laugh, said, "I would have thought you might be grateful that you wouldn't have to explain what I was doing in your room at that hour of the morning."

"Oh please," Colleen said sarcastically.

"What?"

"You knew very well; it was usable. The hinges on the mirror were silent, the electric was working, and there wasn't a speck of dust, or a cobweb anywhere. It looked as if it was in constant use," Colleen retorted.

"Well, it isn't. That's just Joseph's fastidious and tenacious nature," Gordon said in his defense; to which Colleen gave a very unladylike snort of derision. Gordon had had enough of the bickering. He wasn't having any luck in getting her to see reason, nor was he getting any answers from her.

Deciding to change tactics, Gordon asked, "So, basically, what you're saying is that you are jealous. Wondering how many other women I have had staying in that room? Is that the real problem?" He purposefully goaded her, and it worked. She sucked in her breath, and turned blazing green eyes on him, "I--you--oh!" Colleen then promptly turned on her heel, nearly floating across the floor in her angry, and left, slamming the door with such force the artwork on the wall shook.

Quietly chuckling to himself, Gordon garnered the attention of Andrew sitting behind him, keeping Darius company.

"Care to share the joke, Gordon?" Andrew called over the seat.

"Oh, just remembering something amusing," Gordon responded. Gordon wasn't sure what, if anything, the rest of the house had heard... "*Well except for the slamming of the door. Fran and*

Shaun may have heard that two miles away!" Gordon's mind lingered on the memory of her eyes at the height of her anger, *"She was infuriated, but to give the devil his due, so to speak, she was breathtaking!"*

The traffic became heavier, as they neared the city, and Gordon became much more alert and aware of his surroundings. Trying to find his 'city mode,' Gordon attempted to push thoughts of Colleen from his mind; but she wouldn't leave. At times like this, he began to question his sanity. *"Is she doing this, or is it me?"* With a sigh of resignation, and although he wasn't in the driver's seat, he tried to refocus his attention by concentrating on the traffic before him.

When traveling on a highway with multiple lanes, he had always likened the movement of the traffic to a horse race. Cars coming up from behind, drivers' neck and neck, finally one pulling ahead of the other, only to have the one they had just passed to pour on the steam, switch lanes, and reclaim their spot. And so, it went, the drivers and vehicles continuing to jockey for position, until each crossed personal finish lines, the exit that would take them to their destination.

They left the race on I-93 when they came upon the exit that would lead them to the Bilford complex on Commercial Street in the historic North End of Boston. Gordon could remember, as a child, the excitement of going to work with his father; how big and important it had made him feel when he walked by his father's side through the doors of their building. He would puff-out his little chest with great pride when his dad would tell him that someday he would be the boss.

He still felt some of that pride whenever he rolled up to the front of the Bilford Building, the headquarters for Bilford Shipping; but, the little boy's awe and adoration for his daddy had disappeared, never to return. Gordon could feel the familiar ache for the child lost, and the anger building for his paternal nemesis. His emotions began to whirl, as always, whenever he would allow himself to dwell on his father's betrayal.

Suddenly, with no warning or forethought, not only did

Colleen's face block his field of vision but, her perfume, a spicy scent that she always wore, was all around him. He didn't fight it, as he usually did; instead, he put his head back, closed his eyes, breathed deeply, and let it fill him.

"Gordon, are you asleep?" Andrew asked as he touched his cousin's shoulder.

Gordon opened his eyes seeing the front of their building, rather than Colleen's face. They had stopped, and Darius was already out of the car and waiting for them on the sidewalk.

"Uh, no, I was just resting my eyes," he said, as he opened the door, and stepped out. Gordon lingered at the car while Andrew did the same. Tipping his head to one side, Gordon pointedly looked at Andrew and said, "The scenery on the way here was rather overwhelming."

Andrew nodded, and replied, "Yeah, I caught a little of that myself."

Gordon didn't reply, he merely raised his brow in surprise. Even without his key, an understanding passed between the two cousins. From the corner of his eye, Gordon noticed that Darius was studying them both intently, "Yes, well we have this business of a security breach, and a client to deal with currently," Gordon said, and with a tight smile, he added, "We'll talk about the sights later."

"Yes, we will," Andrew said absently while gazing down the street, "Gordon, I finally remember where I have, I seen her before."

"Good," Gordon replied, "Anything that might be of help?"

"Maybe," Andrew answered, still staring down the street distractedly.

Gordon looked in the same direction that seemed to have captured Andrew's attention, half expecting to see the tall, red-headed beauty that haunted him day and night, but all he saw was a bustling street, people moving in and out of the various businesses down the block.

Gordon escorted Darius to the spacious offices that occupied the entire fourth floor of the renovated building. The head of

Alanis House was delighted to wander around the outer reception rooms that featured enough displays, of smaller antique artifacts, to rival a maritime museum. While Darius oohed and awed over fragile yellowed nautical maps, a rare chronometer from the late 1700s, artwork, and model ships, Gordon checked-in with the various department managers that took care of the day-to-day running of the Bilford Complex. The Complex consisted of two buildings with a green space between them. Both buildings boasted various retail businesses on the ground levels with offices; lofts and apartments took up the space on the remaining floors. Gordon's and Andrews expansive apartment, on the fifth floor of this building, had spectacular views of the wharf and the water beyond and occupied the entire top floor above their fourth- floor offices.

It had been decided before they had left New Hampshire, that Andrew would initially meet with the security teams and Gordon would join them after completing the contracts with Darius and the attorneys. After, the last of the documents were signed, and handshakes with congratulations were given all around, the attorneys departed, leaving Gordon and Darius alone for the first time.

"Darius, I was wondering if you would tell me how you know the O'Malley family?" Gordon asked as he pulled out a bottle, to share a celebratory drink of Darius' favorite brandy, from the bottom drawer of his desk, along with two glasses. "The only time I can remember you, and Stavros, visiting was at my wedding to Jeanette. I believe it was about the time the House of Alanis came into being; Stavros was probably sixteen or seventeen then, and the O'Malley's had yet to move to Bilford, on a permanent basis."

Taking the proffered drink from Gordon, Darius leaned back in his chair, took a sip of the brandy while studying his host over the rim of his glass; finally, he said, "I well remember Jeanette, such a lovely girl, and such a shame her life was taken while she was so young, and then your second wife also. A shame."

Dark eyes clashed, and Gordon said with an even tone, "Yes, it is a shame, but such is our life, isn't it?"

Darius must have seen or heard something in Gordon that pulled him up short. He took another sip, cleared his throat, and said, "Yes, well…you were asking about the O'Malley family. Actually, although, Colleen has spoken so often of her Aunt and Uncle I feel I should know them, but I have never had the pleasure of making their acquaintance."

"But you know Colleen?" Gordon asked.

"Ah, Colleen; Stavros brought Colleen and some of her friends to our home after meeting them at a local fair in Greece, they were on holiday. He had had an unfortunate encounter with a woman much older than him, and she married another. The poor boy was absolutely heartbroken. So, I invited his new friends to stay at our villa; I thought it might get his mind off of that which he could not have. They stayed with us for a few carefree weeks, swimming, sightseeing, the usual kind of things tourists do. Colleen was then, as she is now, an absolute joy. Wouldn't you agree?" Darius asked, studying Gordon closely.

Gordon nodded once, and stoically agreed, "Yes a joy."

Darius threw back his head and laughed heartily, before saying, "You know I think Stavros developed a crush on her back then, but they were both so young, and he, was still hurting from his unrequited love." He leaned forward, dropping his voice conspiratorially, "Honestly, I don't think Colleen had any interest, not in that way." Leaning back in his chair, Darius continued, "We have run into her from time to time over the years since, here and there." With that, he tossed back the rest of his brandy and stood to leave. Gordon rose also, and offered to take Mr. Alanis for a late lunch, but, Darius, anxious to meet with his friends and be on his way back to his ship, politely declined.

"Thank you, but, no. I long for my mistress," he said with a chuckle when Gordon extended the invitation, "and the sooner I make my obligatory visits to a couple of acquaintances, the sooner

I can be with her." Darius put his hand on Gordon's shoulder in a gesture of camaraderie as they walked out, "The sea can breathe life into your soul, give you great joy, and nourish you; however, as you should well know, like any woman, she can become fickle if ignored for very long. She can take away your soul, cause you great sorrow, and sap away your strength. Particularly, when there is another storm on the horizon. I want to be well out to sea before it hits."

Gordon had the distinct impression the older man wasn't speaking of the sea, but he decided not to comment on it, and respond to the literal, "I envy you, sir. It has been a long while since I have been in the swells."

"Don't wait too long, Gordon," Darius warned with great intensity, "another could take your helm and your woman if you ignore her." Then with a chuckle, he said, "Listen to this old man, go back to her before too much time passes, you don't want to lose your sea legs."

With that said, Gordon was left to watch the retreating back of the patriarch of Alanis House. He couldn't decide if the 'old man' had been out to sea too long or not, but perhaps his words were worth serious consideration in the abstract. He wanted to tell Andrew of the strange conversation and get his perspective. Was Darius trying to send him a message or was it merely the ramblings of an old man?

Going in search of his Cousin, Gordon found Andrew in his office alone, pouring over the blueprints for the building.

"I have good news and bad news," Andrew announced as Gordon approached the desk and sat down across from his Cousin. "The bad news is that someone hacked into our security system shutting off the alarms and surveillance video feed. The good news is that the electronic door locks held."

"Two questions: What can be done to ensure this doesn't happen again?" Gordon asked, "And, is there any way to trace the hacker?"

"We buy two servers of our own; put the surveillance on one, the alarms on the second. In that way, if one goes down or gets hacked...say the video, the alarms will sound or if the alarms get hacked the video will still be engaged. It will be expensive, but worth it in my opinion." Andrew looked to Gordon, who nodded in agreement, before continuing, "Since, both, a key and code, is needed to unlock the doors to reception, we'll change the locks and the codes. As for your office and mine, we thought a completely different alarm system should be installed; one that is not connected to any of the others. Also, we talked about hiring a guard whose only duty would be to guard the private express elevator and of course our apartment on the fifth floor."

"And the hacker?" Gordon queried.

"They narrowed down the area, considerably," Andrew said, "but, not the exact location. The IT report says it came from within two blocks of the complex; but whoever it was could very well be hundreds of miles away or not." At Gordon's quizzical expression, Andrew added, "Hackers can be anywhere, at any time all they need is a laptop; which brings me to that discovery I mentioned earlier when we first arrived."

"Please," Gordon said settling back in his chair, "continue."

"Not here," Andrew replied with a shake of his head, "security did a cursory sweep for bugs, but I want a thorough check before we discuss certain subjects."

"Where do you suggest we go then?" Gordon asked.

Gordon watched as Andrew picked up a pencil, wrote on a small pad, and slid it across the desk: *Little Irish pub halfway down the next block--Something you need to see.*

Nodding, Gordon stood to leave, Andrew took the note back and put it through the shredder next to his desk.

Once on the sidewalk, Gordon asked, "Why all the cloak and dagger?"

"I finally figured out why Colleen was so familiar to me." Andrew began, "After being in her company several times, I decided I had never met her; yet, I still couldn't shake the feeling of familiarity. Met her…no. Seen her…yes."

"Okay, where?" Gordon asked.

"Here, on this street, this sidewalk, and in the pub where I'm taking you now, which by the way is a Wi-Fi hub," Andrew replied.

"Andrew, I don't understand. A lot of tourists come here, it's the historic district, walking distance to the wharves," Gordon pointed out. "That is the primary reason we are doing so well with the Complex rentals."

"You don't understand, I've seen her here several times. And, I have seen her in our building, too," Andrew said, "but, it's the pub I want to show you."

"What is so special about the pub?" Gordon asked, impatiently, "What? You've seen her there too? Andrew, she's Irish, and I'm sure she can use a computer, it would make sense that she would visit the pub."

"You'll see," was all Andrew would say.

They walked along in silence, each man lost in his own thoughts, until, Andrew veered to his right and opened a door. Gordon looked at the transom above the door for the name before entering. *Kelsey's Celtic Pub* was busy, but Andrew managed to snag two stools at the far end of the bar. They ordered two dark brews, and Gordon gave Andrew a questioning look; it looked like every other bar he had ever been in, people sitting at tables, some talking, some on their computers, some staring into their glasses, the usual barroom patronage.

"They have a lot of interesting photographs of people," Andrew remarked, waving his hand toward the wall behind the bar.

Gordon casually looked in the direction that Andrew had indicated and caught his breath as he saw a dozen or more pictures of Colleen. A younger Colleen, laughing with a group of people. One that Gordon thought could be fairly recent portrayed Colleen sitting perched on the bar smiling down into the face of a man who looked to be a little older than she. Another photo was of

Colleen in traditional Irish dress with three other girls, and the camera had caught them in mid-step of an Irish jig. One picture that Gordon found particularly interesting was a close-up of a younger Colleen singing into a microphone. Several of the others were group pictures, of which, she was a part.

"Gordon," Andrew said very quietly, "did you just feel the shift of the emotional level in the room since we sat down? See if you can get a read on them."

Gordon tore his gaze from the photos of Colleen, took a drink of his beer, and nonchalantly turned his stool a bit, glancing about the room. He looked up at a television running some football highlights, motioning toward it, he then turned to Andrew, and with a smile belying his words, said, "Yes, I do believe we're not wanted here. Something that you did that I don't know about?"

Andrew laughed and answered, "Not me this time, cousin. So, what do you think? Up for a bar brawl, or are you ready to leave?"

Chuckling, Gordon said, "It has been awhile, might even be fun, but maybe we should take our leave. After, I have a word with the barkeep."

Gordon signaled for the bartender that had served them; an older man with a leathery lined face, Gordon suspected the man had spent a lot of time on the water in his younger days with the wind and salt in his face; he was not emanating the same animosity as most of the patrons. Gordon slid a fifty across the bar for the beers, told him to keep the change, and asked if any of the photographs were for sale.

"I can sale," he answered in a heavy Irish brogue, "more can always be taken." Without taking his eyes off of Gordon, he said, "Aye, she is a lovely lass. You're not the first man to be smitten with her."

They settled on an extremely generous price for the photo of the younger Colleen singing; and Gordon, along with Andrew, left *Kelsey's Celtic Pub*, and started back to the Complex.

"Why did you pay so much for that photograph? Why did you

pay anything for it, when you could have just taken it?" Andrew complained.

"Andrew, you know I don't live--"

"Yeah, yeah I know," Andrew said, with a wave of his hand. "But, it's an amateur photograph, not a *Henry*."

Gordon smiled at Andrew's reference to Paul Henry, a famous Irish artist, and one of Gordon's favorites. Although his *Head of an Old Man* is very familiar to most, it is his landscapes of Western Ireland that he is best known for and had earned him wide acclaim as a contemporary landscape artist. Gordon had reproduction prints of *Windswept Trees, Connemara* hanging in his office at Bilford Manor; and *Grace O'Malley's Castle* here in the Boston apartment. "Andrew, outside of the fact that I refuse to use my...ah... gifts, to take whatever I want, whenever I want; don't you think, after the reception we received back there, that we drew enough attention, without stealing?"

"We could have made them forget we were ever there at all, you know," Andrew argued.

"Yes, I know," Gordon replied, "but, like I said, cousin, that's not how I live my life." Feeling they had come full circle, and not wanting to go around again, Gordon changed the subject by asking, "So can we talk, I mean really talk, in our apartment?"

Andrew gave up, realizing he had lost this argument, and said, "Yes, I had a separate team thoroughly sweeping the apartment. They found nothing. We are free to speak there, and we have a lot to speak about; starting with this morning's surprise visitor in your quarters." Then Andrew added, "And Gordon, I have a theory to share with you." Gordon raised his eyebrows, intrigued, at this, and they both picked up their pace in the weak light of the waning day.

I N THE ELEVATOR ON THEIR WAY up to their fifth-floor apartment, Gordon and Andrew decided on pasta from a little Italian place, a neighborhood mom and pop restaurant just a few blocks away; popular with the locals, and they delivered. Andrew went straight to his suite to make a call to the security company to get them started with updating the buildings' computer systems, and Gordon headed to the kitchen to phone in their order while opening a bottle of Chianti to go with dinner.

As Gordon waited for Andrew, he looked around the apartment; the decor was the total opposite of Bilford Manor or the Hideaway in Albany. Where antiques and traditional furnishings dominated every room at the Manor, and the Hideaway could only be described as cozy contemporary, the Complex apartment was urban sleek, and modern. Exposed brick walls, steel trusses, and pipes were complemented by the clean lines of the couches and occasional chairs. Side-tables were constructed of steel frames with glass surfaces, and on the walls hung contemporary artwork.

The entire top floor had been dedicated to their living space; divided into three main areas; two large suites, one for Gordon and one for Andrew. Each had its own small private sitting area that opened into a spacious bedroom and bath. The third area, where he stood now, consisted of a large communal living room, open to the gourmet kitchen, and dining area with floor-to-ceiling windows to take in the view of the busy harbor. One could see every type of sea-going vessel, from sailboats to freighters, and everything in-between, in Boston Harbor. Gordon missed spending time on the water; as he had told Darius, it had been a long time. *"If Andrew is truly willing to stay around a while, maybe I can take some time off and go sailing in the spring,"* Gordon thought, as he stood looking out to the harbor. The doorbell sounded, and Gordon checked the video feed for the lobby elevator. He pressed the buzzer to unlock the express elevator as Andrew came around the corner, "Oh good, is that our food? I'm starving," Andrew exclaimed. Opening the door to accept the delivery, Andrew took the bags, and Gordon paid for their dinner.

As they ate, Andrew brought Gordon up to speed with the plans for the security systems; "They have already started the update, and I gave them the go-ahead to start the installations overnight. I made a call, and we'll have a guard on the elevator by 6:00 am. She, Breanna, is a tenth Dan rank in her field of martial arts. Now I don't know what that means precisely, but I wouldn't want to tangle with her...well, not if she was mad at me," Andrew amended with a slow smile. "She is also an expert in firearms, and of course, she is one of our own. I'm waiting for a call back from Dmitri, another highly qualified guard."

"Sounds like you have it all under control," Gordon said rather absently.

Andrew had noticed that Gordon instead of eating was just moving his food around on his plate, "Okay, we've got all evening, Gordon, start at the beginning. Did you spend the night with Colleen?"

"Yes," Gordon answered. Noting Andrew's smirk, he quickly added, "I hate to disappoint, but it's not what you're thinking. When I went upstairs, last night, I thought I heard her calling out. Thinking she might be ill, I opened her door to check on her; however, she was calling out in her sleep, having a nightmare, and was quite distraught. I stayed to comfort her, at her request I might add, and I fell asleep. I woke up, started to leave, and Stavros came knocking at her door. Realizing it could be awkward to explain my presence that time of the morning I headed to the bathroom, remembering the passage behind the bathroom mirror that leads to my room. Although I had told Joseph years ago to seal the passageway, I know Joseph. Sure enough, he had disregarded my orders, had kept it cleaned and everything in working order, so I went back to my rooms through the passage. I thought she would be happy that she wouldn't have to explain my presence to Stavros." Gordon paused, remembering her reaction, before continuing, "I couldn't have been more wrong."

Andrew, who had remained quiet throughout the retelling of the story, asked with a frown, "How so? And, why did she use the passage later? Not to mention, but I will, what about her '*Thank you*' in front of me? She had to have heard our voices."

"Well apparently, my father didn't keep his private life, very private. Darius knew about the 'mistress suite,' he told Stavros, and in turn, Stavros told Colleen." Gordon sighed, then continued with a brittle smile, "She accused me of flaunting her as 'my whore' in front of a house full of men by purposely placing her in that particular room."

"So," Andrew began, placing the pieces together, "she comes to your room this morning through the passageway, "Thanks" you in front of me, and walks out of the main doors. All of that was to call you out for putting her in that particular room?" Andrew looked to Gordon for confirmation, and Gordon shrugged his shoulders.

"It makes some sense, I guess. Who knows what goes on in a woman's mind?" Andrew continued, "She felt that you made her look foolish because everyone else knew about the room last night, but she didn't know until this morning when Stavros told her how Uncle Gordon used the room. Then you disappear from the bathroom confirming Stavros' story."

Andrew shook his head, "Huh, seems you can't win for losing, cousin." Both men sat quietly for a moment, then Andrew asked, "Wait, what did you say or do to make her slam out of your office like that this morning?"

For the first time since they had sat down for dinner, Gordon genuinely smiled, "She didn't believe me when I told her that I wasn't sure the passageway was usable. She made it sound as if it must have been in constant use, due to the lack of dust and cobwebs."

"And?"

"I asked if she might be jealous thinking of all the women I might have had in there," Gordon said still smiling at the memory of her reaction.

Andrew let that sink in for a moment, then threw back his head with a hearty laugh, "No wonder she nearly broke the house."

"I really shouldn't have goaded her like that, but I didn't care for her accusations," Gordon said. "I told her how ridiculous she was behaving, especially, after the way she had been throwing herself at me. But Colleen completely ignored that part of my argument. She was so angry, but then this afternoon…you saw her?"

"Yeah, on the way here, were you doing that, or was she?" Andrew asked.

"At this point, who knows," Gordon said more as a statement than a question. "I was purposefully trying to put her out of my head, and then I started thinking about how my relationship with my father had changed since I was a child." With a short self-derisive laugh, he said, "I guess I was feeling sorry for myself; then suddenly, she was there." Casting a side glance toward Andrew, Gordon asked, "Did you notice anything other than her image."

"What do you mean? Like her location, or what she was wearing?" Andrew asked as he started clearing the table.

Drawing a deep breath, and glancing back to Andrew, Gordon said, "No, her scent. Her perfume to be more precise, it filled the car, and I felt calmer, comforted."

Andrew sucked in air, and widened his eyes, "Gordon, this

is getting serious. Not only is she able to infiltrate your senses, making you see things that aren't there, smelling a fragrance that isn't there, but she is controlling your moods too?"

"Don't be so melodramatic." Gordon admonished, as he moved to one of the couches in the living room, "All of it could just be me, and you're picking it up. It is what we do after all."

"And, maybe she is putting it all there," Andrew pointed out as he joined Gordon. "Gordon, I hesitated to tell you this, until I had more information; however, with the way things have been going, I think we had better discuss it now. I have been in contact with some people, I've learned a few things, and I have a theory about Colleen."

"Well, don't keep me in suspense, Andrew, tell me your theory."

Taking a deep breath, Andrew launched into the information he had found. "It was your talk of 'light beings' that really stuck with me. The idea there could be others, as powerful as the Fold out there, but working in direct opposition had never occurred to me. But, the more I thought about the possibility, the more curious I became. It seemed like such a thing could be within the realm of possibility; so, I started asking around, and I spoke with some people that kinda' live on the fringes of the *Fold*. Well, actually just one person."

"You mean an Abrogate?" Gordon asked aghast, "Andrew have you lost your mind?" The Abrogates were the 'cleaners' for the *Fold,* not belonging to any one 'House' within the fold. They didn't bother to pretend to be a *Normal*; they did as they pleased for the highest bidder, or sometimes just for fun. Their title, the word Abrogate literally meant "to put an end to." They weren't picky about who they took out either, whether it be a member of the *Fold,* or not if the price was right. They were also known to use whatever information they could gather to their advantage; blackmail was one of their less egregious methods for recruitment. Gordon's mind was reeling, "How much did you tell him, Andrew?"

"I didn't tell him anything," Andrew said with great annoyance, "I'm not stupid!"

Gordon gave him a look clearly meant to put that statement into question.

Andrew threw-up his hands, and just short of yelling said, "This is why I didn't tell you anything about it sooner." Still visibly agitated, but striving for calm, Andrew continued, "I said nothing of you, Colleen, or any of our family. I met up with the guy in a sports bar, and I told him that I had been in a pub in England and heard an 'old one' telling of a legend and I asked him what he thought…myth or truth?"

Warily, not trusting himself to speak at the moment, Gordon motioned for Andrew to continue.

"When I told him that it was about the 'light beings' he laughed and said, 'Oh you mean the Argents, a faction of the Radiants. I played along and said, 'Yeah, that's what the old guy called them.' Then I laughed and said, 'I knew it had something to do with light.''

"Argents? Radiants?" Gordon asked perplexed, Andrew nodded, "Well what did he tell you about them?"

"Gordon, you pretty much hit the truth with your theory. They are as old as the *Fold*. They are our opposite in virtually every way. We have the power to wipe out memories, and they have the power to return them. We can call on the forces to do our bidding, and they can undo it. In other words, they have the capability of reversing what we have done with certain caveats. There is other stuff too; as with the Fold, some of them are more powerful than others, that sort of thing."

"Did you believe him?" Gordon asked, knowing Andrew's inordinate capability of reading others.

"Given everything that's happened in this past week? Hell, yes, I believe him," Andrew stated, emphatically.

"If such a thing as the *Radiants* exist," Gordon was still having trouble wrapping his mind around it, even if he had played around with the idea himself, "don't you think one of our fathers or Joseph would have told us about them?"

"I thought of that too. So, I told the guy that I was skeptical of what the old man was saying, that I had even argued with him because I had never heard of them," Andrew said.

"Did he have anything to say about that?" Gordon queried.

"He just shrugged, laughed and said that since I was a Bilford, I had no reason to know about them." Before Gordon could say anything, Andrew quickly said, "I didn't tell him I'm a Bilford, but he knew." Pausing, briefly to make sure he still had Gordon's full attention, Andrew continued, "Then he said, '*We take care of most problems as they arise, either they go so deep underground they stop making problems, or, if we catch them, by the time we're done with them there's not much left to cause any problems.*' And, that's when I offered to buy him another drink, and I changed the subject."

"And you didn't talk of it again?" Gordon asked.

"I didn't say another word about it. We talked about the game on the bar television; he's a big football fan. But right before he left, he handed me his card, and said, '*That light thing we were talking about earlier?*' I nodded, and he said, '*There's a rumor going around that there may be a coalition forming, there have been a few disturbances lately, you have any trouble you just give me a call.*' Andrew took out his wallet and handed Gordon a card.

Gordon flipped the card over it had one name on it, "Rayne" along with a phone number. "First or last name?"

"I don't know," Andrew said with a shake of his head, "he introduced himself as 'Rayne' and when I asked, he said, "Just Rayne, that's all you need to know. I took him at his word; that's all I needed to know."

"Where did you meet him," Gordon started grilling, "when did you meet him? And, how did you meet him?"

"I called a friend of mine, Karl Woods, do you remember him?" When Gordon nodded once, Andrew continued, "Karl said he knew a guy that could tell me anything I wanted to know, and that he hung out in a bar here in Boston, and that's where he could be found most evenings, unless he is on a job. Here's the thing, he just happened to be in Albany that night; the same night that we were there." Gordon started at that piece of information, and Andrew said, "The bar here in Boston is just a few blocks away if you want to meet him?"

"No thanks," Gordon replied, dryly.

"The thing is that I saw him again this afternoon," at Gordon's look, Andrew added quickly, "he didn't see me, or at least I'm fairly certain he didn't. But here's what I do think; I think he's following Colleen and I think that pub has something to do with the 'coalition.' Especially, after the reception, we received this afternoon."

"Okay, Andrew let me get this straight," Gordon started, "you think the bar where Colleen has, obviously spent a lot of time is a haven for the Radiants, Colleen is one of them, and an Abrogate is after her?"

"Yes," Andrew said without elaborating. Gordon wanted to argue with him, the mere thought of Colleen at the hands of an Abrogate caused a pain to run through him like an ice pick. Everything in Gordon rejected the idea; yet, something inside of him whispered that Andrew was right.

Without a word he took out his phone and placed a call to Joseph. Gordon paced, yelled, and cursed as he questioned, talked, and listened to Joseph. When Gordon finally took a breath, Joseph cut in on his tirade.

"Sir," Joseph began, then with a more personal approach said, "Gordon, I don't know what you want me to say. Far be it from me to speak for your father's, but I'm sure it simply never occurred to them to tell you about the Radiants. I know I never gave it any thought."

"And why not?" Gordon asked brusquely.

"First of all, it wasn't my place to do so, and besides, you're both Bilford's," Joseph replied as if that should explain everything. When Gordon said nothing Joseph continued, "No Radiant, nor, even an

Abrogate would dare touch a Bilford. Apparently, Gordon, your father and Uncle, are far more powerful within the *Fold* than either you or Andrew realizes."

"How powerful?" Gordon demanded.

When Joseph didn't answer, Gordon loudly proclaimed, "It's not right that Andrew and I don't know." When Joseph remained silent, Gordon softened his voice and said, "Joseph, please talk to me."

"You might want to sit down this is going to take a while," Andrew had started to stand up to go to his rooms to give them some privacy knowing Gordon would fill him in later, when Joseph said calmly, "You too Andrew, sit. This concerns you as well."

Andrew had not made a sound since Gordon had made the call; the cousins looked at one another in bewilderment. Chuckling, Joseph said, "Don't be so surprised boys, I have my ways of knowing. Who do you think has been keeping tabs on both of you all of these years?" Having sufficiently silenced them for the moment, Joseph continued, "Your fathers meeting with the Acoorsi sisters did not happen by accident. The women had been experimenting, performing ancient rites, calling upon the dark, and the dark finally answered. Together, the sisters became the *dark messenger*." Joseph paused, before speaking directly to Gordon, "Now Gordon, I know you have never set any store by the meaning of a person's name, but, within the Fold and the Radiant, names have a significance.

"Okay, Joseph," Gordon replied, wearily, "I'll never doubt you again."

Joseph laughed, and said, "Of course you will, just as it should be." Clearing his throat and taking on a more serious tone, Joseph continued, "When the dark messenger moved over the women it destroyed them, but it wanted the twin males. Your fathers, in association with the sisters, had already experienced enough to know they wanted more. You want to know how much power they possess; only the Genesis is more powerful."

With that Andrew and Gordon's heads snapped up to exchange

a look of disbelief, shock, surprise, there wasn't enough superlatives to express their feelings.

Recovering first, Andrew said, "So we were right. That's the reason everyone treats them with such deference, although, I would never have expected them to be that close."

"Andrew, it's not just them," Joseph said quietly, "it puts you and Gordon second in line."

Gordon continued to stare at Andrew, his eyebrows had disappeared again, and Colleen had not been the cause this time.

"Colleen!" Gordon exclaimed, for the first time since meeting her, she had slipped from his mind temporarily.

"Ah yes, the lass," Joseph said, "I took certain precautions to keep her from your mind Gordon while I explained about your fathers. I don't know how much she knows. But it won't last for long."

"So, do you think she is part of the Radiants?" Gordon was asking Joseph, but he knew the answer already.

"Yes," said Joseph without any infliction.

They sat quietly, when suddenly Gordon said, "So you're in my head too Joseph? Do I ever have a minute of privacy?"

"No, no," Joseph said, "You have it backward. I blocked *her* from invading *your* mind Gordon, but I don't know how long it will last."

"And, me?" Andrew asked.

"What do you mean Andrew," Joseph asked his voice tinged with caution.

"Did you block her from me, or do I just see her when Gordon does?"

Joseph fell silent for a moment, Gordon could nearly see the frown on his face, "Are you telling me that you see her when Gordon does?" Joseph demanded.

"Yes, sometimes," Andrew answered, "I nearly hit the ditch, yesterday when we were coming home from Albany. Her image blotted out everything including the road."

Joseph whistled softly and said, "Oh my, I had no idea the lass was that powerful. I thought she was a Paladin, maybe, but they don't have that sort of capacity. She might be an Arc."

Exchanging looks of confusion, Andrew and Gordon both started questioning Joseph at once.

"Boys, boys, let me think for a minute," Joseph said over their voices, "this puts things in a different light, no pun intended."

Seeming to have gathered his thoughts, Joseph began, "Okay, the Argents have a hierarchy much like the Fold. Low to high ranks and the Paladins protect the ranks."

"Ranks?" Andrew interjected, then scoffing said, "You make them sound like an army."

"That's exactly what they are; an army with one single objective," Joseph said.

"Being what exactly?" Andrew impatiently asked.

"Well Andrew, the light conquering the darkness, of course, holding it at bay," Joseph said as if speaking to a child. "I can't say I'm surprised given the current state of affairs that they have mobilized."

Andrew bristled at Joseph's patronizing tone, but, was too curious to complain, instead he asked, "What current state?"

"Joseph you are starting to speak in riddles," Gordon said.

"Andrew, I know you never pay attention to the world of the Normals, but Gordon you read every newspaper you can get your hands on; city, state, national, and international news. Think about it," Joseph said.

"Things around the world are pretty grim right now," Gordon agreed, "authoritarian governments are gaining, relationships between long-standing allies are strained to say the least, and as usual the rich are getting richer, while the poor are getting poorer."

Scoffing, Andrew asked, "Since when do you care about the politics of the Normals?"

"I have to keep abreast of their political whims, Andrew," Gordon argued back, "for *our* business. Our business opens doors that put us in touch with possible recruits for the Fold, not to mention their political whims can determine where we keep our ships afloat."

"Don't lose sight of what we're talking about here boys," Joseph reprimanded them, "the point is that the darkness is gaining rapidly, apparently too rapidly. Things are getting out of balance, and that imbalance has brought out the Radiants."

"So, what is it that they do exactly?" Andrew asked.

"Depends on which ones we're talking about." Joseph answered, "Some are simply do-gooders, working in charities, neighborhood nannies so to speak; while others literally reverse actions of the Fold; for instance; if one of the Fold calls for drought, they will send rain. The ones that are higher in the ranks go after the Fold's recruits, flipping them back. The Radiants that do the most damage to the Fold are the Arcs, they have the capability of reversing tributes, and they will go after the higher ranks of the Fold; either to flip them or to take them out."

Startled, Andrew asked, "They kill them?"

"No," Joseph said immediately, "from what I understand they bind them, a method similar to what the Fold does with tributes, with some exceptions."

"And you think Colleen could be one of these Arc's?" Gordon asked, his voice heavy.

"I honestly don't know what to think about her," Joseph responded. At Gordon's exasperated sigh, Joseph said, "You have to understand that working for the *House of Bilford* has guaranteed that I have not encountered one, I have no personal frame of reference, only what I have heard." Joseph was silent for a moment before continuing, "But, I must say there is a sincerity about her that defies my expectation of an Argent or an Arc."

"I know exactly what you mean," Andrew said suddenly. Gordon raised a questioning brow prompting Andrew to explain, "Gordon, when we were at that pub this afternoon, we could feel the patrons' animosity, but I have never gotten that feeling from

Colleen. You read people nearly as well as I, have you ever felt that kind of hostility from Colleen?"

"I'm probably the last person you should ask, Andrew," Gordon said with a touch of irony.

"But you know when you're in imminent danger, have you… uh…ah…never mind, I see what you mean," Andrew conceded.

"Joseph," Gordon spoke quietly, "Andrew thinks an Abrogate that goes by the name of Rayne is after Colleen---"

"Rayne? Haven't heard that name for a while. I've never met the man, you understand, just heard the stories; he's legendary. But, if he's around, it must be getting serious. Gordon don't trouble yourself about this, you take care of Bilford Shipping, I will see that no harm comes to the lass," Joseph said, reassuringly. "I know what needs to be done to keep her safe from Rayne."

"Whatever it takes," Gordon added.

"Whatever it takes," Joseph promised.

"Well, Hell's bells!" Andrew exclaimed loudly, drawing a chuckle from Joseph, and a frown from Gordon. "Don't give me that look Gordon; just tell me that you're not going to try to marry her too."

Sighing heavily Gordon retorted, "No one said anything about marriage Andrew, I just want to assure her safety, at least for the time being. She is Fran and Shaun's niece." Turning his attention back to the phone, he said, "Joseph, we will be remaining in Boston for a couple of weeks. I trust the younger Alanis is comfortable?"

"He has spent the majority of today with Miss Colleen," Joseph answered, "and seems to be quite comfortable. Plus, I believe I overheard the two of them making plans for this evening."

Gordon's brow furrowed deeper, suddenly remembering what the elder Alanis had warned of earlier today, *"another could take your helm and your woman if you ignore her."* Gordon said, "Joseph, please extend an invitation to Stavros to join Andrew and me here in Boston. He needs to be informed of his responsibilities now that he is in business with Bilford Shipping. I will expect him in my office tomorrow afternoon no later than two o'clock. That should give him time to settle into his apartment before he joins us for dinner at six."

"Uh, sir," Joseph began, "he seemed pretty well settled here at the manor as your father requested."

"Well then unsettle him; he's not staying there," Gordon snapped. "If he can't be here tomorrow, I will have our attorneys contact Darius to let him know that our contract is void."

Gordon braced himself for an argument, but Joseph merely said, "As you wish sir," and when he looked directly at his cousin, Andrew just held up his hands and shook his head indicating he wouldn't argue. *"Good,"* thought Gordon, *"the last thing I need right now is to be at odds with either of them."*

"Gordon, I'm going out for a little while," Andrew said as he stood and stretched, "I have an appointment this evening, and I don't want to be late."

Gordon studied his cousin for a moment, "Are you bringing her back here?" Gordon asked. When Andrew gave him a look, Gordon shrugged, and said, "I only ask, because I don't want to be the cause of any awkwardness in the morning."

Amused, Andrew asked, "Planning on waking me, Cousin?"

"You certainly don't have a problem surprising me in my rooms, Cousin," Gordon reminded Andrew.

Momentarily stymied, Andrew did a slight bow and said, "Touché."

Gordon gave him a questioning look, "You still haven't answered me."

With a slow smile, Andrew, replied, "Well that's because I'm not sure what she will want to do."

"Curious, to my knowledge Andrew has never deferred to any woman," thought Gordon "Since when do you concern yourself with the wants of the lady?" Gordon asked.

"This one is different, Cousin," Andrew replied. Then with a smirk added, "Guess you will just have to *tune in*, Gordon."

Responding with a small shudder, Gordon declared, "Andrew, you are completely depraved."

Laughing, Andrew gave Gordon a salute as he went out the door. "What are we to do with him, Joseph?" Gordon asked, not expecting an answer. "Speaking of 'tuning-in' have you fixed my key yet?"

"Yes sir, it's been repaired," Joseph answered, "We can't trust a courier with it, so I will bring it to you whenever you're ready."

"Just keep it safe for me, Joseph," Gordon said, "I rather like having a small piece of privacy, and I will retrieve it when we come back."

"Are you sure? I think you might be safer if the two of you are more closely connected," Joseph pointed out.

"Why should you worry? After all, I'm from the *House of Bilford*," Gordon responded with a bit of mockery.

"But---" Joseph began.

"Goodnight Joseph," Gordon said interrupting him before an argument could ensue.

OVER THE NEXT FEW WEEKS, GORDON attempted to focus all of his energy on the business. He spent long hours poring over contracts, reaching out to new contacts, and personally checking invoices from the last six months of incoming and outgoing products. An unhappy Stavros came to Boston as ordered by Gordon, and Gordon had taken a quiet delight keeping Stavros either, tied to a desk buried under useless documents, or, on one of the ships running up and down the coast.

Gordon had spent some of his time on the ships in dock; some days working side-by-side with the sailors. It felt good to stretch his muscles and work up a sweat, performing some of the mundane, but all important, tasks necessary in keeping a ship afloat. He had even gone for a short run on one of the smaller vessels down the coast to Newport. *"It was wonderful being on the ocean, for even just a short time,"* Gordon thought, remembering the rush he always got when first losing sight of land, and then finding his rhythm once again of riding the swells was exhilarating.

But, even with the vastness of the ocean and the concentrated effort of immersing himself in his work, Gordon could not block out the images of Colleen. It seemed that when Joseph's magic of blocking her had worn off, the frequency of the images had increased, as if she had known somehow, and wasn't willing to let that happen again. They were so frequent now that Andrew began to stay away more and more, to get some relief. *"Or, at least that was his excuse when he started spending his nights with his friend,"* Gordon thought wryly. Gordon was reasonably sure that Andrew's friend was Breanna, the new elevator guard he had hired to work the day-shift.

Gordon didn't begrudge Andrew the company he was keeping, the woman was quite striking, and he had to admit the images were wearing on him too. This afternoon they were accompanied by intense emotional waves, so much so, that he decided to knock off early today, and go back to the apartment to rest for a while. By the time he had made the short elevator ride, from the office to his apartment, his head was actually hurting.

Before he stepped over the threshold into the apartment, Gordon felt a tremor run through him... *"Colleen!"* Entering the apartment, he whipped his head from side-to-side searching for her. Not finding her in the main living area he headed to his suite. The feeling was so acute that he expected to find her in his private sitting room, but she wasn't there. *"I must be losing my mind,"* Gordon thought, as he went through to his bedroom while tugging at his tie, stopping short at the door; *"or maybe not."*

"Colleen, what are you doing here?" He wasn't going to bother to ask 'how' she had gotten into his private quarters right now.

"Why Gordon, where would you expect your mistress to be, if not waiting in your bed?" Colleen asked, as if she were asking for the time.

Gordon drank in every detail of the picture she presented, she was dressed very casually in jeans and a flowing peasant blouse; her hair was loose, and compared to the last time he had seen her, she appeared to be fairly calm. He also took note that his headache had eased significantly upon seeing her, "You're not *in* my bed, you're on it," Gordon pointed out, as he moved into the room closing the door behind him, and removing his jacket.

"Same thing," Colleen quipped with a shrug of her shoulder.

"Oh, trust me," Gordon said with confidence as he crossed to his closet while loosening his tie, "it's not."

"Didn't anyone ever tell you it's not polite to brag?" Colleen asked.

Ignoring her taunt, Gordon said, "You haven't answered my question." He removed his tie and began unbuttoning his shirt, while pulling it free from his waistband, "And, I thought we had already established that you're not my mistress...yet," he added quite pointedly, his dark eyes boring into hers.

Laughing lightly, Colleen stood up and replied, "I needed to speak to you, face-to-face, and privately."

"Well you have my attention now," Gordon said, as he threw his shirt onto the back of the chair, "what is so pressing that you could not have waited a few more days? I know Joseph told you I was planning to return home before the week's end?" Gordon sat in the chair and toed each of his shoes off and pulled at his socks, watching Colleen the entire time.

"Are you planning on stripping in front of me?" Colleen asked with a plaintive tone, while staring at his bare chest.

Gordon gave her a slow smile, as he stood, reaching for his belt, "Need I remind you that you're in my bedroom, uninvited I might add. I've had a long day, and I'm taking this suit off." Smiling wickedly, he added, "Don't get shy on me now, you have identified yourself as my mistress; so, if that's what you want, I should think that as my mistress you would be helping me."

"I told you I needed to speak with you, and I certainly don't trust the privacy at the manor with its secret passageways," Colleen complained, ignoring his mistress remarks, "and no it couldn't wait a few more days."

"Well, start talking," Gordon said as he pulled his belt from the loops and tossed it on top of his shirt, "Andrew will undoubtedly be here any minute."

Sighing, Colleen said, "Yes, of course, he will. He always shows up at the most awkward of times."

Gordon just smiled as he put his hand on his waistband, poised to unfasten his slacks; Colleen narrowed her eyes at him and set her mouth defying him to go further. So, he released the fastener. Gordon chuckled as she spun away from him only to find herself staring at both of their reflections in the free-standing mirror on the wall opposite of him. Throwing her hands up in aggravation, she went over to sit on the edge of the bed, pulling her feet up, she laid her forehead on her knees, allowing her hair to create a cocoon around her.

Laughing out loud now, Gordon finished undressing, and while pulling on a pair of athletic pants, said, "You lasted longer than I thought you would. You don't scare easily do you, Ms. O'Malley?"

"Is that what you want? For me to be scared," she asked, sounding irritated, but still hidden behind her hair.

Silently, padding across the room, after pulling on a t-shirt, Gordon took hold of her hands, pulling them from her face, he pulled her up, and said, "No I don't want you to be scared, I want you to be willing." He continued to pull her forward until he could loop her arms around his neck, never taking his eyes from her face. Colleen melted toward him, accepting the invitation, leaving Gordon to at long last kiss her with the fierceness, and the longing he had been holding on to since the first time he had kissed her in the observatory.

Colleen broke away from him gasping, and with her eyes still closed, held up her hand, "Stop, we have to talk."

Taking a step back, but not letting her go, Gordon growled, "Too late." Colleen's eyes flew open, and she looked so startled, that Gordon frowned at her until he realized that she must have misconstrued his words, thinking he wouldn't stop; Gordon immediately released his hold on her, and explained, "Too late, *because* Andrew is almost here."

"Damn it," Colleen exclaimed, "can you get rid of him, or is there anywhere we can go where no one will be eavesdropping?"

"You may not understand this, but it is difficult for me to get away from Andrew even when I leave," Gordon said.

Leveling a look at Gordon with more understanding than he felt comfortable with, Colleen asked, "Does he literally know what you're thinking and doing? Or, is it just a feeling?"

Gordon gave Colleen a measuring look, quickly made a decision aware of the implications, and he answered, "Both."

"Gordon!" Andrew shouted as he ran through the apartment.

"I'll figure something out," Gordon assured her in a whisper, "but, brace yourself, if I can't stop him, he may come through that door any second."

"Andrew, I'm fine," Gordon called through the door when he heard him enter the sitting room, "Please stop shouting, I had a headache and was lying down. Give me a minute, and I'll be out. Why don't you go pour us a drink?"

"Are you sure?" Andrew asked, not sounding convinced.

"Yes, yes," Gordon answered, "just let me splash some water on my face, and I'll be right out."

When Gordon heard the door to the sitting room close, he turned to Colleen, pulled her close and whispered in her ear, "Stay here, and I'll try to convince him he can go back to his girlfriend." Colleen nodded her assent.

Entering the living room Gordon found Andrew looking out over the harbor; clapping Andrew on the shoulder as he joined him, he said, "Sorry I didn't call you, cousin, I should have known you would be concerned."

"Yes, I was concerned; I sensed your pain, but I couldn't detect the source. Since when do you get headaches?" Andrew asked, as he handed Gordon a drink, and continued to stare out the window.

"They're rare," Gordon replied, "I think the last time I had one was a couple of months after Jeanette."

"Humph," Andrew grunted, and sat down in a nearby chair, he said, "You need to relax. Colleen is safe enough, I have people watching Rayne, and keeping an eye on the pub down the street.

You're working day and night, just to keep the images away, and I know for a fact it's not helping. You need to get away for a few days."

"I don't know Andrew," Gordon said, realizing that his cousin had just given him the perfect out, "do you really think you could handle things for a few days on your own? Tomorrow alone is going to be a long one. I have a couple of meetings with prospective clients scheduled; and then, tomorrow evening, that dinner with the head of the Durham Corporation, may need to do some hand-holding with Johnathon, he isn't happy with us right now." Gordon knew the quickest way to get Andrew to rise to his bait was to call his Cousin's business acumen into question.

With a snort, Andrew said, "I think I'm capable of schmoozing a couple of new clients and smoothing things over with Mr. Durham. You don't need to play the martyr, Gordon. This is my business too."

Gordon inwardly smiled, to Andrew, he said, "I wouldn't mind getting away from everything for a few days. I would like to be in the mountains, but Europe is out of the question with that benefit coming up so soon."

Andrew rolled his eyes, and said, "Go back to Albany. You have a home away from home there. You might even get in a little skiing, it's not the Alps, but--"

"You know, I did feel like I kind of got cheated out of Albany," Gordon interjected.

"Perfect!" Andrew exclaimed. "Go back to the Getaway. Hike, sleep, ski if there's snow. And, if you would find yourself a little company," Andrew wiggled his eyebrows, "it might do wonders for you."

"Speaking of company," Gordon said dryly, refusing to engage on that subject, "don't you have someone waiting for you?"

"She will keep," Andrew said with a self-assured, smug smile, "it's different having a woman from the Fold; especially, a guard. Quite agile, if you get my drift. You might give it a try sometime."

Gordon just shook his head, and said, "Thanks for too much info, once again, Andrew."

Andrew laughed, and said, "Okay, suit yourself. So, are you going to go to Albany?"

"Let me sleep on it," Gordon replied, not wanting to appear overly eager to take Andrew up on his offer, "I will let you know in the morning."

"Okay," Andrew agreed, "Now that I know you're good, I'll leave; but Gordon I really think you should go, I can take care of things here." Andrew walked to the front door, stopped and turned back, "and Gordon, think about what I said," Gordon gave him a quizzical glance, Andrew clarified, "I really think you need to get laid," and with that, he was out the door.

Gordon just shook his head at Andrew's crudeness, but he wasn't the only one that had been listening, "He really is a jerk, isn't he?" Colleen asked as she came up the hall.

Gordon mildly chuckled, and said, "Yeah, usually; particularly when it comes to women."

"Humph," Colleen said, as she leaned her hip against the kitchen bar, tipping her head to one side, she looked at Gordon with a smile playing around her lips, and widened her eyes, "Guess it's a good thing I'm your mistress and not his, huh?"

"Colleen," Gordon said with a note of warning in his voice.

"You really do need to lighten-up, Gordon," Colleen laughed.

"And you need to stop being so provocative," Gordon shot back, suddenly feeling agitated. "You keep playing with fire, and eventually you will get burned. There are forces out there that can be quite dangerous."

Sobering, Colleen replied, "You needn't worry about me Gordon, I can take care of myself. Nothing happens to me except by design...my design."

"If I conducted myself as Andrew does, your design would be of very little consequence, and you wouldn't care for the outcome," Gordon responded.

"But that's the point, you're nothing like Andrew," Colleen

replied as she pushed away from the bar and came across the room to sit opposite of Gordon, "and that's why I'm here."

Narrowing his eyes, Gordon studied her, but didn't reply; he motioned for her to continue, but Colleen stared back without a word. *"We're at a stalemate,"* Gordon thought, *"neither of us wanting to give anything away."* Gordon's mind started to reel, as in a game of chess he tried to think three moves ahead, *"but, I just don't know enough. I need to know what she knows about the Fold."*

Gordon chose his next words carefully, "Andrew is my cousin, we are blood; we were raised as brothers. Physically, people sometimes have difficulty telling us apart; I would say we're very much alike."

"All of that is true, however; you have a conscience and Andrew does not. He is a lost cause, but there is still hope for you." Colleen replied.

Suddenly, the afternoon of their arrival in Boston loomed large in his mind; when Colleen's image and her scent had brought him comfort. *"Does she know how desperately I want to get away from the Fold?"* Gordon asked himself. His next thought, *"If she does, then she knows about the Fold, and she knows what I am."*

Settling back into the cushions, Gordon said, "This conversation will not go any further until I get some answers; our verbal dance is over."

"I'm an open book, what would you like to know?" Colleen asked, as she too settled back in her seat mirroring his actions.

Gordon shook his head slightly and as his dark eyes bore into her, "A picture book, with lots of pretty *pictures,*" he said, emphasizing the word, "but your book contains very little information."

The corners of her mouth curved as she rebutted, "I've always heard it said that a picture is worth a thousand words."

"At one time that might have been true," Gordon replied, "but, then Adobe came out with Photoshop."

With a soft tinkling laugh, Colleen said, "My, my, aren't you the clever one?"

Gordon schooled his expression and remained firm, "I'm not trying to be clever, and I want some straight answers."

"What do you want to know?" Colleen asked.

Gordon observed her body language as she spoke, she had leaned toward him with her forearms still resting on the arms of her chair leaving her body open. From the right angle, this move would indicate no fear, openness, and honesty.

However, from his vantage point, the move had allowed the front of her loosely tied peasant shirt to fall away from her body, affording him a glimpse of cleavage and a wisp of lace. Inwardly, cursing himself for falling for her gambit, Gordon closed his eyes for a second, before re-opening them to focus on her face, "That's not going to work this time," he warned.

Colleen, again lightly laughed, "Well shoot, it always has before," she said.

Gordon noticed that she was not bothering to demure, nor, did she bother to sit back in her chair either. Much to his consternation, Gordon discovered, that he really didn't care for the idea of her playing at *Mata Hari* or some other femme fatale with other men.

Attempting to concentrate on getting any information, Gordon asked, "Are you ready to answer my questions?"

Without missing a beat, she replied, "I'm always ready."

Blowing out his breath noisily, Gordon choose to ignore the innuendo and asked, "Are you telepathic? Do you put images into people's heads? Can you read people's minds?"

Leaning back in her seat, and with all traces of the bawdy flirtatious humor erased from her face, Colleen said, "And there you have it, the difference between you and Andrew. Telepathic? Maybe, a certain type of telepathy. You see in my world I am known as a projectionist, but I can *only* project successfully if the subject is, either, a willing participant or is struggling with a major conflict within. Then and only then are they open to my projections. Obviously, neither you nor Andrew is willing; however, Andrew is not conflicted, he knows who he is, and he embraces it. He can't pick up my projections." She paused; Gordon assumed that her silence was to give him time to absorb this new disclosure.

Continuing Colleen said, "But you," she flipped her hand toward Gordon, "are a mass of contradictions; therefore, I can project to you." She paused, weighing her next words, "You, Gordon, feel you have been forced into a life that was not of your choosing, you have done things that you regret every minute of every day." She leaned toward Gordon, and said, "There is hope for you yet."

For the first time in a very long time, probably since the night of his twentieth birthday, Gordon felt vulnerable. He wasn't accustomed to having anyone other than Andrew in his head. And even Andrew could not see his emotional state laid so wholly bare, and he didn't like it, "So can you read my mind?"

"No, not really," Colleen answered, "and I'm not trying to be evasive," she added when she noticed Gordon's expression. With a sigh of resignation, she explained, "For some reason, when you are experiencing an overwhelmingly intense emotion, I can feel it, you know? Like, if you're extremely happy or extremely sad. On the day you left Bilford, I have no idea what brought it on, but I do know that you became very distraught."

"Is that normal to have that kind of connection with your subjects?" Gordon asked, his growing irritation evident as he nearly spat out the last word.

"No, never before," Colleen replied frowning, ignoring his anger, "I don't know why my intuitiveness is connected to you so strongly; unless…," she stopped, leaving her sentence unfinished.

"Unless what?" Gordon demanded.

Squaring her shoulders, and looking him in the eye unflinchingly, she responded, "Unless the chemistry between us goes beyond a mutual attraction."

"Oh, and I'm supposed to believe that we have some sort of cosmic interconnection between us, and you're not just playing a game to get what you want?" Gordon lashed out. "Hey, if all of this is a way to get me into bed, all of this wasn't necessary," leaning forward Gordon mocked, "all you need to do is ask; we can take care of that here and now." Gordon felt an unexpected twinge of regret, when he saw the hurt play across her face caused by his callous remarks, but she disguised it quickly.

Drawing a deep breath, Colleen said, "Believe what you will, I have been honest in my answers; and, now it's my turn to ask the questions. Who is Rayne?"

Gordon jumped up, "No more verbal sparring," he commanded. "I want the truth, and I want it now, have you had any contact with him?"

"Calm down," Colleen said wearily, waving Gordon off, "he's being tracked as we speak. He ah---introduced himself to me in Albany, but something felt off about him."

"Damn it!" Gordon shouted, making Colleen jump, "you mean he hit on you."

"Well yeah, but that's not exactly new to me, or any other woman," Colleen said. "But like I said something didn't feel right; I sent him on his way." Hesitantly, she asked, "U mm, so it's safe to assume he's not a friend of yours?"

Gordon snorted, as he replied, "Not hardly."

Gordon stared back at her as she tipped her head watching him, then watched as realization dawned, "Oh," she said, "he's one of the dangerous forces that you spoke of earlier?"

With a suggestive tone, Gordon said, "Yes," his one-word answer speaking volumes.

Feeling like he was about to explode, Gordon started pacing the apartment, as he began firing questions at her, "Did you drive here or hire a car?"

"I drove."

"Did anyone come with you?"

"No."

"Did you go to see anyone else; did you go to the pub?"

Startled, Colleen asked, "Just exactly what do you know about the pub? And, by the way, why did you buy my photo?"

Gordon roared, "Answer me!"

Exasperated, Colleen said, "Yes, I stopped in at the pub, after I drove to Boston by myself; then I came here, and I have been with you since. Gordon, it's okay, I have people watching my back."

"What about the friends that were supposed to visit you?" Gordon asked.

"What about them? They came a day later than planned due to the storm, stayed a couple of nights, and they left." Colleen replied.

"Have you heard from them since they left?" Gordon asked, trying to pull his fury under control, or else, Andrew would be back any second.

"No, I haven't." Suddenly, Colleen's eyes grew round as she sucked in air, "You think something has happened to them." Her phone was in her hand in seconds, "Kelsey," she said into the phone, "has Jacqueline or Tommy checked in recently?" She listened for a minute, "I'm sorry Kelsey," and then putting the phone on speaker, she asked, "Would you repeat that?"

Gordon could tell by his heavy Irish brogue that Kelsey was the barkeeper from the pub, "No one has heard from them since they left your place."

"Oh, Kelsey!" Colleen said genuinely distressed.

"Now lass, we have people lookin' for them. The first couple of days, we didn't think so much about it; we thought maybe they decided to take a little romantic side-trip. But it's been too long, we can't locate them." Pausing he asked, "Where are you right now lassie, we can't locate you either?"

"I'm where I'm supposed to be," Colleen answered, as she shook her head and rolled her eyes toward Gordon, "don't worry about me. But Kelsey I did want to ask if you have found out anything about the man that goes by the name of Rayne?"

Dropping his voice, Kelsey's Irish vernacular became more pronounced as he said, "Aye, he's a merchant for hire. He showed up out of nowhere, we can't find his connections. Colleen, lass, ye need to come to the pub where we can keep ye safe." Lowering his voice, he added, "But I don't understand why we can't locate ye," Kelsey argued, "unless one of *them* is close by." As if he suddenly had an epiphany he asked, "You're with Bilford, aren't you?"

Colleen looked to Gordon, who was shaking his head no, to Kelsey she said, "I'm okay Kelsey, you'll just have to trust me," looking to Gordon again, with a genuine smile, she said, "I'm reasonably sure I'm safe, and in good hands."

"Ah, lassie," Kelsey sighed.

15

"**I** STILL DON'T UNDERSTAND WHY I HAVE to stay with you in Albany, or at the very least why I can't pick up some of the clothing that I left at Aunt Fran's house," Colleen complained for the umpteenth time as Gordon pulled into the garage of the Getaway. "I can take care of myself you know, I have been taking care of myself for years, without you."

"For the last time, we cannot take the chance of you being seen. I have no idea what kind of network Rayne has, but I do know that he followed you here before. I'm not leaving Fran and Shaun's niece to the likes of Rayne. You will stay here with me," Gordon said in a voice that would brook no more argument. He knew she was absolutely seething, but he also knew that for her safety and everyone involved he could not give in to her.

Jutting out her chin and with green eyes snapping, she said, "Planning on tying me to a chair?" Her voice dripping with sarcasm.

"A chair isn't the piece of furniture I would choose," Gordon muttered under his breath.

"What?" she snapped.

"Nothing," Gordon said. He was tired, and in no mood to indulge her arguments anymore tonight. All he wanted at the moment was a stiff drink, a shower, and a pillow; after driving through the night for hours on roads that were only partially cleared, he didn't think that was too much to ask.

Gordon refused to keep arguing with her right now, he got out of the rental vehicle, walked to the alarm panel and punched in the code to disarm the security system. He then unlocked the door that led into the house and started moving from room to room, turning on lights, and turning up the heat too tired to build a fire.

Heading back to the garage to grab his bags from the SUV he met Colleen in the hall, with her hands on her hips, "Were you just going to leave me in the garage?" She asked, plaintively.

"I turned on the lights, I thought you might like to see where you were going, and turned up the heat to take the chill off of the house," Gordon said, flatly, as he moved past her to get his luggage and reset the alarm. "Besides, I'm pretty sure I heard you say you could take care of yourself," he called back.

"I'm sorry, I know I'm impossible," Colleen said, apologetically, as she watched him reset the alarm, "I'm not comfortable with someone else managing my life."

Ignoring her apology, Gordon came back through with the bags and handed a smaller one to her saying, "There are some clean socks, along with an old pair of sweats, and I found a long-sleeved t-shirt never worn, it's too small for me. I know it's all probably way too big for you, but it should keep you warm enough until we can find something better tomorrow."

Gordon dropped his bags at the bottom of the staircase and went straight to the bar, poured himself a shot, and threw it back, before turning back around, "Oh sorry, did you want a drink?" he asked Colleen who was still standing in the same spot.

"No Gordon, I don't want a drink," Colleen answered, "I am trying to apologize for my behavior."

Gordon stared at her for a moment, coming to a conclusion, *"I can't do this anymore tonight, I'm bone tired and not thinking straight,"* to Colleen he said, "Apology accepted, your bedroom is right through there," he said, pointing down the small hall next to the library, "the sheets are clean, and the attached bathroom is stocked. I'm taking a shower and getting some sleep, we can figure out our next step tomorrow," glancing at his watch he amended, "or, later today."

"I must look as rough as I feel," Gordon thought, surprised that she had simply nodded and turned toward the bedroom, *"she's actually letting me go without an argument."*

Gordon checked his phone for messages as he headed upstairs. He did have a couple from Andrew and one from Joseph, but they would just have to wait a few more hours to be answered. He wasn't sure how much Andrew was channeling, but he felt reasonably confident that his Cousin didn't know Colleen was with him; and honestly, as for Joseph, Gordon never could be sure of what he did or didn't know.

Gordon pulled a pair of pajama bottoms from his suitcase and headed for the bathroom. He stood in the shower letting the hot water run over him for a solid forty-five minutes in an attempt to loosen his knotted muscles.

Gordon walked out of his bathroom toweling his hair, when he stopped short, "Didn't we play this scene earlier?" he asked Colleen, who was once again sitting on his bed. This time looking like she had been swallowed by cotton, the clothing he had given her was a tad large. "Is there something wrong?"

"No, I'm fine," she replied.

Gordon frowned at her.

Sighing, she said, "I can't sleep." Then with a pleading in her voice, she said, "Can I stay with you for a while? It's lonely down there." Pausing for a moment, she said, "I thought we could talk for a bit."

Gordon groaned, "Colleen I cannot engage in any more arguments tonight. I need some sleep."

"I didn't say argue, I said talk," Colleen responded, with a tinge of annoyance in her voice, "Besides, how can you sleep with everything that's going on?"

"Is she serious?" Gordon thought as he tried to focus on her. She

looked like a lost little girl at the moment, as she sat cross-legged in the center of his bed, twisting a lock of her hair. Gordon tossed his towel in the corner, walked over to the bed, and pulled back the covers. Sitting on the side of the bed, he flipped the lamp off, "Stay if you want Colleen, but no talking," he said, as he finally put his head on the pillow. Gordon closed his eyes, but he could feel her watching him.

Gordon had just started to drift off when, with no warning, the image of Colleen, when he had kissed her earlier at the apartment, loomed large in his mind's eye. "Knock it off Colleen," he growled.

He felt her jump when he spoke, "What? I'm not doing anything, but lying here quietly, and trying to go to sleep," she retorted.

"You know what I mean," Gordon responded without opening his eyes, "quit putting images in my head."

"Don't be silly, why would I even do that? You're right here, and...," Colleen paused for a moment, "Oh boy! What did you see?"

Sighing heavily, Gordon said, "You know exactly what I saw, you put it there."

"But, I didn't," she said, "I don't think...at least not intentionally."

"What?"

"I was just thinking about everything that had happened over the last few hours," Colleen said. "Gordon," her voice was soft and pleading now, "please tell me what you saw."

Knowing he wouldn't get any rest unless he gave her an answer, Gordon rolled to his side and pushed himself up on his elbow to face her, "Do you want to know what I saw?" When she nodded, he cupped her face with his free hand, and leaning down kissed her as he had this afternoon, "There, that's what I saw," Gordon said, falling back down on his pillow.

Touching her lips, Colleen mused, "I wonder what that means."

"It means you're driving me to distraction," Gordon said grumpily.

"No," Colleen said, "I mean I didn't put that picture in your mind," she paused for a moment, looking over at Gordon, and then added, "It was a private thought. A memory. Are you sure you're not a mind reader?"

Gordon didn't believe her for one second, and putting his hand at her waist, he said, "Oh, well let me help you make some more memories then, better memories," as he pulled her toward him, "I told you all you have to do is ask."

"Gordon, no," Colleen said, pushing the palm of her hand against his chest.

"No? Is that any way for a mistress to speak to her man?" Gordon asked in a mocking tone. "Didn't you tell me, just a few hours ago, that you were always ready?"

"Please don't," Colleen pleaded.

With a dark chuckle, Gordon said, "Yeah, that's what I thought," before releasing his hold on her.

"Could you be satisfied with just holding me for a little while," Colleen asked softly.

"Satisfied? Absolutely not." Gordon said. He reached for her again, this time pulling her up against his body, he felt her stiffen, and he heard her suck in her breath, "But if I do, can you be quiet, and let me sleep?"

Gordon could hear the smile in her voice as she replied, "Yes, I can be quiet."

Gordon slowly became conscious of an annoying buzzing sound, the smell of bacon, along with the fragrance of freshly brewed coffee, and an empty bed. Pulling himself up to a sitting position he grabbed at his cell to see that Andrew had now left him a total of five messages. After splashing his face with cold water, Gordon messaged Joseph that he was fine and would call within the hour. Steeling himself against any thoughts of Colleen he called Andrew.

Andrew answered with a plaintive tone, "Gordon, what is going on, I have been trying to get you since last night."

"Good morning to you too, Andrew," Gordon said, wryly.

"Gordon...," Andrew started with an admonishing tone before

Gordon interrupted, "I'm fine, Andrew. If you had gone back to the apartment last night or went there this morning, you would have found my note telling you that I decided to 'sleep on it' in Albany."

"Why didn't you call or text me?" Andrew asked.

Gordon raked a hand through his hair, and said, "I didn't get your messages until I got here, bad reception I guess; it was late, and I didn't want to uh-ah-interrupt you at the wrong moment."

"Why did you leave so late?" Andrew asked, not ready to let it go yet.

"I don't know," Gordon said, "I decided that I wanted to wake up in the mountains, rather than, the city." Laughing Gordon asked, "What, can't I have a moment of spontaneity once in a while?"

"Okay, okay," Andrew said laughing, "but, you must admit it's a little out of the norm for you."

"Hey Andrew, did you find out anything about your new friend, Rayne?" Gordon asked, trying to sound nonchalant, and wanting to divert Andrew's line of questioning about last night.

"Nah," Andrew answered, "he's been flying under our radar. I didn't say anything before, but the guy reminds me of someone, just can't put my finger on who."

Gordon took note of what Andrew was saying, after all, his feeling about Colleen had been validated; but he didn't want to appear too anxious about it.

After ending his call with Andrew, Gordon called Joseph.

"I wanted to let you know that I am still searching for information on Rayne," Joseph said, "the only thing I have currently is that he is still in Boston, so the lassie should be safe."

"Is it the same person that you spoke of from the past?" Gordon asked, not wanting to talk about the 'lassie.'

"I can't be sure," Joseph replied, "you have to realize it's a name I remember, I'm not aware of ever having met him."

Keeping his conversation with Joseph short, Gordon dressed and headed downstairs. He found Colleen curled up in the corner of one of the sofas wearing yesterday's clothing staring into her phone.

"Hey sleepyhead," Colleen greeted him, with a big smile, "and, before you start lecturing me, it's a burner phone. No way to trace it, I always keep a couple on hand," she said absently. "I raided the freezer, hope you don't mind; so, if you're hungry there is bacon with English muffins in the warming oven, and coffee on the counter."

"Thank you," Gordon said, wondering where all the cheerfulness was coming from, as he went to the kitchen. He hadn't eaten since lunch yesterday, and his stomach reminded him of that fact. After pouring himself a cup of coffee, he fixed two bacon and muffin sandwiches and joined Colleen in the great room.

"Thanks again, for fixing breakfast," Gordon said, "I'll do some shopping and get some take-out for dinner."

"When you go out, I need for you to go to this store, the address is at the bottom," Colleen handed him a scrap of paper, with a list of items and an address, "and pick-up my order."

Gordon glanced at the bottom of Colleen's itemized list, recognized the name of the clothing store, and then softly whistled, it was one of a few high-end boutiques that catered to the very wealthy that came to Albany to ski. "Tell me you didn't use a credit card. If you're being tracked that is the first thing they will watch for."

"Don't be silly, I didn't use a credit card," Colleen said, apparently annoyed that he would think she would do such an irresponsible thing. "I ordered the clothing online, true; but you are paying for my new wardrobe when you pick it up."

"I am?"

"You're the one that decided I have to stay with you and stay hidden," Colleen reminded him, "you owe me."

"I owe you?" Gordon asked, incredulously, "I'm trying to keep you safe." But he could tell by her expression that she wasn't backing down, and this was a battle he had no interest in fighting.

"Okay, I will buy you new clothes, but couldn't you have picked a less pricey establishment?"

Smiling like the proverbial cat that swallowed the canary, she said, "Yes, I could have."

"I don't suppose you would consider doing that would you?" Gordon asked.

"No," Colleen said emphatically shaking her head, "I'm picky about my lingerie."

Holding up his hand, Gordon winced, and said, "Okay, forget I asked," the last thing he wanted to think about was Colleen in her lingerie; because that inevitably would lead to thinking about Colleen out of her lingerie, and his night had been uncomfortable enough.

They sat quietly for a moment. Gordon, sipping his coffee while glancing at the list of items to be picked-up while Colleen watched him still wearing her Cheshire smile. And, before he could say anything, he was assailed with an image of her wearing two scraps of lace, and his hands on her body. Gordon nearly dropped his coffee mug.

"Are you insane?" Gordon asked in with a low rumble.

Colleen laughed, "Gordon, I'm just teasing. I will pay you back when ---"

Cutting her off, before she could finish her thought, Gordon growled, "Yes, that's exactly what you are, a tease! And bordering on cruel. You need to stop now; I'm barely holding it together as it is." At her startled expression, he continued, "Let me put it this way, the next time you put pictures in my head, I will assume it's an invitation.

"I'm sorry?" she asked, sounding bewildered.

Gordon stared at her for a long moment, "Do you do this with all of your subjects?" he asked, his tone hardening as he said the word.

"But, I didn't. What did you see?" Suddenly her eyes grew wide, and she said, "No, I don't. I never...I don't know why...." Colleen stood up, and as she headed for the bedroom that she wouldn't stay in last night, she said, "Please excuse me."

Gordon didn't know precisely what her game was now, but he had to admit that she did seem to be genuinely upset. He instantly felt sorry for speaking to her so harshly, *"but, damn it, I am barely keeping my hands off of her as it is."*

His father, his uncle, and his cousin, along with countless others in the Fold would have bedded her by now, and moved on. *"But I can't do that,"* Gordon thought to himself, *"I won't do that. I don't want a woman that way. I want a woman that wants to be with me of their own free will. If I had to resort to that kind of trickery, it would be absolutely meaningless."* The men in his family considered themselves superior to the Normals, but what they had been known to do with women, from time to time, wasn't really any different than the low-life Normals that slipped drugs into the drinks of unsuspecting girls at bars or parties. It was tantamount to rape. But that was the way of the Dark Fold; steal, cheat, and rape.

Gordon couldn't do any of it; he was proud of Bilford Industries because he worked it clean. The business flourished or failed on the fair deals that he struck, on his acuity for business; not from his capability of mind-bending theft. He was proud of what he owned because he worked hard for everything he had, and when Gordon had a relationship with a woman, it was because she wanted him as much as he wanted her.

As Gordon cleaned up the coffee cups and the remnants of his breakfast, he kept glancing down the hallway toward the bedroom. He was vacillating between tapping on her door to check on her, or just leaving, to give her some space when he found himself outside of her door. Rapping lightly on the door he asked, "Colleen are you, all right?"

Opening the door a few inches, she looked straight past Gordon and with no inflection in her voice said, "I'm fine Gordon, thank you for asking."

Gordon didn't consider himself an expert on women; however, he knew enough to know that when a woman said "I'm fine" the way Colleen had just said it, quietly, politely, completely flat;

nothing was fine, nor was it likely to be for some time to come. Rubbing the back of his neck, and clearing his throat, Gordon lowered and tipped his head attempting to make eye contact as he spoke, "Colleen, I'm sorry if I offended you. I should have chosen my words with more care."

Still staring straight ahead she asked, "Did you mean what you said?"

Pushing his hair back, and blowing out his pent-up breath, he replied, "Yes." He watched as her eyes hardened, and quickly added, "Colleen, please listen to me. You're intelligent, you have a sharp wit, you're beautiful, and any man would have to be dead not to want you. I have been taught most of my life to take without asking." Colleen drew in a breath, and her eyes narrowed as she continued to stare past him. Gordon held up his hand to stop the eruption she was building up, "It's what I have been taught, but I don't live that way. However, it's taking every ounce of strength I have not to act on my wants, especially when you put those kinds of pictures in my head. Can you understand that?"

Finally, Colleen looked into Gordon's eyes, and said, "Gordon, I think what happened just a few minutes ago, was the same thing that happened last night. Will you please tell me, not *show* me," she said with a warning tone, "what you saw?"

Gordon couldn't believe it, and his temper was beginning to flare again, "Seriously?" Gordon shook his head, "What game are you playing now? I just told you I can't do this anymore."

Colleen gave him a brittle smile, "All right, let's try it this way, if the 'picture' that you saw was what I think it was, then once again, you saw a private thought, not something that I intentionally shared."

Gordon's mind was racing, if she were telling the truth, then that would mean....

"You don't get it, at all, do you?"

"You're fantasizing about me! Us...together." Gordon blurted out.

With her color high, she drew in a deep breath, and said, "Yes...and?"

"And, you're putting it in my head," Gordon said, "which leads us right back where we started."

Shoving past Gordon, Colleen went back to the great room, she started pacing back and forth; turning, with her hands on her hips, and her green eyes flashing as she zeroed in on a startled Gordon, who was still standing in the hall and said, "You are so obtuse! I am losing my patience."

"What the Hell are you talking about?" Gordon demanded, his temper was now spiking and would probably have Andrew calling any second, "*I'm* obtuse? *You're* losing patience?" he echoed, feeling she had no right to call him out for either. He strode back into the great room as he built up a tirade of his own, "You're talking in circles, but, *I'm* obtuse and the cause of *your* frustration?" he asked. With genuine exasperation in his voice, he said, "Woman, you are driving me insane!"

"Gordon, how does it work for you and Andrew? To know what the other is thinking, do either of you have to put in any effort?" Colleen asked.

Gordon contemplated her questions, *"The only way to explain it would be to tell her about the keys; I can't do that."* Instead, he emphatically replied, "I'm not discussing that with you."

Colleen studied him for a moment, then said, "Very well, I understand that you don't trust me; however, since I have already told you that I am a projectionist, I may as well tell you that I have to work at putting out an image. And Gordon, the last time I *purposefully* put an image in your mind was the day you left for Boston."

"You can't expect me to believe that," Gordon scoffed, "over the last two weeks your *projections*," Gordon spit out the word, "have been too numerous to count." Colleen shook her head in denial, which further infuriated him. "In fact," Gordon continued, narrowing his eyes, "Andrew virtually moved out of the apartment to get some relief; yesterday they were so vivid it was nearly unbearable, it was the reason I left my office early, my head actually hurt until I saw you."

Colleen's stance softened somewhat, and she asked, "Your head stopped hurting when you saw me?"

"Yes," Gordon admitted, then with a smirk added, "Surely you remember, I walked into my bedroom and found you lounging on my bed like Goldilocks."

"I simply don't understand," Colleen whispered, as she dropped her defensive stance, and moved to a sofa, wearily dropping down on it, and protectively wrapping herself in a throw.

"You are creating all of this, and yet, if I am to believe you, you claim not to understand?" Gordon asked, incredulous at her brazen attempt to shift the blame to the unknown.

"If I am to believe *you*," Colleen said, "then you're right I am creating it; however, I don't understand how or why it's happening." Taking a deep breath, Colleen calmly asked, "Is it possible for you to sit down and help me work through this?"

Gordon was surprised by her request, but cautiously curious about what she had to say. He nodded sharply once, and sat down across from her. Gordon's patience was stretched as he watched her chew her bottom lip, nervously fiddle with the fringe on the blanket, and seemed to struggle to find her first words, yet he was determined to remain quiet and let her say her piece.

"It would be helpful if I could speak to one of my people," she stated, looking at Gordon, who shook his head no, sighing, she said, "But, I understand that isn't possible right now."

Clearing her throat, and looking him in the eye, she said, "From the beginning, I have felt an inexplicably strong tie to you, like nothing I've ever experienced before. It scared me, it still does, so, I pushed really hard to finish what I was supposed to do," at that Gordon sat forward prepared to ask just what her mission was, but, she shook her head and held up her hand, "I'm not discussing that with you. Not now." Gordon sat back, she had just thrown his own words back at him, and oddly he understood. She no doubt had people to protect, just as he did.

"At first, I did work to keep myself in your mind, and although I can't explain right now... maybe never, it was integral to my goal. When you left for Boston, I spent most of the day fuming from our... let's call it a disagreement," shaking her head at the memory, she added, "and trying to avoid Stavros." Colleen laughed quietly, and said, "By the way, 'thanks,' for getting him out of my hair for the last couple of weeks. Wow, I thought I was pushy," she said, more to herself than to Gordon. "Sorry, I'm digressing, like I said, you were on my mind a lot that day; but, suddenly I was," she appeared to be struggling for the right words, "feeling, channeling, connecting," Colleen looked directly at Gordon, and said, "I don't know what to call it, but you were so sad, so hurt, I could feel your pain, and I wanted to comfort you somehow, so I tried something different." She dropped her gaze, for a moment, then faced Gordon again, and asked, "I guess it worked?"

Gordon wanted to be angry with her, but she looked so contrite for just admitting to trying to control him that he merely said, "Yes." He watched her face light up, *"she is very pleased with herself,"* he observed. He frowned at her then, although he was sure it held very little rancor.

"This next part is the most confusing, and more than a little embarrassing, at least for me. I was fairly certain I was successful that day, and that truly was the last time I tried to project anything toward you," she said.

Gordon shook his head as he said, "Colleen, that can't be. I--"

"You agreed to hear me out," Colleen interrupted, in a plaintive tone, "let me finish, please." Gordon's sense of fairness kicked in, so he clamped his mouth shut, and nodded his assent. She took a deep breath and continued, dropping her head letting her hair fall forward, to hide her face, "It was the last time I tried, but it wasn't the last time I thought of you. I thought of you constantly," she said, raising her head just enough to look at him. Drawing a shaky breath, and with flushed cheeks, she continued, "I wondered if you were all right, what you were doing, that sort of thing." Then drawing in a deep breath, "And, then, of course, I was extremely curious about who you might be seeing."

This last statement was said in such a quiet rush, Gordon wasn't sure he heard her correctly, leaning forward to ask, "What?"

"I wondered if you were with another woman. Okay?" This she said with such force that Gordon was taken aback; yet, pleased. However, he didn't think now was a good time to express his feelings; "Okay, continue."

"Yesterday I had you on my mind the entire day because I knew I was going to see you." Finally, Colleen looked straight at Gordon, and said, with unabashed honesty, "Last night, just as I was falling asleep, lying so close to you, made me remember your kiss from earlier. A little while ago when you were reading through that list, I thought of one particular item," Gordon watched as she closed her eyes and dipped her head again before saying, "and a mental picture of myself wearing it for you flashed through my mind."

Gordon sat back, staring at the ceiling, remembering, "Black lace, interwoven with blue ribbons, and the bra hooks in the front?" Gordon asked, quietly.

"Yes," Colleen whispered, barely loud enough for him to hear her.

Gordon couldn't tell if she was merely embarrassed or frightened; perhaps a combination of both. He got up and went to the French doors to look out over the snow twinkling in the sunlight, trying to gather his thoughts, because he didn't know what to think; she appeared to be sincere, but could he trust her?

"Maybe this is my punishment," Colleen faintly said.

Gordon turned to look at her, and felt a twist in his gut when he saw the unshed tears glistening in her eyes; however, he resisted the urge to go to her and hold her until the tears went away. *"Why do I feel such an overwhelming need to protect this woman?"* Unable to answer the question, and not trusting her or himself he stood still.

"Maybe I have been 'the tease' one time too often, and now I can't control my own mind," Colleen's voice quavered. "I can't stay here with you, I can't go back, because I might lead Rayne to people who would die to keep me safe." Burying her face in her hands, she said, "The only thing I can think to do is to leave on my own, I need to lead him away."

"What the bloody Hell? You're not going anywhere," Gordon said, unequivocally, his voice growing louder with each word. "Don't be ridiculous! Why do you think you can't stay with me?"

"I can't control every fleeting thought I have, I'm making you miserable," Colleen said, her voice also rising, "not to mention that you have threatened me if it happens again."

Rubbing his temples, Gordon thought, *"She has to be the most exasperating woman I have ever met!"* to Colleen he said, "Distance doesn't stop the images. There is no point in taking a chance in separating." Going to her, Gordon pulled her from her seat, cupping her chin to tip her face up, he stared into her eyes, "Colleen, I promise you, I will not hurt you, or do anything you don't want me to do. I said that purely out of frustration." Searching her face, he asked, "Do you think you can trust me?"

"Yes," she breathed, in the same moment Gordon was hit with a replay of the images of the kisses they had shared. His eyes narrowed infinitesimally as her pupils dilated. Gordon was struggling to not react, he was, after all, trying to prove he was worthy of her trust. Kissing her on the forehead, he stepped back and told her that he was going into town to get their supplies.

Clearing his throat, he gruffly asked, "What do you want for dinner?"

Giving him a watery smile, she replied, "I want comfort food. Cheeseburgers and steak fries from that little diner over on Main Street."

"Done," Gordon agreed, thinking he could use a little comfort himself but wasn't likely to get any; certainly not with food. "If you go through to the library you will find plenty of books, movies, and music, I'm sure you will find something to your taste. But first, you need to come with me so I can show you how to reset the alarm after I leave."

After going through the steps twice, assuring himself that she had mastered the sequence, Gordon said, "I know it's not pleasant, but please keep the drapes closed, don't go outside, not even on the back deck, I shouldn't be gone too long, a couple of hours or less, okay?"

"I'm serious, Colleen," he said when she frowned at him for adding the deck to the list. "Promise me," he demanded. He watched as she waved him off and shrugged. Gordon didn't trust her dismissive attitude, attempting to lighten the mood, he said, "Don't make me tie you to a chair." But, if her scowl was an indicator, his attempt at any levity had failed miserably. Sighing, he quietly demanded, "Promise me."

Through her frown, and gritted teeth, she answered, "I promise."

With a nod, he said, "Thank you, I'll be back soon. We'll get this figured out, and things will go back to normal, whatever that is."

"**D**O THE HARDEST THING FIRST, RIGHT?" he asked himself, as he drove to the boutique. Gordon had always lived by the rule of, "Do the hardest thing first, then the rest is a piece of cake." Once inside, he went straight to the counter where a pretty young girl greeted him with a bright smile and the usual, "What can I do for you, sir?"

"I'm picking up an order that was made online this morning, cash-on-demand," he explained and handed over Colleen's itemized list.

The young clerk's eyes grew wide as she gushed, "Oh yes sir, we have it ready. Give me just a moment." She slipped behind a curtain that Gordon assumed led to a storage room. After a few minutes, she returned struggling to carry the numerous blue bags and boxes to the counter. "Someone has good taste."

Gordon flashed the girl a smile, and replied dryly, "Well if quantity equates taste, then, yes, I'm sure someone does." The silly girl just kept standing there with a goofy grin on her face, "Ah, could you go ahead and ring it up, I'm in a hurry," Gordon said.

"Don't you want to check it first, and make sure everything is to your satisfaction?" She asked as she started to pull items from the first bag, starting with something filmy, a deep blue in color, and lacy.

Putting out his hand to halt her, "Is it customary for this establishment to make mistakes?" Gordon asked.

With wide eyes and bewilderment, the girl gushed, "Of course not sir."

"Then, I'm sure everything is fine, could you just ring it up please," he requested, yet once again.

For the first time, Gordon used a card that Joseph had insisted he acquire, telling him, "You just never know." A black card with the alias, Jackson Greer.

Gordon quickly made his other stops, striding through the local market, loading up on perishables, and then stopping at the diner for their burgers. He had furtively surveyed every location looking for anyone that might be watching him. He was anxious to get home; he was anxious to get back to Colleen.

"I'm back," Gordon announced as he came through the garage entrance. Not hearing anything he moved into the living area, "Colleen?" he called. When she didn't answer, Gordon felt a shaft of fear pulsate through his body. Moving quickly, he checked each room on the first floor, and then took the stairs two at a time to the second floor.

Opening the door to his bedroom he stopped short, and blew out the breath he had been holding, she was curled up asleep in the middle of his bed, hugging his pillow. Quietly, he backed out of the room and closed the door softly. Once back downstairs he unloaded his purchases, putting the food away, their dinner in the warmer, and made two trips carrying Colleen's 'new wardrobe' to his bedroom. She didn't wake on his first trip, but, stirred when he came in for the second time with the last of the packages.

"Oh," she said, yawning, she sat up and glanced around the room. Gordon hid his smile as she quickly shoved his pillow back in place, "I must have fallen asleep; I came in to make the bed. I thought I would lie down, and just close my eyes for a few minutes, I didn't intend to nap."

"A nap is a good idea, the last twenty-four hours have been rather trying," he stated, then asked, "Feel better? Hungry?"

"I do feel better," she smiled, then bouncing off of the bed, she declared, "and, I'm starving." Looking at the pile of pale blue bags and boxes, each with the store's logo stamped in silver, she said, "Thank you, I'll take care of all this later."

Gordon thought Colleen might think him overly presumptuous for taking her new clothing to his bedroom, but, since she wouldn't stay in the room downstairs last night, and he had once again found her on his bed this evening, he took the chance. Actually, he would feel better about being able to protect her if she stayed near him. Gordon nearly laughed aloud, at his attempt to make up an altruistic motive for what he wanted, *"No matter how uncomfortable it makes me I still want her in my bed, it's that simple, and given our current circumstances that complicated,"* he thought. Gordon decided it would be best not to say anything, one way or the other, *"just let her take the lead, I can take her things back down if she wants."*

Once they were both downstairs, Gordon, flipped a switch and music filled every room. Colleen tipped her head listening for a moment, and then wrinkled her nose at his choice as she went ahead to the kitchen.

"Not a fan of Bach's?" Gordon asked.

"Too intense for my mood tonight," Colleen replied.

"What would you prefer then?"

"My parents raised me on 70's music," Colleen laughed, "I especially like to listen to it when I'm working in the kitchen. My mam and da would sing along when they were both in the kitchen." Gordon watched her face turn dreamy as she remembered, "Sometimes they would dance, and da would pick me up, spin with me while in his arms, and set me on the counter to watch while they worked together preparing a meal." Smiling at Gordon, she said, "I think I know every word of every 70's love song."

"Then, by all means, let the 70's play again," Gordon said, as he changed the playlist. They both started for the kitchen just when Gordon Lightfoot's haunting voice filled the air singing *If You Could Read My Mind*. Colleen looked with surprise at Gordon who shrugged and said, "Don't look at me, I just changed the playlist. Do you want me to find something else?"

Colleen laughed and grabbed Gordon's hand to pull him along. Together they fixed a salad, set the table, and carried their comfort food to the dining area, and talked about their childhoods as they ate. Colleen regaled Gordon with stories of herself as a little girl with her mam and da, as she called them. Gordon could nearly see the love they had for each other and their child, in Colleen's animated face. When she told Gordon it was his turn, he tried to leave his family out as much as possible.

He told her of his first time out to sea, he couldn't remember his age exactly but he was very small, and the enormity of the sea made him feel smaller still. He could remember the panic he felt when he had watched the land disappear as the ship made for open waters. But his father had picked him up, put him on his shoulders so that he could see that the land was still there, it wasn't moving, they were. He had then turned, facing seaward, telling him the ship and the water had become one now, and that he would teach Gordon the secrets of this great lady.

Gordon grew quiet, furrowing his brow as he remembered the trust he felt as a child, only to have that trust crushed as a young man. When Gordon lifted his stormy eyes to Colleen, she sucked in her breath, and immediately reached across the small space to cover his hand with hers, "This is what I felt the day you left," Colleen said, searching his face, "It's your father that is causing your pain, isn't it?

Gordon gave Colleen a tight joyless smile, and said, "My relationship with my father is strained to put it mildly." Gordon checked the time, and not wanting to dwell on his familial problems said, "Excuse me, I need to catch Andrew, before his dinner meeting to make sure he doesn't lose his temper with Mr. Johnathon Durham, and by extension our account."

Colleen tipped her head to the side as she scrutinized Gordon's face, "Gordon do you want me to make the pain---"

Cutting her off, Gordon said, sternly, "No, I do not." Seeing the hurt on her face, he softened his tone, "Thanks for the offer, but I have been living with this for a long time." He abruptly stood, and said, "I will be in the library, do you want anything from that room? A movie? A book?"

Shaking her head, Colleen replied, "No, not now thank you. I will clean this up," she said, making a sweeping motion over the dinner table, "and I need to go through all of those bags upstairs."

"Interesting," Gordon thought, as he retreated to the library, *"she didn't say anything about bringing them downstairs."* Sitting at his desk, he tried to quell the jumble of emotions he was currently experiencing. Thinking or talking about his father always brought up the same old hurt and anger that he had been dealing with since his twentieth birthday. Thinking of Colleen brought on a myriad of different emotions; fear for her life from Rayne, wanting her, trusting her, not trusting her, it was too much to think about right now. He could hear her puttering in the kitchen, and he thought about the pleasant evening they had shared. *"She really does have a very pleasing voice,"* Gordon mused, and he remembered the photograph he had bought of her with a microphone in her hand.

Brought out of his reverie abruptly by his ringtone, Gordon heaved a heavy sigh, before answering, "Andrew, I was just about to call you."

"Yeah, I knew you would call at some point," Andrew said, "I wanted to catch you before my dinner engagement and to let you know that Mr. Durham came by the office unexpectedly this afternoon; however, we worked everything out."

"Just how did you work everything out?" Gordon asked uneasily.

Andrew chuckled, "The old-fashioned way, I did a lot of ass-kissing, that's how. Long story short, we're back in the Durham

Corporation's good graces, and I will be taking John out to dinner in about an hour."

Gordon laughed, relieved that Andrew had not resorted to one his unique talents to close the deal, "So it's 'John' is it?"

Andrew replied, "Yes, I'm good at kissing ass when necessary," he said with a smug laugh, "I may have found a new calling."

All at once, Gordon's mind was bombarded with Colleen in an array of slinky, filmy, lacy clothing. The images were moving so fast, it nearly took his breath away. It was like looking through one of those old flip-books.

"Whoa!" Andrew breathed into the phone. "Can you run through that again, only a little slower this time?" he asked.

"Damn! Andrew had picked that up, she must be unpacking the new clothes," Gordon thought. He couldn't decide which bothered him more; that Andrew might guess that Colleen was here with him, or, that Andrew had been privy to seeing Colleen in a personal lingerie show that would rival a Victoria Secret runway.

"Gordon, you okay?" Andrew asked when Gordon didn't respond.

"Yeah, I'm okay, nothing out of the ordinary here, right?" Gordon decided to play it off as if it wasn't unusual.

"I thought the images were generally your memories," Andrew said, then he asked probing, "Have you seen her dressed like that?"

"Of course not," Gordon declared. It wasn't a lie; he hadn't physically seen her in such items. The two times he had seen her in sleeping clothes she had been forced to wear oversized tee-shirts. To Andrew, he said, "Who knows? Maybe it's wishful thinking?" Gordon hoped she would be done unpacking soon, but he needed to get off the phone before Andrew was treated to another show.

"If you say so Gordon if you say so," Andrew said. Gordon knew he didn't believe him, but he was willing to let it go for the moment. "Hey, speaking of Colleen, I wanted to let you know that Rayne has finally surfaced, and he is still in Boston, at least, he was as of...,"

Andrew paused, and Gordon could hear him shuffling papers, "as of exactly three hours ago."

"Thanks, Andrew," Gordon responded, "I appreciate the update." Still concerned with getting him off the phone, he asked, "Umm, do I need to let you go, your dinner... remember?"

"You're right, I need to call for the car," Andrew replied, "But before I go, tell me what's on your agenda for tonight?"

"Oh, I don't know. I might stay in," Gordon answered, to which he could hear Andrew tsking; wanting to break the connection with Andrew he said the first thing that popped into his mind, "or, maybe go to the tavern for a while, they're having a dart tournament,"

"Just don't forget my suggestion, cousin," Andrew reminded him.

"What suggestion?" Gordon asked, his attention being drawn to noises coming from the second floor.

Andrew laughed, "Find someone and get la--"

"Goodnight, Andrew," Gordon clicked the phone off before his cousin could finish verbalizing his thought.

Gordon had started up the stairs, as Colleen was coming down with one hand behind her back. "I thought I heard something fall. Are you all right?" Gordon asked.

"I'm fine, but you did hear something," Colleen said, mournfully, and held out the hand she had been hiding.

Gordon frowned, it looked like she was holding kindling. "What's that?" he asked.

"It's what's left of your boat. I knocked it off the table," Colleen said, so forlornly that Gordon wanted to laugh.

"Oh, Colleen, that's just a cheap little trinket that I had bought to give to Andrew as a joke," Gordon smiled, "I just forgot to give it to him, the last time I was here."

"Really? You're not just saying that so I won't feel bad?" Colleen asked.

"Really," Gordon replied, and took the sticks from her, "C'mon, we'll use it to start a fire in the fireplace. Why don't you go find a movie for us to watch?"

"Don't you think we should talk, Gordon?" Colleen asked, somberly, "I mean really talk? As appealing as it may sound, we can't hide out here forever."

"Of course, you're right," Gordon said, finding himself once again ridiculously pleased; this time that she found the idea of hiding out with him appealing. "By the way, did you find your new wardrobe to be to your satisfaction?"

Colleen gave him a quizzical look, as they moved into the living room, and said, "Yes, it was exactly what I ordered. Why?"

With an indifferent shrug of his shoulders, Gordon sat down, and said, "Just wondering if I would need to take anything back tomorrow."

Colleen sat across from him, tucking her legs under, "No, it's all fine."

Gordon nodded, and then asked, "So everything *fit?*"

Narrowing her eyes, Colleen studied him for a moment, then her eyes flew open wide, and she said, "Oh my God! You could see me thinking about what my clothes would look like when I put them on?" Her voice had risen an octave.

"Not exactly, but then Andrew--"

"Andrew? No! Andrew could see me too?" She asked her voice lowering, like the calm before the storm.

Turning his palms up in an innocent gesture, "I was on the phone with him," Gordon said by way of an explanation.

"What did he see?" Colleen asked, between gritted teeth, her voice still too calm.

"Judging from his reaction I'm assuming he saw the same thing I did," Gordon replied.

"Which was?" She asked tersely.

Clearing his throat, he answered, "A lot of satin, lace, and bare skin. They were moving so fast it was almost, but not quite, a blur."

Colleen jumped off of the couch and started pacing. Just as Gordon was about to say 'calm down,' she wheeled around, and said, "I have to talk to Audra, now, tonight."

Gordon started shaking his head no, and Colleen, still pacing, said, "Don't even try to talk me out of it. Either, I speak with her or I will bring her here."

With a warning in his voice, Gordon said, "Colleen, please don't fight me on this."

"You don't understand, I *need* to at least talk to Audra," Colleen said, imploringly, "you can listen in if you want, but she is the only one that can help me right now."

More out of curiosity than acquiesce, Gordon asked, "Who is Audra? And, why is she the *only* one that can help you?"

Throwing herself down into a chair, only to jump up again to resume her pacing, Colleen said, "Her name is Audra McMann, she is a very close friend. She might be able to help me to stop unwittingly project."

"If she is such a close friend to you, then her phone may be tapped. I won't take that chance with you," Gordon said firmly.

"Then she will just have to come here," Colleen replied coolly, "If you will excuse me," she said as she started to the bedroom.

"Where are you going?" Gordon demanded.

"I need a place without distractions," Colleen said, calmly, "and you are distracting me."

It suddenly dawned on Gordon that she was planning to contact her friend through projecting, "Colleen, don't do it," he warned, as he jumped up to follow her, having no idea how or if he could stop her, "if your friend is being watched you could put her in danger also."

"Trust me, no one catches Audra unless she wants to be caught," Colleen said, with an air of confidence, "and, even then, they will see only what she wants them to see."

"You don't understand men like Rayne, and what he is capable of doing," Gordon argued.

Colleen glared at Gordon, "He's a cleaner for the Fold, I know exactly what he is capable of doing!" she hissed, "I've seen the handiwork of the Abrogates up close."

Stunned, Gordon said roughly, "If you know about the Fold, and understand it, then you know I am a part of it. I have a station, a role in it also."

"But you don't want to be a part of the Fold," she stated calmly, "you don't play the role any more than absolutely necessary; even then, you're racked with guilt, and revulsion. The same cannot be said for your associates, including your cousin."

Gordon was speechless. *"Obviously, Colleen's knowledge of the Fold was far more extensive than I had realized, along with her knowledge of me."*

"Gordon, you're worried a phone might be tapped; I'm worried about my mind being tapped. If I don't have complete control over my projections, and apparently, I don't, that could be a direct link to Andrew," Colleen explained. "There is too much at stake, too many people that could be hurt. Gordon, I need help, I'm still relatively new to projecting. Please don't fight *me* about this," she added, turning his words back on him for the second time today. "Audra can come here and leave without anyone being the wiser."

Gordon was caught again vacillating between trusting and not trusting Colleen; between maintaining control or relinquishing a portion of it. His gut told him that she wouldn't purposefully put her friends or anyone else, for that matter, in danger.

Taking a deep breath, Gordon asked, "How can you definitively say that she will not be tracked?"

Colleen smiled at him, and said, "You wouldn't believe me if I told you, you will have to see for yourself. Gordon, you asked me to trust you earlier, and now I'm asking you to trust me."

Gordon, still apprehensive, studied Colleen's face, and finding no deception, curtly nodded his assent, and said, "Go do what you have to do."

"Wait till you see her, it will change how you view everyone you meet for the rest of your life; but I don't have to leave if you don't talk to me during the process," Colleen said. Gordon felt as if she was asking for him to stay; nodding he said, "Okay." Then asked, "Anything else?"

"Well, you were going to build a fire, a flame would help, a piece of paper, and a pen." Shifting her shoulders, and rolling her neck, she said, "and, I need to change into something more comfortable."

"Really? A fire, and slipping into something more comfortable?" Gordon asked drily, "Projecting sounds a lot like seduction," he said, bemused.

Colleen just gave him a little smile, then lightly ran up the stairs.

17

GORDON, SOFTLY WHISTLED APPRECIATIVELY, AS COLLEEN came back into the living room, barefooted, and wearing a dark green dressing gown. "Pretty," he remarked.

Rolling her eyes, at his overt display, she said, "I take it you have already seen this little number."

"And, then some," Gordon said, under his breath.

"What was that?" Colleen asked, narrowing her eyes and frowning.

"Nothing important," Gordon replied, looking around the room, he asked, "Is everything the way you want it?"

"Yes, almost," she replied, still frowning a bit at his muttering. Finally, with a small shrug, she said, "I just need to write the note." Gordon stood behind the couch looking over her shoulder as she wrote the words, 'PRIVATE-INCOGNITO' in bold letters and added the Getaway's street address underneath. Glancing back at him, she patted the cushion next to her, and said, "I think it would be best to show Audra that I am with you willingly and that I'm perfectly safe."

Gordon came around the end of the couch, sat down next to her, and she immediately took his hand. "It will be easier if I'm touching you," Colleen said, "I will project the note first, then the two of us. I will need to let her channel my emotions a bit, and that will sap a lot of my energy," Gordon frowned at this; and she quickly said, "She will need to know that I'm not being coerced."

"Okay, I'm ready," Colleen said, as she lightly touched his lips with her index finger, and said, "Sh-h-h." Gordon nodded, as she turned to stare into the fire. Within minutes, she went completely still; Gordon could barely discern her breathing. Slowly, stiltedly Colleen turned to look at the note she had written, and just as slowly with the same posture she turned until she was facing him, her eyes boring into his.

Her grasp on his hand tightened hard, and as he stared into her eyes, he felt as if some inner part of himself was being pulled toward her. As he was drawn closer, he felt a tremor run through his body, and an image of his own face swam before him, then images of him kissing Colleen yesterday, and again last night. But the images were confusing, backward. He wasn't seeing her, he saw himself; after what felt like an eternity, he realized the images were from her memories of the kisses, from her perspective.

About the time Gordon didn't think he could take much more, Colleen's hand relaxed, and she slumped back on the couch, her eyes were closed, her breathing shallow, and her face was covered in a sheen of perspiration. Gordon gently touched her face, her skin felt cold and clammy. He jumped up and ran to the bathroom to get a damp washcloth. Striding back across the living room, he sat beside her, pulled her across his lap, and cradled her as he wiped her face.

"Colleen, Colleen," he called her name, trying to get her to come around. He was beginning to get a little panicky, she hadn't said this would happen, but then, she didn't say what would happen. "C'mon, Colleen wake up." Just when he began to wonder if he should call an ambulance, she stirred and groaned softly. Feeling a rush of relief, Gordon asked, "Are you all right?"

"Hmmm," she moaned.

"What do you need? Do you want me to carry you to bed?"

Gordon asked. Her coloring was coming back, and her breathing was returning to normal; but he was still concerned.

Drawing a deep breath, she opened her eyes, and looked back at him, "Is getting me in your bed all you ever think about?"

Gordon gave a throaty chuckle of relief, and asked, "Do you want the truth?"

Closing her eyes, she smiled, "Maybe not right now. Right now, I feel like I could sleep for a week."

"Then you do need to go to bed," Gordon said, standing he turned and picked her up cradling her against his chest.

Rousing herself, she said, "Put me down, you can't carry me up the stairs. I can walk."

Gordon stopped, he had intended to carry her to the downstairs bedroom, "*...but hey, if she wants to share my bed again, who am I to say no?*"

Gordon carried her to the foot of the stairs and gently stood her up, and when she started to wobble, he put his arms around her and half carried her up to his room. After guiding her to a chair, he went over to the bed to pull back the covers, then picked her up again, took her to the bed, and laid her down.

Gordon pulled the covers over her, and was about to leave, thinking he could use a drink, and some time to process everything that had happened, but then she sighed, and said, "Don't leave me."

He leaned down close, and whispered, "I'm right here."

"Hold me," she softly demanded. Gordon groaned.

"Woman you're driving me crazy," Gordon mumbled, mostly to himself, as he pulled his clothes off, and climbed in to lay beside her. She threw her arm across his chest, and promptly, fell into a deep sleep, as Gordon starred unseeingly at the ceiling for a few hours, before drifting off into a restless sleep.

For the second morning in a row, Gordon woke to find himself alone in the king-sized bed, and to the smell of bacon, and coffee. Dragging himself up, he headed for the shower, needing to feel the sharp spray of water to wash away the remnants of an extraordinarily restless and frustrating night.

Showered, shaved, and dressed, Gordon headed straight for the kitchen, and the coffee. There he paused in the doorway to take in the somewhat domesticated scene of Colleen moving about the room, loading the dishwasher, wiping the counter, and stove, while singing softly. Her hair was down loose, she was dressed in tight-fitting jeans, and a flowing blouse. As if she felt his presence, she suddenly turned, flashed him a dazzling smile, and said, "Good morning."

"Mm," was the only greeting Gordon could manage at the moment. He had suspected it yesterday, and now was positive, *"...she is one of those...a morning person."*

Colleen laughed lightheartedly, and asked, "Need some time to greet your day?"

"Coffee," Gordon grumbled.

Pointing to one of the bar-stools, she ordered, "Sit, I will be your waitress this morning." She placed a coffee mug in front of him and poured it full to the brim. She then pulled a plate heaped with scrambled eggs, bacon, and toast from the warming oven, and set that in front of him. "You eat, I need to run upstairs."

As she was leaving, Gordon caught her hand, and said, "Thank you for breakfast."

Leaning over she smiled, and kissed Gordon's cheek, "Thank you for taking care of me last night."

Gordon was just about to settle into the living room with his second cup of coffee when the doorbell rang. Puzzled at who would be at his door at this early hour, he glanced at the video feed. *"Lost repairman,"* Gordon thought when he saw the white van printed with **Mike's Electrical** on the side panel, and a middle-aged, balding guy standing on the porch. Opening the door, he asked, "Can I help you?" At the same time, Colleen came bounding down the stairs, went past him, and grabbed the guy at the door, exclaiming, "You're here, come in."

Gordon feeling completely befuddled, closed the door and turned to look at Colleen, ready to ask if she had called an electrician. His jaw nearly hit the floor, there next to Colleen was an absolutely stunning woman, with a long dark braid over her shoulder, wide, almond-shaped eyes the color of night, and the kind of creamy dark skin that made it difficult to discern her age. The classic Native American planes of her face begged to be immortalized on a master's canvas.

Colleen stood next to her with a superior look on her face, obviously enjoying Gordon's shock; *"...which must be written all over my face. I think I have truly fallen down the rabbit hole."* Gordon thought.

"Now you know why I couldn't explain. Honestly, would you have believed me?" Colleen asked, with delight. "Oh, where are my manners? Audra, this is Gordon Bilford the III," then turning to Gordon, she said, "Gordon, this is my friend, and my mentor, Audra McMann."

Trying desperately to find his equilibrium, Gordon stumbled over his words, "But, where-how--"

"Colleen, shame on you," the woman admonished, "did you tell him nothing of what to expect?"

Colleen shrugged, and Audra shook her head laughing indulgently, extending her hand to Gordon, she said, "I'm happy to finally meet you, Mr. Bilford."

Gordon shook Audra's hand, still having trouble pulling together a coherent sentence. He glanced back toward the video monitor half-expecting to see the balding middle-aged guy he had seen minutes before on the porch, but the only thing he saw was the white van.

"Oh, don't concern yourself about anyone tracking the van or its plates, it's actually a black Prius, and the plates are not the same, look again," Audra directed, Gordon.

When Gordon looked again, the front end of the van began to shimmer, it was as if it had become translucent, and he could see the front end of a Prius inside. Colleen came to his side, looking up she placed a finger under his chin, pushing his jaw shut, "In and out, no one the wiser," she said, smiling. Gordon looked again and saw a white van in his driveway.

"If we do not want to arouse suspicion from your neighbors we need to start immediately," Audra said, "I would assume that you don't want an electrician sitting in your drive all day. Colleen where did you sleep last night?"

It was now Colleen's turn to look surprised, Gordon smirked, and answered for her, "She slept upstairs."

With a knowing smile, Audra said, "Then that's where I need to start." With that she led the way up the stairs and without hesitation walked straight to his bedroom door.

"It's as if she knows the house," Gordon mused. "I will be in the library if you need me," he called.

Gordon busied himself at his desk, answering a few emails, placing a couple of calls to his managers, and one overseas call. The whole time he kept listening for them to come back down. With nervous agitation he started pacing, he was on his third trip around the room when an image, of he and Colleen, nearly knocked him to his knees. "What the Hell are they doing?" Gordon said aloud.

He quickly strode out of the library determined to demand they cease what they were doing when he met them both in the living room. Zeroing in on Colleen, Gordon asked, "Seriously?"

Ignoring Gordon, Colleen turned to Audra, "What am I going to do?" Colleen asked, "I can't control every fleeting thought I have, Gordon thinks I'm doing it on purpose, and he's a direct line to Andrew."

"Mr. Bilford, please accept my apologies. I needed to see how quickly the images transferred," Audra stated.

Gordon stared at the seer with disbelief, "You did that? It wasn't Colleen?"

"No, no. It was Colleen, but I led her to the...ah...the thought, although she added more than necessary," Audra explained and simultaneously chided Colleen. "She did not intend to send it out." Gordon gave her a look clearly meant to convey his disbelief. "Mr. Bilford, you saw Colleen last night, you took care of her. If she had purposefully projected that image you just experienced, do you think she would be standing here now?"

Gordon threw his hands up, and said, "I really don't know what to think anymore. I don't know what is real and what isn't. The image I just saw has not happened, but it *felt* like a memory." Gordon moved to drop down on one of the couches. Addressing Audra, he asked, "Did you see that?" Audra nodded once, and with a groan, he said, "Well, after seeing that, I think we can agree to dispense with the formalities, please just call me Gordon."

With a smile, she said, "And you can call me Audra. I'm so sorry if you find this embarrassing, but if I am to help the two of you, there are certain things I need to know." Indicating the seat next to Gordon, she said, "Colleen, I need the two of you together." Although Colleen took the seat by Gordon, she wouldn't look at him. Audra, Gordon noticed, looked at them both with exasperation, and sank gracefully on the couch opposite of them. She closed her eyes and went very still for a few moments, reminding Gordon of what Colleen had done last night. Gordon looked to Colleen who put her finger up to her lips to indicate they needed to be quiet.

Finally, Audra opened her eyes and smiled at the two of them. Focusing on Gordon, she said, "First, Gordon, you need to understand that not only am I capable of illusion, but I am also what we, the Argents, call a seer; Colleen's people might call me a *Fili*'," she smiled warmly at Colleen.

"Audra," Colleen called her name in warning.

"He already knows we refer to ourselves as the Argents," Audra said, as she waved off Colleen's concern. Continuing her explanation, Audra said, "Although I am privy to the future, my concentration is more in the past. My powers of observation are strong; I don't miss much."

Gordon wasn't sure what he was supposed to do with this

revelation, but he had a very uncomfortable feeling he was about to find out. Deciding to gather as much information as possible in the meantime, he asked, "Why the past? Why not the future."

Smiling, Audra replied, "Our past events and experiences, molds the events and experiences we create today." Drawing a deep breath, she continued, "I need to understand your past to understand the cause of your current circumstances," she explained, waving her hand between Gordon and Colleen, "I needed to see your combined past."

"And, did you find what you were looking for?" Gordon asked cynically.

"Gordon, don't be rude," Colleen said reprovingly.

Gordon was about to tell her he didn't care for being used as part of their experiment, when Audra said, "You both need to calm down and quit sniping at one another, there is a solution." Having gained their attention, she warned, "However, given at what I'm witnessing right now; it will not be easy."

Wearily, Gordon said, "I'm sorry, what do you propose we do?"

"You will have to open up and be honest with each other," Audra replied.

"Honesty?" Colleen frowned, "We have been honest with each other. I have admitted to Gordon that I am attracted to him, and he has made it quite clear that he is attracted to me."

Audra laughed as she repeated, "Attracted? Child, you are both way past attracted." Shaking her head, she said, "Attraction, desire, or lust, doesn't begin to describe the depth of your feelings for one another. I can't see either of you without seeing the other."

Audra once again smiled, and said, "I can set you both on the path, but you will have to work on it from there. You each must have complete trust in the other."

"And how would you go about setting us upon this path?" Gordon asked, curious despite his skepticism.

Audra replied, "I very much doubt that either of you will like it, but I'm going to start by filling in a few blanks for each of you.

And, Gordon before I say anything, remember that I would not be able to read you so easily if you didn't want me to know." Drawing in a deep breath, she focused on Colleen and asked, "For instance, Colleen did you know that Gordon has been protecting you from the first time that you met?"

Colleen, frowned, "No, I don't know what you mean. I'm pretty sure I have been taking care of myself."

"Stop," Gordon demanded, leaning forward.

Ignoring Gordon's directive, Audra kept talking, "He actually thought about making you a tribute on the night you met." Audra said calmly.

Colleen gasped, and Gordon went rigid.

"However, by the next day, *when* he had sobered up, he changed his mind." Continuing, Audra said, "He has been trying to protect you from himself and the Fold, which, is the reason he keeps running; and he has succeeded in protecting you from his cousin, Andrew, on at least two occasions."

Quickly switching her focus to Gordon, she said, "And, Gordon, did you know that Colleen has been protecting you since the two of you first met? Her job was to get to Terese; if that wasn't possible, she was to lure you in, then, turn you over to the Arcs. But then she met you," Audra paused, looking into Gordon's eyes, she held him there for a beat, "and, she has been standing between you and the Arcs for weeks now." Audra sat quietly, to let them each absorb what she had just told them.

Gordon starring past Audra now was the first to break the silence, "Okay, I will admit after giving it some thought, I didn't want any harm to come to Colleen; neither, from Andrew nor me. I respect and care about Shaun and Fran, so I tried to keep my distance. But, apparently" Gordon turned to look at Colleen, "she was bound to '*lure me in*'?"

Shaking her head, Audra interjected, "No, she could have done that on the night of the party. But, she didn't. Let me rephrase; she wouldn't."

"I've explained this before," Colleen huffed, "I felt--"

"Oh, let me," Audra cut in, holding up her hands, "I've heard it so many times, I have it committed to memory. And, I quote: "I know he can be turned; I saw something in his eyes; I felt the light in him." Turning to Gordon, she said, "So you see, if Colleen were merely doing her job, we would not be having this conversation today, because you would have been *bound* that night." Audra paused, watching Gordon closely, "She has even convinced the Arcs to give her more time. Well, except for Jerad, he doesn't trust you with her." Sharing an amused look with Colleen, Audra said, "Of course, Jerad, doesn't want her around any man."

"Who is Jerad?" Gordon asked, through clenched teeth.

"Calm yourself," Audra chided, "Jerad Evan is a happily married man to his Molly, and he has always been like an uncle to Colleen. However, he is also an Arc; he would find revenge on anyone that would cause her harm," she cautioned.

Gordon laid his head back on the couch and closed his eyes; he spent the next few minutes trying desperately to sort through the new information and make it fit into what he already knew. Plus, his emotional state was...but he pushed that thought away, *"I can't even think about what I'm feeling right now,"* he thought, *"not when I can't trust what I see."* Gordon fixed his gaze on Audra, "Okay, if it isn't just an attraction, a desire, then what? Why?" he asked.

"Your souls," Audra replied, calmly, quietly, "Your souls recognized one another the night of the party, but your minds, your emotions have not had time to catch-up; you are steadfastly intertwined. Honestly, I could count on one hand the times I have seen this before." Looking to Colleen, she said, "Your parents for one."

Without hesitation, or forethought, Gordon automatically reached for Colleen's hand at the mention of her parents, and she grasped his hand like a lifeline. He could see the glimmer of tears that suddenly filled her eyes; he wanted to hold her but refrained.

Smiling indulgently at the two of them, Audra went on, "What

I haven't ever seen, and this is the tricky part; is this kind of soul-mating between an Argent and a member of the Fold."

"So, this 'soul-mating' is what you think is causing Colleen to project without trying?" Gordon asked.

"Yes." Audra smiled widely as if everything was crystal clear. Gordon and Colleen exchanged looks of bewilderment; so, she went on, "On a subconscious level you are both reaching out to one another since you will not allow yourselves to so otherwise," Audra said pointedly.

"There is the part of Colleen that reaches out to you through her most private thoughts, and there is the part of you that is eager to receive her. It is the most basic level between two people in a relationship filled with the complex intricacies as what exists between the two of you." Audra explained with the patience of a teacher, instructing her students step-by-step through a new process. "From what I have seen the images are projected," she nodded at Colleen, "and received," gesturing to Gordon, "during times of high or intense emotion; anger, desire, jealousy, fear of one another, and fear for one another. Your physical desire for one another is the one place that you will allow yourselves to agree upon."

"So, if I understand you correctly," Gordon said dryly, "all we need to do is stop fighting, have an affair, and the images will stop."

Audra startled them both by laughing out loud, "Oh, Gordon, you're such a man!" She exclaimed. "Sex is not the answer to all problems. In fact, my advice is for the two of you to refrain from that particular activity until you can connect honestly on different levels. I realize that comes as a great disappointment for both of you."

"Audra," Colleen admonished.

The seer merely shrugged, and said with a twinkle, "Oh please Colleen you are far from the innocent in this scenario. You have done nearly everything within your power to keep him chasing after you."

Gordon gave Colleen a smirk. Watching this bit of by-play, Audra pinned Gordon with a look saying, "And, Gordon you have been more than happy to answer her siren's call. Seeking any excuse to keep her at your side," Audra added.

Gordon not accustomed to being called out frowned and narrowed his eyes at Audra ready to argue with her.

Audra challenged him as she taunted, "Go ahead, Gordon, tell me I'm lying."

Dark eyes clashed, but Gordon knew when to call it; she wasn't lying. Resting his head on the back of the couch again, he rubbed at his temples and said, "I don't know what you want."

"I want you both to stop acting like children," Audra replied "It comes down to this; learning to trust each other, and that starts with honesty. Learn about one another, talk, listen, spend time knowing each other. It's that simple, and it's that complicated." Audra sighed heavily, "I don't know, you both have lived dancing around the truth for so long, protecting your ways of life, I'm not sure either of you is cognitive of how to be completely honest with another human being. It will be a lot of work, but you must do this for yourselves, and each other." After studying each of them for a few moments, she leaned back into the cushions closing her eyes, "The two of you have exhausted me."

With a bark of laughter, Gordon said, "I can relate to that." After a moment, he said, "Audra, you're welcome to stay here, if you want," he noticed that his offer seemed to surprise her and Colleen, so he added, "Honestly, I think we can use the guidance," glancing at Colleen he quickly added, "or at least I know I can. Of course, considering who I am, what I am, I understand if that's not agreeable to you."

Colleen jumped up from her seat and went to sit by Audra, who had laid her head back and closed her eyes again, "Oh Audra that would be great, you can share my room, there are two master suites upstairs," Colleen enthused.

Gordon gave Colleen a quizzical look, at which she shook

her head, willing him not to say anything about their sleeping arrangements.

Without moving, Audra replied, "Colleen, I consider myself a very liberal person, but there are certain areas where I draw the line. I'm not sleeping with you and Gordon." Gordon tried to hide his laughter, as Colleen made a small gasp.

Audra opened her eyes, looked at Colleen, and said, "When I asked you to show me the image of your and Gordon's last kiss, it appeared that you were purposefully keeping the field very narrow. I was curious as to where it took place, so I widened the field. You have managed to put yourself in his bed for the last two nights, and you," she said, looking at Gordon, "did not make her leave. Despite, your...um...shall we say, frustration? You were willing to spend the nights in extreme physical discomfort just to keep her by your side."

Colleen dipped her head letting her hair fall around her face to hide her embarrassment, and Gordon just lifted his shoulders in a small shrug to indicate he wouldn't argue with her summation.

"I intended to take a room in town for a few days to keep an eye on you two; no one is expecting me back right away. So, I will accept your gracious offer," Audra said, inclining her head toward Gordon; gazing fondly at Colleen, she continued, "and I will stay in the downstairs bedroom, alone."

Standing to wander around the room, she said, "I need to think this through for a minute, it will take a bit of maneuvering," Audra said, lost in thought, "I will need to leave here in the van in case I'm being watched, but, I will need to switch it, and myself, at some point, so I can return. Oh, I know, I believe I remember seeing a drive-thru car wash a mile or so before the city limits." Giving Colleen a wink, she said, "I think I will go wash the van off; the next time you see me, I will be a male business associate in a silver Lexus. May I park in your garage? It will take less concentration to maintain the illusion if it's as close as possible."

"Yes of course," Gordon agreed, "I'll get the spare remote for you,"

DONNA PFANNENSTIEL

When Gordon returned, the balding, middle-aged electrician was standing at the door. Gordon held out the remote, the technician pocketed it, looked at each of them respectively, and said, "While I'm gone, you two might want to reset your breakers, wouldn't due to overload the circuits." With that cryptic bit of advice, Mike headed out to his van.

"WHAT DO YOU SUPPOSE THAT MEANT?" Gordon asked Colleen, as they both watched Mike the electrician, drive away. "I think, she meant we might need to take this time to think and sort things out in our own minds, separately, before we try to work through this together," she replied. "But, Gordon," Colleen laid her hand on his arm, "first, I want to thank you for asking Audra to stay here."

"I thought it would make you happy," he said, quietly. Clearing his throat, he said, "Besides, I think I like her. She certainly doesn't pull any punches, does she?"

"No, she doesn't," Colleen laughed. "She's all about the honesty; whether you want to hear it or not."

"She's right about one thing," Gordon said, as he rubbed the back of his neck. "Out of a forced duty to protect the Fold, I have lived the lies for a long time. It will be difficult to let that go." Gazing intently at Colleen, he stepped closer to her, wrapped his arms around her waist, and pulled her up against him. Starring into her eyes, and seeing no fear there, he lowered his head and kissed her as he had before, thoroughly.

When he let her go, she turned wide green eyes on him and whispered, "What are you doing?"

"We're supposed to practice honesty? And honestly, I wanted

to kiss you, and you didn't seem averse to it, so I did," he answered. With a wink, Gordon added, "It will give you a new image," smiling, he headed for the library, leaving her in the foyer to stare after him.

Once in the library, Gordon poured himself a stiff drink he didn't really want; but he had a habit of sorting out his thoughts while swirling the liquor around the glass and watching the amber liquid create a vortex. *"And, by everything in heaven, on earth, and in Hell; I have a lot to sort through,"* Gordon thought.

When his phone sounded, Gordon checked the ID to see Joseph's number. He was tempted to let it go to voicemail, but he needed to behave as normal as possible, "Joseph, good to hear from you," Gordon said answering the phone.

"Really? I've been receiving some confusion on my end." Joseph replied.

"Oh yeah? Tell me," Gordon invited.

"What? No anger that I'm tapping in on you once in a while," Joseph asked, sounding surprised.

"Not today," Gordon replied with a chuckle. "Besides, I have so many people *tapping in on me* you're the least of my worries."

"Excellent sir," Joseph said, not bothering to ask for an explaination, "But I did want to let you know that Rayne has headed south, Andrew's people have tracked him to Florida."

"As long as he stays away, I'm good," Gordon said. "Thanks for letting me know Joseph."

"Before you go, there is one more thing I wanted to talk to you about," Joseph said, somberly.

"I'm listening," Gordon said, thinking he really needed to go before Colleen came bounding into the room, or sent him another image. *"I wonder if Joseph has seen any of it,"* Gordon brooded.

"You know that I have been with the Bilford family for...uh," Joseph hesitated, then continued, "well, without putting too fine a point on it, let's just say, for many years. I have always been loyal to the family, primarily to your father; but then you came along. I've been by your side since you came into this world, and Gordon you have always been, like what I imagine it would be to have a son. I want you to know that my loyalty now lies wholly with you. No matter what you chose in life, I will support you, and I will stand by your side."

Gordon sat forward in his chair; Joseph now 'wholly' had his attention. "Joseph, why are you telling me this? Why now?"

"Just a few new insights which have been revealed to me recently," Joseph responded, with astonishing candor, "and I believe you have some difficult decisions to make in the near future. Just remember what I said Gordon, whatever you choose, I will support." Then, with a note of conviction in his voice that took Gordon by surprise, Joseph added, "No matter the outcome."

"Thank you, Joseph," Gordon replied, feeling like he had slipped into yet another tunnel from down the rabbit hole. This conversation with Joseph nearly as confusing as meeting the incredible Audra McMann.

"I believe I should let you go now," Joseph said. "It wouldn't do to have too much revealed to me at once."

With that mystifying remark, Joseph, hung up so quickly that Gordon didn't have time to say goodbye. *"Well that was odd,"* Gordon thought, *"he sounded as if he was trying to keep from laughing."* Within, the same moment, Gordon's senses were filled with an onslaught of images starting with the first night he and Colleen had met at the party. Some he recognized, her face, the kisses, the lace, and a few more. Others, he didn't recognize, *"they must be fantasies,"* he thought. Then one projection, in particular, struck him like a thunderbolt. Rather than a single image, it flashed through his mind as a series of photos; but they were moving so quickly, he had the sensation of watching an old movie, one where the scenes jerked from one frame to the next. He and Colleen in bed, touching, kissing, caressing…; *"She is driving me out of my mind,"* Gordon thought as he tried to concentrate on something else, anything else, but the projection was too strong. When they started changing positions in the bed, Gordon could take no more,

"Colleen!" he bellowed. Within seconds he heard a yelp and the crash of pottery breaking.

Leaping to his feet, Gordon took great strides leaving the library in search of the source of the noise. He found Colleen picking up shards of a large platter from the kitchen tiles. Looking up at him, she scowled, "What are you yelling about? You scared me half to death, and I dropped the platter."

"Stop, you'll cut yourself," Gordon said gruffly, the projections had ceased altogether. He went to a pantry closet, pulled out a broom and dustpan; and began to sweep the pieces together.

Adopting her usual stance with her hands on her hips, Colleen watched him sweep the broken platter onto to the dustpan, "Why did you yell at me like that, is something wrong?" she asked with a peevish tone.

Dumping the remains of the platter into the trash bin, Gordon stared at Colleen in disbelief, "You just ran, what amounts to, a pornographic video starring the two of us through my head, and you want to know if something is wrong?"

"I did not...I...O ooh!" Colleen twirled toward the door and stomped out of the kitchen.

"I can't stand this," Colleen said, from the couch. She had pulled her feet up and put her head on her knees. "I can't take not being able to have a thought of my own, without you seeing it. It's beyond embarrassing."

"I understand, you know," Gordon had followed her in and sat beside her. "Andrew has been in my head since we turned twenty." When she didn't respond, he continued, "As for embarrassing? You must know that I have the same thoughts about you. You just don't see them." Still no response, he decided to try one more time, "And, I must admit I was quite intrigued by that last move, I'm not sure it's possible, but your creativity is---"

Colleen's head snapped up, "Oh my God." she exclaimed, cutting him off before he could finish the sentence.

Gordon laughed, "Finally, a reaction, I thought you might be planning on feeling sorry for yourself the rest of the day."

Colleen grabbed a throw pillow and hit him with it.

"Uh-hum," They both turned to see Audra coming in from the garage. "Can't I leave you two alone at all?"

Glaring at him, Colleen primly stated, "Gordon was behaving quite rudely."

"Only because," Gordon rejoined, his eyes twinkling with humor, "Colleen is being naughty again."

"What have I gotten myself into?" Audra muttered as she crossed the room, to sit opposite of them. "Both of you need to get your minds out of the bedroom."

"Talk to her," Gordon said, pointing to Colleen.

Narrowing her eyes at Gordon, Colleen said, "Tell him to stop kissing me whenever he feels the urge."

"Good grief, this must be a match made in heaven, or maybe hell, you're both four!" Audra scolded. "You two have to pull it together, something is brewing," she warned. When they each started questioning her at the same time, she held up her hands to stop them, "Don't ask, I don't know. It's a feeling, a premonition, a shift; I can't identify it yet."

"The last time I felt a shift was when I came back from Switzerland, and Colleen was at the manor," Gordon said, quietly, all traces of humor erased as he remembered his reason for being on the trip in the first place.

Colleen laid her hand on his arm, "That's going to be okay, Gordon," she said, earnestly.

"How is what I did to Terese ever going to be okay?" Gordon asked, anguish coloring his voice.

Audra frowned at Colleen and said, "This isn't the time for that discussion." Focusing on Gordon, she asked, "Is there anyone, anyone at all, from the Fold that you can trust? Anyone that you can talk to openly?"

Contemplating her question, Gordon said, "You know I took

a rather odd call from Joseph this afternoon. He spoke of recent insights that he had received, and he made of point of telling me twice that his loyalty now lay with me. He said, and I quote, *"I want you to know that my loyalty now lies wholly with you. No matter what you chose in life, I will support you, and I will stand by your side."* I had no idea what he meant, and when I asked, he said something about a need for me to make choices in the near future.

"I think I would like to meet Joseph. Can you trust him?" Audra asked.

"If not Joseph, then there is no one," Gordon responded. "My father made it clear to me a long time ago that if I tried to leave the Fold, both Andrew and I, would be killed shortly thereafter. We were told that our lives are tied together, literally dependent upon each other."

Colleen gasped, but Gordon noticed that Audra didn't appear to be particularly surprised. Gordon continued, "Andrew embraced the Fold immediately, I did not. In the beginning, I was in denial; then when I fought against it, my father told me that Andrew's life depended on me. We were raised as brothers, I had to protect him."

Once Gordon had opened the floodgates, he couldn't close them; he felt an uncontrollable need to confess it all. He didn't know if the two women were compelling him or not, but he no longer cared. "I met Jeanette, and married her, even though I didn't particularly like her, but I was young and rebellious, she was a little older than I and sexually very exciting. However, I soon learned that she was one of those overly-privileged people that believed the world was hers for the taking due to her wealth and beauty. And, in her selfishness to get what she wanted, Jeanette didn't care what method she used, nor whom she hurt." With a bitter laugh, Gordon continued, "Actually, she would have been a perfect addition to the Fold. Even with my growing disdain for her, I waited, seeking a way out. I still fought against what I knew I would have to do eventually, make her my confirmation tribute."

Gordon leaned forward, propping his elbows on his knees, his forehead in his slightly trembling hands. "Then, I met Terese. Such a lovely young woman, so kind, so loving, she saw the good in everyone; she was the complete opposite of Jeanette. Although I was never *in* love with Terese, she was easy to love, and I could pretend at a normal life with the knowledge that it would be years before it would be absolutely necessary to bring another tribute as long as I continued to bring in new members. Terese was so easy to please, never demanding; she made it easy for me to travel the world on using Bilford business, as an excuse, when in actuality the trips were to procure new recruits." Lifting his eyes to stare unseeingly at the floor, lost in the past, Gordon added, "I would not have become involved with Terese if I hadn't wholeheartedly believed I could find a way out of the Fold, long before another tribute was needed."

"Gordon, I have a question," Audra said.

"Ask, and I will decide whether or not to answer," Gordon said honestly.

"Why did it have to be your wives? Why couldn't it have been a stranger?" Audra asked.

Gordon sat for a moment trying to decide how much to give away, finally deciding to tell her the bare basics, he replied, his voice rough, "A relationship between member and tribute must be established, a name must be given, and a place prepared; once you start, there is no going back. Andrew has often chided me for 'marrying them.' But I can't do it his way, either." Stealing a glance at Colleen, he added, "I'm not cut out to be that player."

"The night of the Solstice party...," Gordon maintained eye contact with Colleen who nodded, "I was fairly sober when I first saw you, but by the end of the evening I was drunk. I'm not offering that as an excuse, but rather a statement of fact. I was crazy out of my mind with grief and anger. Although, I'm not sure whom I was grieving for more, Terese or myself." Staring off again, remembering, Gordon continued, "By the time I had sobered up the next day, I had thought better of the plans I had made for my neighbor's pretty redheaded niece, that I had met the night before; I had every intention of forgetting you altogether."

"I went through the next couple of days on auto-pilot. I said the things that needed saying, did the things that needed doing; I stayed in character; that of a husband concerned with his wife's health. While in Switzerland I spent much of my time on the mountain slopes," Gordon gave a short, derisive laugh, "I guess I was trying to outrun the demon inside. Then, I tried to drown it with a couple of bottles of bourbon, and I tried to satisfy it with…," Gordon came out of his reverie enough to remember who was in the room with him, "well let's put it this way, nothing worked."

Drawing a deep breath, he looked into Colleen's eyes and said, "I came back to Bilford, and of all things, there you were in my house planning my wife's memorial. I saw you, and suddenly, there was a shift in my entire universe; I became acutely aware of you; drawn to you. I immediately became consumed with the idea of simply taking you; that would have made my father proud," Gordon laughed bitterly. With a penitent smile, he continued, "It's the reason I ran to Boston and stayed away until the day before the memorial. I knew I would blow my carefully contrived role of grieving husband." Dropping his gaze, he continued, "Then, on the day of the memorial I found you on my balcony with Andrew, and I warned him off," Gordon paused here, and took a deep breath. He continued saying, "Which in our world, was my way of laying claim to you, to make the choice with your life." Gordon watched Colleen's eyes widen in shock, then narrow in anger as he spoke of Andrew. "I knew exactly what Andrew would do to you, and I couldn't allow that. My need to protect you overwhelmed my wants. So, I laid claim, and I thought it would just be a simple matter of waiting you out. I presumed that eventually, you would go home. In the meantime, I would avoid you, keeping you safe from Andrew."

"Except, I didn't go away," Colleen mused. "I moved in with my Aunt and Uncle."

"Not only did you not go away, but you also followed me. Not only did you follow me, but your constant sexual innuendos almost made me forget my promise to myself to leave you alone," Gordon took note of the flush that highlighted her cheeks. Suddenly gripped by the horror of another thought, Gordon asked, "How much do Shaun and Fran know about all of this?" When Colleen dropped her gaze, he asked, "Are they Argents too?"

Colleen winced, and slowly nodded her head yes. Closing his eyes, Gordon groaned.

"Look at me," Colleen demanded. Gordon opened his eyes, and she continued, in a softer voice, "They see in you what I see in you. They have from the beginning. They helped me to convince Jerad that I needed more time."

"Gordon," Audra said, cutting across the intensity of the last few moments, drawing his attention from Colleen's gaze, "how do you feel right now?"

Gordon frowned as he looked at Audra, confused for a moment by her question, but he realized that he felt lighter as if the weight of the years past had been lifted. "I feel like I can breathe." Audra nodded, and Gordon thought she seemed pleased by that.

"But I can't feel Andrew," Gordon said; at the same time, his cell phone rang. Checking the ID, he answered putting it on speaker, "Andrew, how are you?"

"I'm fine; it's you I'm concerned about," Andrew replied. "Something just seriously shifted; it was like you disappeared." Gordon noticed that Audra looked surprised. "I mean, even without your key and at this distance, our connection just isn't normally this bad. At the very least I'm always aware of you."

"Huh, well, I'm fine. Maybe, I'm too relaxed, not experiencing so many intense emotions," Gordon joked.

"Maybe," Andrew agreed. "So, tell me what you have been up to, something fun I hope."

"I don't have any salacious stories for you Andrew," Gordon replied dryly. "So far today I have taken care of a few business details. I have returned some calls, answered a few emails, that sort of thing. I did speak with Joseph, and wanted to thank you for keeping a tail on Rayne," Gordon said. "By the way, is Stavros still on his errands?"

With a barking guffaw, Andrew said, "Oh yeah. He is *still* riding the coastline."

Gordon laughed, "It's good for him, keeps him away from trouble."

"You mean it keeps him away from Colleen, don't you?" Andrew asked, with a throaty chuckle.

"That too," Gordon answered. *"No point in denying anything now I suppose,"* Gordon thought looking over at Colleen, who shyly smiled back at him.

"Speaking of Colleen, has it helped to be out of town, to get some rest? Have you had any more lingerie shows?" Andrew asked.

"No. No more lingerie shows," Gordon replied evenly. "Why don't you just forget that you saw that?"

Incredulously, Andrew asked, "You're joking, right?"

"Andrew...," Gordon began, in a no-nonsense tone, trying to keep his temper in check.

"Okay, okay," Andrew laughed, "Hands off, I know. But, after seeing that, I just think it's a waste. It could be great fun while it lasted; until her time."

Gordon sprang to his feet; at the same time an incredible clap of thunder could be heard through the phone; his control over his temper was now hanging by a thread.

"Damn it, Gordon, calm down," Andrew yelled over the din. "Geez, I just meant that if she is an Argent, she is an enemy to the Fold. But, an incredibly sexy enemy, so no one would blame you if you had a little fun along the way, what difference would it make?" Another crashing roll of thunder could be heard, "Gordon!" Andrew yelled again, "Knock it off! It is as dark as pitch here now, and the lightning is continuous. Happy?"

In a quiet voice thick with menace, Gordon said, "No one, including you dear cousin, will touch her. Am I clear?" The noise from the phone grew louder.

"Gordon stop it!" Andrew sounded as if he was running. "You've got the winds at gale force out there, and it's whipping the waves up into walls of water." The roaring and cracking sounds on Andrew's end nearly drowned out his voice. "Great! You just took out two cargo ships in the harbor, and one of them was ours!" Andrew exclaimed. "Tantrum over yet?"

"The building you stand in will be next," Gordon spoke quietly, but with certainty. "I'm going to ask again, are we clear?"

"Yes, yes," Andrew conceded. "No one touches her, including me."

An ear-shattering crack of lightning and a horrendous roll of thunder could be heard, just before Gordon switched the phone off completely. Turning to find Colleen and Audra standing in the middle of the room, their eyes as round as a full moon, and their mouths slightly gaping at what they had just witnessed. G o r d o n had been told that his eyes resembled white-hot coals when he unleashed a portion of his temper, as he had just done. Avoiding direct eye contact with either of them, he said, "Excuse me, ladies, I'm going for a walk." Gordon's temper was still burning, and he headed out the front door without bothering to take a coat, even though the temperature outside hovered just above freezing.

Walking around to the back of the house he started up the trail that led to the woods just past the back deck. Gordon's anger had carried him deep into the timber before he felt his head clearing, and became cognitive of how far he had traveled from the house. Turning back, he took his time heading to the house. Gordon had been aware that Andrew had no interest in keeping Colleen safe, he had made that abundantly clear on more than one occasion. But when he had assumed it a foregone conclusion that her ultimate fate, lie in becoming a tribute Gordon had been enraged. Thinking of Colleen, Gordon wondered how badly he had frightened her. *"My little display may have put a stop to her sexual fantasies about me,"* Gordon thought.

B Y THE TIME GORDON HAD REACHED the house, he felt mentally exhausted and emotionally drained. Entering through the back door off the kitchen, he ran into Colleen immediately. She turned at the sound, giving him a cautious smile, she said, "We didn't get lunch, so I'm making an early supper. Oh, and Joseph called," Colleen said, waving a wooden spoon toward the phone on the counter, where Gordon could see the little red light flashing, "I didn't answer, of course, but I did recognize the number. Did you call him?"

Wearily, Gordon shook his head, "No. But, I can't say I'm surprised, that he called me." Gordon picked up the phone, punched in the code, and listened to the message. Placing the phone back onto its base, he said, "Audra will get her wish; Joseph will be here in a few hours."

"You look cold and tired," Colleen fussed. "Why don't you go take a hot shower, and lie down for a bit? It will be a while before dinner is ready, and if you're still sleeping when it's ready, I can keep a plate warm for you if you would rather wait to eat."

Turning to face her, Gordon said, quietly, "Colleen, I'm sorry."

Gordon watched as Colleen came toward him, there was something in her eyes he couldn't identify. Lifting her hand, she put her finger on his lips yet once again, and said, "Sh-h-h. Go on up."

When Gordon came out of the shower, Colleen was coming through the bedroom door, with a highball glass in hand. Wordlessly, she handed him the drink, and without a word, he accepted it, threw it back, and felt the burn. Colleen walked to the bed, and Gordon followed her. She pulled the covers back and tipped her head, Gordon fell onto the bed, and she tucked the blankets around him.

Leaning over Colleen pressed a soft kiss on his mouth, flipped off the lamp, and walked to the door, quietly closing it behind her. *"She doesn't appear to be frightened,"* was Gordon's last thought before exhaustion overtook him.

Gordon awoke with a jerk and immediately checked the bedside clock. He had slept for almost an hour and a half, slept hard. He felt pretty good, considering everything that had occurred since waking this morning. Stretching, he thought, *"But the day isn't over yet, I still have to talk to Joseph before he gets here."* Knowing that Joseph could arrive anytime now, had Gordon up, dressed, and on the phone.

"Joseph, would you meet me at the tavern for a quick drink when you get into town?" Gordon asked when Joseph answered his call.

"If you like," Joseph said. "I'm about twenty minutes out."

"Okay, I'll get us a table," Gordon replied. "See you there."

When Gordon reached the bottom of the stairs, he could hear the muted sound of music and smell the delicious aroma of whatever they were cooking, coming from the kitchen. Upon entering the room, he observed both women harmoniously working side-by-side preparing food, and quietly singing along with Paul Davis' *I Go Crazy.* *"Back to the seventies again,"* Gordon thought, smiling. "Ladies," they both turned at the sound of his voice, "I'm leaving in a few minutes to meet Joseph at the tavern in town; I need to prepare him for the two of you."

"Gordon," Audra said, "If it would be easier for you to talk here,

I can take Colleen for a drive, she would be cloaked as long as she remains in the car."

Gordon thought for a moment, "Thank you, but no, something could happen that would force her to leave the vehicle; she would be exposed. Meeting Joseph in town will be fine." Gordon laughed quietly, "Besides, given Joseph's resourcefulness, it could be a short conversation." Colleen looked at Gordon with a quizzical expression; clarifying, Gordon added, "Joseph can be quite an enigma. He may know everything already."

As Gordon entered the tavern, he scanned the crowded space looking for a private table that he could request. To his surprise, he saw Joseph already seated in a back corner. Indicating that he had found his party, the harried hostess smiled and waved him on.

As Gordon slid into the booth opposite of Joseph, he noticed that a shot of bourbon was already placed on the table. Raising a brow at Joseph, he said, "I see you made much better time than you thought."

"Traffic just outside of town was lighter than I had anticipated," Joseph replied. "I took the liberty of ordering your favorite whiskey," Joseph nodded to indicate the glass, "I didn't think you would want to be away from your house-guests for any longer than necessary."

Gordon looked directly at his table companion, and with a sardonic smile said, "It's good to see you, Joseph."

Inclining his head in acknowledgment, Joseph replied, "It's good to see you too. I'm anxious to meet your new acquaintance."

Laughing, Gordon stood, threw some money on the table leaving his drink untouched, and said, "Actually, I'm more hungry than thirsty, and there is a meal waiting for us at the Getaway."

Even the ordinarily unflappable Joseph was awestruck when he met James Mitchell the male business associate that stood at Colleen's side; then, before his eyes, the man shimmered, disappeared, and Audra McMann emerged.

After the initial shock had worn off, and Joseph had taken his bags up to the second bedroom; they had all sat down to eat the hearty stew that Colleen had set to cooking that afternoon, keeping their conversation light.

When everyone appeared to have eaten their fill, Audra reached out to Joseph, and said, "Could I have a word with you in private?"

Joseph studied her for a few seconds, and replied, "Yes, I would like to speak with you also. Gordon will have no need of the library for a while," which drew a look of surprise from Gordon.

Colleen looked at Gordon and said, "Will you help me clear the table, and clean-up in the kitchen?"

Gordon nodded in response, as he watched Joseph and Audra make their way to the library, with Joseph firmly closing the door after ushering Audra in first.

"Did you find that odd?" Gordon asked Colleen, nodding toward the library.

Colleen lightly shrugged, as she stacked the plates, and said, "Grab the glasses please," as she turned for the kitchen. "I've learned that it's best not to question Audra; she will talk when she's ready," Colleen added.

Gordon noticed that Colleen kept glancing at him while they worked in the kitchen; she transferred the leftover stew to a container, tidied the counter, and put away the items he had covered. Finally, with the kitchen spotless, she asked, "Are you ready to talk?"

Gordon stiffened slightly; he had known they would have to get around to discussing his exhibition from this afternoon. Taking a deep breath, Gordon asked, "Where do you want to start?"

"Did you really make those things happen; the storm, the ships, lightning, and thunder, or, was it an illusion for Andrew's benefit?" Colleen queried.

At first, Gordon felt surprised that she would think it wasn't real, but, on second thought given what Audra could do... "I made those things happen," he said quietly. "I'm not like Audra," Gordon added. He observed her face carefully, trying to gauge what she might be thinking. He kept his distance, purposefully to give her physical space.

"Did you take down the building?" Colleen asked.

"No, I got the answer I wanted," Gordon said,

Raising her eyebrows, she asked, "Oh, is that always your reaction when you don't get your way? Create a storm out of nowhere? Tearing ships apart? Plunging an entire city into darkness?"

"Only when it's a matter of great importance, life or death. I took care that no one would be severely injured, and I did not plunge the entire city into darkness," he said, gravely, still watching her without approaching. She didn't appear to be scared of him, but he couldn't be sure. He watched as she pushed a footstool over by the bar, and used it to hop up to sit on the island.

She held out her hand, beckoning him; when he stood in front of her, she held out both arms, and he cautiously walked into them, at which point she loosely draped them around his neck. With her sitting on the bar they were eye-to-eye, Colleen held his gaze for a moment and said nothing. Then she leaned forward and hungrily kissed him. His arms immediately went around her as he gently returned her kiss. Gordon was bewildered, but he wasn't complaining and remained determined to let her take the lead. But, when she deepened the kiss, Gordon groaned and his hands began to roam.

"Um hum," Audra cleared her throat, as she and Joseph stood in the doorway. Gordon pulled back, absurdly feeling like a child caught with his hand in the candy bowl.

"I thought I told you two to refrain from that particular activity for the time being," Audra said, sternly. "You both need to focus."

Gordon looked around Colleen to see Joseph standing just behind Audra with a silly grin on his face and a twinkle in his eyes.

After drawing a shaky breath, Gordon said, "It might help if you would tell us just where we are to direct our focus," his suggestion directed to Audra, his voice rough as he struggled to rein in his emotions.

"Honesty," was her one-word reply.

"I *honestly* wanted to kiss him," Colleen said flippantly as she stepped down from the bar. Her comment had Joseph shaking with silent laughter, and his eyes dancing.

Audra rolled her eyes, then speaking directly to Colleen, "Start being honest about a few other things, and then you can kiss him all you want," she admonished. Audra looked back over her shoulder at Joseph and said, "Do not encourage her." Shaking her head, she declared, "I swear it's like working with teenagers."

Gordon raked a hand through his hair, and rubbed his temples between his thumb and fingers, "What things?" he asked, his voice full of the exasperation that had been a constant companion since this morning.

"Those things that you guard so closely; your secrets, your dreams, your past, and the vision for your future," she replied, brusquely. Audra paused, and then softly added, "Then you both will have life-changing decisions to make. What are you willing to give up, and what you are willing to receive, to achieve your heart's desire?"

Gordon glanced at Colleen; who still wore a belligerent expression; sighing, he caught Joseph's eye and nodded toward the library. Joseph turned on his heel, and they both left the women to their own devices.

As they walked across the room, Gordon slightly stumbled, his field of vision momentarily blocked by a virtual image of Colleen and the kiss they had just shared. "Colleen," he said when it cleared, and he saw Joseph frown at him.

"When was the last time you had a vision?" Joseph asked.

"I don't know," Gordon answered, weariness tinging his voice, as he closed the library door. "This morning, I guess, after Audra arrived."

"Are they always sexual in nature?" Joseph asked, as calmly as if he were asking what Gordon wanted for dinner.

Gordon had dropped down in the matching chair adjacent from Joseph. Stalling for time, he said, "Why would you ask that?"

"Had Joseph also been privy to Colleen's most private thoughts?" Trying to decide how he felt about Joseph possibly seeing her projections, Gordon came to his conclusion, *"Decision made; I don't want any other man seeing her as I have."*

Making a teepee of his fingers, Joseph sat back and studied Gordon carefully before answering, "Primarily, because I am so attuned to you. Not that I can read you in the same manner that Andrew does; what I do is more like reading the barometric pressure. I can't see into the future either; however, I know a few seconds, or sometimes a couple of minutes, ahead of time when you're about to take an emotional hit…high or low."

Gordon sat quietly for a moment; that would explain why Joseph had hung up so quickly this morning; he had always known that Joseph had some sort of connection to him apart from that of a mentor. Throughout his life Joseph would always show up when Gordon needed him most; whether, it was to celebrate a triumph or guide Gordon in picking up the pieces after an emotional defeat. Curious, he asked, "Do you have that same sort of connection with anyone else? Andrew? My father?"

"No just you," Joseph smiled fondly at Gordon. "However, because my link with you is, and always has been, so strong I can feel your emotional state. I am aware of your impressions, and reactions to the people around you. Therefore, I do have an inside track to your father, and Andrew, through you," Joseph explained. "And, now Miss Colleen," he added, giving Gordon a knowing smile. "To answer your *unasked* question, no, I have not *seen* the images Colleen has sent to you; but, when you receive the images, your reaction to her is so strong I feel your emotional state of being."

With a derisive laugh, Gordon replied, "Well that's embarrassing."

"You're a normal man," Joseph said, with a slight shrug. "Even if it was only sexual desire that you felt there is no need to be embarrassed with me. But Gordon, the sexual desire is only a small part of the depth of your feelings for Colleen."

Gordon recognized the all-knowing look and tone from Joseph that he had grown up with; he could never lie to the man, because *"the man always knows the truth, sometimes before I do,"* Gordon thought. Wanting to take the focus off of himself Gordon asked, "How did you know that Audra and Colleen were here?"

Joseph laughed, "Audra sent a few images to me. Images of you after you spoke to Andrew. At the time, I didn't know from where they were coming, but now I know it was her." He paused to watch Gordon's reaction before continuing, "I assume she did it in much the same way as what the lass does with you."

For a split second, Gordon was stunned, and a hundred questions filled his mind, but then he thought, *"Why not? It's no crazier than anything else I've experienced over the last few weeks and particularly today."* So rather than to start grilling his mentor, he simply smiled at Joseph, and asked, "Weird, isn't it?"

Joseph laughed, "It is a very unusual sensation."

Gordon waited, knowing Joseph as he did, he knew his mentor had more to say. "But, Gordon," Joseph continued, earnestly, "you need to be honest with yourself, you care deeply for the lass, like nothing you have ever felt before for any woman. Which brings me to my question: Gordon, would you be willing to leave the Fold?"

Shocked that he would ask such a thing, Gordon closely regarded Joseph with a frown, "You know there is no way for me to leave; not without signing mine, and Andrews' death warrant. Father made himself very clear on that point."

Joseph remained quiet for a moment, then slowly asked, "What if I were to tell you, it is possible for you to leave and live; that Andrew could be contained, Terese could be released, and that perhaps your father could be contained as well, or at the very least, his hand could be stayed?"

With a short snort of derision, Gordon asked, "Just who would I have to kill to make that happen?"

"No one," Joseph replied calmly, "but, it would involve treating them as tributes."

"And?"

"And," Joseph went on, "it would require that you flip, their word not mine," Joseph said quickly when Gordon smirked. "You will need to agree to go to the Radiant; become an Argent."

"Me? An Argent?" Gordon questioned incredulously. "After the dozens of people that I have brought to the Fold; not to mention, damning two women to a watery world of existence for eternity," Gordon shook his head in disbelief.

"It is possible," Joseph replied, with assurance. "It would mean turning the names of your recruits over to the Arcs. It would mean pledging your life to the Radiant. It would mean trapping your cousin in that watery world, and betraying your father."

"My father betrayed me a long time ago," Gordon interjected, with a note of hardness to his voice.

"Then, Gordon, if you can do that, it might be possible to release Miss Terese, but the balance would have to be kept. Trading Andrew for her release. The question is, would you consider the possibility?" Joseph asked.

"I could get my wife back?" Gordon asked, incredulous. He immediately felt shame; perhaps the darkness was too ingrained, because his first thought was of Colleen.

Joseph studied Gordon for a moment, "It's possible to release her, but she doesn't have to know that she was ever your wife. As far as the world is concerned, Terese Bilford the III died in Switzerland. The Argents will take care of her, ensuring that she has a new start, without memory of her previous life."

Gordon could make her forget, but he couldn't just turn her out into the world with no memory. "And Jeanette?" Gordon queried.

"Too much time has passed to release Jeanette," Joseph said, shaking his head. "Not to mention there are things about Jeanette that you were not aware of when you married her. I thought you would have figured it out, but since you haven't..." Joseph took a deep breath, and said, "Jeanette had recently been brought into the Fold when you met her. She purposefully set-out to entice you all those years ago. She thought marriage to a Bilford would be advantageous in her ambitions to climb the ranks within the Fold."

Gordon was stunned at first, his mind racing back. But suddenly with absolute clarity, he realized it made perfect sense, "Why didn't you tell me? Why didn't you stop me from marrying her?" Gordon demanded.

Quietly, Joseph, asked, "Could you have been stopped, especially back then?"

Gordon didn't want to admit it, but Joseph was right, he was so rebellious at that time nothing or no one could have swayed him, "They won't hurt her, will they?"

"Audra has promised that Jeanette will not be hurt, but they will not turn her loose either," Joseph said. "The Arcs will not allow her release; she would remain bound in the globe with Andrew."

"And you?" Gordon queried, "How do you feel about all this? What do you want?"

"I go where you go," Joseph replied solemnly. "Whether that be to stay in the Fold or to join the Argents." Joseph rose to leave, and said meaningfully, "You have a lot to think about, but Gordon, you must first and foremost be honest to yourself." Joseph paused to lay his hand on Gordon's shoulder, "It's getting late; sleep on it tonight; they will be looking for an answer soon."

"They?" Gordon asked.

"The Argents," Joseph replied, "and the Arc, Jerad."

Gordon didn't know how to respond. He had not allowed himself to seriously think about leaving the Fold for over a year; seeing no sense in pining for something he couldn't have. After Joseph went up to bed, Gordon wondered out from the library, finding the downstairs quiet, he turned off lights and checked the alarm system. For the first time, in a long time he allowed himself to hope. If Andrew could be contained, he knew he could control his uncle. Gordon had always felt that his father had just a little more power than his twin. Just as Gordon had more power than his Cousin; Andrew knew it too. Otherwise, Andrew would be a complete monster. Gordon shuttered at the thought, *"Andrew left unchecked would be pure chaos for Normals."*

Upstairs, Gordon found Colleen curled into a ball in the middle of his bed. He briefly wondered what the two women had discussed after Audra had spotted Colleen kissing him in the kitchen. Gordon smiled at the memory.

After readying himself for bed, Gordon slipped in beside Colleen as quietly as possible, trying not to disturb her. Lying on his back, he closed his eyes, attempting to focus on the day's events. So many surprises, and so much turmoil had dominated his day since rising this morning; his 'tantrum,' as Andrew had called it, had taken a toll on him. His introduction to Audra had been nothing short of mind-blowing, along with her revelations of his and Colleen's relationship. And then, the information that Joseph had just divulged; urging him, as Audra had, to be honest.

Honestly, Gordon just wanted a normal life. A life free from the tumult that had plagued him for well over the past fifteen years. Free from the anguish of causing others pain, free from the restraints of the Fold, of having others telling him how to live; thrusting responsibilities on him that he never knew existed, he didn't ask for, nor did he want them. Life as an Argent would still have its restraints, he would yet have to answer to others, and no doubt there would be numerous responsibilities. However, the idea of no longer being a threat to mankind intrigued him, but of one thing he was sure about, the Dark would try to kill him first.

Gordon thought about his conversation with Joseph, on one point, Gordon knew with absolute certainty that Joseph was right, he had never before experienced the intense feelings he had for

Colleen, for any other woman. His marriage to Jeanette had, in the beginning, been sexy, exciting, and pure rebellion for the life he had been forced to live; it had also been totally non-gratifying. He had found that he didn't really like her, and he certainly didn't love her. His marriage and relationship to Terese were different; comfortable, pleasant, agreeable, and he believed that he could have been satisfied enough to live out his life with her if he could find a way out of the Dark Fold.

Colleen was different, he felt a level of intimacy, even though they had not been intimate that he had never come close to experiencing before. He thought his heart had been involved with Terese, but every fiber of his being, mentally, emotionally, and physically screamed out for Colleen, in a way he never had for Terese. As he thought of Colleen, she stirred, mumbled his name, and reaching toward him slid her hand across his chest; she then settled, and with her hand resting over his heart her breathing became steady again.

Suddenly, it all became clear, he would do what he had to do just to be near her for as long as he could; for as long as she would allow. Everything else became secondary in his mind to Colleen's safety, and to her happiness. Although he had stayed Andrew's reach, for now, he knew that his cousin wouldn't rest until he had Colleen trapped. Gordon knew one thing with startling clarity, he would protect Colleen with his life.

C OLLEEN, AUDRA, JOSEPH, AND THE NEWEST member of their little conclave, Jerad Evan, an Arc, sat at the dining table the next morning, as Gordon paced the great room. He kept his eye on the man that stood just under six feet tall, middle forty's, his body thick with muscle; he had blondish brown hair, liquid brown eyes, and had had a permanent scowl on his face since he walked through the door. Gordon was struggling with Jerad's presence. The man's powers were comparable to Gordon's, Gordon could literally feel it; his familiarity with Colleen was unnerving; however, as Audra had assured him, it wasn't sexual in manner, but as if he held control over her. Although, Gordon had made the decision to 'flip' he was currently finding it quite challenging to lay bare his past, and the methods he had used to bring recruits to the Fold.

"If you expect the slightest chance of the Arcs sanctioning a relationship between the two of you," Jerad said, waving his hand between Colleen and Gordon; "and according to Audra, it is inevitable, Colleen needs to know all, she stays," Jerad argued, when Gordon had requested privacy for this part of the conversation.

"Seduction," Gordon finally said smoothly, giving Colleen a smoldering look that left no doubt to anyone in the room of the validity to that one-word statement. Returning his attention to

Jerad, he said, "Normals, from all walks of life, are easily seduced with the promise of power, money, and sex. Choosing to join the Fold and utilizing its forces can guarantee all three."

"So, you have no compunction of who you turn? Housewives, business owners, politicians, pastors, or the teen on the corner?" Jerad continued with his questioning with a condemning tone.

"It's preferable to choose those with power, or influence over others," with a shrug Gordon replied matter-of-factly. "The higher up the political ladder, the better, heads of state have the most power; legislators and religious leaders have tremendous influence over large numbers of Normals. They are also the easiest to turn; they already have a taste for power and money. Power and money translate easily into sex."

Gordon could feel the anger the Arc was suppressing as he asked, "How many recruits are you responsible for bringing into the Fold?"

Gordon really didn't want to answer this question, but he quickly did the mental math, and responded defensively, "Fifty," and because he did not want to be pinned down to the exact number, added, "Give or take."

Gordon heard the collective gasp of Audra and Colleen. "I have been active in the Fold since my twentieth year. A member of the Fold either brings a minimum of one tribute every two years or five recruits. I couldn't bear the thought of damning that many people as tributes, so I chose recruits," he explained, "I, at least gave them a choice."

"A choice?" Jerad asked. "Join or die, eh?" he continued derisively.

"Although my sins may be numerous, I am not a murderer," Gordon stated quietly. "If a person declined my offer, I simply made them forget they ever met me."

"And how many out of the fifty, give or take," Jerad added snidely, "did you bring to the Fold by seducing to your bed?"

Jerad was purposefully pushing his buttons, Gordon narrowed

his stare, and could feel his anger building. *"Don't let him goad you into losing it,"* he warned himself, *"nothing would make the Arc happier than for me to blow in front of Colleen and Audra,"* to Jerad, he snarled out, "None of your damn business."

Clearing his throat, Joseph, ever the diplomat said, "I believe what Gordon is trying to say is that, regardless of the methods employed, he has brought, approximately, fifty members to the Fold." His attempt to pull Gordon's focus from Jerad unsuccessful.

Jerad scrutinized Gordon carefully, and Gordon knew what the Arc could see happening; his eyes altering. First, an eerie ring of white would encircle the irises, and if he could not hold his temper in check…. "And, for the record," Gordon flipped his hand toward the clipboard Jerad held, "I have never needed, nor used, the powers of the Fold to force any woman into my bed."

Jerad then looked to Audra who frowned and slightly shook her head. Sighing heavily, he moved to his next question, "The unexpected storm that hit Boston yesterday; you were responsible for that?"

Gordon still feeling incensed answered, with a clipped, "Yes."

"From what I have been told, you put on quite a show. So, you have a little control over the elements?" Jerad prodded.

Gordon and Joseph exchanged glances. Jerad looked back and forth between the two of them, "What?" he demanded.

Gordon looked at Joseph again who nodded his head in encouragement, but Gordon shook his head 'no.'

"What?" Jerad asked again, still watching them. "You blew up a storm that turned the skies black, whipped up gale force winds over the water that took out two cargo ships, and threatened to take down a building all in a matter of a couple of minutes. Is that, along with the ability to make people forget, the extent of your talents?"

Gordon had stopped his pacing to stand in front of the French doors leading to the back deck; watching a brilliant red cardinal hop from one branch to another of a balsam fir that rose like a sentinel over the house, and served as a respite for the furred and feathered creatures, "Not exactly," he replied.

"Well, then *what else* exactly?" Jerad asked impatiently. "You could have taken another ship, a building or two, decimated the entire block? Make everyone forget it ever happened? What?"

When it became evident that Gordon was not going to answer, Joseph solemnly interjected, "Gordon could have ripped the entire eastern seaboard apart if he had chosen to do so." Continuing, Joseph added his opinion, "Given his inordinate desire to protect the lassie, he displayed extreme control in the situation. *Localized chaos* is how we refer to such an event."

"The entire seaboard? Localized chaos? An event?" Jerad asked disbelievingly. Joseph nodded. "He could have injured or killed innocent people," Jerad ranted, "as it is, he caused a great deal of monetary damage that will adversely affect innocent people."

"No one was severely injured or killed," Gordon said, absently, still staring through the glass door. "I will see to any monetary damage that incurred; I always do; much to the displeasure of my family."

"Speaking of your family," Jerad said with a slight sneer to his voice, "you threatened to kill your cousin?"

"He threatened Colleen," Gordon responded quietly, matter-of-factly, as if that should justify any steps he had taken. "And, if I had really wanted to kill Andrew, I could have taken the top floor of our building and placed it, along with Andrew, in the middle of the Atlantic. He is still a threat, and I may have to take him out yet."

Jerad rose slowly from his seat to face Gordon, "You're trying to tell me…tell us, that you could have taken one floor of a building and moved it to sea?" He asked with disbelief, both, coloring his voice and written on his face.

"Yes."

Jerad shook his head, looked at Joseph, and questioned, "Localized chaos?" Joseph merely shrugged. Rubbing the back of his neck, Jerad said, "Well, I guess that could explain some unusual events in the past. Instances of great devastation due to storms, horrible vehicular accidents, and yet, miraculously, no one is killed."

Gordon smiled tightly, and with a tinge of sarcasm, replied, "I can't take credit for all, but, perhaps, one or two."

Audra was the first to break the silence that ensued, "Well I think it's time we take a break," she said as she rose, "I, for one, could use a cup of coffee; anyone else?" Joseph stood while exchanging a look with Gordon, with an imperceptible nod, he followed Audra to the kitchen, and Gordon turned on his heel going to his library, slamming the door behind him.

Gordon walked straight to the bar cart in the corner of the room, snatching up the first bottle he could lay his hands-on; twisting the lid, he tipped the bottle to pour, stopped, swore, and promptly threw it against the wall. Gordon watched as shards of glass flew, and whiskey ran down the wood-paneled wall, *"I am probably actively pursuing one restrictive hell for another,"* he thought, as he turned away, and sank onto the couch. Laying his head back to stare at the ceiling, Gordon took deep breaths to rein in the maelstrom of thoughts swirling in his mind. He became aware of the door opening quietly, looking around, he saw Colleen hesitantly step through the door. "Mind if I join you?" she asked.

Sitting up, he replied, "Did you get permission from Jerad to speak to me?"

"I don't need anyone's permission to speak to you," Colleen said, defensively. Looking around the room, she sighed when she saw the broken bottle. "You made a mess," she said, as she bent to pick up a couple of the larger pieces and place them in a nearby trash bin.

"Leave it," Gordon commanded, "It's my mess, I will take care of it. Didn't you hear me out there? I'm accustomed to cleaning up my messes." Colleen picked up one more piece of glass, disposed of it, and came to sit beside him pulling her legs under her as she faced him. Gordon studied her face for a moment and then said, "Jerad thinks I have seduced you, using the power of the Dark, doesn't he? That's the reason he is so interested in my methods of recruiting isn't it?"

Colleen laughed a little nervously, "Jerad knows better, or he should."

Curiously, Gordon asked, "Why do you say that?"

Leaning into him she whispered, "He knows that it has been the other way around, it's what I requested."

"You *acquired* his permission to seduce me?" Gordon asked astounded.

Colleen shrugged lightly, staring at Gordon's lips for a moment, "Sort of, I told him I needed time to get to know you; that I could feel the conflict within you. I needed time and space to work on getting you to see things my way, and that always involves a little flirting," she added with a little smile while chewing on her bottom lip.

"That's what you call a little flirting?" Gordon asked incredulous.

"Things happened differently with you," Colleen pouted.

"Humph, perhaps he should be questioning *your* methods of recruitment," Gordon observed. "Like your X-rated projections, for instance."

Emerald eyes collided with onyx, and Gordon grabbed her about the waist pulling her across his body, his mouth covering hers when she gasped at the swift movement. Previously, Gordon had been vigilant in maintaining his control when he had Colleen in his arms; but this time, when Colleen wrapped her arms around him and returned his kiss with an urgency all her own, it was the only encouragement that he needed to let go of that restraint.

When she pulled back to catch her breath, he drew her closer, leaving a trail of kisses down her neck, and across her collarbone; his hands roaming over her body pushing her clothing aside. Having momentarily forgotten that anyone else existed, much less anyone in the house, Gordon swore under his breath when interrupted by a sharp rapping on the door; at the same time, Colleen moaned plaintively, opening her eyes to look up at him. She trailed her fingers down the side of his face and reached up to place a soft kiss on his mouth before sitting upright, both of them needing a minute to calm their breathing.

Gordon stood first, as he pushed one hand through his hair, he held out the other to assist Colleen to her feet, and said, "Back to the inquisition."

Swaying a bit as she stood, Colleen placed her palms on his chest, and said, "I'm so sorry, but if we don't want you to be bound by the Arcs, it's necessary."

"You really believe they could bind me?" Gordon asked bemused, watching her face.

"Well, yes," Colleen replied with a frown. "Isn't that one of the reasons you're going along with this?" she asked. "To keep from being bound?"

"No one can bind me, Colleen, unless I allow it," Gordon responded. "I am doing this because I never wanted any part of the Fold," Gordon cupped her chin, tilting her head back slightly, "and, I want you," he murmured against her lips.

Another tap at the door, and it opened just enough to allow Audra to step inside, "Gordon we need to finish; Jerad has just received a message, Rayne is on the move again."

Gordon released Colleen, and headed toward the door, he chuckled softly as he heard Audra say, "Colleen, you...uh... might want to pull yourself together before Jerad sees you; I really don't need to hear another of his rants about your virtue."

Gordon had never given any real thought to Colleen's past. He preferred to focus on the future; assuming he had one when this was all said and done. If he survived, and if she would have him, he had every intention of being the last man in Colleen's future.

Gordon found Jerad in the kitchen with Joseph. The two men seemed to be deep in conversation, but, when Gordon walked in, Jerad gave him a thunderous look, and Joseph appeared to be holding in laughter.

"Keep your hands off of Colleen," Jerad growled, "she's an innocent."

Gordon tried to control his expression, but he was stunned by both the venom in Jerad's voice, and the claim he had just made. *"Surely, he doesn't mean that literally, does he?"* Gordon looked over at Joseph who merely raised his brows and still had a smile playing about his mouth, obviously finding Gordon's current predicament amusing.

"Audra said that you received a message concerning Rayne," Gordon said evenly, ignoring Jerad's statement.

Jerad narrowed his gaze, "We'll talk about Rayne when I understand that *you understand* that you will not hurt that child in there. She is not to be used as another proverbial notch in your bedpost."

"Joseph!" Gordon snapped angrily, not taking his eyes from Jerad's, "I would like to speak to you privately in my rooms, please." Gordon turned on his heel and started for the stairs with Joseph close behind, just as Colleen and Audra came out of the library.

Slamming the door to his bedroom so hard the sound resonated through the house, Gordon rounded on Joseph, "Just what in the Hell were the two of you discussing down there? And, what was that about Colleen being *an innocent?*"

Joseph calmly looked at Gordon, and quietly said, "Apparently, the lass is a virgin."

Gordon stared at Joseph for a beat, his mind racing, then said, "I highly doubt the validity of that claim, given the way she has thrown herself at me on every turn." Joseph remained placid and mute. "It just can't be, at her age? How would he even know if that's true," Gordon demanded.

Joseph shrugged slightly, and said, "The lass is very close to her Aunt Fran, and confides in her. She also confides in Audra. The women talk," then making a circular motion with his hand, he said, "Mrs. O'Malley tells Mr. O'Malley, and so forth." Continuing, Joseph explained, "According to Jerad, the loss of Colleen's parents had a profound effect on the little lassie's capability of bonding with new people. Probably, due to her young age at the time of the accident, coupled with the understanding of the dangers that revolve in the lives of the Argents. She clung to those she knew around her, but would not allow anyone else to get close fearing more loss." Pausing to gain Gordon's direct attention, he added, "There is certain evidence that Abrogates had a hand in her parents' accident."

Gordon wanted to argue, but instead, grew reflective suddenly remembering something Fran had said to him weeks ago, *"...but she seems so comfortable around you, which is quite unlike her, honestly. She doesn't always take to people so quickly."* Running through his mind certain pieces of conversation with her, Gordon began to put together a new impression of Colleen, to view her through a new filter; *"I've seen the handiwork of the Abrogates up close."* Musing to himself, he thought of their first night here, when she had asked, *"Could you be satisfied with just holding me for a little while?"* Gordon had thought that she was playing at another game; but now, viewing it through the lens of sexual inexperience...maybe not. He thought about her embarrassment when she had admitted that she was jealous, her anger and indignation when she had discovered the dual purpose of the Mistress suite, and when he had called her out on her sexual fantasy yesterday morning. A woman of experience, at least the ones he had known, would have turned it to their advantage, but Colleen's mortification had been undeniable.

Dropping into a chair as if the wind had been knocked out of him; he looked up at Joseph, "She's a virgin?"

"That's what the man said," Joseph replied, grinning from ear to ear.

Gordon groaned, "Joseph, you have a strange sense of humor."

Smoothing his face, Joseph replied, "Sorry, sir."

Gordon noted, however, that his mentor did not appear to be the least bit remorseful. Rising from his chair, he said, "I need to speak to her."

"I don't think that would be wise," Joseph cautioned, as he stepped between Gordon and the door. "It would probably cause her a great deal of embarrassment if she knew that something as personal as her 'status' so to speak, was a topic of discussion among the men around her."

Gordon's brows drew together in thought, then with a sigh, he said, "You're probably right. Considering the night of the storm, she accused me of treating her like my whore in front of a houseful of men."

Both men sat lost in thought for a few more minutes, before Gordon said, "This really doesn't have anything to do with the issue at hand; keeping her safe from Andrew and Rayne."

Going back down, Gordon and Joseph paused at the foot of the stairs, unabashedly, listening to the heated discussion between Colleen and Jerad.

Colleen sounded livid, "I will thank you to stay out of my personal business."

Gordon didn't need to see Colleen to picture her green eyes snapping.

"You have no experience with men like that," Jerad said insistently. "How do you know he hasn't already done something and made you forget?"

"Just what are you asking of me Jerad?" Colleen hissed.

"Jerad!" Audra admonished. "Have you lost your senses? Do not push this."

"Are you ignoring what Audra said?" Colleen asked.

"Pfff!" Jerad snorted. "Soul-mating?"

With a threat in her voice, Colleen retorted, "I'll be sure to let Aunt Molly know how little regard you have for the concept."

At that, Audra laughed, and said, "I don't think Molly would be too pleased to hear of your ridicule for the very thing that brought the two of you together."

As much as Gordon was enjoying hearing the two women gang-up on Jerad, he cleared his throat to announce his and Joseph's presence. As they entered the great room, Gordon addressed the Arc, "Mr. Evan, I believe you, and I should speak privately," indicating the door to the library.

Gordon waited as Jerad closed the door, and turned to him, "I believe we have gotten off-track of our main objective."

"And what do you consider our main objective?" Jerad asked, pacing the room.

Gordon took the seat behind his desk, and replied, "My main objective is to keep Colleen safe, then if it's possible to 'flip' me from the Fold to the Argents."

Standing in the middle of the room, Jerad said, decisively, "We agree on one thing, my primary objective currently, is to keep Colleen safe, and I think that will best be achieved by keeping her away from you."

Mockingly, Gordon said, "I tried that, even when I went away, she followed."

"That's because you, no doubt, did something to her," Jerad railed.

Feeling himself start to bristle, Gordon made a decision, leaning forward in his chair, he waved toward the two chairs opposite the desk, inviting Jerad to sit, "If you would care to listen there are one or two things I need to tell you about my personal life, and my role in the Fold." Jerad hesitated for a moment, staring hard at Gordon, and then sat down. "First for your edification," Gordon started, looking Jerad in the eye, he said, "Colleen and I have not had sex. Now, if I were to put into practice what I have been taught…pushed to be, Colleen would have lost her 'innocence' weeks ago, but I prefer my women willing, not comatose."

Gordon observed Jerad's color beginning to rise, "And, second, if and when we do, it will remain strictly between us." Gordon remained quiet as he watched the Arc struggle to maintain his temper; once he seemed to have a rein on his emotions, Gordon continued, "One more thing you need to know, and it's important, I have recently learned that I am only one generation removed from the Dark Genesis." If nothing else Gordon had said mattered to Jerad that seemed to catch his attention.

Gordon continued, with candor, "I never wanted any part of the Fold, I was introduced to it on my twentieth birthday, at first I was in complete denial, later when I realized..." Shaking his head to clear those memories, he went on, "anyway, I have been trying to find a way out ever since. I do not live by the tenets of the Dark Fold any more than absolutely necessary, but I don't know if I can be *flipped*," Jerad frowned at him. "Not that I'm opposed to it," Gordon amended, "In fact, it would be gratifying to, in some small way, atone for some of the things that I have done, or turned a blind eye to things that others have done to appease the Genesis. However, I am assuming the Dark will try to kill me first, but I have made a decision; as dramatic as it may sound, I would rather be dead than to continue living like this. My only concern right now is to keep Colleen safe, to do that, my cousin Andrew will need to be contained; and regardless as to what you may believe, you cannot contain a Bilford, I will have to take care of him, but I may need help."

"And you don't have a problem with that, containing your cousin? Your blood?" Jerad asked still skeptical.

Gordon leveled his gaze on the Arc, before replying, "I would kill him if that were all it took to keep Colleen safe, but it isn't; danger would come from another direction." Jerad seemed to be taken aback by Gordon's callousness in speaking of the demise of his cousin, by his hand. Gordon ignored the Arc's look of surprise, and continued, "With control of Andrew, I can gain control over his father, my Uncle; and if I can control my father's twin, it might give me some leverage with my father."

"You see, I believe that just because you can do a thing doesn't mean that you should. On the other hand, Andrew thinks that he should *because* he can," Gordon went on to explain, "Andrew believes he is entitled, taking, forcing, and doing as he pleases, because Andrew is the epitome of what it is to be the Dark. He believes that Normals are inconsequential, beneath us, disposable, and he believes the Argents are our enemy. Actually, I suppose he has that last one right if one is loyal to the Fold." Gordon paused, knowing that what he was about to say might have Jerad ranting again before he could finish. "I warned Andrew off of Colleen the day of the memorial for Terese, even though, or maybe because, I knew something was changing, shifting; also, I didn't want Fran and Shaun hurt by involving their niece in our world." At this, Jerad shot Gordon a look of skepticism. Leaning forward in his chair, Gordon looked directly into Jerad's eyes, and said evenly, "Believe what you will, but I do care a great deal about both of them."

Jerad studied Gordon a moment before replying, "They have said as much."

"Anyway, in our world, the warning I gave Andrew meant that I was laying claim to Colleen," Gordon saw the fire flash behind Jerad's eyes, but he pushed on, "I did it in order to keep her safe, to keep him from doing the very thing you feared I had done or will do in the future. Later, we had reason to suspect that she might be an Argent, which in Andrew's mind makes her an enemy of the Fold, and again in Andrew's mind that makes her fate inevitable, he said as much to me yesterday. He had to be warned again, and by warning him, I have once again, laid claim to her. She continues to be under my protection."

"Ah," the light dawning on Jerad, "the storm."

"Yes, the storm," Gordon responded. "I had to make sure he understood that I would protect her from him, and all others, at any cost." Gordon spread his hands, "Otherwise...."

Both men grew quiet, the Arc deliberating and once again pacing the room, and Gordon awaiting his decision. Appearing to have reached a conclusion, Jerad finally spoke, "Because you are willing to come to the Radiant, I think we can handle that, and keep you alive." Gordon smiled blandly, not nearly as confident as the Arc. "As for Colleen, I will stop fighting her about you, she has in no uncertain terms reminded me that she is no longer a child;

but, it's hard for me to let go, I have been protecting her for a long time." Jerad paused, studying the wide gold band on his left hand, turning it around a couple of times with his thumb, before adding, "And for what it's worth, Audra is never wrong." Returning his gaze to Gordon, he warned, "But, understand this, Colleen has already been hurt more than anyone deserves, so, I will always be watching."

"I would expect nothing less," Gordon responded solemnly.

The two men studied one another for a long moment, each coming to a non-verbal truce; Gordon broke the silence by asking, "Shall we get started?"

ORDON AND JERAD HAD DISCUSSED, CUSSED, planned and schemed, until the early hours of the morning. Gordon had acquired new insight into the Argents and the hierarchy of the light. For instance, the Argents were just part of the authority of light.

"Really, it wasn't much of a hierarchy," Gordon thought, *"Basically, they were all equal, with each grouping having special abilities. The Paladins are the guardians, Argents are in the field, each with their own unique talents; like Colleen projecting, and Audra as an illusionist/ seer. The Arcs are the protectors, the most powerful of the group, capable of pulling strength from all elements in their environment, living and non-living; given the motive was pure. Telekinesis, much like one of my capabilities, is common among the Arcs. The three factions collaborated seamlessly, and collectively made what they referred to as the Radiant."*

He had also learned that Kelsey's pub was a lair for the Paladins and that it had been a group of Argents that had hacked into Bilford's security system. *"Little wonder that Andrew and I had felt such animosity that evening in Kelsey's,"* Gordon thought. Gordon told Jerad of Rayne's remark alluding to a coalition forming, and that he was to be called if there was any trouble.

Gordon had assumed that he would be stripped of his powers once his transformation began, but Jerad had said, "As long as your talents are being used for the good of humankind you will have full range. However, if you are using them only in a fit of anger that could cause harm, you will be rendered incapacitated, bound, and make no mistake, as an Argent you can be bound."

They, Jerad and Gordon, had decided that Gordon would extend an invitation to Rayne using Andrew's name; inviting him to Bilford Manor for the benefit gala. Gordon thought the Bilford name should be enough to entice the Abrogate to the party, neither man felt comfortable using Colleen as bait; however, they both understood that the Abrogate was following Colleen, and he would know she would be in attendance. They had both decided the party would be the best cover to bring in more Argents and Arcs, intermingling with the guests, to give them their best advantage in capturing Rayne. However, it didn't give them much time, the gala was to take place one week from tomorrow.

This would entail Gordon to get back on speaking terms with Andrew. Gordon had also explained to Jerad the significance of the keys, not only for the specially made snow globes, but the ability they afforded him and his cousin to see what the other was seeing, feeling, and thinking. Gordon had held a tiny spark of hope that perhaps Andrew could be swayed to leave Colleen alone, but after their most recent conversation, that spark had been extinguished. They had to get Andrew's key; Joseph would hang on to Gordon's key for as long as possible.

At some point during their deliberations, Jerad received yet another message from his people that Rayne was in D.C. Gordon merely arched a brow when Jerad relayed the information, "Always a fertile ground for the Fold. Have you read the papers lately?" Jerad nodded with understanding.

They had a reasonably solid plan for containing Andrew; and together, they tried to create a contingency plan for every possible scenario to entrap Rayne while keeping Colleen safe. They had to hammer out a few more details, and then, of course, there was always the unknown possibilities for which they couldn't plan. But, when Jerad seemed satisfied with their progress, he left for his hotel in town to catch a few hours of sleep, and Gordon took a quick shower, before finally getting to bed about 3:30 in the morning.

There was just enough moonlight bouncing off of the snow outside to cast a glow in the bedroom for Gordon to make out Colleen's form in the bed. She was sound asleep, facing away from him. However, she was apparently dreaming, considering the moment he laid down next to her he was hit with more images, incredibly intimate images. But it was different this time; this time it wasn't just the images, he was consumed with her emotions also. Emotions of her yearnings and needs strong enough for him to have an immediate reaction that had him considering another shower. A cold shower.

Touching her shoulder, Gordon whispered, "Colleen, honey turn over," thinking that if he could get her to move, she might stop dreaming, but she just moaned. Just about the time Gordon thought he might move to the couch downstairs, she turned toward him, murmuring his name. She slid her hand over his chest, down his stomach, and then he caught her wrist before she could go further.

Colleen's eyes popped open, and she jerked her hand back, and said, "Sorry, I was dreaming."

"No kidding," Gordon muttered under his breath, but once she had awakened, the intensity of her emotions had subsided; to her, he whispered, "it's okay, go back to sleep."

"I'm not used to having someone in my bed," she mumbled, as she snuggled tightly into Gordon's side.

With a smile, Gordon whispered, "You're a wanton woman, Colleen O'Malley, and you're in *my* bed," he emphasized.

With a tiny smile of her own, she sighed, "Same thing," before drifting off again into a dreamless sleep.

The next day brought another round of questions for Gordon about the Fold from Jerad, interspersed with planning strategies. During one of the planning strategies, Jerad saw firsthand the effect that Colleen's images had on Gordon when Joseph had barely caught Gordon right before he walked into a wall. He even went so far as to suggest that perhaps Colleen should go stay with his wife Molly, in upstate New York, for the next couple of days; until Gordon explained that distance only made it worse.

"I've never seen anything like this; on the other hand, I've never seen a connection between the Dark and Light like this either," Jerad exclaimed. When Gordon froze again, for the second time, while drawing and explaining the layout of the Manor, Jerad jumped up and yelled for Audra, who came running into the library.

"Make her stop," Jerad ordered.

Looking at Gordon, Audra shot back, "You make her stop. She isn't even aware she's thinking of him, it's in her subconscious." Audra drew a deep breath, "Jerad they need time to know each other; all of Colleen's time has been spent in the work of the Argents; Gordon's, the Fold, and now you're here. They have barely begun to know each other, to trust each other outside of their sleeping arrangements; give them some space."

"We haven't got that kind of time," Jerad argued immediately; then he stopped for a moment, squinting at Audra, he then turned to stare at Gordon, fire shooting from his eyes, as he asked, "What do you mean outside of their sleeping arrangements?"

Audra sighed, "Their relationship has more or less started at the end, they haven't had a beginning yet. Jerad, remember how things were for you and Molly? Each of you knew that your lives would be spent together the first time you met, but neither of you would own up to that to the other. The two of you had time to learn about one another, to build trust in each other; they haven't had that time."

Jerad opened his mouth to continue the argument, but Colleen walked in, surveyed the room and with her signature stance, hands on her hips, ordered all of them out of the library. Gordon had felt instant relief and release from the image when Colleen entered the room, he was amused when she ordered them all to leave and surprised when they went without an argument.

Turning to face him as she closed the door behind Jerad, Colleen gave Gordon a brilliant smile, sat on the leather couch, and patting the cushion next to her, said, "Come sit with me."

"Yes ma'am," Gordon said, with a bemused smile as he sat facing her. *"What is she up to now?"*

Colleen stared into Gordon's eyes, then took a deep breath, "I need to tell you something; something that I think I have figured out about my spontaneous projecting, but I have been afraid to voice it; however, I think once I do, I might stop projecting my every thought to you."

Extremely curious now, and with an encouraging smile, Gordon said, "I'm listening."

Colleen continued to stare into his eyes but didn't say anything. Gordon could feel her inner struggle, and he wanted to pull her close, but she suddenly looked so fragile he was afraid to touch her; as if she might go to pieces. Gordon watched her intently, as she dropped her gaze to her twisting fingers in her lap, and chewed her bottom lip.

"Colleen, talk to me." Gordon urged softly.

Clearing her throat, Colleen finally said, "Gordon, I've never really been in a relationship, any kind of a relationship, with a man before. When I lost my parents, I had a problem, for years, of letting anyone get too close, I was afraid if I did, I would lose them too; therefore, I have always kept anyone new in my life at arm's length."

Gordon nodded, and said, "That's understandable." Watching her closely, Gordon wondered, *"Did she just tell me she's a virgin?"* Then a different thought crossed Gordon's mind that had his gut twisting, *"Or, did she just tell me she has decided that she doesn't want me."*

Continuing, she said, "I mean I've dated, there was this one guy, but…," she paused, and Gordon braced himself, "but, I've never felt this way, I haven't been able to keep you at arm's length."

Gordon was the one struggling now, "And this frightens you

in what way?" he asked. "Is it that you don't want a relationship with me?"

Drawing a shaky breath, Colleen said, "I don't even know how to express myself correctly."

"Just tell me," Gordon said roughly, preparing himself for the worst.

She looked at him then and said, "Remember when you called me a tease?" Gordon nodded, "You were right," she continued, laughing lightly. "In part, being a tease is sort of my job description, like playing a role, enticing men to come to me, and then I back away to let the Arcs take over. It came fairly easily to me; since I never wanted anyone, much less anyone from the Dark Fold that close to me, I was able to detach from the situation easily, and never look back." Drawing a deep breath, Colleen's green eyes bore into Gordon's, and she said, "Then you became my next assignment. I began as I always do, except this time I couldn't detach."

"And, that's what scares you?" Gordon asked stoically, "you're afraid of becoming involved with me, and you don't want to be involved."

Sighing deeply, Colleen murmured, "I have no experience at this; I'm saying it all wrong." Gordon watched her warily, feeling vulnerable, and cursing himself for allowing his feelings to get to this point.

"Gordon, I don't want to detach from you. You see, I do want a relationship with you, but," she blew out the breath she had been holding, and said in a rush, "I want a real relationship, not just sex, I want it all." Her cheeks flooded with color, but she seemed determined to explain. "My fear is that you don't feel the same; that the only thing you want is an affair. So, I think the reason I keep subconsciously sending you images, images that are always sexual in nature, is because I *know* you want me in that way, and projecting is my subconscious attempt to keep you connected to me. To keep you interested."

Feeling a flood of relief course through him, Gordon thought,

"She is looking for a declaration of my feelings for her." Gordon closed
the space between them, gathered Colleen in his arms, and held her
quietly for a moment before saying, "Colleen, if I survive turning
against the Dark Genesis, I can promise you that I will stay by your
side in whatever way you will accept me, for as long as you will
let me." He held her away from him anxiously searching her face,
waiting for her reaction.

"That may be for a *very* long time," she whispered.

Gordon smiled, as he whispered back, "I'm counting on that."
Then he pulled her to him, kissing her tenderly at first, then with a
hunger that Colleen returned with eagerness.

Gordon had felt her hand on his chest but hadn't realized that
she had very deftly unbuttoned his shirt until he felt her fingers on
his bare skin. With regret, he pulled his mouth from hers and said,
"Hey, whoa, what are you doing?"

With a sultry smile, she replied, "I wanted to touch you."

He gently pulled her hand out of his shirt, and kissed her palm,
as he softly chuckled, "You know you're driving me crazy, right?"

Sliding her hands over his shoulders to interlace her fingers at
the back of his neck, Colleen smiled into his eyes, and said, "That's
my job, remember?"

Smiling indulgently, Gordon started to re-button his shirt, and
asked, "Speaking of jobs, did Jerad tell you that Joseph and I will be
going to Boston later today? You, along with Jerad and Audra, will
stay here tonight, and then we will meet at the manor tomorrow."

Colleen frowned as she let her hands drop to her lap, and said.
"I don't like it. I'm going with you."

"That's not possible, Colleen," Gordon responded firmly. "It will
be difficult enough for me to run a bluff on Andrew, I have to focus,
and I can't do that if I'm worried about you." Gordon recognized
the familiar stubborn set of Colleens chin, and said emphatically,
"You're staying here, where I know you will be reasonably safe."

"You need to remember, I am an Argent," Colleen said, evenly.
"I can take care of myself."

"Better tread lightly here ole' boy," Gordon told himself, as he chose his next words carefully, "Colleen, I do not doubt *your* abilities, it's *my* ability to keep Andrew out of my head that is in question. If you're near, you will be on my mind; and he will pick up on that." Gordon watched her face as she mulled over what he had said, then added, "Joseph will try to block Andrew from my mind. He did it recently, with you actually, and it worked for a short period of time. But, the connection between Andrew and I is different; and there is no guarantee it will work at all. If it does, there shouldn't be any problems; however, if it doesn't, I will be forced to improvise." He could tell by her expression that she knew he was right, so he added, "Colleen, members of the Fold do not normally work in a unit, as does the Radiant, simply having Jerad's men there will be new to me."

After a moment, Colleen sighed deeply, and said, "I still don't like it, but I understand; I will stay here. But what if something goes wrong and you need more back-up? The Paladins and Arcs that Jerad has chosen are good men, but they don't know you as I do."

"My physical powers are greater than Andrews, if I have to, I *will* put him in the middle of the Atlantic until he can be subdued," Gordon stated matter-of-factly.

With a sharp knock, the door to the library swung open, and Jerad, along with Joseph, stepped in while announcing, "Okay, time to get back to work."

"The taskmaster returns," Gordon whispered in Colleen's ear.

"Yes, the taskmaster has returned," Jerad said mockingly while as he gave Gordon an appraising glance.

Stifling a giggle, Colleen said, "Uh, Gordon, when he chooses, Jerad's hearing is beyond extraordinary. It's one of his talents."

Gordon groaned, turning to Joseph he asked, "So is the concept of privacy simply an elaborate illusion?"

Glaring at both of them, Jerad asked, his voice dripping in sarcasm, "If you two are done 'talking' can we finish up now?" Gordon knew the Arc had not missed Colleen's kiss-swollen lips, nor him refastening the last of his shirt buttons.

GORDON SAT BACK IN HIS SEAT as he and Joseph headed south to Boston. He had been able to finish the diagram of Bilford Manor, for Jerad, with only minor interference from Colleen's images. She was still projecting, but now the images were more like a television's picture within the picture, not totally obscuring his field of vision. Apparently, their talk this morning had some impact. But, since separation from each other usually made the images more frequent and vivid, Gordon had conceded that it was best for Joseph to do the driving, just in case.

They were hopeful that Joseph would be able to block Andrew from picking through Gordon's thoughts, but Gordon feared the proximity would be hard to overcome. *"If the block worked, then that would beg the question: Would Gordon be blocked from Andrew's mind? This was all new territory."* Gordon heaved a heavy sigh that drew Joseph's attention.

"Gordon, try to relax," Joseph encouraged. "Remember we have it worked out so that when you make contact with Andrew, I will contact Jerad, and Colleen will send a projection. Then, hopefully, by Andrew's reaction, you will know if my block is working, or, even if he is trying to fool you into thinking that he isn't receiving; you should be able to get a read him."

They had reason to be hopeful that Andrew would be blocked;

after Joseph had performed the necessary procedure, Gordon had felt a loosening within himself as if a string that had been pulling at him was suddenly cut. *"The only thing is Andrew probably felt the disconnect too."* Gordon thought.

After making a stop at the vault, Gordon stood quietly in their Boston apartment as dusk began to settle over the harbor, waiting for Andrew; thinking about the enormity of what lay ahead, yet he felt utterly calm in his resolution.

He could hear Andrew whistling just outside of the door as he keyed the lock. As Gordon turned, the whistling stopped, and Andrew stared at Gordon, "Well this is a surprise," Andrew said, "and it really shouldn't be, at least not to me." Looking Gordon up and down, feigning a nonchalance Gordon could feel as false, he asked, "What are you up to now, Cousin?"

"I thought I should visit with you in person since our last conversation was cut short," Gordon said smoothly. At the same time, an image of Colleen wearing a gossamer, nearly transparent negligee floated in front of Gordon. *"She's doing something new,"* Gordon thought. The image was translucent enabling him to see through it, and still observe his surroundings. Clamping his mouth shut, Gordon tried to gauge Andrew's facial expression, but his cousin gave no indication of seeing a nearly nude Colleen. Gordon began to focus on Andrew's mind searching for deception.

"Cut short by you as I recall," Andrew sneered. "If memory serves, it was right after you ripped one of our ships apart."

"I have already seen to the damages, and made up the missed wages to our workers," Gordon replied calmly; while at the same time marveling at Joseph's ability to block Andrew.

"Money wasted due to your baseless tantrum," Andrew shot back, pointing an accusing finger in Gordon's direction.

"I can promise you that won't happen again," Gordon said, noting that Andrew seemed surprised by his declaration. "As long as nothing happens to Colleen. Problem solved."

"So, you're back on her again, huh?" Andrew scorn evident in his voice. "I had hoped that with some time away you would be more reasonable on the subject of Ms. O'Malley."

Gordon drew a calming breath, the image of Colleen had ceased, "Andrew, I have repeatedly told you that Shaun and Fran's niece is not to be harmed. Colleen is primarily a minor annoyance; you can't honestly believe she can cause any real disturbance." Gordon paused, before adding, "However, if the O'Malley's niece goes missing, then we have a problem."

"Why?" Andrew questioned. "People go missing all the time."

"Not the niece of my neighbors. The O'Malley's are close friends; not to mention that Colleen has been seen with the two of us on several occasions. She is also the person that is overseeing the benefit that will honor Terese, which in turn honors the Bilford name," Gordon replied.

"I still don't like it," Andrew said sourly, "Did it occur to you that all of the O'Malley's might be Argents? Or, their friends? How many of them are going to be at this gala?"

"We don't know for sure that Colleen is an Argent," Gordon argued, to which Andrew just snorted. "Okay, what would make you feel better?" Gordon asked.

"Well for a start, if you would take your position within the Fold seriously, I would feel a whole lot better." Andrew challenged, his emerald eyes hard and boring into Gordon's. "We are, after all, only one step away from the Genesis. That means something to the members of the Fold."

Gordon stared back scanning Andrew's mind, and thought, *"Andrew feels our new-found station has given us even more power and should excuse his every whim."* Gordon nearly groaned aloud, *"As if he needed to feel any more entitled,"* then said, "Andrew, I never asked for any of this, I never wanted it. You know that." Gordon was hoping to appeal to what humanity his Cousin might still have.

"Yeah, I know; but it is who you are," Andrew stated. "Maybe you need to learn to love yourself," he added sarcastically, "and put aside all of those misplaced feelings of yours for those that are beneath us."

Gordon's already small hope for swaying Andrew, was shrinking rapidly, "Would it make you feel better to ask your friend, Rayne, to attend?" he asked.

"Really?" Andrew asked, in disbelief. "I thought you didn't want anything to do with Rayne or the Abrogates."

"I don't want anything to do with the Abrogates, I think it's a mistake to become involved with them, but if it would make you feel better…" Gordon shrugged, as he let the suggestion hang in the air.

"Considering we might have a house full of Argents, I think I will give him a call," Andrew said defiantly.

"You could send an invitation by special courier if you know his address, then follow-up with a call," Gordon suggested.

Carefully scrutinizing Gordon, Andrew said sneeringly, "I really don't believe that Rayne concerns himself, as you do, with the social niceties of the Normals. A phone call will suffice."

Gordon shrugged in feigned nonchalance, and said, "You would know, more than I, on how best to handle the Abrogate."

Andrew stood a little straighter and squared his shoulders, and took on a somewhat condescending tone to match his posture, "And, Gordon what about your key? I would have thought that Joseph would have repaired it by now, and brought it to you."

Gordon snorted, and shook his head, "You're starting to worry like an old woman. As for the key, I don't take chances with it," Gordon lied, "one never knows what can happen when on the road. It has been repaired and safely tucked away at the manor, I will be home tomorrow, and I will retrieve it then." Cocking his head to Andrew, he said, "We seem to have done all right without it, don't you think?" Gordon had been wondering if Andrew had felt a significant shift since Gordon's defection to the Radiant.

Andrew narrowed his eyes as he scrutinized Gordon's face, "I guess so. Although, I do feel as if we have been out of touch since the day of your storm."

With pinpoint clarity, Gordon recalled the red cardinal flitting from branch to branch in the fir behind the Getaway and opened his mind to Andrew.

"Okay, so you're still into bird watching," Andrew drawled. "Got anything else you would like to share with me Cousin?"

Gordon allowed his mind to wander the streets of Albany a little, and he flashed on Colleen's face briefly.

"Can't let her go, can you?" Andrew complained. "Is she the reason you're blocking me, Gordon?"

Shutting down the corridor to his mind that he had opened for Andrew, Gordon knew his response would be crucial; he had to temper it with the right amount of anger and indignation without going too far. He also resigned himself to the fact that to have any hope that Andrew might be enticed from the Fold was an exercise in futility. It was time to set their plan into motion. Taking his time, wandering over to the windows to gaze out at the harbor lights, he began, "Andrew, do you really want to push me like that again?" Gordon asked, with a warning note. "You told me you understood my message, were you lying to me?"

"You're in love with her," Andrew stated flatly; it wasn't a question; it was an accusation.

Still staring out the window, Gordon took a moment before responding. Andrew had struck a nerve; Gordon had been avoiding admitting this even to himself. He had never told any woman that he was 'in love' with her, including his wives. In place of 'I love you,' he had used phrases such as, *'I love how you make me feel, I love being with you,'* but never I love you.

"I will deal with Colleen in my way and in my own time," Gordon, finally responded smoothly, "You need to trust me."

"Trust you?" Andrew scoffed. "I'm supposed to trust you? You can't trust yourself. How would you know if what you are feeling is real? How do you know it's not just her controlling you now?"

DONNA PFANNENSTIEL

Andrew demanded. "Why can't you just use her and lose her? Best of both worlds that way. You might as well because you know what will happen to her anyway; but we could have the added bonus of using her as a tribute, rather than someone from a different house."

The floor began to shift, dishes in the cabinets started to rattle, and the hanging art began to dance across the wall, "Andrew, I'm not having this discussion again," Gordon's voice was deadly calm, and it saddened him that there was no hope for his cousin.

"Damn it, Gordon!" Andrew shouted as he braced his feet apart. "Control your temper! Are you going to tear the building down over some woman?"

"That's up to you Andrew," Gordon responded in the same level tone, staring unseeingly at the harbor. He could feel the power of the elements surge through him as he allowed the Dark to creep into his mind.

"So, you would rather rip us and this building apart over a woman that is our nemesis?" Andrew yelled. "Can't you see how absurd you're behaving? She is nothing, a guard dog to the Normals; and she is controlling you."

"And you, Cousin, are so controlled by your fear, of a mere woman, that you are ignoring my orders," Gordon replied.

"Your orders?" Andrew scoffed. "I answer only to the Genesis," he added smugly. Turning to focus his gaze on Andrew, Gordon heard his cousin's gasp as he looked into Gordon's eyes, "Gordon you really need to pull back."

"Are you ready to pull back Andrew?" Gordon asked as he gave a slight mental push causing the earth under the building to shift just enough for Andrew to feel it, once again. Gordon could feel the potency of the Dark moving over him; however, for the moment he still held control over the power.

"I will not hurt her Gordon, and I will not order a hit," Andrew conceded. "But I will not protect her if another member of the Fold goes after her." Andrew held Gordon's gaze defiantly, and added emphatically, "Ms. Colleen O'Malley? I'm done."

Gordon moved to the small case he had brought with him and had placed on a nearby end table. Opening it, he retrieved a bundle wrapped in black velvet, and placed it on the coffee table, speaking softly he said, "Yes Andrew, you are done." Gordon removed the velvet covering to reveal the snow globe that ensconced Jeanette and Terese frozen in their watery world. Quickly, inserting the key, the one he had told Andrew he didn't have, into the hidden lock, he gave it a twist; the snowy glitter within the globe swirled, and the figure of Terese disappeared as Andrew begin to shimmer. At that moment a ripping sound tore through the building, the portal was now open. The door to the apartment slammed against the wall, and four men that Gordon didn't know entered followed by Joseph.

Gordon took no joy in seeing the shock of betrayal on his cousin's face as the two Paladins, and the two Arcs seized him; holding him as Joseph snapped the chain that secured Andrew's key from his neck. The lights flickered, then the apartment was plunged into darkness for a moment. There was just enough light from the harbor and the city streets below for Gordon to see the two Paladins rush toward the center of the room just in time to keep Terese from hitting the floor and place her on the couch.

Gordon looked up to where Andrew had been standing between the Arcs to see that he had been replaced by a flame that writhed, hissed, and then suddenly extinguished. Spinning around to look at the globe Gordon watched as the glittery snow inside swirled into a tight vortex, and when the funnel broke apart, it revealed his cousin arm-in-arm with Jeanette on the little path near the pond, wearing a look of confusion that matched Jeanette's.

Gordon looked down at Terese, and dropped to his knees beside her; struck as he always had been by her ethereal beauty, thinking, *"She is just as exquisite as the last time I saw her."* But she hadn't come around yet, and he shot an anxious look to Joseph as the Paladins gently wrapped her in the blankets that Gordon had hidden under the couch when he had first entered the apartment.

Placing a hand on his shoulder, Joseph stood next to Gordon, and quietly said, "Miss Terese will be fine; they told me it could be a couple of hours before she wakes. But they need to take her immediately; there are members of the Radiant waiting for her at the hospital. Gordon, it will be all right; she won't remember any of this."

"She might not remember, but I will," Gordon responded, filled once again with self-loathing as he stood. "Due to my arrogance and selfishness I stole ten years of her life; she didn't deserve that," then placing his hand on her forehead in a gentle caress he pulled from her the memory of their first meeting.

The first time they had met was at a street fair in Boston's Historical Section. He had planned the Grand Opening of the Bilford Complex to coincide with the festival. He had been intrigued by her as he had watched her approach the various vendors. She appeared genuinely delighted with their handmade wares and had laughed as carefree as a child with her companions as they pulled her along with them. He had watched the cheerful little group as they enjoyed the festivities and each other. He envied their bright, carefree afternoon, the only worry they had was in deciding which street food to sample next.

It was here that he had introduced himself to the enchanting Terese. Gordon decided to change her memory of that meeting into nothing more than a smile and a nod from a passing stranger; leaning down he placed a kiss on her forehead, and in a voice heavy with remorse, whispered, "I'm so sorry,"

The Paladins carefully picked Terese up and headed out the door; as Gordon watched them leave, he was momentarily lost in his memories of his life with Terese, and the excruciating emotional pain of what he had done to her.

The Arcs stood by quietly waiting for Gordon; the Radiants would take no chances; the Arcs had stayed behind for two reasons; first to bear witness to Gordon completing the task at hand, locking Andrew in the vault, and second to assist Gordon if there was any interference from the Dark Genesis.

Gordon led the way to the private elevator that would take them to the business offices on the fourth floor when he was suddenly filled with Colleen; her face, her fragrance, and her emotions were coming on strong. Joseph knew something was coming and grabbed Gordon seconds before the projection to keep him from falling, the two Arcs looked at Gordon, and then at one another knowingly. The one called Larry said, "Wow! Colleen's at it again, even I can feel that." Turning to his partner David, he said, "Try to contact Jerad, maybe he can interrupt her before she inadvertently causes this guy," pointing to Gordon, "to get hurt. If she causes anything to happen to him," he shuddered at the thought, "let's put it this way, I don't want to deal with an unhappy Colleen."

"It's worth a shot, but, maybe you should hold on to that globe before he drops it," David said, as he pulled his phone from the inside of his jacket, and stepped away punching in the numbers, "we have no idea what kind of trouble that could cause."

Although Gordon could still see and feel Colleen the initial surprise and intensity had marginally subsided, and he told them, "No, I'm all right, the globe cannot be out of my possession, and the vault will not open for anyone but my Cousin and myself." With a grimace, he corrected himself, saying, "Actually, I suppose it won't open for anyone but me now."

David took a few running steps back to catch them as they boarded the elevator, informing them that, "They are going to try to distract Colleen, but Jerad said that she was beside herself and kept saying, "He's in pain" over and over again. I assured him that Mr. Bilford had no injuries, and was perfectly all right."

Larry looked over at Gordon, and then said quietly to David, "It's his emotional pain that she is picking up." Clapping Gordon on the shoulder, he said, "C'mon man, you're going to have to pull it together to get her to stop."

"It's a little better now," Gordon replied. "The original onslaught was draining, but she has dialed it back." However, when the elevator doors opened, Gordon sucked in his breath and became stone still... hyper-aware of his surroundings. Joseph once again grabbed at Gordon, only this time rather than an attempt to keep him from falling, Joseph pulled him back and jumped in front of him before Gordon could stop him.

Joseph went flying backward, slammed into the rear wall of the elevator, from a flash of what looked like a fireball hitting him square in the chest; he landed in a heap on the floor. The Arcs were looking around in confusion, but Gordon feeling a pull, stepped out into the hallway; there, several feet away to his left stood Andrew Bilford the II. Behind, Uncle Andrew, billowing, swirling, pushing and pulling was the Dark.

"Good evening Gordon," the elder Bilford greeted sardonically. "I believe you have something that belongs to me." With eyes that glowed a murky green, he added, "Give me my son."

"I'm afraid that isn't possible, Uncle," Gordon replied keeping his voice level. As Gordon observed his Uncle, he couldn't help but notice that the man looked ten years younger than the last time he had seen him; and that had been more than fifteen years ago. Briefly, Gordon wondered how many tributes Uncle Andrew had taken to achieve his present youthful appearance.

However, Gordon didn't have the luxury of time to dwell on his Uncle's perverse activities; he could instantly feel the energy of the Dark, pushing against him; intent on dominating him by literally trying to bring him to his knees. The Dark energy was probing and testing Gordon's mettle; its draw was potent; Gordon could feel it pulsating through every fiber of his being. It would be so easy to give himself over to the Genesis; yet, Gordon held steadfastly, he had resolved that he would die before bowing to the Genesis of the Dark ever again.

The Arcs, Larry and David, after having checked on Joseph and had gotten him on his feet inside the elevator, came to flank Gordon; one on each side, both stood with their shoulders squared and their hands hanging deceptively loose. Peripherally, Gordon could see that Joseph was injured, his left arm dangling at his side.

"Gordon, I care for you," his Uncle began, "but, this is a betrayal," he motioned to the two men that stood at Gordon's side, "it is an affront to your birthright, your family, and the Genesis. Release my son now, and we will let you go to live your life as you see fit."

"My family?" Gordon asked in disbelief, "My family betrayed me! Forcing me into something I never asked for, nor did I want." As Gordon spoke the Dark swirled faster and started to creep along the walls, ceiling, and floor; framing his uncle in black shadow. Gordon could feel it probing at his mind, draining his energy, *"It would be so easy to give in,"* Gordon thought, but he gathered what strength he had and remained stoic in his resistance. "You don't honestly expect me to believe you now, do you, Uncle Andrew?" Gordon sneered as he flipped the snow-globe into the air, in the same manner, one would toss a baseball, but instead of catching it as it descended, he made a rapid circular motion with his hand, and the globe came to settle at eye-level, floating in the air.

"I would advise you to take your leave and take your unwanted guest with you," Gordon said calmly. "You don't want any trouble, right Uncle? You don't want me to let the globe drop." Gordon heard his Uncle Andrew draw in a sharp breath as he watched the globe with his son inside dance in mid-air, then Gordon allowed it to plunge about two feet above the floor. At the same time, he could feel the Dark reaching out to him as a low screeching filled the hallway, like fingernails slowly scratching on a chalkboard, "You do know what will happen if it drops and breaks, right?"

"Gordon, son, be reasonable," his Uncle said beseechingly. "You don't want to hurt your cousin."

"You're right," Gordon agreed, "I don't want to hurt him, but he threatened the life of someone I care for deeply---"

"An Argent," his Uncle sneeringly interrupted. "Yes, I know all about it. I also know that you are choosing a woman, an Argent woman, over your own blood."

"My blood," Gordon emphasized mockingly, "knows that

by threatening anyone under my protection is an equivalent to threatening me. And that is why he will be kept here," indicating the globe, "where I know he will do no harm." Gordon clapped his hands twice, and the globe disappeared. Gordon could feel an odd energy coursing through him, like a shot of adrenalin, and realized that it came from the Arcs that stood beside him. He could feel his eyes altering as they always do when angered and he called upon the energy; but it was righteous anger this time, the energy was coming from the light not from the Dark, "If you leave here, stay away from me, and those that are under my protection, then your son will be contained, but safe."

Suddenly the lights began to flicker rapidly in a strobe-like effect, and the only sound that could be heard was an ear-splitting screech from the Dark, along with what sounded like a hundred harmonizing hellions. It crawled rapidly along the walls, ceiling, and floor, filling the hallway, and billowing toward Gordon. The Arcs raised their arms to throw-up a glimmering shield to block its path, but not before a portion of the swirling darkness had slipped past along the walls; glowing pinpoints of flames tossed the Arcs sideways, isolating and surrounding Gordon, lifting him close to the ceiling. Gordon could physically feel the Dark leaving his body to join with the Genesis and then slamming him to the floor, left to lie motionless, before receding. The Arcs, who had regained their footing, moved forward, pushing their shield before them, and as they did the hallway filled with light, but, both Andrew Bilford the II and the Dark had vanished.

Joseph immediately went to knell beside Gordon, who did not appear to be breathing; and David quickly began to administer CPR as Larry called their contacts at the hospital.

23

WEARY AND WITHOUT REGRET, THE TWO Arcs, Larry and David, along with Joseph and Gordon left Boston in their rear-view mirror to race through the wee morning hours to reach Bilford Manor hoping to get some rest before sun-up. Larry was at the wheel since Joseph was unable to drive due to his left arm being tied up in a sling; a displaced shoulder and a reminder of the harrowing night he would carry for a few days, courtesy of Andrew II. David, sat up front with Larry, quietly talking to Jerad on his cell.

"Yeah, he's going to be okay," David said as he reported to Jerad. "The doctor sedated him, so no concussion. He does have some bruising on his legs and backside, but the worst is his ribs; we tried to cushion him from the floor, but with keeping the shield in place, there wasn't time. However, the doc said nothing was broken, but that he probably pulled every muscle in his body. He will be sore, in pain, and will need to take it easy for several days." David listened for a moment and then chuckled, "Yeah, he kind of scared me, I thought we had him protected within the shield; but somehow it slipped through just enough to pick him up and slam him to the floor. I thought his heart had stopped, that's the thing that scared me; but I guess it just knocked the wind out of him because when I started giving him CPR, he came to and tried to punch me."

Gordon, although still groggy from the drugs, was listening to David's conversation from the backseat. He didn't have the energy right now to explain that it wasn't the lack of their protection that caused him to be lifted and then get slammed on the floor. It was the Dark taking its own back from his body, leaving him suspended in midair briefly. That, the force of the separation, coupled with the vindictive retaliation of the Genesis, had hurtled his body downward.

After making sure everyone was all right both in Boston and in Bilford, David ended his call with Jerad only to have his phone to go off less than a minute later. Looking at the caller I.D., David groaned, "Colleen."

"What do you want to bet, that you and I will be to blame for his injuries?" David asked Larry, who responded with a grunt. "Hey, Colleen," David answered cheerfully, hoping to ward off the unpleasantness of being taken to task. Gordon couldn't make out her words, but he could hear her rising voice through the phone. "Yeah I know," David said heavily, "everything was going exactly to plan until his Uncle showed up...along with his company from Hell." David paused and held the phone away from his ear; Gordon could nearly make out her words as Colleen began a rant that had him smiling.

"No, you can't talk to him," David said when she demanded he hand his phone over to Gordon. "He's sleeping right now, he was injured, and he needs to rest Colleen." When she started raising her voice again, Gordon tapped the back of the seat and held his hand out for the phone, wordlessly David handed it over.

"...if he wakes up before you get here, have him to call me," Colleen demanded.

Gordon smiled and, in an attempt, to placate and lighten her mood, said, "*He* woke-up. What can *he* do for you, ma'am?" For a second Gordon thought the connection had been cut-off. Then in a rush, Colleen hit him with a barrage of images, images of every kiss they had shared, his hands on her body, her hands on his body, and emotions of fear, relief, need, want, and yearning so strong that his breath caught in his throat. She still hadn't spoken, but he answered her, softly saying, "I will be home in less than an hour. I am all right, and so is Joseph, we're just a little bruised and banged up. I'm mostly exhausted and need my bed." Without hesitation, he added, "And Colleen, I need to see you as much as you need to see me." With that, he ended the call, handed the phone back to David, and giving in to the drugs and the fragrance of Colleen's perfume, promptly dozed off.

Gordon woke as they were heading up the drive to Bilford Manor, which was ablaze with lights. Chafing to be out of the confines of the car Gordon tentatively stretched only to find himself gasping in pain as every muscle screamed in protest. The gasping itself caused pain to explode around his mid-section. As he modulated his breathing the pain tapered off somewhat, and he glanced around to see Joseph watching him, "How are you doing?" Gordon asked, through gritted teeth.

Joseph smiled wanly and said, "I'll survive. I'm just sorry I couldn't keep the Dark from hurting you."

"You can't be serious," Gordon responded. "If it had not been for you taking that first hit, I would never have gotten Andrew to the vault." Shaking his head, he continued, "Our bruises will heal, but you, Joseph, you saved us and I wouldn't be here now, had it not been for you first and then the Arcs."

Parking the car at the front entrance to the manor, David and Larry, opened the back doors to assist Joseph and Gordon into the house. Gordon's eyes hungrily scanned the foyer, stopping when he saw Colleen at the foot of the stairs; in a green dressing gown, her braided hair over one shoulder, and her eyes shimmering with unshed tears. As always, the moment he saw her, his body became taut with want, and that in turn, made his bruised muscles protest once again, causing his attempt at a smile of welcome to become a grimace of pain.

Colleen sprang into action at once and began handing out

orders. "Jerad help me to get Gordon upstairs. David go get the ice packs from the kitchen freezer, and Larry, help Audra to get Joseph settled."

Everyone immediately started to move following the orders they were given, leaving Colleen, Gordon, and Jerad in the foyer alone.

Pulling himself up a little straighter and squaring his shoulders, Jerad said, "Colleen, I still have a few questions about this whole sleeping arrangement thing."

With a roll of her eyes and a harrumph, Colleen said sternly, "Well you're not getting any answers!"

"You two are unbelievable! I swear you both would rather argue than to eat when you're hungry."

Gordon carefully turned his head to see this latest newcomer. She was a petite woman wearing a flowing flowery dressing gown; her soft fawn colored hair curled about her heart-shaped face emphasizing ice blue eyes, and a smile that was at once warm and brilliant; she came to stand next to Jerad.

"Mr. Bilford, it is a pleasure to meet you; I am Molly Evan, Jerad's wife." She stepped away from Jerad and extended her hand to Gordon. "I have heard so much about you, some good, some bad, and all very interesting; I can't wait to get to know you."

Gordon liked her on the spot, and took her hand replying, "Please call me Gordon."

Inclining her head, she said, "And you shall call me Molly." To her husband she spoke softly saying, "Jerad, I think it would be an excellent idea for you to assist Gordon," she turned to smile sweetly at Gordon, before turning the same sweet smile back on her husband, "to prepare for bed, unless you would prefer to leave that to Colleen?"

Jerad's eyes grew wide as he started to bluster, "No, no of course not. I will take care of helping Gordon get ready for bed."

"You're such a darlin'," she said, her cultured voice slipping into an Irish lilt as she laid her hand on her husband's chest and she stared up at him with that same sweet smile.

If Gordon had witnessed this bit of byplay from most of the women that he knew, he would have done a mental eye roll, but he truly believed she was sincerely complimenting her husband. To Gordon, she said, "I'm sure you must be in some pain and absolutely exhausted." Pointedly looking at Jerad first, then to Gordon, she continued, "I'm certain the only thing on your mind right now is to get some rest." Turning her attention back to her husband, she patted his chest, and softly said, "I'll be waiting for you dear."

Gordon wanted to laugh at the great Arc for being manipulated so successfully by his tiny little wife, but he refrained, for one thing, it would hurt like Hell to laugh right now.

By the time Gordon had climbed the stairs, pulled his clothes off, used the bathroom, and maneuvered himself into bed, all with Jerad's assistance, he had a fine sheen of perspiration covering his face. Colleen placed plump pillows on either side of him to help keep him still and went to get his pain meds from David.

Jerad stood uncertainly at the foot of the bed and finally said, "From what I hear you did great tonight. Thank you."

"Thank you for giving me the opportunity, and most importantly, for making sure that Terese will get the life she deserves," Gordon responded with sincerity.

Colleen returned with Gordon's pain pills and a glass of water. Facing the Arc, she said, "Thank you Jerad," and in a tone meant clearly to dismiss him she continued, "I will see to Gordon now, and I will call you if I need you."

Jerad narrowed his eyes as he took in her defiant posture, but before he could question or argue with her, she sweetly reminded him, "Molly is waiting for you."

Jerad sighed deeply, and said, "We'll talk later Gordon."

When Jerad had closed the door behind him, Colleen held out her hand, "Here take your pill; it should help you to sleep," she said softly.

Gordon motioned for her to come closer, Colleen leaned over a little and Gordon motioned again for her to come closer. "What is it? Is something wrong?" she asked anxiously.

"Yes," Gordon said. Then in a plaintive voice added, "You're making an injured man work too hard for a kiss." Cautiously, so as not to jostle him, Colleen leaned forward and lightly pressed her lips to his, as she started to pull away, Gordon, with his hand on the back of her head, pulled her back and deepened their kiss. *"Colleen appeared to be more than happy to comply,"* Gordon thought.

Finally pulling back with a sigh, Colleen said again, "Take your medicine like a good boy, and maybe you will get another kiss before I leave."

Frowning, Gordon demanded, "Where do you think you're going at this time of night?"

Laughing softly, she replied, "To bed, silly. I will be in the next room." Giving him a meaningful look, as she handed him his pill for the third time, "You remember, the Mistress Suite?"

"No."

With a cajoling tone, Colleen said, "C'mon, you need to take it, it will help you sleep."

Gordon shook his head, took the pill from her hand, and swallowed it, "I meant, no, you're staying here with me."

"Gordon you need to rest, I'm afraid I might keep you awake or hurt you with my tossing and turning," Colleen argued.

"You have been in my bed every night since we left Boston," Gordon said, "I have had a very trying day, I'm hurting from head to toe," to prove his point he stretched his legs, grimacing slightly, "I need you next to me tonight."

"Are you trying to play on my sympathy?" Colleen asked him with a raised brow.

"Maybe," he said with an impish grin, then asked, "Is it working?"

Colleen studied his face for a moment, then with a sigh and an indulgent smile, said, "Yes." When Gordon tried to move the pillow, she shook her head, and said, "Uh-uh, I will lie on the other side of the pillow, so I don't accidentally roll into you."

Beginning to feel the effects of the painkillers, Gordon murmured, "I want to hold you."

"Hush, I'm right here," she ordered, as she laid down and placed her hand lightly on his chest over his heart.

"I still don't understand it, but her touch feels so right, soothing and comforting. As if we have always been together," was Gordon's final thought as he gave over to the drugs and the exhaustion.

Over the next few days, Gordon stayed in a perpetual state of drugged conscientiousness. He knew that at some point they had brought in a nurse, a male nurse, at Colleens' insistence. Gary, the nurse, had been assisting Gordon, during the day, with going to the restroom, and bathing, while monitoring both Gordon's meds and his progress. But Colleen had stayed by Gordon's side every night, and Gary slept in the Mistress Suite.

By the fourth day, Gordon could breathe a little easier, his ribs starting to heal, and the rest of the bruising looked much worse than it felt. Deciding he didn't care for the dull, fuzzy feeling, Gordon had begun to refuse some of his pain medication. By the morning of the gala, feeling more like his old self, Gordon was up and dressed on his own. He could take a fairly deep breath with only minimal discomfort, and the rest of his bruising had been reduced to a minor annoyance.

Standing at the foot of the stairs, after slowly making his way down the main staircase, Gordon looked around in amazement at the transformation of the foyer and great hall. Black tulle with dark red satin ribbons, along with long strands of white beading, had been draped as individual canopies over small round tables around the perimeter of the room; tall green plants were interspersed between the tables, offering a bit of privacy for the guests. Strands of tiny white lights softly lit the tulle and glowed against the satin. Completing the setting were small vases of red, pink, and white roses set in the middle of the tabletops that were draped in black coverings.

Gordon wandered into the formal dining area; here the theme had been continued, the long table covered in black with rose-filled vases of varying heights added interest. The chairs from the table were pushed to the perimeter of the room. In between the chairs were small covered tables just big enough for a guest to set a drink or a plate. As Gordon approached the observatory, he could see a soft purplish-blue glow illuminating the vast area. Here the greenery had been left to serve as the decor, and colored lights were used to highlight its natural beauty. Not surprisingly, it was here that he found Colleen.

Gordon stopped, once again ogling her from the entrance of the observatory, except this time she stood with her back to him on a short step ladder halfway down the middle path. She was barefooted, wore tight black jeans, and a loose, gauzy black top, the solid black of her clothing highlighting her deep red hair. Gordon gave a low whistle of appreciation, and she turned toward him.

"Gordon!" she exclaimed excitedly, as she scampered down and came running toward him. "Are you sure you should be up?" she asked when she reached him.

"I'm nearly a hundred percent," he exaggerated, as he tucked a stray tendril of her hair behind her ear, then slipped his hand around to cup her neck. Gordon grinned, and asked, "Want me to prove it?"

With eyes twinkling she gave him a little smile; Gordon decided that was a 'yes' as he pulled her closer to kiss her, at the same time he slid his other hand down her back to the curve of her hip, and then under the hem of her blouse to her bare back.

"Okay, you have made your point," she said, breaking their kiss with a smile as she pulled back.

"Are you sure?" he asked, and then with mock innocence said, "I could offer more evidence."

"No doubt," Colleen laughed, "but you need to take it easy for a few more days, and I have more work to do. Why don't you go check in with Joseph?"

Immediately sobering, Gordon frowned asking, "Is something wrong with Joseph?"

"No," Colleen answered, "but, he has been anxious about you. He is still fussing because, and I quote, *'he didn't keep you safe.'* He has apologized to me every day. Why don't you show him you're up and coherent?"

"I'll go find him," Gordon said, then shook his head, "Joseph takes too much on himself." Looking deeply into Colleen's eyes, he asked, "Will I see you later today?"

"Later as in this evening? At the gala? Yes." Colleen replied. Looking around the observatory, she added, "I have a couple of errands in town this morning, a few things to see to here, and then I need to go check on my guests that are staying at my house, and get dressed."

Gordon frowned, "I will go with you to run your errands," he said, not wanting her to travel alone.

"Larry and David will be with me," she sighed. "You know," she turned back to look up at Gordon, "you have been pretty out of it for several days, and nothing has happened to me."

Still not happy about the situation, but knowing he was probably behaving unreasonably, Gordon acquiesced, "Very well, I will see you this evening; but be warned, I have every intention of keeping you by my side tonight."

Reaching up to lightly kiss his lips, "And, I wouldn't have it any other way," Colleen said with a smile, as she left.

Gordon followed her with his eyes and decided that as long as he could be reasonably sure that she would return, he would take this opportunity to appreciate the view of her walking away.

ORDON DECIDED TO STOP BY HIS office, to check on the mail he was sure was piling up after the last few days, before searching for Joseph, only to find it locked. Pulling his key from his pocket, he went in and saw Joseph sitting inside.

Joseph jumped up to greet Gordon with a huge smile, "Sir, it's so wonderful to see you up and about. Are you still in pain? Sorry about the locked door, but I didn't think you would want people wandering in here. I felt like I was in everyone's way out there, so, I locked myself in here. The lassie seems to have everything under control," Joseph finished his rush of words with an expectant expression on his face.

Gordon smiled, as he said once again, "You don't need to call me 'sir' and yes, I'm feeling much better, Thank you. And, you're right, I don't want people poking around in here. Colleen has transformed the Main Hall and Dining room beautifully," Gordon gave Joseph an appraising look, and asked, "How about you? How are you feeling?"

"I'm healing," Joseph replied, wincing slightly as he attempted to physically shrug-off Gordon's concern, "I don't have to wear the sling anymore, so that's progress. I won't be lifting weights anytime soon, but I'm much improved. It's you I'm concerned about."

Gordon knew this would be the case, and had prepared himself to have a frank talk with his mentor. Motioning for Joseph to sit down, Gordon took the chair across from him, "Joseph, I need for you to understand that no one could have prevented my injuries."

Gordon acknowledged the look of skepticism on Joseph's face, "Let me explain?" Joseph nodded, and Gordon continued, "I never understood the strength of the Dark's hold over me until we physically occupied the same space. It took everything I had to resist its power. It was as if I went through some sort of physiological change; it must have been the presence of the Arcs. The energy from the Dark's expulsion from my body pulled me up and off of my feet; once it was drained from me, in retaliation, I was flung to the floor." Gordon watched as Joseph grimaced, apparently remembering, and said, "But, Joseph, I had to go through that in order to be rid of the evil. Quite frankly, I went into this prepared die, but I didn't, I have been given a second chance at life, thanks to you, and the Radiants," looking past Joseph, deep in thought, Gordon said, seeming to affirm to himself, as much as to Joseph, "I don't want to waste it, I want to make it a good life."

"And, you want that 'good life' with the lass, I presume," Joseph grinned, knowingly.

"It's what I want," Gordon agreed, as he stood and made his way to the windows overlooking the front lawns, "but, I have much to work through before I can make such an offer; and, of course, she might not agree."

Joseph smiled, "I don't think that will be a problem. She would hardly let anyone near you these past few days."

Gordon felt abundantly pleased to hear this. But, remembering there were others that still needed to be dealt with; Gordon said, broodingly, "Uncle Andrew may be on a short leash for now; but my father still needs to be dealt with, not to mention Rayne," turning to Joseph, he asked, "have you heard anything on either of them."

"No," Joseph answered, gravely. "As you said, your Uncle has gone underground, completely off radar; but, according to Audra something is brewing and will happen soon. Audra said they think it could be as soon as tonight during the gala."

Teasingly, Gordon asked, "*Audra* said, huh? I presume that the two of you are getting along well?" Gordon watched with amazement, and delight as the normally imperturbable Joseph's cheeks colored slightly, and then, with a clearing of his throat, replied rather defensively, "Yes well, you were not the only one to experience a transformation Gordon."

"No, I guess not," Gordon replied, still grinning. "I know there are still some issues that must be dealt with, but I feel buoyant; as if a terrible weight has been lifted. You?"

"Well, I don't think it's quite the same for me," Joseph replied, "but, yes I do feel less encumbered."

With a nod of understanding, the two men sat in comfortable silence; each lost in their thoughts. Yawning, Gordon said, "Since the preparations for tonight seem to be humming along nicely, and I couldn't persuade Colleen to stop working and spend the afternoon with me, I think I will go to my rooms for a while. From the look my desk, I have some correspondence I need to attend to; I might lie down for a bit before the party tonight, maybe you can keep an eye on things down here." With a wink, Gordon added, "You could see if Audra needs any help."

"As you wish sir," Joseph responded formerly, and with a twinkle in his eyes, said, "I will be more than happy to carry out your instructions and assist Audra in any way that I can."

Gordon chuckled as he headed upstairs going to his balcony first. He flung the doors wide to breathe in the salt air; he couldn't fill his lungs yet, due to the soreness lingering in his ribs, but still, it felt wonderful to have the cold breeze blowing in his face and to taste the salt on his lips.

Absently, out of habit, he reached for his key which he still wore; even though, he no longer felt the presence of Andrew or the pressure of the Dark laying on his chest. Andrew's key had been melted down to the size of a dime, permanently sealed in a clear acrylic block that had been placed in what appeared to be a simple metal lock-box, and stowed away here at the manor, in Gordon's private vault.

Gordon hadn't had time to mourn for the loss of his cousin. Even though Andrew's removal had been his decision; and, although Gordon felt no regret, he still felt a sense of loss. *"Mostly,"* he thought, *"it is the loss of hope; the hope that someday Andrew and I could be as we had once been, more like brothers,"* Gordon allowed a glimmer of a smile, as pictures ran through his mind of the two of them as children. *"Comrades in arms, that's what we called ourselves. Us against the world turned out to be us against one another,"* he thought sadly. *"The Dark Genesis had a hold over Andrew that even our blood bond could not sway."*

Although he hadn't been up long, Gordon was feeling his bruises and beginning to tire quickly; glancing at his watch, he decided to take one of his pain killers, and lie down to rest up for the gala tonight. He needed to conserve every ounce of strength he could; especially, if Rayne showed himself, and Gordon was sure he would be there. Rayne would not miss such a blatant opportunity to go after Colleen.

"God, I hate that Colleen is being used for bait," Gordon chaffed at the thought, *"but, she wouldn't listen to me; arguing that had always been a part of her job as an Argent."* Thinking of Colleen, Gordon allowed himself to drift into a fitful slumber.

"He's still asleep," Colleen whispered to Audra.

"Just leave his lunch on the nightstand," Audra replied, "he will be hungry when he wakes up, this way he won't have to go downstairs."

Gordon could hear the two women talking, but he was feeling too woozy from the meds, and he couldn't open his eyes yet. Besides, he dreamed of Colleen so often he wasn't sure if he was awake or not.

"What am I going to do, Audra?" Colleen asked softly.

"What do you want to do?" Audra asked.

"I almost hurt with wanting, yet at the same time...," Colleen trailed off. "But, I'm afraid to push him away for very long. I mean, for one thing, he knows!" She added emphatically, "Good grief, he apparently has seen every fantasy and thought that has flitted through my mind. It's so embarrassing!"

"I don't think you're giving the man enough credit, Colleen," Audra said.

"What do you mean?"

"Colleen, has the man ever forced himself on you in any way? Has he harassed you into going further than you wanted? Pushed past your objections?" Audra asked.

"No," she answered quietly.

With humor tinging her voice, Audra said, "No, he hasn't; even after the Hell you have put him through with the realistic projections of your erotic fantasies, *and* your insistence on sharing his bed." More seriously she added, "You know, some men wouldn't have taken no for an answer."

"He has been understanding, never crossing the line I've drawn; but, I'm just afraid he will grow tired of waiting and move on," Colleen said wistfully. "I could lose him."

"Colleen, if sex is all he wanted, you never had him," Audra said gently, adding, "But, he is still here, waiting for you."

Their voices began to grow fainter as if they were leaving the room, and Gordon strained to hear Audra's last remark, "Remember, the advice I gave you that first day in Albany? I still think that is the path the two of you need to follow."

When he was confident, they had left the room, Gordon opened his eyes to stare at the ceiling.

"*Well that was informative,*" Gordon thought wryly. "*On the plus side...Colleen* **wants** *me and is afraid of losing me; on the deficient side... Colleen wants me and is* **afraid** *of losing me.*" Sighing heavily, Gordon thought back to the day Audra had been introduced into his life, and he could recall her advice quite vividly, "*Oh, Gordon, you're such a man!*" She exclaimed. "*Sex is not the answer to all problems. In fact, my* *advice is for the two of you to refrain from that particular activity until you can connect honestly on different levels. I realize that comes as a great disappointment for both of you."*

Colleen had told him that she had never really had a relationship and that she had only dated occasionally with one short-lived exception. Although, Gordon was no novice to sex, and even though he had been married twice he had no more experience in an honest relationship than Colleen. He had rushed into both of his marriages for all the wrong reasons, there had been no honesty, and he had used his wives selfishly as a means to his ends. *"Disappointment hardly begins to describe my sexual frustration then or now,"* Gordon mused. *"But I can live with that. The last thing I want is for Colleen to feel fear or to feel coerced into my bed before she is ready. What did Jerad say to me? 'For the record, Audra is always right.' I assume this is no exception, especially, if Colleen is not comfortable with our relationship yet."*

Still, Gordon had no such qualms. The feelings he had for Colleen were like nothing he had ever experienced before; yet, somehow deep inside he knew this was what he had been searching for, and never found. He would not push her about a sexual relationship, he didn't want to push her away.

With the rest of the afternoon ahead of him, Gordon mentally framed out his plan of action. He then went to work on his computer to take care of the more pressing matters at Bilford Shipping and the Boston Complex, and then he made a few more calls; the last one to Jerad Evan. Gordon had cleared his calendar freeing up the next several weeks. If Colleen needed time, he would give her time.

25

ORDON DESCENDED THE STAIRS OF HIS home into a lover's grotto. He paused at the foot of the stairs to give his eyes time to adjust to the low lighting. Soft music floated through the air, the strands of white lights in the canopies surrounding the private tables, gave off a soft glow to the center of the great hall where several couples were already dancing. Gordon immediately started searching for Colleen, as he moved past the dancers into the dining area. Here too, the lights had been dimmed, he stopped a waiter for a flute of champagne as he made his way into the main salon still searching. The salon was crowded, but he followed the sound of Colleen's twinkling laugh and spotted her on the other side of the room.

Gordon started to make his way to Colleen but was besieged by one acquaintance, and neighbor after another. People exclaiming that the gala was a smashing success, and thanking him for continuing Terese' charity work. The silent auction, being held in the library, was a huge hit from what he was hearing. He accepted everyone's congratulations, belated sympathies, and gratitude as he did his best to tell them they should be thanking the O'Malley family for the success of tonight's festivities; all the while trying to keep Colleen in sight.

Gordon was just about to leave the library to make another

round through when he felt a strange, yet familiar, drawing sensation. Stopping where he was, he scanned the area and felt a tug from the other side. Someone from the Fold was here. Gordon felt surprise that he was still so attuned to the Dark since it had left him days ago, but there was no denying its force; he even had a tickling vibration from the key he still wore around his neck. The source of the pull felt strongest coming from a tight group of people chatting and laughing with one another, Gordon recognized most of them as local neighbors, but there was a man and a woman that was not familiar. He couldn't get a good look at either of them, but the palatable energy came from the man of that there was no doubt. *"Whoever he is he must be quite powerful, since I can still feel him,"* Gordon thought. Gordon would lay money that the man was Rayne. He really needed to find Colleen.

Taking up a position in the centrally located dining room would give Gordon the advantage of keeping an eye on the comings and goings of the guests from all party spaces. Fortunately, the library had large double doors, and Gordon could still see the group that held his interest while making small talk with various partiers as they passed.

Gordon was relieved when he finally spotted Colleen in the library, he mentally sighed in relief, *"She's okay, but the mystery man is gone."* Catching her eye, he nodded his head to indicate she should join him.

Gordon appreciatively watched Colleen's hips sway as she made her way across the crowded room, toward him. Although, he wasn't too thrilled with the attention that she garnered from every other male in the room. Not that he could blame any of them, *"She is extraordinary,"* Gordon thought.

He had noticed, when her back was to him, that she had pulled her hair up from her face on each side to gather at her crown, allowing the length of it to fall in a cascade of curls down her back, which naturally led the eye down to her shapely backside.

When she had turned to face him, he took in every detail of the black gown she wore, not only did it have a plunging neckline, but it was split down to her navel. It looked as if the only thing holding it together was a ribbon lacing that crisscrossed the median of her body in the fashion of a corset, and ended between her breasts with an emerald clasp in the shape of a Celtic knot. She stopped to stand directly in front of him.

Gordon had been so focused on her attributes that he was taken aback by the picture she currently presented; arms crossed, foot tapping in aggravation, and green eyes snapping. *"This isn't good. I don't envy the person that brought about this level of her ire."* Gordon said to himself.

"Would you like an introduction?" Colleen snapped at him.

"Not exactly the greeting I had anticipated," Gordon thought, *"Okay, I guess I'm to feel sorry for myself."* Perplexed by her question, and her angry tone, he cautiously asked, "An introduction to whom?"

"Oh please," Colleen mocked. Continuing she said, "To the blonde, the one just over my left shoulder. You know, the one you have been *staring* at for the last five minutes."

Unable to keep himself from looking over her shoulder, he finally noticed an attractive blonde-headed woman halfway across the room talking and smiling with her circle of companions, the circle from which he had felt the pull.

"Don't be ridiculous, I have not been staring at that woman," Gordon said defensively. "I was just gazing."

"Ah!" Colleen's eyes grew wide, then narrowed, "Are you kidding me?" she fumed. Turning on her heel, she flounced away toward the conservatory. Feeling more than a little aggravated by this turn of events, Gordon drew as deep a breath as his healing ribs would allow, and mentally counted to ten before following her.

He found Colleen pacing up and down one of the paths in the west corner, *"Still quite livid from the look of her,"* Gordon thought. She stopped pacing when she saw him, squaring her shoulders and jutting out her chin. Gordon had had every intention of explaining what he had meant, but with one look at her obstinate face, he muttered, "Oh to Hell with it," and blocking her only exit, took hold of her shoulders pulling her to him, and covered her lips with his just as she sucked in her breath.

Colleen stood stiff for about five seconds, then slid her hands inside of his jacket and leaned into him. Gordon smiled inwardly and more than a little triumphantly, deepening his kiss as his hands found their way down her back, pressing her firmly against the length of his body. She broke their kiss and leaned back from him, but Gordon didn't release his hold on her; instead, he stared into the depths of her eyes watching them dilate as he traced the neckline of her gown with his fingertip starting at her collarbone and then dipping down to the emerald clasp that matched the color of her eyes.

With a husky voice, Gordon asked, "Are you willing to let me explain now?"

Halfheartedly slapping at his hand, Colleen narrowed her eyes, and asked, "Do you think that all you have to do is to saunter up to me, all tall and dark; try to seduce me with a mere kiss, and I will automatically forgive and forget your behavior? A little too cliché don't you think?"

With a slight smirk, Gordon replied by repeating a line that Colleen had used on him, "Well shoot, it's always worked for me before; you must admit it was a great kiss." As she narrowed her eyes, Gordon smiled slowly, and in a silken voice breathed, "Tell me what else I'm allowed to do, other than kiss you, and I will be more than happy to oblige."

"You're incorrigible!" Colleen retorted.

"And, you're beautiful," Gordon rejoined, pulling her in tightly, trapping his hand between their bodies.

When Colleen stiffened somewhat, and her eyes took on a wary look, Gordon loosened his hold just enough for him to once again find the trail along the edge of her dress, where the fabric met her skin. "I was trying to see the man on the *other side* of the blonde lady..."

"Catherine," Colleen interjected.

"Catherine," Gordon repeated, never taking his eyes from Colleen's face, nor did he stop running his finger over the top of her breasts. "She was blocking my view of a man that I don't know, but he *felt* familiar. I wasn't staring at her; she was in my way." When Colleen didn't respond, Gordon continued, "We're still looking for Rayne, and I think there is a good possibility that *Catherine* was talking to him." Gordon could tell that Colleen was struggling, trying to decide whether to believe him or not, and he said, "You're the only one that has seen him, I don't suppose you noticed to whom Catherine was speaking?"

"Humph! No, I didn't notice who she was talking to, but I did take notice of the man that was staring at her," Colleen said primly.

"Colleen, don't be absurd!" Gordon gently admonished. "You want to talk about staring? I have had to stand by and watch every man here tonight eat you alive with their eyes; unable to do anything about it due to my current status, that of a grieving husband." Colleen ducked her head, and Gordon asked, "Why on earth would I look at any woman other than the woman in my arms right now?"

Shaking her head, Colleen whispered, "Because I'm such a child, twenty-six years old with no experience." Looking at him, her eyes filled with doubt and brimming with tears, she added, "And, I'm not giving you what you want right now, but other women will. Undoubtedly, Catherine would."

Expecting some sort of snippy comeback from Colleen, Gordon was stunned by her abrupt admission, and once again, was unnerved by her vulnerability. *"It's not the best timing, but this, plus what I heard this afternoon can no longer wait, I have to straighten this out... now,"* Gordon decided, as he put his hands on either side of her face. She was struggling to hold back the tears threatening to spill, and biting her bottom lip to keep it from trembling, Gordon gently kissed her, before saying, "Colleen, I won't lie, I want you with everything in me, with every fiber of my being. But, more importantly, I want you to come to me when you can trust me, trust us. Not out of a fear that I will grow tired of waiting and lose interest in you; but, because it's what you desire with no reservations, no regrets. Because you know it's right."

Colleen's eyes grew wide, "Oh my God, you were awake! You heard Audra and me talking!" Her cheeks flushed and grew warm under Gordon's hands.

Gordon smiled ruefully as he admitted, "I did hear a little, enough to know that Audra is right. We need a beginning; we need time to know each other on different levels...with honesty." Kissing her again with more than a little passion, Gordon continued, with an appraising smile, "I think we can both agree there is no doubt that we have the chemistry. But the trust isn't there for you, is it?" Gordon asked.

When Colleen dropped her gaze and didn't answer, Gordon said, "Colleen, I'm not looking for a one-night stand. If that was all I truly cared about, then this—us, would have been done before it started."

"And you're willing to give me time?" Colleen asked, seeking reassurance.

"No, I'm willing to give *us* time," Gordon responded. Releasing her, he took her hand and led her to a small bench that was hidden behind a clump of ornamental grasses. "My previous relationships were based on lies; Audra was correct, in that I have lived with the lies for so long that I find the truth hard to come by, I don't want that for us. Not to mention that I will need to get to know myself in this new role in my life."

Looking at Colleen, Gordon continued, softly, "I was thinking about us earlier; you're worried about being inexperienced; but the truth is, I don't have any more experience than you when it comes to an honest relationship with a woman. I have never felt as close to anyone as I do to you; yet, we really don't know each other's likes, dislikes, thoughts, opinions, or our dreams for the future."

Gordon watched her face as she mulled over what he had just said, continuing he said, "I'm tired, Colleen. I'm tired of the secrets and the lies. I have been trapped in a bizarre version of a life I never planned for and one that I did not want."

"And now?" Colleen asked.

"And now, I feel as if I'm at the threshold of something wonderful, a life that could have real meaning; I want a real relationship, a partner in that life," Gordon earnestly replied. "I'm afraid I don't know how to go about it, but I'm willing to try, and I want you to try with me."

"You do know that I have had to do a fair amount of dancing around the truth myself?" Gordon nodded, and with determination, Colleen said, "I want the same thing that you do; so, maybe we can figure it out together?"

"We will figure it out together," Gordon replied, with confidence.

With that said, she sealed their bargain with a kiss, and then, frowning, she asked, "Do you really think Rayne is here?"

"Yes," Gordon replied, "even though the Dark has left me, I could feel a powerful, familiar pull from the man, maybe I have met him at some point, but I couldn't get a clear look at him. Perhaps you could give me a description of the man you met in Albany."

"Because *Catherine* was in the way," Colleen spat. Gordon raised his eyebrows in surprise. He had not expected that sort of venom from Colleen, *"Maybe that's a story best left to another day,"* Gordon mused as he watched Colleen furrow her brow in concentration, she said, "Hmmm, a description. I have already projected an image to all of the members of the Radiant while you were convalescing, but we haven't the time for that now. Keep in mind that we were in a bar, the lighting was low; however, I did get a pretty good look at him. Let's see, he is about your height maybe a tiny bit shorter, very muscular, jet black hair, long, straight, shoulder length. But it was his eyes that was so striking, so unusual. I suppose it could have been the lighting, but they were as dark as ink, yet they were rimmed in cobalt blue."

"Colleen!"

"That's Jerad," Colleen whispered.

"Of course, it is," Gordon groaned, then kissed her quickly once more time, before rising and stepping out of their hidden corner.

"I've been looking for you Colleen," Jerad said plaintively as if speaking to a child when he reached them.

Frowning at the Arc, Colleen replied in a firm voice, "We were simply talking, Jerad."

Glancing back and forth between them, Jerad slightly shook his head, "Uh huh, I'm sure you were just *talking*," he mocked. "You two need to stay where we can keep track of you both. You just can't run off like this."

Gordon sighed, as he watched the struggle between the two Radiants. It was a power struggle, akin to what occurred every day around the world, control versus independence; the battle between parents and their children. However, he had thought he and the Arc had an understanding; especially, after their conversation this afternoon. *"However, I suppose if I were in his shoes, I wouldn't trust me yet either,"* Gordon thought.

"Our apologies Jerad," Gordon replied, cutting through the tension. "You're right, we shouldn't have added to the stress of the evening."

Colleen looked surprised, and Jerad a little skeptical, but he gruffly replied, "Well, you're both okay, that's really all that matters. It looks like things are starting to wind down a little out there; a few of the guests have left, and some have ordered their cars to be brought around. If Rayne is going to put in an appearance, it will be pretty soon."

"Gordon thinks he may be here, already," Colleen said. "Why don't you two make the rounds among the guests, I gave Gordon a description of Rayne, and I need to announce the winners of the Silent Auction."

Gordon and Jerad each stood on either side of the library while the various winners were called and made their way to the little stage where Colleen stood with a microphone in hand. When the last one had been called, and the proceeds had been tallied, Colleen made an announcement of how much money had been raised for Therse' charity and thanked everyone for making it such a success. After a hearty round of applause, she announced the close of the evening, by saying, "I would be honored if Mr. Bilford would escort me in the last dance." Everyone started clapping again, and some of the more boisterous guests were chanting his name.

Putting up only token resistance, Gordon made his way to the stage, and turning to address the onlookers, he said, "As a sincere expression of my gratitude for all of her hard work for this evening; I would consider it my privilege, to escort Ms. O'Malley to the dance floor for the last dance of the evening." Leading her from the library to the great hall Gordon leaned in to whisper, "You're a hit Ms. O'Malley, but I wonder what these good people would think if they knew where you have been sleeping lately?"

Colleen immediately flushed and shot Gordon a warning look, which had him laughing as he pulled her into his arms to begin their waltz. They were soon joined by quite a few other couples that wanted one more turn around the floor before the end of the festivities.

"We fit together quite well; wouldn't you agree?" Gordon asked Colleen in a hushed voice, as he led her around the dance floor.

"Gordon," Colleen replied quietly with a warning tone, "Behave yourself."

Gordon gave Colleen a slow smile, saying, "Ms. O'Malley, you wound me." Adding with a deceptively innocent tone, "No pressure, simply an observation. I only meant to point out that I think we move together in perfect rhythm and quite harmoniously."

With a playful smirk, Colleen said, "Un-huh, no innuendo

intend…Oh no!" Without warning, Colleen sagged against Gordon heavily, as if her legs were buckling. Gordon held her up, searching her face, "Colleen what is it? Are you in pain?"

"Jacqueline!" She gasped. "She's here!"

"What? Jacqueline who…your missing friend?" Gordon asked, his mind reeling, and eyes darting around the room, trying to make sense out of what she was saying.

"Jacqueline is here," Colleen replied in a halting voice, "I can see her in your office." With eyes wide, she whispered, "She's scared, and Gordon she's not alone."

"Rayne?" Gordon asked, his voice hard.

"I think so," Colleen responded.

Still whispering as they made their way through the crowded dance floor, Colleen said, "I know your office was locked because I checked it before the first guests arrived. I suppose the use of locks for safe-keeping doesn't mean much around the Fold or the Radiants, do they?"

"There is no such thing as *safe*," Gordon replied emphatically. Continuing, he said, "Normals need to have a feeling of security. Locks, walls, and fences are the tools used by the Normals to feed their illusion of safety. But in reality, whether an intruder is a member of the Fold, Radiants, or Normals, if someone is determined enough, they will find a way around any obstacle."

"We have to get these people out of here," Gordon said, catching sight of David and Larry he gave them the prearranged signal, Larry nodded, and they both started moving.

26

OUTSIDE THE DOOR TO HIS OFFICE, Gordon paused to listen, then twisted the knob while pulling Colleen behind him. Pushing the door open with his foot, he flipped the light switch that immediately illuminated a young woman, huddled and softly sobbing, sitting in the corner of the leather sofa.

Colleen who was peeking under his arm squealed, "Jacqueline!" and ran straight into the room before Gordon could stop her. At the same time, Gordon saw a young man up against the far wall... halfway up the wall, hanging there as if he were a piece of art from the Dada movement.

Gordon quietly shut the door, and quickly scanned the room, taking in the minute details of his office looking for anything different, or out of place when he noticed that his high-backed desk chair was facing the French doors. At the same time, he saw a man's hand rise, and with a snap of his fingers the young man plastered to the wall slid with a thump to the floor, the young girl that Gordon assumed was Jacqueline was suddenly frozen into place, as was Colleen.

"You must be Rayne," Gordon said, addressing the back of the chair.

As the chair slowly swiveled to face Gordon the man spoke,

"That is one of my many monikers, but you know me by another, Gordon."

One look into the man's eyes told Gordon what he had secretly suspected as soon as he had heard Colleen's description, he did know this man. The hair was longer, blacker, without a trace of grey; the face was smoother and younger, but the eyes said it all, and Gordon remembered what the man had said to him at one of their last meetings, *"This time when I go away, I won't be coming back, at least not in this role."*

"So, father, you come back in the role of a rogue Abrogate? As Rayne?" Gordon questioned.

Gordon the II slowly looked his son up and down while maintaining an air of superiority, that Gordon remembered well, before replying, "All Abrogates are rogue, son. And, speaking of going rogue, it seems you have traveled down that road yourself." Slowly shaking his head, and tsking, he said, "Aligning yourself with the Radiant. Your Uncle is extremely distraught and put out with you Gordon. I don't know how long I will be able to keep him away from you."

Gordon shrugged slightly, and said, "Let him come." Taking a few steps toward the center of the room, Gordon tried to insinuate himself between his father, who now called himself Rayne and Colleen. "Of course, if he does then Andrew will die."

"You can speak of your Cousin's death with such insouciance," Rayne, observed shaking his head, "that I don't know whether to be appalled or awed by you."

With a snort of derision, Gordon said, "I was educated by the best," mocking he added, "I suppose one could say I excelled under my father's tutelage."

Rayne tipped his head, scrutinizing Gordon, "I'm not so sure about that. Your father offered you boundless possibilities, so many choices, laid the world at your feet, and look at the manner in which you have responded. I set everything into motion to give you nearly infinite power over the Normals to choose their destiny, to rule over them on behalf of the Genesis."

Standing he came around to the side of the desk to face Gordon, "You defy not just me, your father; but the Genesis? And for what? A woman?" Throwing his hand out indicating Colleen. "And not just any woman, but a member of the Radiant! You have wounded me deeply son, and you have brought shame to the House of Bilford."

Gordon had stood silently as his father rebuked him, his anger building with every word, "I never asked for, nor did I want, infinite power over the Normals, to lord over them. You claim to have given me possibilities and choices? The only choices I was offered as I recall was to join or die!" Gordon had not raised his voice, but he could feel his eyes changing, and he felt the rawness of a power coursing through him, unlike anything he had ever felt before. "*You* allowed yourself to be seduced by the power, and *you* bargained away your soul to embrace the Dark. That was your choice, your desire; it was never mine."

With that said, Gordon's father suddenly became enveloped in a dark haze that undulated and swirled around him; his eyes were now as black as his soul, rimmed in a thin circle of cobalt blue, "How dare you! I handed you an abundance of wealth, an established thriving business, a magnificent home, and I, quite literally, gave you a key that would allow you to fulfill your slightest whim. Rather than display any gratitude, you continue to wound and provoke me. How could my son reject the legacy of the Genesis? Do you not understand my eminence within the Fold?" And as if to prove his point, Rayne threw up a shield of fire with a flick of his wrist. Like a living entity, the flames flicked from around its edges and thrusting toward Gordon.

Gordon could feel its heat and hear its hiss, as it reached for him, "with *talons from Hell*," was his thought as he sidestepped, and dodged its grasp. Gordon raised his hands, and a brilliant opalescent shield appeared behind him protecting the frozen Argents from Rayne. Speaking aloud, he declared, "I reject my father, I reject my dynastic legacy, and I reject the Dark Genesis." Through the French doors, Gordon could see balls of flames raining from above, as the Dark shadow billowed out to fill the room looking for a way around Gordon's iridescent barrier.

Gordon seized the distraction to call forth what looked like a waterfall from the ceiling, but was actually millions of fine shards of light that showered over the fire. The fire shield hissed louder as it began to solidify like cooled lava; the talons of fire were now blackened, turned to rock, and frozen in claw-like hands still reaching.

The air became filled with a breathtaking acrid stench; and the Dark screeched, as parts of the falling rays of light touched the shadow and wafted away into nothingness. Gathering itself into a dark funnel on the far side of the room, it then rolled across the ceiling, and came straight at Gordon. Gordon tried to summon another barrier, but the shadow was moving too fast, and Rayne was simultaneously advancing. Rayne was trying to make his way past Gordon and toward Colleen. His eyes were glowing and reflecting what was left of the fire shield. Caught between the two entities, and desperately wanting to protect Colleen, Gordon took his eyes off of the Dark and focused on Rayne.

Gordon shouted at Rayne, "Do not touch her or I will kill you." Rayne stopped and turned toward Gordon, suddenly transformed into a vision of the man that Gordon remembered as a very young child, "My son, you can't mean that you would kill your father."

Momentarily shaken, but not falling for the ruse, Gordon snarled, "Harm one hair on her head old man, and you will die." Gordon, the father, instantaneously dropped his facade and Rayne reappeared.

"My, my, she must be quite the intriguing little piece for you to defend her so vehemently," Rayne taunted, "Tell me is she really that good in bed? Good enough that a man would choose to kill or be killed? I can hardly wait to find out for myself," Rayne flipped his wrist, and Colleen came out of her frozen state, never taking his eyes from Gordon's, Rayne raised his hand, and Colleen started moving, almost floating toward him, stopping short at the glimmering shield. "You will have to choose your opponent; you can't fight both of us at once. Choose wisely and remember the second this barrier drops she's mine, and then I will find her worth."

Gordon's heart felt like it had ceased to beat when he realized that although Rayne could not cross the light barrier, he still held control over Colleen. Already feeling the strain, in his not yet healed body, Gordon started to calculate his odds quickly. Although his heart was now pounding in his ears, he knew he couldn't become distracted by the thought of Colleen at the hands of Rayne, that's exactly what Rayne wanted. However, the devil was right; he didn't know how long he could keep the barrier in place and fight the Genesis at the same time. *"I have no choice,"* Gordon decided, *"I can't fight Rayne if the Genesis kills me first. I will have to fight the Genesis, pray that I survive, and can keep the barrier in place so I can then deal with Rayne."*

Turning his back on Rayne, Gordon closed his eyes to help him focus. Somehow, from somewhere within he suddenly knew what he had to do; he just didn't know why. Gordon called on the light from every source in the manor plunging it into darkness, then faced the Genesis. With a rising screech, it swirled toward him with great speed; the sound was more piercing than it had been in Boston. Gordon waited for as long as possible then dropped to the floor, allowing it to roll over him.

Gordon could see the wraithlike creatures that were in accompaniment, and a part of the Genesis, pushing toward him their mouths gaped open, and their eyes blazing in the darkened room. One was close enough to reach out a twisted taloned hand, and create a long, searing gash along his left arm. He closed his eyes, mentally begging for strength when he felt a raw shaft of adrenalin course through his body. The boost had him raising his hand to find he had been provided with a weapon.

It was a shaft of light, the light from Bilford Manor. *"It must* be a weapon from the Radiants," Gordon thought, but he had no time to ponder the origin of the gift as he thrust the light weapon upward slicing through the shadow. The cacophony of screaming, screeching, and wailing was deafening as a portion of the phantoms were severed from the contingent. The Genesis shot upwards, gathered what was left of itself, and came at Gordon again, dropping even lower, but this time Gordon was more prepared and sliced upward with the shaft of light again, but not before another wraith succeeded in gashing Gordon across his chest.

Nearly spent, Gordon tried to prepare for the Genesis to make a third pass, just as it rolled over him to deliver what no doubt would be its death blow, Gordon was suddenly enveloped in a cocoon of light. The Dark's momentum brought it crashing against the cocoon with a screech that ripped and reverberated through the room. The sound was unbearable, and Gordon could feel a warm trickle of blood running from his right ear, encased in his shimmering blanket, he watched the Dark recoil and then to funnel tightly until it vanished. Surprised by its hasty retreat Gordon rolled to his side to see that, Jerad, along with four other Arcs had entered the room, explaining the sudden withdrawal of the Genesis.

Rayne stood his ground as the Arcs were attempting to subdue him; laughing at their efforts, as he raised his hand lifting them from the floor to send them flying backward into the great hall and slamming the doors shut after their departure with a flick of his wrist. Turning to Gordon, he proclaimed, "As it has been said before, you may have won this battle son; but you have yet to win this war." With that said, the flames that had been dancing around his feet engulfed him, and he too vanished, but not before lighting afire the entire room.

"Colleen!" Gordon rasped out before he lost consciousness, overcome from the excruciating pain of the jagged rips to his body from the Dark, and from breathing in the black smoke from the flames that raced up the walls.

Epilogue

GORDON SETTLED INTO THE LEATHER-SEATED BACK of the SUV watching the scenery fly by as they left Boston Hospital. Up front, Jerad Evan was behind the wheel with his wife Molly by his side. Gordon was heading into upstate New York, to the Evans' home nestled in an area near Ferris Lake Wild Forest. Their home, situated in the middle of a 150-acre tract of land, served as both a retreat for the Radiant members and as a training site for certain recruits.

Due to his injuries and his new found life commitment, Gordon would be using their place for recovery and then for training to the ways of the Radiant when he was healed. The gashes to his arm and his chest had required some stitching, but it was the inhalation of smoke so soon after his last visit to the ER that had kept Gordon in the hospital for observation during the previous two days. Joseph and Colleen had rarely left his side.

Love songs of the seventies from Molly's playlist filled the interior with REO, Foreigner, Dr. Hook, Fogelberg, and more that he couldn't identify. *"What is it with these people and 70's rock music?"* Gordon idly wondered. He was sure that Colleen would know them all… if she were with him in the vehicle, but she wasn't. *"And in as much as I didn't want to leave Colleen, I have to see this through,"* Gordon thought with renewed resolve. *"Not to mention that it will give both of us time to get acquainted on different levels, something that she needs.*

Gordon smiled at the way she had argued when he told her he would be with the Evans for a few weeks. Just a few hours ago, they had stolen a few minutes of alone time in his hospital room to say goodbye. He explained that along with Jerad he had made this decision before the gala, "I thought you wanted some time for us to get to know each other, right?"

"Yes," Colleen conceded, then pursing her lips in a pout, said, "But, I didn't think that meant we had to be apart."

"I'm still a widower in mourning, remember?" Gordon gently reminded her, "We can't be together right now. That wouldn't do either of our reputations any good, and I want to do the things that are best for both of us."

"Yes, I know," Colleen sighed. "But you better be prepared, the images could get worse."

Brushing her hair back from her face, Gordon said, "That's okay. I'm kind of getting used to them, and some of them are more than a little interesting. I'm still curious as to how that one move would work," Gordon teased, enjoying the way she blushed.

Colleen dipped her head, and said, "This is all so ridiculous, I feel ridiculous."

"It's what we agreed upon, more time," Gordon said, then asked, "so why should you feel ridiculous?"

Her blush deepening, Colleen responded, "Because I feel like I'm about to go up in a flame most of the time."

"Oh yeah?" Gordon queried with a self-satisfied smirk. "Well we have a bed and we could lock the door; I'll play firefighter."

Colleen looked up at him then, and laughed, "Seriously? Here? You know, Jerad would break the door down."

At the mention of Jerad, Gordon replied with a heavy sigh, "No doubt."

"What am I going to do with myself while you're gone?" Colleen mused, as she wrapped her arms around Gordon's waist and laid her cheek on his chest.

"I had a thought," Gordon said, "but, only if you are really interested, it would be a big job." Then added, knowing his next statement would pique her interest, "Say no if you don't want to, okay? I can get someone else."

"Get someone else to do what?" Colleen demanded.

"Well," Gordon began, "as you know, Rayne did a number on my office with the fire; plus, according to Joseph there is a lot of smoke and water damage to several of the rooms." Gordon took a deep breath, and said, "Since you have studied architecture and design, I thought you could oversee the renovations."

Colleen had seemed rather surprised by the offer, but he could tell that she was also intrigued. Deciding to sweeten the deal, Gordon added, "Since I am turning over a new leaf, it would nice if my home had a new look. From what I have seen you have excellent taste; you could design and decorate Bilford Manor the way you want it, free rein."

In the end, she had agreed to redo his home and agreed this would be an excellent starting point in getting to know each other better. Many changes were coming in Gordon's immediate future, and he had to admit he felt a thrill of excitement at his prospects.

Gordon made a mental list of all that he had done over the past couple of months in an attempt to make some of the changes he needed, "I have fought back against the Fold, and lived to tell the tale. I have neutralized my cousin; which in turn has neutralized my Uncle. The lessor of the evils, so to speak," Gordon mused. "Most importantly, I have turned my back on my father's dynastic plan for my life. My new life might not be considered normal, but at least it will be one of my choosing, and be more in-line with the way I have always dreamed of living."

Thinking back over the chaotic hours after the gala, Gordon tried to wrap his mind around the most jarring of revelations; his father, Gordon Andrew Bilford II had traded his identity for the Abrogate Rayne. Even Joseph had been surprised by this turn of events. He had no idea that the man he had served, Gordon Bilford II and the Abrogate Rayne, was one and the same.

From what Gordon had learned while in the hospital, Rayne must have followed Colleen's friends, Tommy and Jacqueline, from Colleen's house after the snow storm. The last thing her friends remembered was waving "goodbye" to Colleen, and the next thing they remembered was their awakening in Gordon' office with Rayne. They had lost weeks.

Rayne had scrubbed their memories. No one had a clue as to where he had kept them; but, Jaqueline, a projectionist similar to Colleen, knew immediately that something had gone wrong when she suddenly realized that she and Tommy were at Bilford manor. Much against her will, Jaqueline had connected to Colleen. Even after Rayne had threatened them both, she resisted, until he slammed Tommy up against the wall, and left him hanging there. Begging him not to hurt Tommy anymore, she did his bidding by projecting an image of herself in Gordon's office to Colleen. Rayne was confident that if he could lure Colleen into the office, then Gordon would soon follow; allowing him another chance to manipulate his son into coming back to the Fold by threatening Colleen.

What Rayne had not counted on was the support that Gordon had received from the Radiant. The Arcs had provided the blanket of light that had saved him from the Genesis, but the shaft of light that had suddenly appeared in his hand was a mystery. When Jerad and the other Arcs had questioned him, Gordon attempted to describe it, but all he could tell them was that something told him to pull the energy from the lights of the manor, then it was in his hand. It had no weight, it was neither hot nor cold, but he could feel a power emanating from it unlike anything he had ever felt before, and then it had disappeared as quickly as it had appeared when the Dark Genesis took its leave.

Jerad had told him there were various legends concerning a sword of light, but he had never seen it. He had gone on to tell Gordon that from what he had witnessed and from what Gordon was telling him now none of it seem to fit into the most popular scenarios of its legend. Jerad theorized that since Gordon was neither dark nor light at that moment, but was fighting for the light, that the collective Radiance had sent it to him.

"I don't care where it came from," Gordon had said, "I'm just thankful it showed up."

"I'm sure," Jerad chuckled, "You know, I have been in a few battles before, but nothing like that." Studying Gordon for a moment, Jerad seemed to have come to a decision, as he said, "I will need to confer with the counsel, but this may change your starting position within the Radiant, Gordon. But I want to keep that quiet for now, agreed?"

Gordon wasn't sure what Jerad was alluding to, but at the time, still lying in his hospital bed, he didn't have the energy to do anything more than to nod in agreement.

Gordon was brought out of his reverie when Jerad stopped for a late lunch at one of Molly's favorite cafes, on the border of Vermont and New York. Jerad requested they be seated in the open-air dining area, even though the weather was still very chilly. He picked a table located in a small alcove tucked around the corner of the building near an outdoor heater. Jerad had purposely chosen this table for a little privacy.

While waiting for their meal to be served Jerad had started peppering Gordon with questions about the Fold. Gordon was doing his best to answer, but at the moment he was being highly distracted. Molly laid her hand on her husband's arm in the middle of yet another inquiry, and said, "I can't seem to find my phone. It must have fallen out in the SUV. Would you be a dear and go look?"

"Molly," Jerad frowned, at being interrupted.

Gordon watched with veiled amusement as the Arc's little wife tipped her head to one side, pouted her lips and said, "Please?"

Heaving a heavy sigh, Jerad said, "Okay, I'll go look."

"You're such a love, thank you," Molly beamed at her husband.

As Jerad weaved his way around the now filled tables on the patio, Molly turned her brilliant smile on Gordon.

Gordon smiled back and raised his wine glass to her, saying, "You're very good at getting him to do what you want, aren't you?"

"We take care of each other," Molly replied, with a toss of her caramel-colored curls.

"I'm sure you do, but I could have sworn you put your phone in your pocket when we got out of the vehicle," Gordon replied.

Molly laughed lightly, and said, "Okay you caught me; but honestly, I thought you could use a break from Jerad's incessant line of questioning."

Gordon inclined his head, and said, "Thank you. I am having a little trouble focusing."

"Ah, Colleen is invading your line of vision, again," Molly grinned.

"A bit," Gordon replied. "Please don't say anything to Jerad right now. I still don't have his trust where Colleen is concerned."

Molly stared into Gordon's eyes for a moment, then said, "I believe you care deeply for Colleen, but you will have to be patient with Jerad. You see, Jerad blames himself for her being an orphan."

"Really?" Gordon frowned, "But her parents were killed in a train accident."

"Well, there is more to it than that," Molly confided. "But we will save that story for another day," she said before Gordon could ask. "For now, suffice it to say that Jerad feels a certain responsibility for Colleen. He is a good man, Gordon, give him time."

"Did I hear my name?" Jerad asked as he stepped around the corner.

"I was just telling Gordon what a good man you are, sweetheart," Molly answered, with an innocent smile, "Oh, and I found my phone, it was in my pocket. I'm so sorry I sent you to look for it."

"Really? Now, why am I not surprised; do you think?" Jerad asked, smiling indulgently into Molly's eyes. "Okay, Gordon I will lay off the inquisition for now." Turning to his wife, he asked, "Happy?"

Gordon watched in amusement as the husband and wife performed their verbal dance right through their lunch. Observing Jerad and Molly's tender bantering made Gordon wistful for

Colleen, wishing she were here by his side. Suddenly, with great clarity, Colleen answered his unspoken wish, filling his mind with enough intimate images to have him excusing himself from the table, telling his companions he would meet them at the vehicle. Jerad tossed him the keys and waited with Molly for the check.

As soon as Gordon was reasonably sure that he was outside of Jerad's hearing range, he made his call.

"Hey there lady," Gordon said, when Colleen answered, "just what are you up to?"

"Too much?" Colleen asked.

"I'm not sure on how to answer that. I'm leaning toward not enough," Gordon replied.

Colleen laughed lightly, and said, "You were sad; I just wanted to make you feel better."

"I was missing you," Gordon replied.

"I think I've changed my mind," Colleen said, "this is all so silly, we know each other pretty well, don't you think?"

Gordon smiled, and said, "Did you know that anticipation can be a great aphrodisiac?"

"I don't think either of us needs one," Gordon could hear the pout in Colleen's voice.

Gordon chuckled, and said, "Promise me one thing?"

"What?"

"Keep the fire burning for a while longer, okay?" Gordon asked in a husky voice.

"Fire?" Gordon spun around to see Jerad and Molly approaching, "Did the fire reignite at your place?" Jerad asked.

Molly, who was studying Gordon, smiled knowingly, and said, "Jerad, let Gordon finish his call." Then, tugged on his arm to bend down as she tiptoed to whisper in his ear.

Gordon made a Skype date with Colleen for later in the evening before settling into the backseat again. He steadily met the frowning eyes staring at him from the rear-view mirror, before Molly drew her Arc's attention with her chatter.

"Jerad and Molly, would be reaching their destination soon, home," thought Gordon. "But for me, it will be the first stop on my journey. A journey that will hopefully lead me back to my home, back to a certain green-eyed lady, and back to my soul."

Need a little more time with Gordon and Colleen?
Turn the page to read the first chapter
of their upcoming sequel in:

Summer Solstice

By:

DONNA PFANNENSTIEL

Light and Dark
Compromising, blending,
At days end,
Dominating, receding, again, and again.
Each struggles with the other.
Radiance dances with shadow,
Argent light perseveres--
Burning deep within the Fold of Darkness,
Bursting forth,
Trapping, smothering
Darkness overtakes the light
Becoming one.
Dusk
-DP-

Chapter 1

Light breaks where no sun shines
-Dylan Thomas-

Colleen O'Malley, felt as if she had a hundred things to check on before Gordon Bilford III returned from upstate New York to his newly renovated home in Bilford, New Hampshire; a small seaside town named for the Bilford family.

The last time they had spoken Gordon couldn't tell her exactly when he would be back, it could be a few days or a few weeks, but Colleen wanted everything to be in place when he did arrive. Colleen took a break from studying her to-do list to look around the great hall of Bilford Manor with a critical eye, trying to get a sense of how Gordon would view the space when seeing it for the first time since the fire after the Valentine Charity Gala.

He had hired her to renovate his home and had given her a free hand to do the job as she pleased. Mostly new color, some furnishings; minimal structural changes. The décor of the manor had been kept very traditional for decades. Of course, the traditional style had its own beauty; but Colleen viewed all of the somber colors, heavy damask draperies, and dark antique furniture as being rather oppressive. She had lightened the wall colors, changed out the window coverings, and replaced many of the antiques to bring in a lighter and airier atmosphere. She had purposely kept the color palate muted; occasional chairs and sofas upholstered in shades of cream; touches of ocean blues and greens in the floor coverings and cushions, lent a calming quality; and were a reflection of the New Hampshire coastal manor. Colleen hoped that the changes she had made would meet with his approval. As a part, of their agreement, she and Gordon had kept in constant contact over the past few weeks; although he hadn't disagreed with any of her choices, Colleen still fussed.

Feeling a familiar curl of desire pulsate through her body every time she thought of Gordon, which was quite frequent; Colleen smiled in wonder as she thought about how different things were between them now as compared to the first time they had met.

Curling up on the seat beneath the bay window Colleen let her mind wander back to the first time she had entered Bilford Manor; accompanied by her Aunt and Uncle, Fran and Shawn O'Malley; dear friends and neighbors to Gordon and Terese O'Malley. They were there by invitation attending Terese O'Malley's Annual Winter Solstice Party, and to aide Colleen in carrying out her mission for the Radiant against the Dark Fold.

Colleen knew something was amiss as soon as she stepped through the door of the stately home known as Bilford Manor. Her feelings were quickly confirmed, and she knew she was too late when Gordon Bilford III announced that his wife Terese was unable to attend their annual winter solstice party due to a migraine. Unbeknownst, to the rest of the party-goers, Terese Bilford would be lost to this world, frozen in time for eternity, unless the Radiants could find her and reverse this cursed situation in time. Colleen tried her best not to show any overt emotion to the announcement. Her only reaction was a small gasp as she reached for her aunt's hand. Colleen's aunt, Fran O'Malley, gave her hand a reassuring squeeze, and an understanding nod. Her uncle, Shaun O'Malley, immediately stood a little straighter and squared-off his shoulders as if he had just suffered an insult and prepared to face a confrontation, but a quick warning glance from his wife had him relaxing his stance.

Colleen watched and listened as Terese's husband made the excuses for his wife's absence.

"However," Gordon announced, "as most of you know Terese does have a certain fondness for Christmas." Nearly all of the guests, especially those that knew Terese well, laughed knowing what an understatement that was. "So, she asked me to say 'please, please stay and enjoy' and I second it." He raised his glass, toasted his guests and said, "To Terese, we will eat, drink, and be merry."

Mr. Bilford, played it off to the hilt. He circulated among his guests, stopping to listen to a joke or a story, shaking hands with the men, and kissing the cheeks of the women, inviting them to sample the buffet, "... because Terese had agonized for days rearranging the menu at least a dozen times, and it would be the first thing he would have to report to her." He also made sure that none of his guests' glasses went empty for too long, nor his own Colleen observed; in short, he was the perfect host.

However, Colleen could feel something a bit off about Mr. Bilford's bright, solicitous, facade. She took note that his laughter never seemed to reach his eyes; and when one of the guests had lamented on the absence of Terese, Colleen not only watched as a look of pain flashed across Gordon Bilford's face, but she could feel an incredible sadness emanating from their host, before he murmured in agreement and turned away. The expression of pain was quickly hidden when another gentleman cornered him and appeared to be regaling their host with a rambling tale; however, his sadness slammed into Colleen's soul. This was a new experience for her, never had she been so in tune to a subject before. Feeling more than a little confused by this eruption of new emotions Colleen went to find her Aunt and Uncle; this man of the Dark Fold was different, he might not be the demon in this Greek tragedy, she needed more time.

Colleen quickly conferred with her family members, and they agreed to send word that the Arcs needed to stand down for now. Colleen surreptitiously kept her green eyes on Mr. Bilford quite aware that his eyes along with most of the men in the room were on her, exactly as she had intended when choosing her clothing for the evening.

Colleen had chosen a black sheath dress a perfect foil against her creamy skin and her long flaming red hair. The gown featured a nearly non-existent back and a plunging neckline in the front. It hugged her tall, nicely rounded body in all the right places, then flared slightly from just above her knees to allow for freedom of movement. Aunt Fran laughingly called it her 'hunting' dress. Uncle Shaun wasn't amused as evidenced by the drawn down corners of his mouth when he saw her attire; declaring he would have to spend the night running off the wolves.

Colleen wasn't particularly proud of using her body as a means to an end; but she had been sent on an assignment; usually, that required her to lure the quarry into a vulnerable position and then step aside to let the Arcs take over. She had learned some time ago to use whatever she had available to see it through to the end, and tonight she would be both the hunter and the bait. Colleen knew the Fold primarily consisted of men, and it had been her experience that men tended to let down their guard when distracted. And nothing distracted a man more than an attentive woman with a soft voice, and a voluptuous body.

She had been making the rounds among the guests as her aunt and uncle introduced her to new people and reintroduced her to those that might remember her as a child when she had first come to live with them in Bilford after her parents had been killed in an accident. With the absence of Terese, making the introductions were now critical to Colleen's mission. It was imperative that she get a read on as many people as possible.

Not only was Colleen checking for possible new members of the Fold, and regardless, of the confusing signals she was receiving from their host she still had to search for a particular artifact...a snow-globe. "Such a bizarre choice of vehicle to imprison what they referred to as their tributes," Colleen thought, as she let out a tiny sigh, "but, if the legends are true, it is a choice unique to the House of Bilford." She moved about the great hall taking note of no less than a dozen snow-globes placed within the holiday arrangements that adorned nearly every surface. "And this was only one room," she groaned inwardly. She would need to search furtively for Terese so as not to arouse any suspicion from Gordon Bilford.

Keeping to her character as just another party-goer, Colleen made her way to the formal dining area. As she approached the table, she noticed yet another snow-globe in the center of the elaborate buffet; it stood nestled in the artfully arranged greenery that ran down the center of the table.

Colleen immediately recognized this one as being completely different from the others. When compared to the ones she had seen in the hall this one stood taller, the globe much larger, and the ornate base appeared tarnished with age. "He wouldn't be that blatant, would he?" Colleen inwardly queried.

Colleen deftly lifted the globe and held it gently trying not to shake it too much as she examined the wintry diorama within. There she observed a stand of pines, a small pond that was encircled with a worn path and two women, one dark and one fair. The dark-headed woman was wearing a forest-green gown and standing on the pathway; while the blonde-headed woman sat on a small bench that sat at the apex of the path framed by the snow-covered pines. Colleen felt an overwhelming sense of sorrow, and simultaneously, immense anger. How could she have made such an incredible mistake; he was that blatant.

From the pricking of her senses, Colleen knew she was being watched. She looked up in time to see Gordon Bilford walking toward her. She gently placed the globe back in its place of honor; it would appear that Terese was in attendance after all.

Colleen steeled herself to stay in character as she turned to face her host.

"Good evening, we haven't been formally introduced, I'm Gordon Bilford," he said as he stood near her. "I noticed that you seemed intrigued by this Christmas trinket."

Colleen's trip down memory lane was interrupted when Joseph, Gordon's mentor-friend-and the person that was the heart of Bilford manner, came in pushing a handcart loaded with boxes from her most recent purchases for Gordon's office. Colleen followed him into the office, saying, "Joseph could you put them against the back wall in front of the bookshelves, please?"

"Yes, ma'am," Joseph smiled, as he maneuvered the cart carefully so not to mar any of the new furniture. "Will you be joining us for lunch? We're going to try the new bistro in town?" He asked Colleen.

Colleen grinned widely, assuming the "us" he referred to

consisted of he and Audra McMann, Colleen's mentor and friend. Much to Colleen and Gordon's delight, the two had become very cozy.

"No, you two go ahead without me," Colleen replied still smiling, "I want to get Gordon's office completed today; I'll make myself a sandwich later."

"Very well, but leave the boxes," Joseph instructed, "I will recycle them when we get back."

"Okay, they will be emptied as soon as possible," Colleen responded, anxious to get the boxes unpacked. Since Gordon had lost everything in the office from the fire-fight with the Abrogate Rayne, Colleen wanted to do something special by creating a personalized library for him. She had ordered new books featuring his favorite authors to replace the ones he had lost. She had learned from one of their late-night phone conversations that Gordon's taste ran from political biographies to Hemingway, Stephan King, and to the raw, suspenseful writing of James Patterson.

Standing on a step-stool reaching up to put the last of the books on an upper shelf, Colleen realized that she had worked through lunch when she heard the door open. Without turning, she called over her shoulder with a smile, "You two weren't gone long. What did you think of the new bistro?" Neither Joseph or Audra replied, instead Colleen heard the door click shut followed by footsteps on the highly polished wood floors; she turned still wearing a smile to see who had come for a visit.

However, Colleen's welcoming smile was replaced with a look of surprise, her eyes widened, her mouth went dry, her breath caught in her throat, and her heart began to race when she caught sight of the man that had just entered the room. His purposeful stride as he moved across the room had her frozen in place, but the unwavering gaze in his dark eyes took her breath away.

Without a word, he swept her from the footstool into his arms and captured her lips with his. Colleen helpless and thrown completely off-balance had no choice but to return his kiss with complete abandon. He held her tightly, touching her everywhere at once. When she tore her lips from his, he started walking her backward, never taking his dark eyes from her face, until they tumbled onto the couch. When she began to speak, he stole away her words by claiming her mouth once again. Finally, he released her lips, to trail kisses across her jawline, and down the side of her throat.

Catching a quick breath, Colleen said, "Gordon, are you going to talk to me?"

Gordon Andrew Bilford III pulled away long enough to say, "I like my way of communicating better."

With a throaty laugh, Colleen remarked, "A man of few words, huh?"

Gordon gave her a slow, sexy smile, and said, "All we have been able to do for weeks is talk; I hunger for touch." Gordon noticed a little smile playing about Colleen's mouth as she stared at his chest. He looked down to find his shirt hanging open; every button was undone or missing. Sliding one hand under the hem of her loose blouse, and the other to draw her close once again, Gordon said, "It would appear we have the same hunger."

Printed in the United States
By Bookmasters